THE THREADS OF FATE I

REIGN OF THE GLITTERING FLAMES

Elizabeth F Starling

SEVEN
SISTERS
FABLES

Seven Sisters Fables
401 N. Mills Ave
Ste B PMB 1032
Orlando, Florida 32803

Book cover illustration by Patricia Gutierrez, patriciagutierrez.art@gmail.com.

Interior illustrations & maps by Elizabeth F Starling

1st edition 2025

Reign of the Glittering Flames is a fantasy romance adventure set in a world filled with magic, different planes of existence, fictional creatures, mysteries, and twists and turns. This adventure includes elements such as violence, murder, death, graphic language, blood, loss of family, and explicit sexual content written on the page. This book is intended for adult audiences, so please use reader discretion.

When you are ready for a map, one can be found at the end of the book.

For my soul mate.
If I am your world, then you are my star.
My constant in an unkind universe,
guiding me towards joy.
It was always you.

PROLOGUE

I jolted awake.

My heart raced, and my hand flew to my chest to steady the thrumming that vibrated through my bones.

I had always felt it—a metaphysical pull on the center of my being—for as long as I could remember. The *thread* was usually a soft tug, a loving caress that had comforted me in times of solitude. I rubbed my chest at the new, stronger pull that had jerked me awake. In all my twenty-five years, I'd never felt it pull *this hard* on me.

Tonight it burned with a buzzing current, magnetizing me to move forward as if that metaphysical tether intended to pull me to a particular place. I glanced over to my roommate and best friend of fifteen years sleeping soundly across our dormitory room. Freda shifted slightly before rolling over to her other side. I wouldn't drag her into this. Not yet. And not literally three days before the spring semester courses started.

I swung my feet out from under the blanket and to the floor. The thread hummed as if resonating in agreement with the movement. I stepped forward, and the tension released slightly in a gratifying caress. I took another step and another, and slipped into the hall. The thread warmed, tightening and releasing its pull with every step. Maybe if I kept following it, I would finally learn what it wanted—

And just like that it melted away. Back to its original, ambivalent, soft tug. My fingers twitched and tingled in the sudden absence of the more intense current. What the hell had just happened? I retreated to the room and slipped back into my bed quietly.

I stared, wide awake, as the darkness of the room shrank in around me, and I settled under the sheets. I'd never felt the thread like that before. There had never been anyone I could ask about what it meant. My grandfather was terror incarnate. My mother wanted nothing to do with me. My father ... where could I even begin?

"Reign?" Freda's sleepy voice sounded from across the room. "Are you okay?"

The cold darkness around me warmed just a little bit as I remembered I was not alone. Perhaps with Freda I could find answers. Two best friends and studious wizards—what couldn't we find out?

"Will you come to the library with me tomorrow? I need your help with some research," I said.

"Seriously?" She let out a teasing laugh. "The spring semester hasn't even started and you're already having bad dreams about exams?"

"No! But it will be interesting, I swear."

"Get some sleep or we won't be up early enough to get the good pastries. And I can't research without a cinnamon bun."

"Alright!" I pulled the comforter up higher as I eased deeper into the bed. I would figure this out—what this thread was and wanted. "Goodnight."

After acquiring Freda's cinnamon bun the next morning, we settled in on the first floor of the campus library and began our research with the set of books we pulled. Freda tied her wavy, copper hair back behind her head and plucked a book out of the pile. I scanned the first title in front of me.

Arcane Contracts

I cracked the book open to the index and began searching for the word I knew I wouldn't find.

Infernal

I heard the bookshelves to my left creak and saw the shadows of two students in whispered confidence staring at me.

If they had seen me without the spells I often used to hide my infernal traits—horns, pointed ears, and spade-tipped tail—I doubt they would be so bold as to even whisper this close. And if they saw my real eyes under the spelled walnut brown ones, they would start running.

I pulled my limbs in closer to take up less space. This was the other reason I wanted to leave as soon as I could. I wasn't a human like them. Like Freda.

I looked like my father, with all the same infernal features including pale scarlet skin and his eyes—glowing irises set like two, rose-colored rings on black sclera. The eyes of a devil. I had been taught to carefully hide that feature in particular—which helped me masquerade as if I was simply a hellborn. While those infernally cursed mortals were still regarded cautiously, they were far less threatening than an actual devil.

Perhaps I should be grateful that my petite stature helped me sink away in the background. It didn't stop me from hearing the muttered comment between the bookshelves, though.

"Did you see that creepy looking girl?"

Freda's green eyes flashed up to me, then she whipped her head to the other row of bookshelves. "Want to say that a little louder?"

Heads twisted towards us followed by a cacophony of shushes. The two students fled.

Freda's head turned back to me. "Sorry ..."

"It's okay." I pulled the book on arcane contracts closer. "I don't want to cause a scene."

Freda pressed her lips together. "Why are we wasting our time in the Midor's Academy library when we know it's not going to have what we're looking for?"

I glanced up at her. She wasn't wrong. But I'd hardly ventured out anywhere beyond the academy with the tight leash my grandfather kept on me.

Freda continued, "The library in Brunalin has subjects that are restricted here. Maybe we can find information about your dad or your mother's contract—" Her words choked off into silence and I followed her gaze to see my boyfriend, Luka, approach from behind.

I quickly pulled the book to my chest so he wouldn't see the title. I knew *exactly* how he would react to it.

"Classes haven't even started and you are already studying?" Luka said, then planted a kiss on my head.

Freda's eyes darted between the two of us, before narrowing on me. I knew what she was thinking.

I swallowed hard. "We're actually trying to find more information about ... my thread ... and the contract—"

"Why?" Luka said.

"The pull surged harder last night, and if it's related to my father maybe I can—"

"Reign." Luka pulled the book from my grasp, eyeing its title. "Why can't you just let this go? Your father is dangerous—all devils are. Trying to find him is the same as a death wish."

Those words coming from him hurt more than anything because I knew they weren't true. I had met my father once. He had been the first person who had ever shown me love despite what he was. And the thread had always offered me comfort and warm companionship. Nothing about its nature was malevolent. If anything, it felt *loving*.

Luka glanced between us at our shared silence. "Come on—surely there is something better to do with classes starting soon." He set the book on the table, just out of arm's reach.

Freda's green eyes shot to me in challenge. I knew I should say something, but I didn't want to keep fighting about this with him. Every single time my father, the contract tied to my birth, or my thread came up, we would argue. He had never tried to empathize with my situation. Admittedly, it made me wonder why we were still together.

"Maybe we can make sure we have all our supplies," I said, looking at Freda.

She raised her eyebrow in curiosity. We'd both already gotten all our supplies a few days ago. Then, she smiled and played along.

"Right, my supply list is on my desk," she said smoothly, rising from the table.

From then on, we conducted our research in secret.

After scouring the library, we resorted to asking professors *hypotheticals* about magic threads. Especially since I couldn't bring it up around Luka nor use his master student status to get access to the restricted sections without another fight. We searched and searched but nothing here shed any light. I seemed to be the only one who ever had a *thread*.

Over the course of a few months the surges became more frequent, longer. I struggled to stay focused as each yank caused me to drop a pen in a class, fall against a wall, or even cough repeatedly when the breath felt sucked from me. I forced myself to continue my steps in the direction of my classes, my dormitory, and the halls of Midor's Academy for Arcana. At the end of the semester I turned in my final papers and took my final tests.

When I left the Transmutation exam hall, I caught Freda huffing as she ran up alongside me. "Professor Morrel practically kicked me out after the fifth follow up question about magic *threads*." She laughed.

"Thanks for trying." I winced, rubbing my chest where the pull had been strong for hours. Freda's eyes flashed up at me with only the determination a best friend could have.

"After graduation, let's go to the Brunalin Library! Sarah said there's a whole section on the Nine Circles."

The thought of going beyond what we had access to in Midor's and into the city of Brunalin sent an uneasy dread through my stomach. My grandfather had never knowingly let me venture out that far. Even if we could, we needed something to focus our research. Something he'd also never let me *knowingly* see.

"If I can get my mother's contract when I go back to the estate, it might help us when we go to Brunalin Library. Maybe we can pull words from it to translate."

Freda's eyes went wide. "You think your grandfather will just give it to you?"

I looked down, watching my steps down the hall continue taking me away from the pull. "I'll figure out something."

If I couldn't get the contract and find clues in the Infernal written there, perhaps the only way I could get my answers *was* to follow the thread blindly. I'd have to leave Midor's. I'd have to venture into a world I knew so little about thanks to my sheltered childhood. It could very well be dangerous. What was at the end of an unknown, undocumented, unexplainable pull against my very being?

My graduation ceremony was in two weeks, and there was one last thing for me to do. So, later that week, I drifted closer to the admissions counter.

A woman with frizzy, silver hair sat behind it. She pinched over a form, pounded Midor's approval stamp across it, then flicked her fingers out for the next one.

I cleared my throat.

"Apprentice Graduation forms?" she said without even looking up.

I slid my own form to her.

"Master's program forms?"

My stomach turned at the assumption. Almost every wizard student here continued on to become a master. Luka certainly expected me to join him in his master's classes. I had been at this academy since I was ten years old, and I still felt just as far away from everything I wanted to know as I did now. Was this right? Should I follow the thread?

The thread surged powerfully and I sucked in a breath. It was as if it was answering that silent question in my mind with its tingling, pulling force—pleading with me.

Take a step. You belong with me.

I leaned towards it and felt the immediate relief of tension. My answer.

"Forms?" the woman said again.

I crumpled the master's program forms in my hands. I don't know why I had even filled them out.

She finally looked up at me. Her eyes went wide when she realized who she had been talking to.

I lifted my chin. "No forms. I'm discontinuing my education. I'm leaving Midor's."

Relief washed over me as if the decision was one of those tension-releasing steps in the direction the thread was pulling me. Perhaps I *had* shifted a step closer.

And then I knew. The way the thread seemed to speak to my very soul told me.

It had to be *him*.

PART I

THE THREAD

CHAPTER ONE

Luka frowned at me. "Seriously?" he said tensely, arms crossed, seated across from me at the same table in the library he'd found Freda and I at months ago.

Luka and I had studied here together, read together, and sipped coffee and cocoa from these dark wood chairs for the last two years. At the moment the library was deserted. Other wizard students were off applying for or stalking professors for practicums. Tomorrow, I would walk up the platform with other undergraduates and accept my apprentice title papers—*graduation ceremony complete.* Now all that was left was the form resting on the table in front of Luka.

I watched him scan the empty lines of bureaucracy and tradition printed on that parchment. Five hundred years ago, some pompous wizard decided master's students should *report and observe* the mastery of the apprentice students to the dean to formally qualify them for graduation. Today, it was simply a required paper trail, a formality—and I had forgotten that months ago I had listed my now *ex-boyfriend* to carry it out for me.

"Can we just get this over with?" I pleaded.

Luka sighed. He pulled the parchment in closer, snapping his fingers and a fountain pen appeared in his hand. The faint blue glow subsided, an indication of magic or *arcana* as the wizards who studied it academically called it.

I leaned forward slightly in anticipation.

He held the pen nib still over the first empty line. Hazel eyes flashed back up at me.

Something inside me twisted.

"Reign, leaving Midor's is a mistake," he pleaded. "I understand that you had a troubled childhood and you want to find some closure with your father, but this is not the answer."

Troubled childhood. I stiffened at how nonchalantly he mentioned it. He knew what this meant to me and still did not understand. I crossed my arms. "Just fill out the form, please."

He heaved a sigh, but scratched in my name with strokes of black ink. Then he filled out some of my personal details—birthday, room number, specialization—he had known it all.

"Reason for not continuing to master's?" He flicked his eyes up to me as he read the post-graduation section aloud. He knew why. It had been the entire basis for our break up.

"Just write it's to be closer to family."

He exhaled sharply, gripping the pen tighter. I recalled his words, of how it was *ridiculous* not to continue my studies at the master's level like he'd done. How following the pull of the thread was too dangerous a path—not because it would lead me into the unknown, but because of *who* we both guessed it might lead me to.

He had almost convinced me it was too dangerous to pursue information about my father, *a devil.* To seek answers to my origins and the thread. I thought being at Midor's would help me find answers while I learned to wield arcana. But the more spells I acquired the skill to execute, the further I was from answers about my origins. I couldn't—wouldn't—let *this* hold me back from the thread's new surge. It had to be directing me to the answers I desperately wanted. The family I wanted.

I watched Luka's hand sweep across the bottom of the page in the flourish of his signature, his brows terse with anger. Then his expression shifted to sadness, as if signing this form finalized our break up.

He opened his mouth, swallowed, then tried again. "I wish I could convince you this is a mistake. I wish you wouldn't chase this."

I narrowed my eyes. "I want a relationship with my father despite *what he is*. So either support me, or let me go."

"If you stayed," he gripped the form tighter, "we could research it between your—"

"Freda and I already looked. There is nothing in the library or any professor's brain—nothing in this entire academy about what this thread is." I eyed the form. Was he intending to withhold the paper I needed to graduate to continue this argument?

"What if you find out the truth and you don't like it?" he spat back. "I know you think because of one childhood birthday visit that devils are kind, but—"

I lurched forward as the thread surged. Gods, this was starting to drive me crazy. It had become more nagging every day I did not follow its pull. I breathed deep, steading myself before glancing back up at Luka.

His expression had shifted to worry. He knew what it looked like when the thread surged. He'd been watching it torment me for months all while trying to convince me to ignore it. Like *that* was even a remote possibility.

My eyes shot down to the form.

His grip had loosened.

I snapped my fingers, and the tips tinged with the arcana of spellcraft. A ghostly, floating blue hand appeared—my *Mystic*

Hand—and snatched the form. It raced toward me, spectral dust scattering through the air in its wake.

Luka frowned. He could have stopped the spell. He was a more studied wizard than myself, already well into his master's program. But he didn't. He just stared at me. Then the chair groaned as he stood from the table.

"Maybe it makes me an asshole," his face tightened to a pained expression, "but because of *what he is,* I really hope you don't find him."

I crossed my arms, form in hand, and held his stare. I'd backed down too many times before. I wouldn't this time.

He sighed and the tightness melted to resignation. "Goodbye, Reign."

I watched him walk silently past the other empty tables. The doors at the end of the hall slammed shut behind him, rattling the books on the nearest shelf. The strong pull eased as if in relief of the closed argument.

I felt a sudden sense of freedom tangled with a growing anxiety. He was not the only thing I needed to free myself from. After the ceremony, I would have to travel back to my family's estate and find my mother's contract. Emancipating my grandfather and mother would likely be more ... difficult.

My family—the Vendelfrey's—were high ranking nobility in our region with a vast estate and a variety of business ventures thanks to my grandfather. However, I would inherit none of it. I was seen as a tool, an unfortunate mistake to be used in my grandfather's business theatre.

I started the five minute walk back to my dormitory, the click of my boots echoed through the corridor. The gray, stone-hewn halls arched to high points over me, and passing students ducked their heads to avoid my gaze. One poor young student turned in a completely different direction upon sighting me. Each reaction hurt. I just wanted to belong somewhere—somewhere I could be my true self.

I'd fantasized about where the thread might lead me and often imagined my father there waiting for me. I hoped the thread had something to do with him. How could it not? The day I was born I emerged with his appearance and the thread drew taut. If translating the contract yielded no answers, then finding him might. If I *could* find him ... Devils—being immortal and infernal creatures—lived on an entirely different plane of existence.

The Nine Circles of Hell.

I knew that if my father had wanted to see me, he probably would have made a stronger effort to visit me more than once over twenty-five years. He had told me it would be a long while before we'd see each other again, but I was tired of waiting for him to come to me. Tired of waiting for answers. The rising pull of the thread had to have some purpose. It was time for me to make the next move and find out why I was so different. This was my chance to drive my own fate—find my own answers.

I refused to let Luka, Midor's, or even my family get in my way.

My stomach twisted as I reached my room door. Despite my determination I knew I needed help, but I hesitated at the threshold of my next conversation. Valid danger aside, Freda was not going to let me hear the end of it if I didn't bring her with me.

CHAPTER TWO

I unlocked my dormitory room and slipped inside. Freda's head tilted up from packing her bag, green eyes lighting up between her loose copper curls as she sighted me.

"So get this," she said excitedly. "Sarah told me that not only is there a section on the Nine Circles at the Brunalin Library, there's an entire room that has preserved rare texts—possibly infernal topics." She raised her finger as if to silence me from reacting. "And the best part—is it's open to the public." She grinned mischievously.

I smiled back at her. She had been the first human that had truly accepted me. I thought about our first year at Midor's with all the other ten-year-olds in foundations courses. When I had first entered this room, almost all of my infernal traits were on display. Freda had looked at me with the same welcoming warmth then as she did now, whether my eyes were rich brown or glowing red rings in a black void. I loved her for it.

Freda's eyebrows turned up. "What's wrong?"

"Well ..." I began, gliding over to my bed and plopping down with an exhale. "I forgot to remove him from my Observation Form ..."

"Ha!" Freda belted out. "So Luka had to sit there and write to the dean about how great you are and basically why you broke up with him?" She smirked at the notion he might have suffered. To be fair she'd seen how much pain our unraveling relationship had caused me. Her tone shifted low and caring. "Did your father come up again?"

"Of course." I pressed my lips together.

"Well at least it's over," she said as she pulled her bag in closer and stuffed another folded shirt inside. "Happy Reign deserves to stay, no more *rain* cloud."

I felt the corner of my mouth turn at the play on words. "Have you decided what your new area of focus will be for the first year of your *master's?*" I said with excitement.

She glanced up sheepishly from folding more clothing into her bag. "You know, I was kinda thinking I'd try Transmutation?"

"Really?" My eyes widened and a fanged smile burst across my face upon hearing my own focus area—my passion for all five years of my apprentice program—named.

"I totally get the appeal." She winked at me. "I mean, think of how much money I can make transmuting iron to gold, wood to stone."

"All lies!" I teased at the common joke between transmuters. Most arcana used to transform things was temporary or an illusion, like the spell I used to camouflage myself to look less infernal.

My stomach twisted as I realized I wouldn't be going deeper into my Transmutation studies in the master's courses. I had always been interested in understanding the potential of transmuting living creatures instead of objects. It was completely theoretical, of course, outside of an illusionary *Polyform* spell. True transformation was as rare as my own circumstance.

I watched Freda pack presents for her family—small trinkets—into her bag. My hand drifted to the button I had threaded through a loop around my neck, tucked under my blouse. It was the only gift I had ever received from my father.

Despite my research, accounts of devil-produced offspring with mortals was unheard of. To complicate my situation, I had been born of two human parents. Even then I was destined to be a bastard—a human one—when my mother had to make an unthinkable choice. In desperation to save both her lover and me, she made a deal with a devil—my infernal father. As soon as her signature in blood dried on the contract, something transformed me. Not long after, I came into the world with the likeness of *him*—the likeness of a devil.

It was easier and safer to tell others I was hellborn, as long as I kept my eyes magically altered to look like one. Genuine hellborn had been the product of cursed bloodlines. An ancient pact was made with a devil generations back, cursing all offspring with the infernal design, but they retained their human eyes. It made me wonder if what had transformed me was similar to that ancient deal, since nothing about it was biological.

I brought my wandering thoughts back to Freda's choice, her soon-to-be experienced master's classes. I wondered for a moment if I had made the wrong decision, and perhaps joining the master's students could help me learn *something*.

"Why the sudden interest in Transmutation?" I kicked my dangling feet over the bed to chase away the doubts creeping in.

"Abjuration is getting boring." She snorted, pulling open her bedside drawer. "There are only so many wards I can place on my family's home. Plus, I'll miss you," she said, her voice cracking a little. "And I haven't tried Transmutation yet beyond the foundational courses. I figured if I take a few classes it will give me an excuse to *Mindtell* you asking you to tutor me." She feigned a laugh, shoving a few more items into her bag. The thought did make me a little teary-eyed. I would miss having her around me every single day when the semester resumed in the fall.

"I'll miss you too ... If I do find my father and he takes me away, I'll find a way to communicate with you. Even if we're across planes." The promise felt hollow. The short mind to mind communication allowed by the *Mindtell* spell didn't work across planes, even for the most powerful mortal wizards. But I would try. Maybe I'd be the first to figure out how to do it.

She pulled out a spell material—aluminum filament. It sizzled and I heard her voice tingle across my mind with the arcana of the *Mindtell*. *"Even the answers to all my Transmutation exam questions?"* She laughed in my mind.

"Help you cheat? Never!" I teased back through the free reply the spell's design always allowed.

Freda laughed out loud, then tilted her head up to me. "Do you have to start the break by going back to the estate instead of coming to stay with me? My mom will be at the seamstress shop most of the time with my aunt, so who knows what kind of trouble we'd get into."

I had never been allowed to visit her home. But the thought of being there with a real caring family warmed my soul. "I want to do this properly. So I'll ask for my freedom and pack my things." I eased up from the bed and began to discard my boring uniform to don clothing more suitable for a young, female, *probably*-hellborn wizard. I smiled at the all-black items I pulled from the wardrobe as I slowly began changing into them.

Freda relocated the small items from her bedside drawer into her bag. "Have you told your mom you're looking for your father yet?"

I swallowed the anxiety that crept up my throat. Despite how utterly close Freda and I were, I had never gone into great detail about why I'd never written a letter to my mother, let alone sent her a *Mindtell* while I was at the academy. "No. I don't see the point in telling her. Unless I can't find the contract." She knew the sub-context. That we didn't really have a relationship. I slipped a black blouse over my head.

"Did your father ever give you any hint of how to find him? Other than the mysterious arcane thread."

I blinked my eyes, surfacing the memory that often replayed in my dreams. My sixth birthday—the one and only time I'd actually met him.

He'd sat in a big chair in my grandfather's lounge. He had offered me his hand, a pale scarlet—just like mine. Even if it was simply an arcane transformation, something else was there. The warm current glittering in my soul that told me with unwavering doubt that I belonged to him. He had shown me the Nine Circles of Hell and given me a button from his jacket to remember him. He had instructed me to use it to draw on my own power, to focus my arcana. That I was powerful. That I could actualize the things I desired. That he loved me.

It was the first time I had heard those words uttered to me. It was all I needed to know. Despite the circumstances, he was my true father.

"Reign?" Freda's eyebrows raised, catching me lost in the memory.

I winced an apology. "He said it would be a while before we'd see each other again."

"I keep forgetting that you have actually been to the Nine Circles." Freda shifted to a seat recalling the story I'd told her numerous times. Travel from our own plane, Novus, was rare even for wizards. For mortals, travel to the Nine Circles was usually a deadly, one way trip. "How do you think you'll get there?"

I tilted my head, thinking. "Only the older master's students learn the spell for opening portals to other planes. So since I don't plan on hanging out here another eight years, I'll have to find another way ..." I looked down to the floor silently as even now the thread hummed its typical soft tug in me.

"Well, step one, we go to the library—"

"Freda ..." I smiled. "Are you really planning to spend your whole break between semesters helping me do research?"

A wide smile cracked across her face. "Hell yes I am." She drew the drawstring taut on her bag. "What other students get to study off-limits subjects? And I have to check out your father and make sure he's cool before I let him take you away."

I burst out laughing.

"I'm serious!" She laughed back.

I wiped the tears from the corner of my eyes. "In all seriousness, I'm nervous about bringing you into this. If there was anything Luka was right about, it's that devils and humans aren't exactly on the best of terms."

It wasn't the clearest way to express the real danger in letting my human friend get anywhere near infernal creatures, let alone a devil. But I knew she knew what I meant.

"I know ..." She sighed. "Pretty sure I'd take one step into the Nine Circles and become a toasted marshmallow."

"I would be worried about you if you went. I wouldn't want you to get hurt or ... " I smirked, "become enslaved to an infernal!" I laughed, trying to lighten the mood. "You are always welcome to sign your soul over to me for safekeeping." I winked at her. Like I knew *anything* about soul collection—the favored past time of devils.

Freda started laughing. "Right. If you ever learn how to write your own devil contracts and my eternal soul is to be damned to the Nine Circles, I will gladly accept your offer!"

We joked, but it was a reminder of a real outcome for many mortals—especially humans. Mortal souls were currency and a power status in the Nine Circles of Hell. Depending on the owner of your soul, your eternal existence could be quite grim ... or so I'd read. The hierarchies of the Nine Circles were all based on one's power of arcana, with devils particularly high in those ranks.

"Maybe we can make a deal." I smiled softly at her. "After I get the contract, you help me translate it and research the topics, but if it comes down to it, and I can find a way from Novus to the Nine Circles ... You have to let me go alone."

She sighed. "You are mortal too, you know."

I pressed my lips together. "Please. Basically if it gets too dangerous or we reach the end of the summer break—you won't follow me. You'll come back here where it's safe."

She blinked at me, holding my stare as if to test my will.

"Yes, it's dangerous either way," I conceded. "But I know my father will protect me if I can find him."

"Fine ..." She rolled her eyes. "Deal." She lifted herself from her bed, flattened out her blankets, then turned back to me. "Want to grab dinner?"

"No, I have some things to take care of."

Freda raised an eyebrow at me.

"And I just need some quiet time after that encounter with Luka!" I laughed. "Go, enjoy your dinner."

Freda slipped through the door, clicking it shut. Twisting anxiety immediately surged through my body. I had not told her what I actually wanted to do. Because I wanted to prove to myself that I could do it.

Alone.

I laid back on my bed, waiting for it to happen. The thread surged more at night than it did during the day. I glanced down to my now completely original outfit. Black silks and frills covering as much of my skin as possible to hide what I was. I stared at the ceiling, air-tapping my foot, syncopating the seconds that passed.

Then it whirled into me—the surging pull of the thread. I seized with tension as its electric current melted over me. *Finally.*

I sprang up from the bed and snatched the spell materials pouch resting on my nightstand.

I had been afraid to do this. I just wanted a trial run. See if there was anything to learn by just following the thread a little bit. Not past Brunalin. I wouldn't leave the city ... yet.

I felt awful not telling Freda. But this was explicitly *not* research in a library. And I needed to get a taste for what kind of danger I might be pulling her into.

I caught a glimpse of myself in the mirror as I reached for the door. My shoulder-length hair fell in soft black waves, concealing my pointed ears. Little flecks of sanguine freckles painted my pale scarlet skin, just like my father's. I had still used the spell *Modify Self* to hide my tail, red-black rams horns, and eyes. It made me long to be somewhere I wouldn't have to hide like this.

I let out a deep sigh, releasing lingering anxiety.

Maybe I'll find you tonight ...

CHAPTER THREE

With the night as my cover, I made my way up the sloped streets that led into the heart of the Northern District of Brunalin. Every step, with the train bringing me into the heart of the city, the thread surged and released as it tightened its thrall on me. I knew I was getting closer ... but how much further would it be? What were the chances it would literally lead me to somewhere in Brunalin?

The darkness didn't do well to conceal the cracks in the stone walls of the buildings I passed, nor its defacement with black ink—likely code to those who understood it. Brunalin was famous for its ancient design with layers of human—and wizard—history. During the daytime the new businesses breathed life back into the cardinal district, which made it a popular destination for cafés and small boutique stores. After the bustling noise of clinking cups and rustling shopping bags subsided, the businesses closed for the night and it was quiet—too quiet.

The street sloped up and I breathed heavy climbing deeper and deeper into the district. That otherworldly thread pulled stronger, thrumming in my chest with the electric current that had been plaguing me for months. My pace slowed as the thread tightened in front of a closed café. The dark street alongside its storefront was empty.

I shut my eyes and concentrated on the directional tug. I took a blind step forward towards the café. It felt like I was being pulled down instead of forward. I opened my eyes and instantly spotted a red, glowing lantern hung at the dead end of an alley between the café and its neighbor.

Spooky lantern, dark alley. Yeah this was *exactly* the kind of risk I did not want to subject Freda to.

I crept silently towards the lantern until the two buildings loomed over either side. The brick walls were lit red with the lantern's light, making it look like it might actually lead into the Nine Circles. I paused in front of the lantern, where I now saw an unmarked door.

I jiggled the handle. Unlocked.

My heart pounded. The thread felt charged, surging more as it pulled me towards the door. I panted a breath like it was being stolen from me in the moments I remained still. Why would my father plant such a sensation in me if he did not intend for me to give in to it? Or at least reach where it might lead me? I couldn't help but quiver from the nerves rattling me as I tried to keep my hand steady on the handle.

I breathed in slowly and opened the door to find steps descending downward into darkness. I could see better in the dark than my human peers, but to eliminate any surprises, I swirled a finger and cast *Mage Lights*. Floating balls of blue light inflated like small bubbles into the air around me and drifted ahead of my descent. The thread thrummed, sending an exhilarating excitement down my spine.

My *Mage Lights* halted, casting their blue light on another door at the bottom of the stairs. I took the remaining steps downward and the pull roared like I was caught in a rushing river, moments away from losing complete control and being swept away in its current. It narrowed my vision and I slowly wrapped my fingers around the handle of the door. I turned it and that sensation—the electric, thrumming pull of the thread—slipped away like sand through my fingers.

Wait!

I shoved the door open.

Dim yellow light and voices flooded my senses as I took a step through. A long bar stretched down the left side of the space with a crowd of all kinds of folk leaning into it. A tall, elven bartender dressed in dark leathers turned back to a wall of bottles, then shifted half-full glasses of amber liquid to patrons. To the right were rows of packed tables barely visible by the light of the crude, candlelit structure hanging from the ceiling and aged sconces plastered to the walls. A variety of mortals stood shoulder to shoulder packing the room: humans, elves, dwarves, and even other hellborn. My eyes landed on one of the hellborn—and their human eyes—and I felt like a bit of a fraud. But if the crowd here saw my devil eyes, I wasn't sure how far I'd make it. I wove through the patrons and spotted a halfling and a gnome pushing between taller folk as well.

Most of the individuals here wore dark-colored cloaks that obscured their faces in shadow and threw suspicious glances as they neared one another. Coin purses were pulled in tight and heads shifted closer in whispered confidence. I was pretty sure I saw the glint of a dagger or two resting under palms. It didn't surprise me now why the entrance was unmarked.

I was not in the heart of the Northern District. I had stumbled into its underbelly.

Patrons pushed on either side of me as I slipped between them, finding a break in the crowd. Across the wall in front of me was a short, raised platform with a single unoccupied ornate chair. I crept closer until I stood right in front of it. The seat was upholstered with black velvet and gold grommets that were nailed into dark-colored wood with intricate, swirling, flame-like carvings on their joints. There was a smell hovering in the air, and I leaned in closer and inhaled. A smoky, cinnamon aroma, as if someone had dried and burned bark from a sweet tree.

"Girl."

I jumped at the voice that abruptly called me from behind. I turned and was met with the towering presence of a man with wiry, gray hair, clad in old, worn leather. My eyes caught on the glinting of axes, looped into his belt.

"I've not seen you around here before. Are you looking for someone?"

My eyes flashed up to his face as I considered how to handle the situation. A whiff of the lingering smoky cinnamon drew my attention back to the black chair behind me. "I'm looking for the owner of this chair," I said in my best attempt at confidence, searching the old man's face for any form of acknowledgement.

He leaned back on his heels. "Ah, yes ... Well, you've missed him, I'm afraid. He comes and goes when he pleases, especially if he's not seeing clients." A wobbly smile of missing and yellowed-brown teeth painted his face.

"When was the last time he was here?" I knew this would probably be the last question I was afforded. I had to make sure—that it was *him* that had drawn the thread so tightly.

"A few moments ago. Terrible timing for you, I reckon." He tilted his head, looking at me from head to toe. "I wonder what a nice-looking girl like you was going to offer for a deal?" His eyes searched my body, assessing the value of my clothes, belongings, and anything else visible to him.

A deal? Certainly sounds like my father.

My skin crawled as I noticed the attention of others seated in the crowd watching me. My gaze shot between each of them—their drawn hoods, the tattered edges of cloaks, dark soils on their sleeves and knees, and hands all resting on hilts as they listened for my next words.

I only just realized that I stuck out like a sore thumb in this crowd. Not because I was a hellborn in disguise—I stood out because I was obviously wealthy and woefully unguarded. Ready for every piece of me to be sold to the highest bidder.

I took a quick calming breath in as I employed my already planned escape route. *"I'll see myself to the door."* I muttered the arcana-laced words—the spoken word material required to cast my *Mystic Door* behind me. The crowd burst into gasps and chairs groaned. I took a quick step backwards and crossed its spectral blue threshold.

Blue arcane light clung to me as I stepped down from the floating door into the alley. Cool, clear air rushed in as the door dispersed like glittering smoke in the air. The alley was darker now, the red lantern extinguished.

And so I ran. Back to my dormitory. Freda was already asleep, so I slipped in quietly. At least now I knew. It was *him*. He was at the end of this thread.

The next morning, my apprentice graduation proceeded to be perhaps one of the dullest, least important moments of my life. The Arcana Prima, Lorrel, slipped me a small scroll as I shook her hand crossing the outdoor platform erected in one of the green fields. I turned the scroll in my hands. It wasn't my certificate, another professor had handed me that. This scroll was intended for my grandfather. Probably filled with the typical pleasantries that were given to all the noble human families that attended here for generations. I knew better than to open things addressed to my grandfather.

I was careful to avoid Luka after the ceremony, but I found Freda quickly among the other graduates on the green. She was hugging her mother and Mabel, her younger sister.

"Hello, Reign!" her mother said as I joined their group. It had been five years since I'd seen either of them, and Mabel was looking more and more like her mother the older she got. Mousy brown hair and blue eyes, and a kind and caring expression. I'd never met Freda's father, who I assumed is where she got her red hair and green eyes from. He'd fallen ill shortly after Mabel was born and had been confined to bed rest ever since.

Freda swooped in and embraced me as I greeted her family.

"Nice to see you, Mrs. Rye," I squeaked past the tight hug. I used the smile reserved for putting humans at ease—the one that hid my fangs.

"Reign!" Mabel burst out. "Freda won't tell me if you have a tail!" Her eyes sparkled with excitement.

Ahh, to be ten-years-old and so unbiased by this world. I imagined she hardly remembered me from our foundations graduation five years ago.

"Mabel!" Mrs. Rye scolded her.

"It's okay," I said. I looked down at Mabel with a more mischievous smile. "Since I'm a wizard," I waved my hand in the air in demonstration, "I've learned what materials and instructions unlock the magic all around us to do my bidding." I winked at her, then snapped my fingers. The illusion hiding my tail flickered away, glittering, red light dissipating around it. I immediately wiggled it towards her and poked her side with its spade tip. She jumped and we giggled together. I glanced up at Freda and she rolled her eyes in amusement.

"We're going to get dinner tonight to celebrate—nothing fancy," Freda said. "Want to come with us?"

I smiled to myself. I still had not told Freda about the night before—and that I was planning on trying again if the thread surged. I knew she would insist on ditching her family and coming if I did. Plus, this would be my last chance to try before I had to return to the estate.

"Thanks for the invite, but I think I should make sure I have everything packed." I feigned an innocent smile.

Freda gave me a curious look as we finished our goodbyes. I was certain that if anyone could catch me in a lie it'd be my best friend of fifteen years. I was grateful she didn't pry further.

I would tell her later.

I spent the rest of the day getting prepared. I chose clothing that matched what I had seen the others inside that basement bar wearing—a long black cloak and black leathers.

And I waited. Waited and waited. The sun set, and I finally rose from my desk impatiently. The powerful surge of the thread had not come, so I decided to start walking to the basement bar anyway.

I had just slipped out of the corridor when I heard a rattling boom, the sound of stones clashing together, followed by shouting.

I rushed towards the dusty plume spilling into the courtyard. Students were scattering into the dust cloud, yelling.

"Where is Quinn?" a voice shouted from the cloud. "What happened?"

"It backfired." Another voice coughed.

My eyes went wide. They sounded young—like foundations students. I ran into the cloud pushing through the silhouettes of people doing the same. I flew forward till I saw the spilled broken rock, burn marks on its surface just barely visible through the haze.

Backfired indeed. Evocation—the elemental school of magic—was not taught till the apprentice level because of risks like this.

"Here!" a student shouted. I followed the obscured movements in front of me till a half-dozen students stood around a boy, his legs pinned under a massive piece of the stone building.

Oh shit.

The younger students began pushing against the stone as if to move it.

"Wait!" I yelled through the dust. "Go find the campus cleric!"

One of the young girls ran out of the dust in the direction of the infirmary.

"We have to move it—"

"If you had taken your Evocation safety courses, you'd know that moving it will make him bleed out!" I realized all the barely-visible faces around me were so small, even compared to me. Just barely adolescents beginning their studies. I was the only titled wizard among them.

Dust whooshed by and I saw the white robes of the cleric rush to the boy on the ground. "What happened?"

They looked at each other tight-lipped to prevent self-incrimination. The cleric's hands flew to the boy's legs and I heard him groan in pain. Sparkling, white light pulsed everywhere her hands trailed.

"His legs are stabilized, but I can't move this stone!" she shouted.

"I can!" I replied, quickly pulling a bit of crushed marble from my spell material pouch.

I whipped my wrists in a flowing motion, rubbing the powdered marble between my palms. The younger students gasped as the ground rattled around us, sending up more dust into the air. The stones began to vibrate, rotate, and lift as I steadied my hands. The Transmutation spell, *Manipulate Rock,* flowed through my fingers in blue, glittering streams, wrapping and forcing the stone to retake its previous shape—transmuting it back into the wall it once was.

The cleric snapped her fingers. An arcane wind blew the dust away and I finally saw the boy. He was wide-eyed, but safe. I breathed a sigh of relief.

I heard gasping to my left, and when I turned I saw four boys and two girls staring at me, mouths agape, hands at their sides trembling.

My stomach twisted as I realized. The dust had been obscuring me. One of the many small reminders of how much of an outsider I was at this mostly human academy.

The cleric glanced between us all, then back to the foundations students. "To the dean's office, now!" She lifted the boy in her arms and the kids scattered. He gripped her white tunic, blinking at me.

She sighed. "Thank you." Then she carried the boy towards the infirmary.

My mind wandered with the sudden isolation. I was an outsider in the basement bar too—but because I came from nobility.

Dark thoughts began to surface. What if I was an outsider in the Nine Circles of Hell? Or wherever my father was.

I wondered if perhaps my father also felt the thread's pull. If so, it didn't seem accidental that it had suddenly vanished when I finally got close enough to him.

What if ... my devil father, the only other family I had, also didn't want me after all? What if he regretted visiting me, no longer loved me as he had said—felt I was a mistake?

I tried to banish my spiraling thoughts as I made my way back to my room in defeat. I waited, wishing the thread would surge again, just so I could feel that powerful reassuring pull. The comforting caress that made me believe it was all intentional. I had to believe it would lead me to somewhere good.

Somewhere I belonged.

CHAPTER FOUR

"See you soon." Freda winked as the horse-drawn carriage slowed to a stop at the campus coach area.

I pressed my lips together. "If all goes well, you should hear from me in a few days."

My single chest was loaded on the back of the family carriage. Then the coachman turned the handle to the door and opened it wide for me. I turned back to Freda and squeezed her into a tight hug.

"You travel safe too," I said as we parted.

"It's just an hour train ride."

I knew that, but I worried for her all the same.

We waved our goodbyes and I climbed into the coach, settling myself against the plush velvet bench before pulling out my spell book, journal, and a short history of famous wizards and their achievements. My entertainment for the next six hours. A solitude I would be grateful for as I drew closer to my human family.

I watched the west towers drift by as the steel-lined wheels below me clicked against the brick roads. The west towers had portals to help students commute across the continent to their families quickly, but my grandfather didn't like the idea of anyone popping in without warning, so the estate had glyphs against teleportation.

I watched the coachman's coat edges flap in the wind through the small window at the front of the carriage. I wondered if my *human father* still drove a carriage like this one.

Thinking through the story of my human parent's affair again, I wondered how much was true and how much my mother had made up. Between her, my grandfather, and overhearing rumors spread between staff, I had pieced most things together.

My mother had been in love with one of the Vendelfrey family's carriage drivers. After many secret, torrid nights in the coach, she became pregnant with me. When it became too difficult for my mother to hide her condition, my grandfather found out. He was furious. However, a rich, incredibly powerful wizard can literally get away with murder—which my grandfather often did. My mother had panicked at the prospect of losing her lover and searched for a way to save him.

In her desperation, my mother had found a devil and signed a contract with him. She had simply wanted to save her lover, but the devil—my infernal father—explained that life cost life.

And thus, an unthinkable choice.

But she had pleaded with him. Back then, she still wanted me, or at least the idea of me when I was set to be human like her. The devil agreed not to harm me and let her lover live—but he was to have all his memories of her burned from his mind.

However, devils are known to only write contracts that benefit them. He must have seen something advantageous about my situation that appealed to him. He had secretly sealed my fate in the fine print, but she had not known and signed in her blood anyway.

And so, I had been born—with the appearance of my infernal father instead of my human father. Considering how hellborn were usually sired, I didn't think she ever imagined I might have received an infernal design. I had always wondered, was I still a human on the inside? Could I be half-devil? Or perhaps was I, regardless of how unique my origin, simply a hellborn?

The story behind my birth outside the estate was different. My grandfather used every opportunity to make himself look like a selfless servant of philanthropy. He had made sure that the story that actually spread was that a hellborn had forced himself on my mother and that my grandfather had accepted and adopted me as a babe despite it all.

He mentioned that oration of my story during every trade contract negotiation. Who would deny the selflessness involved in caring for an unexpected child of rape? The parties of other lords and dignitaries would watch me, fascinated, like I was some kind of rare pet, and their amusement would lower their prices and allow favorable terms to slip into the agreements. And to curb all suspicion of any devil's involvement, he made sure that when I was paraded around he'd used his own skill as a wizard to modify my eyes to look like other hellborn. In fact when I was older, *Modify Self* was the first spell I ever learned. One of his first orders for my arcana education.

The narrative didn't stop at the meetings with lords and dignitaries. Everything that was given to me was to be used in the narrative, or to keep me in the background. When my mother eventually married another noble family's son and had three completely human children, she left me fully to my grandfather as a required material to his negotiations.

Convincing my grandfather to sponsor me at Midor's was when things had changed for me. I was free of their abuse for eleven months out of the year. Each time I returned for the summer month break, my mother's neutral expression melted to a pained scowl. It was as if she had forgotten about me while I was away and seeing me broke her happy illusion. As the years went by, I wondered if she would be relieved or devastated when I aged out of use in my grandfather's public image, especially with my graduation behind me now.

The shadows lengthened, stretching towards the carriage till it turned past the tall spiraling topiary trees on the last stretch of road that led to the estate. The horseshoes clicked on the cobblestone between the ornate fountain and the front of the main house as we slowed to a stop. The coachman opened the door and extended a hand, helping me down.

The estate house towered at four floors high with rows of glimmering windows set in a sandy-colored stone. It covered me entirely with its shadow. The anxiety already churned in my stomach as I walked up the cream marble steps to the double front doors. The solid, carved wood stretched up twelve feet with one door left ajar for me to enter through. My grandfather had ordered the estate expertly designed shortly after my birth. The grandiose features—large double doors engraved with runes, wide marble steps, towering scalloped columns, and a Sapphire Coast rug outside the front door—were all actors in the manipulation of his guests.

I passed into the foyer, another conspirator in his carefully crafted theater of power. With marble floors and walls polished so smooth, it took effort to keep my feet from sliding as I crossed them. Twin curving staircases opened up into the vaulted mezzanine between the two wings of the estate. Between them, a marble bust of my grandfather sat at the center of the foyer atop a small table carved from solid green malachite gemstone. I stopped and examined his likeness. Furrowed brows, sharp cheekbones, a thin but angular slant of lips—harsh features to match a harsh person. Eyes embedded with enormous diamonds in an expression of raw power.

Then I heard his voice, an emotionless dark echo in some far-off room to my right. He was probably in his office connected to the drawing room. I felt the anxiety shift to a nervous tingle in my hands. The contract had to be recovered before he realized I was home.

I had only seen it once. It was shortly after the one and only visit from my father. My grandfather had been highly concerned with the contract after that and, one day while sneaking around, I had glimpsed it rolled out on his desk. Heavy stones in each corner had held open the narrow, tan scroll. Its script was a dark sanguine that had shimmered with a gold sheen in the light. Despite only getting a glimpse, I had known what it was. It pulled similarly to the thread when I was near it. After learning more about arcana, I figured it had something to do with my ties to the contract and this thread that was planted in me. Knowing my grandfather, he'd keep the contract somewhere I couldn't randomly stumble upon it. He had a carefully crafted lie to protect, after all.

I crept up the stairs, pausing at the top and focused on the pulling tingle I felt. I walked down the corridor slowly, pausing every few steps and closed my eyes to focus. I suspected it might be in the room he kept other archives in, but I had to be sure. I passed several doors—a study, a sunroom, and a storage room. A few more steps and I stopped in front of the archive room. I could feel the tingling pull of the contact beyond the seal of the locked door. My grandfather was in the habit of locking all his doors—even his smoking parlor—with arcane locks. This was also where the glyph originated, the one that prevented portal travel. The powerful glyph spanned the entire main estate. I knew how arcane locks worked, if I could disengage the lock, my grandfather would sense his spell was disturbed.

I had always daydreamed about subverting the restrictive arcana and sneaking around the estate, but there had never really been a reason for me to actually test its limitations ... till now.

I pulled a pinch of black sand from the small pouch and held it tightly in my fist as I sidestepped to the wall next to the door. I stretched my fingers up the wall as high as I could and began outlining a large circle, all while I mumbled arcana-laced words to the wall.

"Give a passage to me."

The spell *Passage* bloomed across the wall in a shimmering green light. A hole large enough for me appeared where I had traced my fingers. I cackled quietly to myself. The Transmutation spell didn't technically invoke a *portal*.

I noticed the glyph on the floor immediately. Inlays of intricate, swirled metals glowed blue, forming an angular symbol across the tile floor. It was indeed the Palisade glyph. I stepped through the threshold I'd created and looked around.

Shelves were filled with all matter of rare and exquisite items my grandfather collected. Across each of the highest shelves sat a knife on a wooden stand. A flare of the tingle compelled me to look to the left side of the room. I took measured steps toward the cabinets and shelves that lined the wall.

I pulled one drawer open slowly. A collection of velvet wrapped items sat neatly before me, but my eyes drew to the first one. I picked it up and felt that tingle trickle through my fingertips. I unwrapped the velvet's edge to reveal the warm, narrow tan parchment of my contract.

I quickly wrapped it back in its velvet sleeve and tucked it into my inner jacket pocket. Then, I closed the drawer and slipped back out through the entrance I'd created before dispelling it. I was grateful my connection to the contract had helped me recover it quickly, but something bore a pit in my stomach.

Had it been too easy?

CHAPTER FIVE

I watched my footing as I snuck downstairs, lifting my head at the last step to check for my grandfather's butlers—and almost bumped face-first into one standing in the foyer.

"Ah, Miss Vendelfrey. The Master would like to have a word with you." The man gestured towards the drawing room.

I straightened my jacket and walked in. The drawing room always had cut flowers positioned on tables under each tall window that lined the wall. It would have been a benign decorating choice to any other person. I saw them for what they were. Trapped—forced to decay indoors instead of thriving in the sun. It was how my grandfather treated everything he controlled. The expansive, brightly lit drawing room felt at odds with the dark connecting hall that led to his office. I slowed before the door, left ajar, and listened. Suddenly, another voice spoke and I froze.

"Is that your decision?" My mother asked in a frustrated tone.

There was a long, tense silence before my grandfather answered.

"What would you have me do, Lydia?" His emotionless voice reverberated in the air between me and the door. "She's decided she's done with training. Now, we can make use of her."

What?

My stomach twisted as I awaited my mother's reply.

"You're not worried about potential retribution?" There was a sharp bite to her voice. "What if the family realizes what's been done?"

"I've already seen to it that won't happen. The girl will marry the Gisenwald's second son, and you'll never have to see her again."

I waited for her reply. My heart pounded in my ears as each second moved on.

"Paul's been in contact with the Silver Sands. The captain will take the meeting to show you what they have on board." My mother went on, changing the subject to my stepfather's work.

Paul had married my mother shortly after I was born. He'd never spoken a single word to me. They had three daughters together, my half-sisters: Cordelia, Amberlynn, and Lynette.

I let my mother and grandfather toil on into more mundane conversation and my nerves began to settle. I might as well confront them now. See if my exiting the picture of my own volition would free me of the fate he described.

I glanced behind me towards the entrance to the drawing room. The door was still open, good. I swirled my finger and summoned a *Mystic Hand.* It flew across the room leaving a trail of blue spectral dust in its wake, and pulled the door shut as if I had just entered. The sound of the door echoed across the room and the conversation in the study fell into a guarded silence. I counted to ten in my head, breathed in quietly, and gently knocked on the half-open door.

"Grandfather?" I asked, speaking softly and waiting for permission to enter. I knew he would be pleased if played submissive to his control.

"Ah, it's you, Grace. Come in."

I sucked in a breath before walking in. It always felt unusual to hear the name they had given me. My birth name, *Grace*. I much preferred my chosen name—the name that freed me from them.

I pushed the door open and saw my mother leaning against a built-in bookshelf that spanned the entire wall. She had her arms crossed and head tilted, looking down at me with deep blue eyes flanked by dark lashes. Her brown hair, laced with gray, was braided up around her head, crowning her gaunt face—which looked even more sallow since the last time I had seen her.

My grandfather sat in a massive, fur-lined chair behind his grandiose desk. Parchments were spread all across the shiny, cherry-colored wood. His signing quill—a single plume of golden peacock, the rarest variety—rested on its stand close to him. He motioned for me to sit in the single, plain chair across from him, the one reserved for those he subverted his power over.

Strike one against me.

I lowered myself on the edge of the chair. I felt like a child again, waiting in this very chair to be told what I must do to garner sympathy and influence his bargains with other lords.

His cold, gray-blue eyes targeted me from his towering vantage point. "How was your graduation ceremony?"

I reached into my inner jacket pocket. I pushed the velvet-wrapped contract aside and pulled out the small scroll from Arcana Prima Lorrel. Lowering my head first to show respect, I extended it towards him. He opened a drawer and pulled out a small set of bifocals, placing them towards the end of his nose before he accepted the rolled ivory parchment. He pulled the indigo ribbon, breaking the wax seal. The scroll unrolled and he read it out loud.

"Esteemed Lord Bernard Vendelfrey the Third, we have the utmost joy in informing you that your adopted granddaughter, Grace ..."

Even Arcana Prima had been enthralled with this narrative.

"... has received the highest marks ever recorded upon completing her apprentice program in the School of Transmutation. We will record the Vendelfrey surname upon the wall of noteworthy wizard graduates, between the famous M. Vanguard and C. Wayne." He lowered the scroll, eyes darting between my mother and I. "Michael Vanguard, he's the one that invented the airship, yes?"

Mother curled her eyebrows up in disinterest.

"Yes, Grandfather," I answered in an obedient monotone. "He used a mixture of Evocation and Divination arcana to craft the first thruster that later evolved to the modern ones used today, like in the Skyliner Twin Thruster airship."

He shifted that icy gaze to me, but he nodded in approval. "Ah yes, the Skyliners ..." he trailed off in thought.

I was skilled at behaving how he expected me to, being what he wanted me to be—anything to keep his ire away from me.

He readjusted his bifocals and returned to reading the scroll in his hand. "We would love to continue Grace's education if she chooses to return. She need not apply formally, only send notice of her arrival for the next term. It would be an honor to further elevate Grace's skills ... blah blah blah." He flipped the small scroll over to see if there was anything on the back. "Well, that was nice of Mrs. Lorrel," he said.

"Grandfather," I said swiftly, "I have immensely appreciated your support as I achieved honors at Midor's." My voice trembled as I recited the practiced lie. "And—and I do not wish to place any further burden on you, so I would like to accept a job offer performing Transmutation ... so that I may fund myself. There—there's a research facility that—" I wavered when he brought his hand up to silence me.

"Yes, I thought that after graduating you'd want to get out and experience life beyond the estate." He added volume to his voice as if it made his words more important.

My stomach twisted again. I glanced at my mother. Her eyes were fixed on me in a dead stare. It was a familiar look—a warning—the closest thing to kindness she'd ever given me. I clenched my hands in my lap, wondering if I'd already lost the battle.

"So I've made arrangements for you to marry Heinrich Gisenwald. In exchange, Lord Gisenwald is going to permit me to expand my mining operation into his territory with only a twenty percent cut on the exported materials."

"Marry?" I said, stunned. "Why would they want me? I—I don't ... Please ..."

Grandfather slammed his hand on the desk. The sound made both my mother and I jump. I felt the warmth drain from my body.

"This is not a request," he said firmly, a sharp sear to his words. "What you have, *Grace*, is a name. My name. My name means that your body is worth something to my allies. And now, with the prestige that academy awarded you, I can negotiate a higher value exchange for you," he sneered.

Tears started welling in my eyes. "Grandfather, please let me serve you in another ..." My words faded as soon as I saw the muscles in his face twitch.

I lowered my eyes to his desk as he opened a drawer. He pulled out a bit of aluminum filament, pinching it tightly between his fingers where it sizzled—a *Mindtell*. A moment later, one of his tall, scarred guardsmen bound in leather led a woman by the arm. The guardsman threw her on the floor between my mother and me, the soil-stained apron of the gardeners fanned across her legs. The woman began crying in a panic.

"Please my Lord," the woman groveled, "I don't understand what I—"

"Quiet!"

His order cut off her pleas, silencing her.

He dug through his drawer and targeted me again with his gray-blue eyes. "Now that you're such a practiced student of Transmutation, I'm sure I don't need to explain to you which advanced spell I'm going to use." He set a small lodestone on the desk, its dull, porous surface seemingly innocuous—until the even smaller blue container was laid next to it.

I froze. He was gathering spell materials.

I was vastly outmatched against my grandfather. With the flick of a finger, he'd have this whole room in flames if he wished. Could I do anything? If I interfered, he could turn the spell on me—or something worse. My mind raced for any solution.

My stomach dropped when I saw the powdered gold that he pinched from the blue container. He rubbed the powder between his fingers and it glowed as it fell slowly through the air towards the lodestone. The dust shifted into little runes along its surface. He lifted the stone—an amplifier— in his palm and then looked at the woman who was still sobbing softly on the ground.

"This woman stole from me," my grandfather said.

"Please, my Lord," she begged. "I promise I won't—"

"Cyrus." Grandfather looked at the waiting guardsman.

Cyrus stepped closer to the woman and kicked her side with his dark leather boot. She wailed and curled up on the floor, clutching her ribs and sobbing.

My body went rigid in the chair, as if even the slightest movement would draw the aim of that lodestone. Powerful spells required precise concentration to focus their deadly aim.

"As I was saying, I take stealing very seriously. Especially concerning items from my private archive." His eyes locked on me.

Did he know? He had to know. But why was this woman here?

"Thanks to your foolish mother, you bear my name. If you disobey me, attempt to steal its use from me, your fate will be much worse than this." He stood from his chair.

I gripped the armrests to mask my shaking limbs and slid my eyes to the side. My mother's expression was an emotionless mask—like she'd watched him do this a thousand times and was numb to it.

"Wait!" I pleaded. "She didn't steal anything, I was the one that entered your archive." I shook as the rattling words spilled from me.

"I know," he said, leaning over his desk. His eyes flicked between me and the woman crying on the floor. "You can keep the contract, Grace. I won't have a need for it anymore after I send you to the Gisenwald's."

He lifted the lodestone, now fully glowing like the dust, and extended his hand to the woman on the floor.

"Let me demonstrate the consequences of stealing."

"No—wait—!" the woman wailed.

The glowing stone focused into a pulsing beam, shooting across the desk and piercing the woman lying prone on the floor. She let out a sharp cry of pain before her mouth stretched unnaturally wide. Her skin twisted away and her clothing began crumbling into pieces.

Memories I had long since buried and forgotten resurfaced. Moments with my half-sisters where we heard sharp cries and sizzling through the all-too-thin windows of one of the lounges.

The beam of light finally narrowed and then blipped out. The woman's grayed, contorted figure held its form for just a moment, then it spilled like fine dust across the floor. A thin, silvery stream of smoke floated up from the heap of dust as if he had snuffed out an incense. I had never seen the *Deteriorate* spell cast on a living creature, but it was more brutal and horrifying than I had imagined. My grandfather looked on at it with disinterest, as simply a mess for another servant to sweep up later.

"Now," my grandfather's voice boomed, and I flinched again, "in three days, I'll deliver you to Lord Gisenwald." He sat back down in his fur-lined chair. "Don't steal from me again, Grace." He placed the lodestone and blue tin back in the drawer and slammed it shut. "Leave us. I have other matters to discuss with your mother." He shuffled parchments on his desk, searching for a specific one, as if ending the poor woman's life was a mundane task.

Wasting no time, I got up, turned around—not daring to look at my mother or the gray pile of human dust spilled on the floor—and retreated to my room. My skin crawled, feeling as if his cruel eyes followed me mercilessly, no matter the floors or walls I put between us.

CHAPTER SIX

I rushed up one of the curved staircases of the foyer. My vision darkened as I passed the quarters for the maids. I could hear my heart pounding in my ears as I reached the end of the women's wing and slipped past my door.

Shutting the door behind me, I pressed my back into the wood, still trembling in silent shock. I surveyed the room like any shadow or crevice might conceal some danger. But my room was as I had left it, only dustier. That was nothing unusual. The unfinished wood floor panels met four plain walls as they always did. A patchwork quilt Freda had helped me sew a few years ago laid spread across my bed. Light reflected off the thin layer of dust on it. Just like the gray dust now scattered across my grandfather's office.

Her scream, how her clothes and skin stretched—

My reality flooded back over me and I sank to the floor. If I hadn't stolen the contract, would she still be alive? Had he planned on killing her anyway? Had this been his plan all along? That, on the threat of death, I was to be sold. For access to land and reduced tariffs.

For a few moments, I regretted leaving Midor's after gaining the apprentice title. If I had stayed and continued my studies into my master's, maybe I would have prolonged the inevitable just a little. Maybe my father would have come back for me. But ... the thread had changed—changed how it pulled on me. I couldn't stand the thought of being trapped there when my real fate—that tug of the thread—was pulling so forcefully on me.

I had to get out.

Freda and I had agreed to meet to do research. I needed to tell her what was going on—to help me plot an escape.

I scrambled for the opening of the silk pouch in my pocket, and pulled out a bit of aluminum filament. I slipped the cool metal between my fingertips and concentrated.

"Freda? It's worse case scenario here—I need your help—"

The filament flashed hot orange and I yelped, dropping it to the floor where it melted into molten bubbles before burning a hole in the wood floor and disintegrating.

I blinked, looking at the faint burn marks across my fingers. That was unusual. I was lucky too—whatever hellborn traits I had been given, resistance to heat was one of them. A human would have lost a few fingers.

I snapped a finger to cast *Mage Lights*—and a sharp, sparking flash popped between my fingers.

"Ack!" I shook my hands out.

It ... couldn't be.

I leaped up and turned to the door, cracking it open. Down the long dark hall towards the mezzanine I saw one of my grandfather's guardsmen, carrying a melon sized red glass orb. He set it delicately on an obsidian pillar at the table there.

Of course. I clenched my teeth and swallowed the groan that crept up my throat. I clicked the door shut and collapsed on my bed. The red orbs ... I knew what they were.

Mordoch's Void.

Enchanted to emit an invisible field for a set diameter that prevents the use of magic. I recounted what was common history to the students of arcana. Midor had been the scholar and founder of the academy. His brother Mordoch, had been the tinkerer. Their sister, Morgana, had been described as the pragmatist. Little was known about her but she had a knack for showing up when her brothers least expected and finding the one detail of their plans that made the entire thing fail. I huffed out a breath. If only you could pray to a long dead ancient wizard instead of the gods—perhaps I could find the flaw in this plan to detain me.

The next day I began my Morgana-inspired approach by charting the field diameter and location of each void orb. I memorized each calculation, before retreating to my room to transcribe the notations in a notebook. Everywhere I ambled I was watched. I almost relished it—the thought that my grandfather was suspicious of my ability to unravel this arcane prison.

Sitting at the desk, my eyes flowed down each diagram and calculation I'd drawn. I had hoped there was a gap in the fields. Some part of the estate where two orbs didn't quite overlap. I sighed, closing the book and shoving it across the desk. I turned my attention to the contract, still wrapped in velvet and waiting at the edge of my desk to the left.

I reached for it and rolled it open. The sanguine ink shimmered with a gold tint in the light just as I remembered. The script flowed across the scroll in tight lines first—the common language. I scanned the angular, slanted script below it. I admired it for a moment. The ways the characters connected and filled the negative space of each row of words. How parts of it looked like the tips of flame. The Infernal language was so beautiful. I wished I could read it. Infernal, along with just about everything having to do with the Nine Circles of Hell, was off limits at Midor's.

My mother's signature at the bottom was a deep brown—her blood had long since coagulated and dried with the sealing of my fate. I brushed my thumb gently over the blood inked signature. I recalled a time when her hands had been speckled with the spray of long dried blood.

It was a year after my father had visited me. I'd heard the coach bring her back late at night, and I'd crept through the shadows to find her alone. I clutched the button my father had given me. It pushed me to be brave enough to beg her for what my soul desired.

She had been curled up in a blue cushioned chair in front of the fireplace in the lounge room. She stared into the wavering fingers of flame as she clutched a glass of amber liquid in one hand. Dirt was packed under her fingernails and dark flecks—like her dried signature on the contract—had been sprayed across her hand.

I crept free of my hiding spot and swallowed past a lump in my throat. "Mom? Can you send me away to live with my father?"

I realized later when I was older how much it had probably hurt to hear me address the devil who had deceived her as such.

"You can't leave the estate, Grace," she said to me, still staring into the flickering flames. "He won't let you."

"Can't you convince Grandfather?" I asked in a whimper. "Please?"

"He doesn't listen to me," she said quietly. Her eyes had shifted from the flames over to me. "I can't leave the estate either, unless he orders me to."

"Like today?" I asked.

She ground her teeth, pressing her lips tight as if recalling what she'd been forced to do that day. Then she blinked it away, shoving it behind a practiced shield. She took a sip of the amber drink.

"If you are lucky, you won't have to do the things I've had to. You'll be married into another family, and this won't be your fate." Her hand trembled.

It had been one of the few times I heard her express something positive about my future. My eyes drifted back to her blood-splattered hands, and she caught my gaze.

Raising the hand in her lap, she fanned her fingers across the other, casting the spell I now knew to be *Spotless*. The dirt and blood shimmered pale blue then vanished. She switched the glass over and repeated the spell to make both hands pristinely clean.

I remembered staring wide-eyed. I hadn't known she was a wizard. Like my grandfather. Like me.

"Go to sleep, Grace," she breathed. "He'll be arriving soon." She fixed me with her deep blue stare and whispered, "Don't let him see you."

I wondered now if my fate had originally been worse, and she'd negotiated a marriage arrangement for me ... It didn't matter. I didn't want to marry a stranger even if it was a means of escape. I already knew where I wanted to escape to.

I rerolled the scroll and wrapped it in its protective velvet, placing it carefully in my travel bag alongside my spell book.

By the end of my third day under estate arrest, my research paid off and I had found a small space in the corner of the patio greenhouse where the two nearest anti-arcana fields didn't overlap for about a foot and a half.

I squeezed my body into the exact spot, pretending to take an extreme interest in the half-dying plant on a shelf so I could be out of view of the guardsman assigned to shadow me. Cyrus stood at the greenhouse foyer, drifting between plants and monitoring each exit. I waited till he turned away and slid a small bit of aluminum filament out from my sleeve, concealing it between my fingers.

Casting *Mindtell*, I concentrated on Freda before I sent the message.

"Freda, it's Reign. Things have gone bad here. I need to escape. How do I get to your home? Reply now—there's void orbs."

As I finished, my filament sizzled and crumbled in my hand. I let out a sigh of relief. No backlash—no flashing hot pain. It had worked. I felt guilty not already knowing the answer to my question, having never been allowed to visit her like a best friend should. I had never been allowed to leave the estate. Midor's was the most freedom I had been allowed. Grandfather didn't want outsiders prying into my origin, challenging his carefully crafted lie.

I glanced back over to Cyrus. He turned towards one of the nearby doors and then the entire garden was flooded with the cackling of my two eldest half-sisters. I spun around to face them as they entered my section of the greenhouse, careful not to move my body from the secret opening I'd found.

The older of the two, Cordelia, led my middle sister, Amberlynn, between the rows of plants by their linked arms. They looked pleased with themselves, an air they usually had when they returned home from the local town to purchase ribbons, gawk at boys, or whatever pointless activities they deemed worthy of their time. They often left my youngest sister, Lynnette, behind. Cordelia was tall, like my mother, with brown hair and the same indifferent stare. Amberlynn was a bit more eccentric, with golden hair like Paul, though her gaze also felt like the cold steel of a blade on my skin. They both wore matching blue dresses today, each in a different design.

Cordelia towed Amberlynn closer, her eyes on me like a panther between the green palms. She brought them to a halt about six feet away, their dresses swaying with the abrupt stop. I braced for the strike of words I knew was coming.

"Let me guess, Grace," she sneered. "You are so lonely you are trying to commune with the horticulture?" She used the nasally tone typical of high-born ladies. I thought it sounded ridiculous.

I said nothing and held her stare. What was taking Freda so long to answer?

Amberlynn leaned in, her eyes wide and a crooked, unsettling smile painted on her face. "Maybe she's picking out flowers for her wedding?" she crooned in a soft, melodic tone.

The mask I wore to hide my emotions dropped and I scowled as a mixture of both fear and revulsion surged through me.

Cordelia smiled. "Oh dear Amby, I think you've upset her ..." She leaned in towards me and shifted her tone lower. "I hear Heinrich won't even let the family dogs in the house. What's he going to do when he sees you have teeth and a tail?"

"Maybe he'll cut it off." Amberlynn made a motion with her fingers like the snipping of scissors.

This was their preferred method of bullying me. Attempts to fill my head with images of losing the parts of me that made me different. The parts I always carefully hid. A thousand cruel things I would say to fight back burned up my throat, but I needed to hold out long enough to hear from Freda.

As if on cue, Freda's voice flooded my head.

"Home is too far for Mindtell directions. Meet at mom's sewing shop in Camber's Province town square."

I let out a shallow breath of relief, trying to reassemble my mask. Freda was right, *Mindtell* limited the length of communication. This was faster.

I pushed myself away from the gap in the void orb's field, brushing past the girls without saying a word. I knocked shoulders with Cordelia, unlinking her from Amberlynn. "Sorry," I mumbled to curb suspicion of my true intention to rile her. I slipped around Cyrus, who seemed to disregard the entire interaction as quarreling sisters. Good.

I passed the twin staircase in the foyer and wondered if the Gisenwalds had as grandiose a house as this one. I had never met Heinrich Gisenwald. I had hardly met anyone who would have been considered eligible in my circle had I been born a human. Even if he was nice, it would be difficult to fall for someone when it was arranged like this. And then there was the thought of having sex with someone who was practically a stranger. Even when things were at their best with Luka, I'd always wondered if that kind of intimacy was always supposed to feel … mechanical.

What was I thinking? It didn't matter if intimacy with Heinrich would feel different. I needed to focus on my escape plan.

I laid on my bed and stared at the ceiling as I mulled over my options. Priority number one was to get as far away from my grandfather as possible. He wouldn't fall for illusions or tricks like his guardsmen might.

Grandfather hated taking the coach and would likely send me off alone. When the driver stopped to water and feed the horses in the next town, I'd cast *Arcane Twin* and send my arcane duplicates off in several directions. Then I could make it the rest of the way on foot, hidden. How many guardsmen would he send with me? How many duplicates could I make at once? What if they brought a void orb on the coach?

I spent the night and the following morning reviewing *Arcane Twin* transcribed in my spell book and imprinted it in my mind. Its material requirements were simple ones, a bit of parchment and ink. I was glad I had practiced it before and this was just review. At Midor's we transcribed, over and over, the directions for casting. Then followed them methodically like science. Over and over and over. At that thought, a sinking feeling weighed heavy in my stomach. How did wizards outside the academy learn anything new? How would *I* learn anything new?

I waited and at nightfall, right on cue, a pair of guardsmen escorted me to the foyer downstairs. My enchanted chest was placed on the floor by the guardsmen, but my bag, tight against my back, held my most important possessions.

I stood as far as I could from the green bust's diamond-eyed stare in the dimly lit foyer, waiting for the man himself to arrive to send me off. I listened at the front door a few times, waiting to hear the clatter of the coach. But no such noise came.

I heard the click of boot heels approaching on the marble and my stomach twisted.

"Are you ready, Grace?" My grandfather turned the corner.

I looked back at the front door. Still no coach noises. I bit the inside of my cheek as I searched for the right thing to say—to find out what was happening without setting him off. The room seemed weighed down with a sudden darkness, the fear and anxiety closing in all around me.

"Did you think I'd really let you travel there in a mundane way? A way where many things can happen?" He pulled filament from his pocket as he strode closer.

My fingers turned cold as I realized he was preparing to cast. Was I to be teleported straight to the Gisenwald's estate?

A tingle flitted through my mind—he had lowered the fields of the void orbs. He turned away and held the filament before his face—probably to *Mindtell* Lord Gisenwald of our arrival. Had he deactivated the Palisade glyph as well?

This was my chance. I had to try something—another tingle rose up my back followed by a warm brush of arcana.

Another spell was being cast.

I turned my head and caught sight of a shadowy, black smoke flowing up from the marble floor directly behind me. The ribbons of shadow bubbled until a translucent, humming door hung in the air like dark mist. The shadows swirled, hardening into a single, obsidian knob—the only materially solid thing on the door.

I peeked back over my shoulder to see that my grandfather was still communicating with Lord Gisenwald. He had not noticed.

I squeezed the prepared slip of parchment in my pocket, and cast *Arcane Twin*, sending my duplicate running past my grandfather. It caught his gaze immediately and he began shouting. I gripped the obsidian knob and twisted, pushing the shadow door open, and rushed past its misty veil. I whirled to pull the door shut behind me. At the last second I caught sight of my grandfather. He'd stopped short of pursuing my duplicate and was beginning to turn around.

I slammed the door shut.

Chapter Seven

Utter darkness.

That's all that was left after I slammed the shadowy door shut. I felt the obsidian knob dissipate into a dry mist.

I took a step towards the door, but there was nothing. My hands flew across the empty space, grasping for something—anything.

Nothing.

Sliding my foot along the floor, I knelt down and felt cold stone. I rose and snapped my fingers, sending *Mage Lights* out from my hand. They illuminated a square room with a faint blue light about thirty feet across, its floor, walls, and ceiling made of solid stone. It was bare of any furnishings and completely enclosed with no discernible entry or exit.

What had I done? I had seen a mysterious door appear and stepped through it? No questions asked? My mind raced as I tried to think rationally. *Mage Lights* worked, perhaps other spells could too. I shoved my hand into my pocket and pulled out aluminum filament.

"Freda?" I felt the filament warm in my hand. *"I escaped, but I'm stuck. I'm not sure where I am. Help."*

As the *Mindtell* finished, the filament disintegrated, but a tingling static filled my head as I sensed the arcana of the spell melt into the air around me. I'd never felt that happen before. Perhaps spells are contained to this room? I wondered if my message was received.

I sat down on the floor, the blue orbs of *Mage Lights* floating around me, and thought. I pulled my bag around and flipped open my spell book. After twenty minutes and wasting spell materials on *Passage* and *Mystic Doors*, and any other escape attempts I could think of, I slammed the book shut. There were clearly some kind of arcana restrictions at play here. I sighed. Was this really the extent of my practical knowledge?

And there was still no reply from Freda.

I leaned back on my hands and closed my eyes, feeling for the thread. I had not felt it surge since the night I had followed after it. Now it was simply its usual, soft tug. The same ambivalent pull that had always been a comfort my entire life, as long as I could remember. I concentrated on the feeling of it delicately pulling on me. Soft and caressing like a gentle, warm wind.

I sensed a faint shift to my left. I turned—and sat up when I saw a bead of light rising from the floor. I jumped to my feet, steeling myself for ... whatever might come. The bead of light rose upward, drawing a vertical line up past my head, then it made a horizontal right angle, then bent again, rushing back towards the ground.

A door ...?

A door!

I shoved my spell book into my bag and threw it over my shoulder. Light outlined the door, as if it were bleeding from the other side. I approached slowly to examine it and noticed another obsidian knob. Well, here goes nothing.

I twisted the knob and pushed the door open. Warm air and light flooded my senses and I blinked rapidly. As my eyes adjusted,

I saw a dirt road connecting a few small townhouses and the orange-tinted sky of the sun on the horizon. I heard chirping and a bird flew by.

I swung the door wider, rushed out of the small stone room, and collapsed onto the grass. I breathed in deeply and smiled before flipping on to my back and letting the light of the sun wash over me. Looking up, I saw the door—another veil of smoke and shadow from this side—swing shut and dissipate into mist. I stayed on the grass for a few moments, relieved that I was free, not only from the mysterious room, but from my grandfather.

"Reign?"

I sat up abruptly and spotted Freda rushing through the gate of a painted white fence surrounding a small brown townhouse. I didn't know how she had managed this, but I was so relieved. I sprang up and rushed over to her, embracing her in a hug, my arms pressing against a pack on her back.

"Thank you! I was so worried you didn't get my *Mindtell!*"

Freda pulled me away from her. "I haven't done anything yet! I was actually about to leave to look for you." She cocked her head to the side in confusion.

"It's okay! Wait—" I shook my head. "That wasn't your door?"

Worry scattered across her green eyes. "No ... and I haven't heard from you since we agreed to meet at Mom's shop. That was a week ago!"

What? Freda and I had had that conversation yesterday. I looked side to side, trying to make sense of it. The shadowy door, the loss of time ... Where had I been?

Who had sent the door?

CHAPTER EIGHT

Ceramic cups rattled on the tray Mrs. Rye lifted as she stepped into Freda and Mabel's shared bedroom. "Girls, I made you some tea."

Freda rolled her eyes. "Okay, Mom ... thanks." She clamped her lips tight as we watched her mother set the tray on the floor between us. I felt a pang in my chest. I wished I'd had a mother who thought to bring me tea.

The door clicked shut and Freda leaned forward on her hands, gripping the rug under us.

"Okay, so what's our game plan? Library to research the contract and mysterious shadow doors?" Freda said excitedly. Then a wry smile spread across her face. "Maybe it was your father. But why would he send a shadow door and not just save you himself?"

My father, the one who had visited me on my sixth birthday, then never spoken to me again. Not one word. No letters. No sign that he wanted anything to do with me. All I had was this thread, my contract, the button, and his promise we'd meet again.

"If it is him ..." I paused, looking into the tea between us. "What I don't understand is why he's helping me, but then avoiding me when I try to contact him."

Freda's eyes widened. "You tried to contact him?"

I recounted my trips to the basement bar before graduation. The alley, red glowing lantern, the vacant chair, and the smell of smoked cinnamon.

"We could go back there—" Freda started.

"Do you hear that?" I held my breath, trying to listen.

A faint sound—like a horn blowing—rose and fell in pitch somewhere far off in the distance. Freda and I stared at each other. We fled her room, rushing down the stairs and caught up to Freda's aunt, Leanna.

"Can you hear that?" she said, wringing her hands. I heard movement in the room down the hall, and Freda's uncle, Oskar appeared.

"Leanna, have you seen my sword?" He pushed past us.

I caught a glimpse of Freda's mother pulling Mabel into the room Oskar had left, closing the door. The room Freda's father lay bedridden in.

Freda and I led the way and burst through the front door. There was a plume of smoke climbing above the trees in the distance. I heard chatter behind us and realized Freda's family had gathered near the door and were staring at the same rising darkness.

"What direction is that?" I asked as we pushed through the gate.

"It's ... Brunalin," Freda said.

Then, the hairs on my body rose and my stomach twisted as my grandfather's voice invaded my mind like poison.

I don't know where you've been hiding, Grace, but I warned you. If you do not come home by tomorrow night, Cyrus will retrieve you alive. Only you. See you tomorrow.

Tears burned in my eyes. Would he really hurt Freda? Her family? The gardener flashed in my mind. The beam of light piercing her and spilling her disintegrated ash across the floor.

Freda noticed my look of horror and turned in close to me. "Reign? What's wrong?"

"My grandfather just sent me a *Mindtell*." My voice cracked. "He said I have to come home tomorrow or he'll find me, and he knows we're together—"

"Wait—do you think ...?" Freda scrambled for her spell material pouch, pulling a small bit of clay powder from a tiny aluminum container. She blew it into the air around us, with the arcane laced words, *"Show me."* Then she snapped her fingers. I watched as a blue bubble in the air popped, raining small silver dust particles. "This is why you don't over index in one school of arcana. He was watching you through the Divination spell, *Scry*. It's gone now, but I had to cast *Unveil* to even see the thing to get rid of it."

My eyes widened as I wiped the tears from my face. "Then we can't stay here." I looked at Freda. "Your family can't stay here. He would not hesitate to hurt you or your family."

Freda's eyebrows pressed together in a nervous panic. "I knew you didn't get along with your family, but—seriously? He'll try to attack us?" She exhaled in a gust.

"I'm so sorry, Freda." I bit the inside of my lip. My eyes burned with tears. I'd never shared the details that would make my grandfather's threat heavier—stumbling upon red-spattered floors, the screams that pierced the walls, the dead look in my mother's eyes when she returned late at night with blood-soaked fingertips. I knew it was another form of control he'd exerted over me. Silent obedience. Before now, I had never dared to try anything that would put me at risk.

This was my fault. Why had I brought Freda into this? I had been so focused on the danger of the Nine Circles that I hadn't considered the imminent danger of *Lord Vendelfrey*.

Freda watched that look of horror take over then quickly grabbed my hand and squeezed it, pulling me back to her. "There's a neighbor. The *Scry* spell doesn't give a ton of details and you can only target those you are very familiar with or have an object that belongs to them. So, I ... just need you to help me move my father. Then he won't know where they are at least."

"Of course!" I sniffed, rubbing my nose. "Freda I'm so sorry—"

"It's okay! Nothing bad has happened yet, and we're going to make sure he doesn't follow you here." Freda reassured me. I knew the only reason she had been so calm was because she had not seen what I had. A pile of ash spilled across the floor like it was nothing. A silver stream of smoke rising from it, a parting goodbye.

I stood there alone for a moment, watching her return to her family and feeling my skin tighten as the tears dried. I looked back at the plume still rising over the wail of the sirens. If my father had helped me escape this mess, it seemed as though an even bigger one was unfolding right before me.

As I watched the plume rise into the sky, the thread finally surged. The electric pull had me swaying closer to the plume, the city. He had come back. I stuck my hand in my pocket, folded my palm around my bit of aluminum filament, and closed my eyes.

I pictured him, offering me his hand when I was six years old. Heard his voice saying he cared for me and comforting me. I imagined him sitting in the vacant black chair in the bar—smoky cinnamon aroma and all. I envisioned myself reaching inward to the thread thrumming in my soul. As I touched it I became warm, like my hand had warmed when I touched his.

"Help me. Please."

The filament sizzled and crumbled in my hand, and I knew the spell had been cast.

CHAPTER NINE

A neighbor two doors down would take them in. Mabel kept asking why, *why* they had to leave home. Each "why" had me feeling more and more like I had betrayed them—condemned them to a horrible death.

While I helped Mrs. Rye pack, Freda's uncle transferred Mr. Rye from his bed onto a small cot. Freda's entire family worked so well together, helping pack and arrange things. Even in how they included me, where I helped pack things and moved them towards the door. What little feeling I had of belonging to such a caring group by association to Freda was tainted—pain in my chest like a blade piercing my heart.

I had always been pushed away by my own family, hidden, unless I was needed to perform my role as an adopted, hell-born granddaughter. My first real friend had been Freda. Now I watched her across from me, both of us lifting her father's cot on one shoulder. This was the first time I'd ever seen him. He looked so much younger than I imagined for having such a terrible disease. Freda had told me what he was like before he'd lost his memories and the ability to care for himself. Eccentric, resourceful, clever—just like Freda. But now ... he was confined to a bed, and seemed to have no recognition of his family. I watched his head bob slightly as we navigated the front steps to a neighbor's, his stringy, long red hair caught in the wind. My heart cracked. I was responsible for shattering their safe haven.

After Freda and I said our goodbyes, I numbly followed her to the train station and began to watch the buzz of the city slowly melt in on the hour train ride into Brunalin. Landscape outside the window changed from farmland, dirt roads, and small buildings to apartments, cobbled streets, to eventually tall climbing buildings. If we were spotted with *Scry*, we could easily slip away into some other part of the town. I needed to evade my grandfather long enough to translate the contract, and find the end of this thread. To hopefully, find *him*, and then leave this plane. When the train slowed at the station closest to the city center I sighed. There had been no reply to the desperate message I sent an hour earlier.

The doors to the train opened, and Freda and I spilled into a chaos of people pushing in all directions. An unusual anxiety hung in the air, a heavier pressure than the typical evening rush hour. Some people held bags lifted above their heads as they squirmed through the densely packed crowd. Others bore a mixture of swords, belt knives, axes—I even saw the limbs of a strung bow.

A guard's voice boomed across the platform from where he stood higher than the rest on the steps. "The Trade District is closed until further notice! Keep moving!"

We swapped glances, but followed the flow of the crowd to the exit. The Trade District was still several blocks away, but a faint smell of smoke and dust hung in the air. I wondered if parts of a building had collapsed. If anyone were trapped there and needed help. I thought of the boy, trapped under the fallen building.

Focus on your own problems, Reign!

We booked a room at the nearest inn and Freda and I settled in, before sprawling the contract on the floor between us.

"Is it okay if I look at it closer?" Freda leaned in towards the parchment.

"Sure!"

She lifted it to her face, eyes scanning the slanting and swirling marks of the Infernal language. I watched her expression shift to awe, green eyes lighting up with curiosity. "I feel like I have to know what this thing says now that your grandfather is willing to threaten people over it." She laughed.

I smiled faintly. I supposed I wondered what it had actually said too. I assumed it was the Infernal translation of what I had already known ... but somewhere dark inside me always wondered what else had been tucked away in the deal. What had made me look like my father. What had planted the thread in me. It would be becoming of a devil to conceal those things.

"Well," Freda said, "I for one, am ready to learn some forbidden knowledge." She smiled. "Enough to contact your father and emancipate you from your grandfather."

My grandfather ... The cries I had heard from outside windows and through the walls of the estate echoed louder in the recesses of my mind. The blood splattered across my mothers hands. The dust of that gardener piled on the floor. They flashed in my mind one after the other.

But the thread had pulled on me ever since I could remember—a soft reminder that I was different. And then there had been the visit on my birthday—the way my father had given me a fanged smile, how he'd held my hand as he gently led me through the pink and orange clay streets of the Nine Circles. He'd given me the button and told me, as if he might not see me for another lifetime, that he loved me.

It was as if he had been waiting for me to be and loved me the moment he'd seen me. The thread felt like proof of that. Perhaps it was naive hope, but it had wrapped around me and held me together in one piece every day of my life. Freda ... had no such hope to wrap herself in. Only risk.

"I'm worried." I gripped the edges of my skirt. "About how far down this path you'll go with me. If you will get hurt. Devils ... are not exactly saints."

Freda laughed, "I thought we already talked about this?" She rolled the contract up and handed it back to me. "I want to help you. And I will—with research." Her voice shifted to a more serious tone, straightening her back. "I'm worried too, if I am being honest. Even if I didn't follow you to another plane, what if we meet him here at the bar? Aren't devils evil? What if he hurts *you* as well?"

I gripped the rolled parchment, wrapping the protective velvet back around it. "They *are*, at least by most accounts I've read. But, when I met him ... I knew deep in my soul he would never harm me."

For a moment, only the sounds of the downstairs patrons readily enjoying their food and ale echoed through the floor below us.

I cleared my throat. "I'm not afraid of him. I know it's hard to understand. When the thread pulls on me ... every movement in that direction feels right. Like my soul shines brighter."

Freda gave a little half smile. "I won't pretend that I'm not scared to meet a devil. But the way you talk about him gives me hope that things will be different. Besides, like I said—I need to make sure he's cool before you leave me behind." Freda's face lit with a determination usually reserved for our antics between classes. She held up a finger as a proclamation. "*Operation: the devil is in the details* is now in motion!"

I belted out a laugh. "This is why I love you." I smiled.

I spent the rest of the night laying next to Freda in bed, telling her more about everything I'd hidden about my family. Things

I was conditioned to never speak of. She was silent for most of it, with a few bursts of outrage. I think if she ever met my grandfather, she'd try to pummel him in the face based on her hand twitches.

I smiled as sleep took me. I was so relieved to no longer harbor all those horrible memories on my own. Freda was so willing to listen to it all. I was grateful to have a friend—a chosen sister—like her.

CHAPTER TEN

My mother swung open the door to my room. Worry flooded my body. Had I done something wrong? She stooped before me on the floor and wrapped her fingers tightly around my arm, yanking me up from the small toys scattered around me.

"Come, Grace," she barked, pulling me towards the door.

She dragged me across the house to the wing my grandfather usually stayed in, now empty with his absence. I wished the time he spent away working lasted longer than a few months. The afternoon sun stretched beams of light across the floor of the large meeting room she pushed me into.

A horned figure sat in the chair reserved for guests.

My mother released her grasp on me and addressed the dark figure. "Here she is." She took a few steps back and paused, observing the broad-shouldered guest's expression.

He leaned forward into a beam of light.

He looked like me.

Eyes like mine—solid black voids with blazing, red irises.

"I'll prepare tea," she muttered, leaving me with him.

I watched her exit and then I turned back to look at him. Every similarity drew me into him. Pale scarlet skin with dark flecks. Two, red-black horns curled around his head, short black hair neatly tucked around them. He wore a dark-colored suit and jacket with embellishments of gold.

His expression was warm and soft, not cold and calculating like my mother and grandfather's gazes.

"Are you my father?"

I opened my eyes and stared at the wood panels of the ceiling. I always wished I could stay inside that dream, a replay of that memory of our first meeting. I wondered how he had even known it was my birthday ...

I had hoped, deep in my soul, that once I found him—my father—he'd accept me into his family. That I could leave this plane and be gone from all the terrible people in my life and start a new one. I'd miss Freda, but we'd find ways to see each other, I knew it.

Freda and I made our way downstairs for breakfast, then started on our path to the library, stopping by a shop to refill our spell materials along the way. Then we passed by the Trade District and caught our first glimpse of the aftermath of the plume of smoke.

Charred, stone walls of a large building rose up with sweeping architecture, carved columns, and steps leading up to a looming entrance. Every inch of its gray stone was covered in superficial ash and black burn marks. Despite that, the building was mostly intact, its neighboring structures left completely unmarred. We exchanged looks, silently acknowledging that it was a little odd. Magical fire—a result of arcane spellcraft—could be controlled like that, but only by the most powerful wizards.

We skirted around temporary wood gates and guards, following the flow of the crowds till we finally arrived at another enormous stone building—the library. I gazed up its towering, black stone stature, then back down to large, stained glass windows with depictions of what I guessed were heroes lost to history.

We climbed the steps and entered through two large oak doors, and approached a librarian, an older woman with neat gray hair pulled to the top of her head in a bun. She gave us a long look at our request, but helped us pull texts about the Infernal language. Then we sat around a table with the contract spread between the texts, and flipped through to begin translating.

The sun crawled across the sky, casting colored light from smaller stained glass windows to shift across the floor like a chromatic sundial. We must have scoured through nearly fifteen books and scrolls by the height of our pile when the librarian left us tea and biscuits.

I pulled my notebook in. "Well ..." I said nervously. "Remodeus, First Prince of the Nine Circles of Hell is what the author's name translates to."

Freda sipped her tea before speaking. "So basically, you're a princess."

I scoffed. "No!" I leaned back in my chair and plucked up my own teacup. "I mean, I don't know what it means. But I suppose that's my father."

My eyes drifted down the flame-like text of the contract at the bottom. I recognized every ten words or so by this point.

"And then there's this other guy." I leaned in to read my notes. "Leander, Prince of the Fire Circle."

"Maybe you have two dads." Freda shrugged.

"There's a word in the clause with him I don't recognize ... *inferos*." I did my best to pronounce the infernal words.

Freda twisted her lips in concentration. "Oh! I think I saw that." She set the cup down and ran her finger across her notes. "Yeah ... Roughly it would translate to ..." She looked up at me with her lips pressed tightly together in a look of shock.

I blinked, pausing with my cup almost to my lips and stared back at her.

"Um ..." Freda swallowed. "I think it means *soul mate*."

I choked and fumbled my cup back onto the table. "What? What does that mean?"

A coy smile spread across her face. "Guess it means he's not your other dad."

My stomach twisted in a ball as I stared at the infernal lettering. Why would my father include something like this in my contract? Had he been no better than my grandfather? Trading me away for some other purpose? But then why had he visited me? Why had he told me he loved me? I looked up at Freda between the piles of scrolls and books, afraid to say anything that would acknowledge the revelation we'd just discovered.

Freda broke the silence. "Maybe there are other libraries that have experts who can help with a proper translation of that last part?" She smiled weakly.

Soul mate. I knew what the meaning among mortals was. But for it to be written in a contract like this ... the Infernal meaning remained a mystery.

"I need to walk," I said, pushing my chair out from the table, and rolling up the contract . Freda shifted as well, but I held up my hand. "I won't leave the library. I just need to take a breather."

She raised her eyebrows, but sat back down. *"Mindtell* me if you need anything," she said.

I nodded and strode off.

I had spent a lot of time in the library at Midor's. I cherished the peaceful environment, the quiet flicking of turned pages, and the freedom. Freedom to learn anything you wanted and roam where you liked. A kind of freedom I had never been granted at the estate. Discovering something new had always been so thrilling.

I passed aisle after aisle, books and tomes older than me—probably even my grandfather—stacked high to the ceilings. The smell of dust, paper, and glue filled the spaces between shelves. I crossed a foyer and climbed a flight of stairs, drifting into another aisle filled with yellowed pages bound in dark leather. I trailed my fingers along the spines as I walked. Surely some of these books and scrolls were older than Midor himself—maybe even as old as Brunalin.

I edged past a few half stacks when I noticed a lone desk with an elf sitting behind it. Light from arcane lanterns above and sconces reflected off the yellow manuscripts she was reading, illuminating her tawny face with a gentle, gold glow. Her hair was a deep forest green, neatly braided to the side, only one of her elegant pointed ears showing. Although she wore the same uniform as the librarians, she had made several modifications to it—the sleeves were removed, and she had added a leather bracer around her left forearm. In that regard she looked nothing like the others employed by the library. Her lavender eyes flicked up to me as I crossed to her.

"Hello Miss, are you looking for special collections?" she said in a surprisingly sweet tone that didn't match her edgy garb at all. She noticed the confusion wash over my face and recited, "Special collections is an area of the library that contains rare and unique items which are fragile. We remove those items from circulation and tend carefully to their preservation in the collections chamber."

I thought of what we had managed to translate. "Do you have texts about ... Remodeus, First Prince of the Nine Circles of Hell? Or—" I swallowed, considering. "Leander, Prince of the Fire Circle of Hell?"

One dark green eyebrow raised. "We have a few texts about the Princes of the Nine Circles," she replied. "Are you ... a cleric?" She glanced up and down at my all-black garb.

"Well no, I am not a cleric ... Do I need to be one to see the texts?" I asked with disappointment.

"Not necessarily. I will need some kind of identification. It's policy to keep a record of everyone who enters special collections." She pulled out a logbook and a quill.

I froze. I didn't want to tell her who I was, in case she was one of the many under my grandfather's network and influence. Even though we were on the lookout for *Scry* attempts, she could simply *Mindtell* and my grandfather would be here in an instant.

Her eyes sparkled with silver light as if she were reading every muscle movement in my face, searching for insight.

I stilled. Would she recognize me and tell him anyway?

"Is everything okay? Are you in danger?" Her voice dropped to a more direct tone. I ... had to take the risk of trusting her, especially if I meant to learn more.

"I am ... sort of." I reached into my bag and pulled out my identification, handing it to her. "My name is Grace Vendelfrey."

She opened the small, red leather booklet that bore my family's seal on the cover—an osprey clutching five spears. Inside, a card with my name described my likeness opposite a small painting. It was the typical identification for nobles.

Her eyes widened at first, then she frowned a little. "Are you here on behalf of Lord Vendelfrey?" The direct tone shifted to something much sharper.

"No ... I am actually trying to avoid my grandfather," I mumbled.

She looked at me carefully, her eyes inching across my face, reading every movement. She closed the leather booklet and handed it back to me.

"Good," she said. "Come with me."

She stood up from the desk and placed her hand on the glyph encrusted door knob behind her. The knob glowed blue, then the door creaked open. She stood aside and gestured for me to enter. I followed quickly and entered the viewing chamber of Special Collections.

CHAPTER ELEVEN

The chamber stretched across about fifteen feet. A central cabinet with a wood top was positioned in the center of a solid stone floor. Several other doors with no discernible handles lined the walls. I didn't see any books, scrolls, or shelving as I had expected. I wondered if all the treasured and rare items lay beyond the handless doors.

The elf opened a drawer in the center cabinet and pulled out a set of white cotton gloves, which she handed me, and another set of blue leather gloves which she donned herself.

"Please wear those while you handle the materials I am about to show you," she said.

"Thank you," I replied, taking the gloves. "I'm sorry I didn't ask before. Your name is ...?"

"Alàntriel, but please call me Alàn." She adjusted the gloves over her hands.

"Thanks, Alàn."

She smiled. "Alright, which prince are we looking for first?" Her lavender eyes sparkled with excitement. Whatever read she had gotten on me a few moments ago must have been enough to gain the trust of revealing her authentic self.

"Let's look for Remodeus," I answered.

My father.

She flipped her hands over and I noticed that embedded in each palm of the gloves was a sapphire with gold-embroidered runes encircling them. The pair of sapphires flashed with light before a hefty tome appeared within a glow of arcane glitter above them. Her hands lowered with the tome's weight as it materialized fully.

I blinked in surprise.

"You're a wizard?" I asked in amazement.

"Not really, though my line of work required me to pick up a few arcane skills." She winked one sparkling eye at me, handing me the book.

I didn't let my mind linger on the possibilities of what she meant by that, and set the leather-bound tome down on the table. I lifted its broad rectangular cover and gingerly began turning the yellowed pages between two fingers.

My pulse increased with excitement as I scanned page after page—the left side written in the Infernal Script and the right in the common language. One more page turn, and I was met with an illustration. A diagram depicting the hierarchy of The Nine Circles. At the top of the diagram I found Remodeus's name written with a label of *Prime Circle*. I searched the names until I spotted Leander's name coupled with *Fire Circle*. Each of the circles—physical layers of hell—appeared to have their own prince and a distinct element associated with them. I listed them off in my mind, trying to memorize them. Prime, Fire, Ice, Bone, Ash, Acid, Blood, Poison, Shadow ... They were stacked, one on top of the other, like a floating toy top suspended in the ether of space.

I turned past a few more pages and caught mentions of the words *Veiled Ages*. It sounded slightly familiar, but I wasn't sure where I'd heard it from. I looked up at Alàn.

"Do you know what the Veiled Ages are?"

"It's part of the history of Brunalin," she replied.

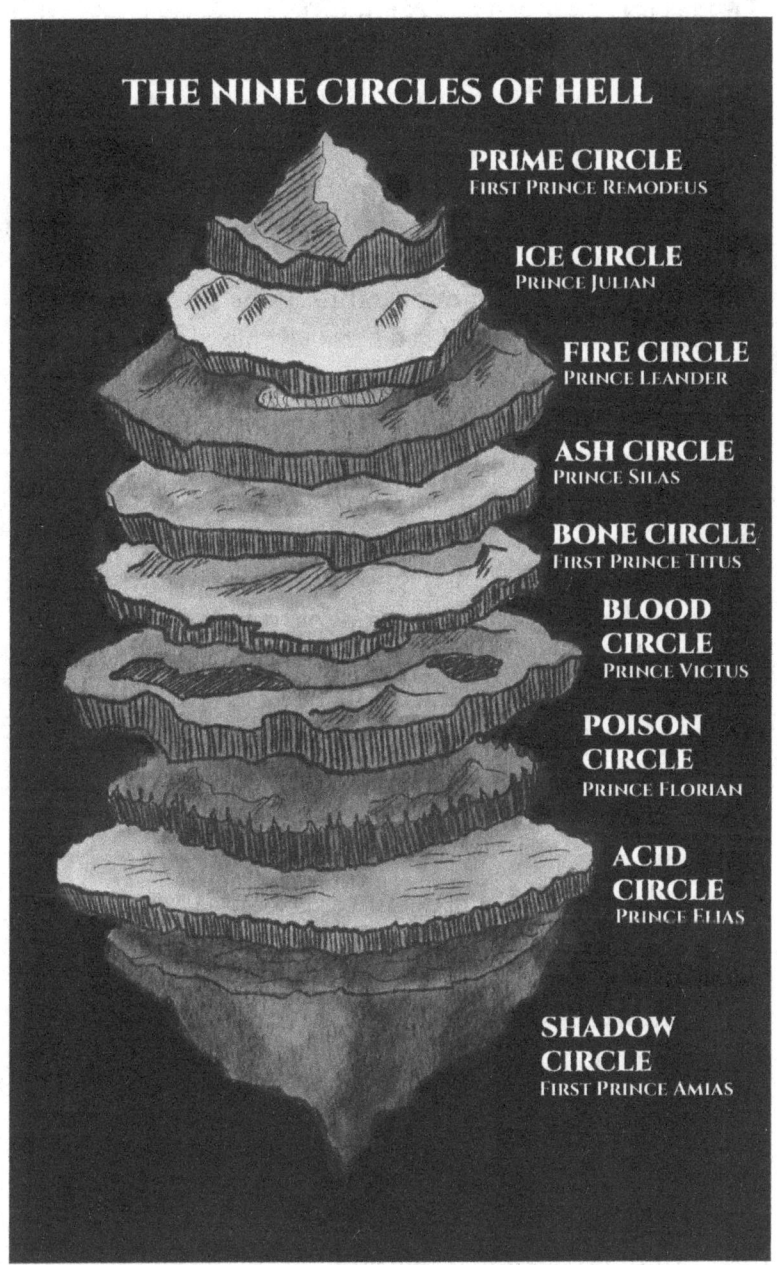

THE NINE CIRCLES OF HELL

PRIME CIRCLE
First Prince Remodeus

ICE CIRCLE
Prince Julian

FIRE CIRCLE
Prince Leander

ASH CIRCLE
Prince Silas

BONE CIRCLE
First Prince Titus

BLOOD CIRCLE
Prince Victus

POISON CIRCLE
Prince Florian

ACID CIRCLE
Prince Elias

SHADOW CIRCLE
First Prince Amias

I chuckled to myself. Human history had never really interested me and now I was paying the price. I could make up for that now.

Alàn continued, "A thousand years ago, devils, and other infernals of the Nine Circles of Hell, preyed upon this entire region of the continent—it was called the Veiled Ages."

My interest piqued. Perhaps I had come across the Veiled Ages while trying to research Infernal history. I felt a little silly for being so focused on contracts and the Nine Circles of Hell in my research over the years. I had narrowly missed the connection Brunalin had with devils in the process.

We slid the tome to the side and she held out her hands again. The sapphires flashed and another book appeared. She set it on the table and flicked her fingers, her arcane touch turning to the right page.

Her voice turned theatrically grave as if telling a haunted legend. "Infernals slaughtered humans so devils could claim their souls to please the god of the Nine Circles. They built much of the wealth of their plane on the souls collected during that time. Many tried to fight to free themselves from that fate, but none could combat the combined power of Remodeus and the most powerful weapon of the Nine Circles: Leander. With Remodeus organizing tactical efforts from the Nine Circles at their god's command, Leander was here laying waste to Novus. His mere presence would cause the ground he stood on to incinerate, and, when angered, his form would shift into a shadow and ember hellhound of colossal size." She flipped a few more pages, showing me an ink illustration.

Walls of monochrome flame swirled around the dark, smoky form of a hound. His long, pointed snout led up to a glowing eye. His teeth stretched to many long, sharp ends, dripping with blood. In the flames circling the hound were tiny shadows—which I realized were humans.

They were stretched upwards as if being vaporized by the hellfire. Based on the scale between the humans and Leander's form in this illustration, he'd be larger than any airship or dragon, and tower over even the tallest buildings in Brunalin today.

I blinked and broke from my trance, realization seeping in. I asked nervously, "*Was* here?"

She flipped to another section of the book revealing an illustration of humans carrying sweeping banners ending in burnt, tattered points, wearing the symbol of a twelve-pointed sun on their plated armor. "Clerics and paladins of the goddess Lumoniel saved these lands, bringing an end to infernal soul collection."

The goddess Lumoniel. Her name was also familiar. I had seen it plastered all over Brunalin. Obviously this was why.

"They found a way to lure the god of the Nine Circles to Novus using souls. Then, Lumoniel herself descended from the Ethereal Planes of the gods, and intervened to banish him to a void plane. He drifts there, forever a prisoner to the void of Abyssus. They imprisoned his counterpart, the goddess of the Nine Circles, in an arcane dungeon.

"The banishment and imprisonment of the infernal gods resulted in an opportunity for the clerics here in Novus to overpower Leander. Lumoniel herself cornered him and decapitated him."

I scanned the illustration in surprise. "So he's ... dead?"

Alàn laughed. "Devils can't actually die. When you kill them they return to the Nine Circles. Scholars say it takes them centuries to gain the power to travel planes again. Could be why you see Remodeus listed as the present reigning leader of the Nine Circles despite Leander being the more powerful one. He kinda got knocked down a peg."

I blinked in shock, staring at the text. My father was the ... *ruler* of the entire Nine Circles? That means Leander was ... what? The most powerful—and apparently most deadly—prince among the

Circles? I knew devils were immortal, but I didn't realize their physical connection to the Nine Circles was so strong.

I looked up at her. "Neither of them returned to continue soul collection after that?" I wouldn't mention the basement bar, which definitely seemed like suspicious activity.

"Not that anyone knows. The clerics did their best to seal off the Nine Circles with wards, but over the past millennia, things have slipped through. It's been about a thousand years, so theoretically he could return if he wanted. Perhaps the seal holds enough. That's the least of our worries with the incident yesterday ..." she trailed off.

My eyes flashed wide. "Do you know anything about that building in the Trade District?" I leaned in closer. "What happened?"

Alàn grimaced. "I shouldn't have said anything ..."

"Please, I'm curious." Sensing her reluctance I straightened and smiled. "What if I offer you an interesting piece of knowledge in exchange?"

Alàn raised her eyebrow. "Go on ..."

I opened up my jacket and pulled out the contract from my inner pocket. "Would you like to see an actual contract between a human and a devil—a genuine artifact?" I couldn't help but smile enough to show my fangs.

She didn't seem to be alarmed by them, but she squinted. "Show me first, and if you are telling the truth, I'll tell you what I know." Her tone was wary, but I could see the glittering excitement in her eyes.

I relished the thought that showing her the contract meant that even if she betrayed my trust, I might harm the image my grandfather had carefully crafted for himself. I unrolled the contract across the table. The script shimmered under the arcane lighting from above and I watched in relief as she scanned it curiously.

"May I?"

I nodded, and she held it closer to her face, eyes scanning each line. After a few minutes, she set it down on the table, allowing it to curl back up.

"This is fascinating ..." Her lavender eyes flicked in calculation, then they shot up to me. "This contract is about you?"

"Yes ..." I replied quietly. I guessed she could read some Infernal. I wondered how many languages she might have had to learn through her work.

"No wonder you are curious to learn about Remodeus and Leander," she mumbled, looking aside, deep in thought. Then she held out her hands again. The two sapphires flashed, and a long, rolled canvas dropped into her hands. "Help me slide these books to the side so we can unroll this?"

I obliged and started making room on the table. She set the canvas down and began unrolling it. We flattened out a detailed oil painting, Alàn pulling glass weights from a drawer below her to hold each corner. The composition was laced with a few cracks and flaked spots from being rolled up for such a long time. She ran her fingers over them, and the cracks glowed slightly as they were restored. I smiled. *Renew* was a Transmutation spell.

The painting was of a seated, broad-chested male. He had a deep red skin tone and two black horns curled back from high on his forehead. His black hair was swept back as if to accentuate them. His monochromatic clothing had a dated look with laces and frill trims at the sleeves and neckline. The billowing unbuttoned shirt formed a deep triangle to his navel, exposing well defined muscles. The sloped line of his neck led to a captivating expression. His smile curled at the corners of his lips, exposing the tips of his fangs and creating the epitome of a devilish grin. The allure on his face sent chills down my spine. I had never seen such a beautiful hellborn before.

But ...

My gaze traced back to his face. His eyes were voids of black with glowing orange irises, bright like a burning hellfire. Not the eyes of a hellborn, but the eyes of a *devil*. I knew it wasn't my father based on what I remembered of him as a child.

Only when Alàn shifted did I remember her presence.

"Who is it?"

"This is Leander, Prince of the Fire Circle of Hell," she said, gesturing to the painting.

"He looks so much like a hellborn?" I knew my father looked like I did, hellborn, but this surprised me after seeing the ink drawing of the hellhound creature.

Alàn shrugged. "I think devils can be anything they want, but the ones I've seen in paintings look like hellborn. Or perhaps hellborn look like them," she clarified.

It reminded me that the original hellborn were known to gain their appearance through ancient pacts with devils. I'd considered that perhaps the reason for my appearance was just a remnant of a curse from my contract.

I looked back down at the painting and compared it with the ink drawing of the hellhound from the second book, now pushed to the right. I couldn't imagine how such a beautiful creature could transform into something so terrifying. I hadn't quite known what to expect when I'd pictured what *other* devils might look like, but definitely not so handsome. Not all of them could be as fair and friendly as my father. Then my stomach turned. What did it mean that I was bound to such a deceptive creature?

My rational mind finally caught up and I blurted out, "Do you have a portrait of Remodeus, too?"

I had to know if the portrait of him matched my memory.

She nodded before producing another object, this time a small framed portrait the size of a serving platter. She held it out to me and I grasped each side of its ornate, wood frame.

My body stilled.

It was him.

His skin was pale scarlet with sanguine flecks, like mine. His red-black horns and eyes—black voids with glowing red irises—were as I remembered. The expression, however, was different—colder. I glanced up at Alàn and I could see that she recognized the likeness between us. Despite my use of *Modify Self,* we looked related, exactly how one would picture a father and daughter. I glanced back down at it again ... the memories that felt more like dreams *were* real. Despite the fact of Remodeus being the ruler over all the Nine Circles making me nervous, I still wanted to contact him. I had to believe he would treat me the same as he had when we'd met all those years ago.

I set the portrait gently on the table. Of course, another problem to sort out was what else my father included in my contract. Why had he assigned me as a *soul mate* to the most powerful devil in the Nine Circles? If I let myself go into my father's care, would I be safe? Or would I suffer a similar abuse to what I had already faced my entire life?

I comforted the anxiety rippling through my mind by calling up my memory of him. When he'd held my hand gently, so much smaller in his, and looked at me with such affection. He had spoken so kindly—had told me he *loved me.* Whatever reason he had to involve another devil in our contract must have been to benefit me in some way. I had to trust that it would be okay.

This was what I was meant for.

I looked up and realized Alàn had been watching as I processed silently. I reminded her, "It's your turn. Please share what you know."

She smirked, her eyes glittering. Maybe she'd hoped I would forget our agreement.

"I have a contact who works in the Citadel of Light's archives," she began. "The archive is mostly a private collection maintained for the Brunalin Council. The Council members called my contact shortly after the incident at the Merchant's Hall to do an audit of the their archives. He reported a few missing objects, all rare arcane knives." She slowly removed her gloves. "Those archives are incredibly difficult to access and, in my humble assessment," she gave me a wry smile, "if something is difficult to steal, it helps to make a big distraction. The authorities still haven't figured out why Merchant's Hall was ablaze. No evidence of a motive yet, other than a ... *sizable* distraction."

I tapped my fingers across the table. So ... the building in the Trade District was Merchant's Hall. As interesting of a puzzle as it was to contemplate, it had nothing to do with my current issues. I still had so many questions, and I knew there was only one person who could answer them. But first, I'd need to copy some new spells into my spell book.

CHAPTER TWELVE

Freda was slumped over our pile of open books when I returned with a new text tucked under my arm. I set it on the table between us.

Freda popped her head up reading its title. "Mistress Deidra's Guide to Practical Conjuration?"

"I want answers," I said. "I'm going to force him to talk to me."

I had come to the conclusion that the only reason my father would flee—at the exact moment I tried to enter the basement bar—was because he was avoiding me. The thought of it was so absurd it was ... humorous. The ruler of the Nine Circles of Hell avoiding a mortal girl?

Freda's eyes were wide with excitement.

I lifted my chin. "I want to ask what his intentions are with me." I pulled the conjuration book closer to my chest and considered the boldness of my plan. "If he's as powerful as I think he is, it doesn't matter what I do. He could do whatever he wants with me, but so far, he hasn't acted. There has to be a reason."

Freda raised her fingers to her chin in thought. "How will a Conjuration spell help force him to talk to you?"

I began flipping pages in the book.

"Neither of us are skilled enough to teleport, but we can use the techniques in this book to draw a temporary teleportation circle that is connected to the bar." I turned the book and slid it across the table, open to the spell diagram. "I think when I approach on foot, he senses me like how I can—through the thread—and he ... leaves. But if I can use this to jump in instantaneously, he won't be able to avoid me. Or at least he'll have to look me in the eyes as he retreats."

Freda tapped her fingers against her chin. "It's sneaky." A smirk crooked her face. "I like it."

"We just need to get lapis lazuli chalk, some string, and copy the spell from this book."

"We only have a few hours before nightfall. I'll go to the shops and get the supplies, while you copy the spell." Freda cocked her head to the side and raised her eyebrows. "Then, I guess ... we're committing our first crime together."

I let out a short laugh. "What do you mean?"

"How else do you think were going to get into the bar to draw the circle on the floor?"

I blinked nervously. Right ... I suppose we would have to break in to do that. Anxiety started to twist inside me.

"It will be fine." Freda sighed. "Two freshly titled apprentice wizards let loose in the city with a mission. What could possibly go wrong?" She grinned.

I narrowed my eyes at her. "I transcribe quickly so you better get a move on."

"I'm going! I'm going!" She laughed and stood.

An hour later we met outside the library and made our way to the basement bar together. During the late afternoon, the street leading to the cafe was filled with people who moved between the shops, cafes, and boutiques. We followed the flow of the crowd as I led us into the Northern District. Eventually, I directed Freda off the busy street, pulling her into the alley.

"See the lantern down there?" I gestured towards the end. "That's always lit red when he's here."

We examined our surroundings then snuck towards the door. The crowd flowed by on the street seemingly unaware of us standing in the shadows between the buildings. I twisted the handle.

Locked.

We stared at it for a moment. I glanced back down the alley, then brought my hand up, concentrating.

"*Open up*," I sang with quiet arcane words. The spell *Enter* activated with a loud click in return that made us both jump.

Freda laughed. "Damn, Reign. I didn't realize you were a professional criminal."

I elbowed her, twisting the now unlocked door open, and pulled her past the threshold. I flung my *Mage Lights* out in front of us and we raced down the stairs.

"We have about ten minutes before that door will lock again," I whispered.

We inched open the door at the bottom, watching for any movements. The basement bar was dark and quiet. I sent the *Mage Lights* on and we rushed in along the bar.

"I'll do a sweep to make sure we're alone," Freda said as she turned for the bar.

I wove between tables to the center of the room, right in front of the black chair on the small stage. I inched up to it and ran my finger along the velvet of the armrest. A shiver went down my spine. Had my father really sat here? Would ... our plan work?

The thought was enough to break my trance and I backed away.

Freda exited the storerooms next to the bar. "We're good. Let's be quick."

The *Mage Lights* cast the tables and chairs in blue light as we moved them to expose more of the floor. I pulled the lapis lazuli chalk and string out of a pouch. Freda held one end of the string to the floor to mark the center. I looped the other end around the chalk, pulled the string taut to two and a half feet, then began drawing the circle on the floorboards. Once finished, I retrieved my spell book from my bag, opened it to the appropriate page, and handed it to Freda.

"Hold it up for me," I instructed her.

She followed me as I crept around the circle, angling the pages towards the *Mage Lights*. I referenced each rune before I drew it on the floorboards, focusing on the angle of each stroke and connection of the characters. Freda glanced about every so often, keeping an eye out for movement.

A few minutes later, we moved the chairs and tables back and examined our work. The dark chalk was almost imperceptible on the wood floors, the edges of the circle slightly covered by the furniture.

"Well ..." I said, studying the teleportation circle inscribed below us. "Now we just wait to see when he comes back."

We slipped back up the stairs and through both doors quietly shutting each behind us. Daylight flooded our eyes as we spilled into the alleyway.

"Let's—" I got out before my body froze. A cold tingling arcana fluttered over my entire being, freezing me like ice. I ... couldn't move. A spell was restraining me!

Freda looked at me curiously, then her eyes focused on something I couldn't see behind me. She stumbled towards me.

"Shit!" She wrapped her arms around my torso and began dragging me across the stone. She twisted and I was able to see three, dark leather-clad guardsmen. The center one I knew.

Cyrus.

I wanted to scream, but nothing would come out. I couldn't even blink. The cold arcana gripped me like an ice sculpture.

Freda Freda Freda! I shouted in my mind. I knew she couldn't hear me, not without an aluminum filament for a *Mindtell*.

Cyrus emptied a small wooden box, dusting out what I imagined were the spell materials used to freeze me. He twirled his fingers and more spell materials flashed in his hand.

A Mystic Door! Throw us through a Mystic Door! I pleaded to Freda in my mind as she tried her best to drag me away.

A Mystic Door!

Freda halted. "Ugh, of course!" She squeezed me tighter.

Could she ... hear me? How? I had no filament.

"A door!" She gritted the arcane-laced words through her teeth and pulled me backwards. The glittering blue threshold flashed past me and we fell till I landed on her. All I could see was the stone floor beneath Freda and the edges of a decorative, metal rail.

His concentration! Break it! I pleaded again.

"Calm down, I'm on it!" Freda muttered.

She *could* hear me ...

Freda scrambled to her feet then scanned something below her. She snapped her fingers and her *Mystic Hand* appeared in the air next to her. She flicked a finger and it flew from the balcony.

I stared between bits of blue sky beyond the awning above me and Freda's eyebrows pinched in concentration. What was she doing?

Freda formed a fist and—I heard a groan echo below us. She snickered, shaking out her fist from the magically linked hand. She had punched Cyrus with her *Mystic Hand*.

Then that icy cold arcana that had been flowing over my body melted away. I gasped.

"Freda!"

She looked down at me with a smirk. "I can't believe that worked." She leaned down to me and lifted me to my feet. "Let's get out of here."

We fled into the apartment the balcony was connected to. I realized Freda had sent her *Mystic Door* to the safest spot she could see—a third floor balcony behind the guardsmen. No one was home, thank the gods. We wouldn't have to explain.

Chapter Thirteen

We returned to the inn and I sighed, collapsing across the bed.

"What if they are waiting for us when we go back later?" Freda said, collapsing next to me.

"They probably will be," I replied. "We should rest as much as we can now so we can go in prepared to face them again."

Somehow the next words were frozen in my throat—like when Cyrus had cast that spell. I took in a deep breath. How had she heard me when I had been arcanely held? There were no spell materials—it shouldn't be possible.

"Could you ... hear me?"

Freda sat up. "What do you mean?"

"That spell Cyrus cast on me. I couldn't move at all, not even my mouth."

Freda blinked, creasing her eyebrows. Then her eyes went wide.

"Wait—you were ... *Mindtell* casting?"

"I ... guess?" I looked up at the ceiling, then turned my head back to her. "I didn't use an aluminum filament. I don't even know what I was trying to do—I was just panicking and screaming in my head to you—"

"Yeah, I heard you loud and clear." Freda huffed, then gave me a long stare. "Add it to the list of questions to ask your dad. Maybe he gave you princess powers," she teased.

My frown cracked into a smile. She always knew how to lighten the mood. "I'm not a princess."

"Of course, *your majesty*."

I elbowed her and she laughed.

We spend the next few hours sneaking to shops and gathering supplies. Now that we knew my grandfather's guardsmen were in the city, we took extra care in casting *Modify Self* as well as *Unveil* to check for the *Scry* spell's floating orb.

Freda found some interesting velvet pouches at the spell materials shop. Each could summon any spell material placed in them directly to your hand with just a thought. A few students at Midor's had such things, but the school had banned most useful items like this even at the Master's level. They wanted us to be practiced in manual methods instead of relying on advancements in enchanted objects. Typical ancient wizards making the rest of us suffer because of how *they learned*. We played with them as we picked up dinner and brought it back to our room.

"Have you felt anything yet?" Freda asked between bites of her meat pie.

There was no table in the room, so we sat cross-legged between the bed and the door while we ate.

"No," I answered, "just the same faint pull as before. I don't think he's there right now."

"Well, it's a twenty minute walk to the basement bar," Freda said. "I think I should go ahead of you and make sure Cyrus is not waiting."

"Technically," I said, "you could come through with me." I looked across the floor at the teleportation circle we had drawn before dinner, a twin to the one in the basement bar.

"We shouldn't go in blind. Besides, we don't even know if he's coming back tonight or not."

She was right. It had been so many days since I felt the thread surge. So we waited. We burned through candlelight playing games and telling stories. I recounted the memory-like dream in as much detail as I could about my father. The paranoia Grandfather had displayed after my father visited me. Then finally we went to bed for the night. I didn't stay asleep for long.

I lurched from the bed, feeling it wash over me—that surging pull of the thread vibrating through me.

I reached to my side and shook Freda. "He's here!"

Her eyes popped open and she rubbed her face.

Nervousness hit me in a wave with the hum of the surging thread. Was I ready to confront my father now that I knew he was also the ruler of the Nine Circles of Hell? I ... wanted answers. I wanted to know why he'd made me, a mortal, his daughter—and why, in the same stroke of blood, signed me into a soul mate bond with another devil. And ... what exactly did it mean to be soul mates with a devil? I imagined it must mean something specific to devils if in a contract.

"Alright," Freda breathed. She rose from the bed and dressed herself. "I'll send you as many *Mindtells* as I can describing what's going on, and I'll pick the most dramatic moment for you to teleport in!"

"Okay." I mustered a half smile. "Get going! I'll wait for your cue before I try anything. I promise!" I waved my hands for her to leave.

And she did.

Waiting for a *Mindtell* from Freda was a practice in patience—especially with how the thread caressed me with that heightened pull. Imagining my father at the other end helped recenter my mind. My memories drifted back to the last time we'd spoken and I focused on his affection, love, and his promise.

Then anxiety wiggled its way back in, taking space away from the caressing pull. What if he didn't want to see me? What if something changed between when I had been a child and now? What if he didn't recognize me because of my *Modify Self* spell?

What kind of message would it send if he saw me, his chosen daughter, hiding the parts of me I got from him?

I sat there for a moment looking at my hands. Each little freckle of dark red on my skin was like a reassuring nod. I looked up at the small mirror in the room, straight into my disguised, brown eyes.

I dropped the spell, and my infernal, black eyes lit like rose-colored flame blinking back at me. My red-black horns curved out from my hair, and my tail drew around from a flap in my skirt. The real me. Not Grace ... but *Reign*.

Freda's voice flooded my mind.

"I don't see Cyrus or his buddies, but it's packed in here." I waited for more, scanning myself in the mirror again. *"There is a long line of people waiting to speak to him. It ends right where you drew your circle. Good guess."*

I sighed in relief. How many people were in line? Could Freda get closer without drawing unwanted attention?

I used the free reply. *"Can you see him?"*

"Oh yeah." Her *Mindtell* echoed in my mind. *"Not gonna lie, Reign, your dad is kinda hot. He's got a whole ass aura to him."*

I breathed a laugh. I had always thought he was pleasant looking. Not terrifying like devils were made out to be. I had thought he must have been an outlier, but then I saw Leander ...

"Just join the line and let me know when you get to the front."

"On it!" she replied.

I wrung my hands while I waited, alternating between pacing and perching on the edge of the bed. After about twenty minutes, my practice in patience faltered and I summoned an aluminum filament from my new pouch. *"Are you close to the teleportation circle?"*

"There are three people ahead of me!"

I stood up from the bed and readied myself, straightening my blouse and fixing my hair around my horns. Standing in the center of my teleportation circle, I waited with my lapis lazuli chalk in hand.

After twenty years, I would see my father again. The hope started burning in my chest. Hope that the eyes that met mine were the same caring ones from all those years ago. Hope that twenty years had not changed the tenderness in them.

"Now!" came Freda's voice in my head.

Finally.

Couching down, I added the two missing runes to the circle. When I scratched the last line with the chalk, the characters glowed with violet light. I clutched the chalk in my hand and stood as warm beams of arcane light stretched across me. I felt my body drop into the floor between space and dimension. The disorienting swirl of cold and tingling arcane winds blew around me, but I could feel the thread's drag on me strengthen as I was reeled closer to him. Like he was the guiding star orienting me in the swirling chaos.

Then I felt the wobbly, ethereal dimension waver, and the physical plane locked into place. The violet light warmed with a surge upward and I rose from the floor. My skin tingled as residual glowing arcana clung to my arms and legs like flames.

I blinked towards the platform and then froze in shock. I recognized his smug grin from the oil painting at the library ...

It was *not* my father.

It was Leander, Prince of the Fire Circle.

Chapter Fourteen

The thread's vibrating pull was so forceful now that I thought it would drag me, feet sliding across the floor, toward him—*him*. Not my father, but this other devil staring wide-eyed down at me, the orange rings of hellfire in voids of black sclera completely visible.

My contractual *soul mate*. I clenched my fists tight, one still around the chalk, and pressed my toes into the floor to keep myself planted.

At first, Leander's shocked expression matched mine, but then his eyes narrowed on me as if he recognized who I was. A blink and the recognition was gone. He tilted his head back and looked me over.

I felt as if my gaze was trapped, fixed on the sharp angles of his jawline, the twisting curl of his black horns, and the deep crimson of the exposed triangle of his chest through a half buttoned shirt—I couldn't stop staring at him. It felt like a mortal trap to get stuck in every edge and detail of him.

I shook my head to snap out of the trance and realized that everyone in the crowd was either silent out of reverence or fear. Then I felt the weight of his warm dark aura sink in around me.

I wondered if he couldn't contain all of it to his body, and had to let pieces of the hellhound out to play in the shadows. I drew a shallow breath and the smoky cinnamon engulfed me. It was *his* scent.

Keeping his hellfire eyes on mine, Leander motioned to a hellborn on his left and whispered something concealed to him. Out of the corner of my vision I caught a flick of red—a spade-tipped tail curled through and opening in the chair. It was larger than mine. Everything about him was larger. The hellborn slipped away leaving the stage, and Leander re-adjusted his posture in the chair, leaning back and relaxing as if finally ready to deal with me. I was wasting time. I opened my mouth to speak—

"What's your name, my dear?" Leander purred in a dark velvety tone that wrapped around me, asphyxiating my first question.

The thread hummed with his voice and it took everything not to give in and be dragged to him. No, I had to stick to the plan. Leander was the most dangerous and powerful Prince of the Nine Circles and he obviously knew my father. I could offer a quid pro quo.

"Reign," I said. I stood straighter, planted like a stone that wouldn't give in to any of this.

Displeasure tilted the corners of his mouth down, but then he raised one dark eyebrow and the devilish grin he'd worn in the painting returned.

"Reign ..." he repeated, like he wanted to taste my name. He flicked a speck of something from his fingernail. "You don't have to lie to me. Tell me your true name." His burning orange eyes glittered in the low light of the room, wholly focused on me.

I held my breath as I stared back in silence. Sure, Reign was not my given name, and my birth name was not in the contract, but I knew he had to know who I was—had to be feeling this thread thrumming between us. At that thought, the caution began to melt away. The thread had never harmed me—and I wanted answers.

"Why did you hide from me when I came here?" I snapped back.

Leander's eyes lit brighter, his fanged grin turning wicked. "Why are *you* so hell-bent on finding me?"

"I'm not trying to find *you*. I'm trying to find my father."

His wicked grin faded and his face slackened to displeasure again.

I heard Freda shift to my left and I finally afforded her a look. Her eyes were wide in an expression of surprise. Ah, that's right. She would have assumed he was my father up til now.

"Sorry to disappoint you." He sighed and continued in a melodramatic tone. "If you mean Remodeus, can't really help you there, we're not on speaking terms." The corner of his lips turned up with the reply.

He was *toying* with me.

I squeezed my fists tighter and I gritted my teeth, the chalk digging into one palm. I was angry—angry this was not my father, that he'd made me soul mates with a stranger, and every answer I was so close to finally getting miles away. And Leander ... was not taking me seriously.

It happened so quickly. I blinked and the next thing I knew, I had launched the lapis lazuli chalk at his face.

"Help me!" I demanded.

It sailed across the space between us and bounced off his right horn, shattering on impact. He must have sensed how terrible my aim was because he didn't even flinch.

He loosened his jaw and waved his hand to figures in the shadows. Perhaps no mortal had ever spoken to him that way. Maybe my relationship to Remodeus and the contract was not enough.

The figures moved across the stage towards me. The thread pulled on me harder, a relentless current at my back. I refused to give it a single inch, at least not until I had what I came here for. A way to my father. Not a *distraction*.

The crowd erupted in a cacophony of shouts and chairs groaning as the two men—humans—grasped us. The guards dragged us towards the exit and the thread yanked on me. I looked back at Leander between the chaos of the crowd.

"Wait!" My protests were swallowed in the noise.

Leander's gaze remained fixed on me, but his eyebrows had tilted up. Something in the embers of his orange eyes had flickered to a heavy grief as he watched me disappear beyond the door and into the dark stairwell.

The guards shoved us through the front door and into the alley. We fell into each other stumbling onto the cobblestones. I turned my head and a halfling appeared with a white slip of paper in their hands. They pressed it firmly into my open palm, and slipped quietly back into the shadows. I hid it in my pocket. It had to be from Leander, and I wanted to be alone when I read it.

I stared at the lantern by the door again. The glowing red light and the pull of the thread remained. He was still here. Sitting down there in that chair as if it was his throne in Novus. This couldn't be it. I had more questions—I needed his help!

Just as I was about to march back down the stairs, the light flicked out, and the pull of the thread faded to a softer, distant tug. The cold blue of night settled around us and I sunk into myself. My eyes burned with tears as I realized how much I'd hoped to see the same devil that had visited me on my birthday.

"Reign?" Freda tugged on my sleeve. "Let's go back to the inn. We'll decide what to do in the morning."

I sighed and nodded before following. This had been it, the best chance to find my father.

I had failed.

Chapter Fifteen

I laid on the bed at the inn staring into the darkness of the plaster ceiling, unable to fall asleep. If I could get in front of Leander again, would he help me? Or continue to toy with me? Maybe the contract was a joke to him. The interaction left me feeling unaware of my purpose with two greater beings moving me around an invisible chessboard. It was maddening.

I turned away from Freda and ducked my head under the comforter. I pulled out the note I assumed Leander had sent to me and unfolded it. My unaltered eyes emitted a low, rose-tinted glow against the paper. It was ... spell instructions scribbled in black ink.

Draw these runes in grave soil.

Below that was a drawing of an enneagram—a circle with nine points—an infernal rune in each. I had seen patterns like this before in books. The arrangement reminded me of texts about the Conjuration school of magic, which meant ... a summoning spell. *What* I would summon was another question entirely. I ran my fingers over the script. The hum of the thread tingled against my soul.

I laid there considering the possibilities. What if I summoned something dangerous? If Leander and I were soul mates, would harming me be against his best interests? Would he harm Freda? While I still didn't understand the mechanics of the infernal soul mate bond, I knew what the meaning was conceptually among mortals.

Lovers bonded for eternity.

I felt my cheeks warm. Was giving me this spell his way of *being nice to me?*

Was it dangerous to assume that *soul mates* meant something benevolent to a devil?

Probably.

Was it dangerous to imagine what lovers bonded for eternity might be like with a fiery Prince of the Nine Circles?

Definitely.

I pictured those two orange hellfire eyes ... then blinked myself out of it. Alright, there's no way I'm bringing Freda into this mission. Not when I have no idea what I'll actually summon and if it's dangerous. Or summon ... Leander.

Emerging from the comforter, I slid off the bed. I changed into my day clothes and grabbed my bag with my supplies, spell book, and materials. Then I tiptoed to the door, pausing at any creek of movement from Freda, until I had slipped out. A few soft steps and I was down the hallway before reaching the stairs that led down to the bar and dinner tables.

Patrons were still awake drinking despite the late hour, and a woman was cleaning cups behind the bar. She looked up at me as I approached and flinched back upon seeing me. My stomach sank as I remembered I had dispelled my *Modify Self* spell before I had gone through the teleportation portal. It was a sad reminder that this place didn't seem to want me. I recast *Modify Self*, blinking my eyes back into their walnut brown color, and shaking my horns into hair.

"Sorry, it was a costume."

The woman's face relaxed a little to an awkward smile.

"What can I help you with, lass?" she asked, a little nervously.

"I was wondering if you could direct me." I began the lie. "I was trying to find the cemetery that's nearby ... " Who knew if there was one. "I got a little lost, but I recognize the area, and I know it's got to be close. A relative is buried there," I added softly.

"Do you mean the cemetery at Ripple Creek?" She arched an eyebrow, drying off the cup in her hands.

I smiled, being careful not to expose my fangs. "Yes! How do I get there?"

She gave me directions and I began the five minute walk. There was a soft wind in the now cooler night. I looked up to our room window as I left. If Freda had woken up, there would be no stopping her curiosity. I needed to do this on my own. She had already taken too much risk to help me.

The cool brisk air cut through me as I surveyed the Ripple Creek Cemetery sign hanging under wrought iron arches, open for anyone to enter. I followed the cobbled path, looking down each row of grave markers. A light mist flowed between the variety of headstones, bits of moonlight caught in the swirl. It was quite beautiful. I halted at a stray dirt path and I found a small, secluded section I could use to cast my spell.

I unfolded the note and opened my spell book, copying the diagram and runes into it. The waxing moon was almost full, and provided so much light I hadn't needed my *Mage Lights*. Finished, I set my spell book down as a reference and began drawing the runes into the soil with a finger.

I dragged the dirt down and then angled up, curving like smooth flame, transcribing the infernal runes. I wasn't sure if they meant anything in particular. They looked more like combinations of infernal characters I'd seen when we translated the contract.

I tilted my head as I laid one rune after another in each of the enneagram's points. Was ... this a summoning spell for a *familiar?* I was semi-aware of the pattern. Usually you needed expensive materials and a special type of vessel to cast it. I never got to try it myself. Midor's rules prevented arcane helpers like familiars.

I felt my cheeks warm again. Leander seemed to think that not only had I trained in arcana, but that I didn't need *any* of the materials. My mind drifted back to when Cyrus and his guardsmen had cornered us. I hadn't needed aluminum filament to *Mindtell* Freda. It shouldn't have worked *at all.* My hand drifted to my father's button hanging by that necklace inside my shirt.

I would try anyway.

When the drawing was complete, I crossed my legs and pulled the button from inside my shirt. I closed my eyes and held it firmly—like my father had held my hand when he had taken me through the portal to the Nine Circles.

I stilled my mind. I felt my body warm. Then I sensed a light shift, and when I cracked an eye open the lines in the dirt held a faint glow. I held my concentration there for several minutes. The glowing continued. I could feel the warm tingle of arcana spread down my body and to my fingertips where it felt as if it were being plucked from the air and deposited into that circle. I maintained my focus. Thirty minutes went by with no disturbance other than the wind, and the drawing still only glowed. I started to feel weak. How much would it cost me to perform this summoning?

An hour had gone by, then there was a sudden flash. My eyes popped open to the drawing in the dirt pulsing with bright violet light. A chill ran down my neck as a stiff wind blew the dirt, obscuring the drawing. Then, I felt heat rise from the spot like fire, as if what was coming was from the Nine Circles itself.

A bubble of hot air popped through the loose dirt, then another, as a small creature clawed its way from the soil, into the violet light.

Then the light flashed out and I blinked as the heat of the small summoning portal was quickly taken over by the cool air of the cemetery.

All that was left was a *cat*.

Its dark fur refracted the moonlight with a deep black-blue shimmer, like a raven's feather. I looked into its eyes, two large black marbles speckled with tiny points of light like stars, set above an abrupt pink nose. The only thing with any solid color on the entire creature. It wrinkled its nose, and glanced around as if assessing its new surroundings.

It was most definitely a familiar ... and it was so cute!

"Hello." I peered down at it. "My name is Reign. Do you have a name?" I smiled, extending my down-turned hand closer to its face so it could sniff me.

Its mouth did not open, but in my mind, I heard a raspy, immaterial voice answer.

"My name ... is Emrys," he said.

My eyes widened. "Emrys! Nice to meet you. Are you my familiar?" I tilted my head at it.

"Yes..." his voice crackled with a hiss in my mind. Emrys smiled, revealing two rows of very un-cat-like sharp white teeth. Each one came to a swift point, like a needle.

A huge grin fell across my face, exposing my own two fangs. "You are *perfect!*" I squealed.

I'd never had a pet, let alone a familiar. I opened my arms a little in a gesture to invite him closer. He popped up from his sitting position, arching his back in a stretch on all fours, and crawled into my lap. I started petting his small, soft head and he let out an audible purr. A purr that I think if anyone else had heard would have been mistaken for a growl.

I stared at his closed eyes and scratched his folded-back ears. I had heard that wizards had telepathic bonds to communicate with their familiars. I turned inwards, concentrating my mind as if I were to cast a *Mindtell*.

"Emrys? Can you hear me like this?" I thought, sending the message into the void, willing it to reach him.

"Yes ... " he answered with the same familiar crackle as before. I cackled back in return.

I could feel Emrys's warm body relax in my arms as he sunk into the sensation of my petting. Emrys, I assumed, was some kind of infernal creature from the Nine Circles.

Was Emrys a gift to me? From ... *Leander*? Familiars usually acted as companions to wizards, protecting them, and helping them. Was this Leander's way of helping me? I could feel my stomach flutter as I thought about it more. I shifted a little and Emrys perked up.

"Let's head back to the inn," I said to him through the telepathic bond.

Emrys skittered between the shadows, flicking his black tail about in the air as he scouted the surrounding area for me. When we reached the alley behind the inn, Emrys sprinted ahead and crossed my path, stopping me. His hair puffed up as he hissed at the darkness ahead.

I froze, waiting to see if anything in that darkness would take form. Out of nowhere, I felt icy hands on my face, covering my mouth. The hands pulled me back a few steps, and I saw another figure emerge from the shadow ahead of me. It was one of the guardsmen. I fought the grasp of the man behind me to free my mouth so I could cast something. Emrys growled and stood between me and the approaching man. I spoke through the telepathic bond.

"Emrys! Help me!" I pleaded.

His distorted crackle replied, *"A command ..."*

Emrys began shifting larger in size, his growl deepening to a rumble that shook the earth we stood on. The hackles along the arch of his scruff rose to points. His rows of needle teeth stretched long and glowed in the moonlight as he widened his mouth into a snarling grin. He had to be the size of a horse—bigger than any predator cat of this plane—towering over the man and occupying almost the entire width of the alleyway.

The man in front of me stumbled backward in panic, his face washed in pure terror as he attempted to escape the grotesque hell creature before him. Emrys lunged, ensnaring him like prey between the knives of his teeth. The man let out a yelp before Emrys clamped down, rending his head clean off, flinging it to my feet like it were a toy.

The grip from behind me loosened slightly. I broke free and pushed my assailant away, jumping over the severed head and rushed towards Emrys. He lifted his blood stained hellish grin towards me, then to the guardsman behind me. Emrys's eyes flashed, and he lunged again—right over me as the man attempted to make a run for it. The guard didn't take but a few steps before Emrys pounced. He growled and a wet crunch echoed in the alley as he bit down on the man's shoulder. The man screamed and Emrys ripped his arm off, tossing it to the side. The screams were quickly muffled by Emrys biting down on his head, then he ripped it from his body as well.

Emrys sat up, looked back towards me, then licked his paws clean.

I stared at him in shock.

Emrys was no ordinary familiar, that was for damn sure. I'd never read about any this size, or this *deadly.*

Everything had happened so fast. I realized I was just standing here in the alley, with two decapitated bodies—in a major city—no attempt to be quiet.

"Emrys!" I said through the telepathic bond. He scuttled over, shrinking back into his regular-sized cat form. *"Can you make yourself even smaller? So I can hide you in my bag or clothes?"*

He tilted his head, blinking at me. Right before my eyes he shrank down to the size of a tiny black kitten, cleaning his blood-stained whiskers and chin. I scooped him up and dropped him inside my shirt where he settled between my breasts.

Panic set in as I located the bodies. Each lay there decapitated with a thin, silvery light pooling and drifting up from their chests, forming a ribbon into the air like smoke. I had seen that before when my grandfather had disintegrated that gardener. So, not an after effect of the *Deteriorate* spell then. Perhaps something else?

I lifted my arms into the air, concentrating on my arcana, and I whispered the arcane-laced word, *"Hide,"* casting *Obscuring Mist.* A low fog materialized in the alleyway as I backed away, obscuring the bodies for now. I felt a warm tingle of arcana as I maintained the spell. I had to keep calm, keep the mist in place long enough for us to leave.

I turned the corner and walked back into the inn, slipping up the stairs, and clicking our door shut behind me.

Freda was still asleep.

We needed to leave immediately. I didn't think anyone saw Emrys and I, but it would not be unusual to wrongly blame a hellborn when two dead bodies show up in a dark alley. Although I suppose in this case, it would not be *wrongful.*

I crawled onto the bed and started shaking her. "Freda, get up."

"What is it?" She wiped her face, rising from the sheets.

"We need to leave, now."

The arcana of my *Obscuring Mist* tingled warmly before dissipating into cold nothingness.

Oh shit. Someone dispelled it.

I rushed to gather our remaining things and pack.

Freda scrambled up. "What happened?" She frantically shoved items into her bag.

"I'll explain everything later," I replied, scooping up shirts, and random items I'd left out and shoved them into my own bag. "We need to move."

"Just a little context as to what we're running from might be helpful," Freda ground out.

"Em—" I froze. Should I tell her now? "Um ... I went out for some fresh air, and I ran into Cyrus's men—"

"What!"

"I'm fine, but ... I killed them—in self defense," I mumbled.

"Wait—"

I pushed against Freda, turning her towards the window. "We need to go!" I said again, urgently.

I flung the hinged windows open. Soft wind and the sounds of shouting in the distance flooded the room. I glanced down towards the awning below us and the road beyond it.

"Ready?" I whispered.

"What, are we jumping?" Freda whispered back.

"Do you have a better idea?"

"Yeah I do, actually." Freda lifted her palm, summoning a small leaf to it. It crackled with blue glowing energy before turning to dust. She clapped her hand on my back.

"Jump!"

I smiled. I knew the spell she had just used. *Floating Fall.*

I climbed onto the awning and launched myself into the night. Instead of falling, I gently drifted to the road like a leaf in the wind.

I heard Freda do the same above, and I afforded a quick glance at Emrys tucked inside my shirt. He peered up with me with the cutest half-closed eyes, small inner eyelids sleepily shut. I let out a sigh of relief.

"Let's run!" I said to Freda and we darted into the dark road, the opposite direction of the alley and the shouting.

I would tell her what really happened. I would. But right now, we had to get out of here.

CHAPTER SIXTEEN

Three times. Cyrus had tried to *Scry* on our location three times since the *alley incident.*

We rushed through the streets for hours, changing direction with each *Scry.* Eventually gold light pushed through buildings and I knew the sun had risen. We hadn't stopped to catch our breath all night. I knew it was too much. I had cast *Mage Lights* at one point in the night and it barely worked. Two measly dim blue lights sputtered to existence. Even though we had our spell materials, no sleep was a major limitation to practitioners of arcana. I could hear professor Yun's voice in my memory.

A poorly rested wizard is as effective as a stale biscuit.

So we trudged into a bakery a little after sunrise. I had hoped after a warm drink and a few pastries each we'd have a bit more energy, but we still struggled to stay awake. Freda rubbed her eyes, and stretched her mouth wide in an attempt to stay alert. I could only imagine how terrible I looked.

I watched the milk in my tea swirl. What were we even doing anymore? The thread had taken me not to my father, but a distraction. Two-thirds of the men chasing us were very publicly dead. We had definitely passed the deadline set by my grandfather, and now I was sitting here with crumbs on my mouth and a secret cat familiar in my shirt wondering if I'd collapse asleep before we figured out our next move.

Despite the mess, I couldn't stop looking for him—my father. And ... maybe Leander was a way to get to him.

I sighed across the table to Freda. "I just want to sleep."

No snarky comment followed so I glanced up to see her head collapsed on her folded arms on the table. I could feel my eyelids getting heavier and thought about joining her. It would be a short nap, a quick rest of my eyes really ...

My head was starting to dip when I heard a familiar voice call out to me. "Miss Vendelfrey?"

I jerked my head up and concerned lavender eyes gazed down at me. I blinked as my thoughts creaked into motion. "Alàn?"

She crossed her arms over her simple, black cloth and laced up leathers as she eyed Freda carefully. She leaned in closer to me.

"I wasn't sure I'd ever see you again. We need to talk," she said in a hushed tone, eyes quickly flicking towards Freda.

"You can trust her," I whispered back, and nudged Freda's head on the table. She peered up at me through half shut eyes before looking up. "Freda, this is Alàn. She helped me with my research on the Nine Circles and got the texts for the teleportation circle."

Alàn straightened and checked her surroundings.

"Not here," she said. "Follow me."

She slinked between patrons and out of the bakery without a sound. We gathered our things and followed.

We weaved through the streets, doubling back and slipping into the shadows of buildings and alleys until we reached a small apartment on the outskirts of the district. Alàn pulled out a handful of small tools from her belt pouch and crouched down to eye level with the lock. She slid the tools in, carefully maneuvering them till we all heard a small click. She rose silently and slipped past the opened door first before gesturing for us to follow. Freda raised her eyebrows curiously at me. I shrugged back at her with a smile and walked inside.

The apartment was well-decorated, giving it a warm and inviting feel. A bright and ornate-looking wallpaper plastered the walls. Matching oak furniture provided several places to sit.

"Is this your ... apartment?" I turned the room, eyeing each bit of bright color. It didn't really seem to match her at all.

Alàn crossed her arms. "No."

"Right." I winced and lowered to the sofa. Freda slumped next to me.

Alàn watched us.

"Is anyone following you?"

I sat up straight. "I don't think so."

"You are both wizards, yes?" She uncrossed her arms, resting them at her hips. "Cast *Unveil* to make sure we're alone."

Freda sighed pulling the necessary materials from her pouch, the air glittered for a moment. "All clear." She slumped back into the cushions.

"I'll make this quick." Alàn took a step closer towards me. "Grace ..."

I winced. It was never a joy hearing my birth name, but I would correct her later.

"... does your grandfather include you in his meetings with his business partners?"

I tilted my head, pondering. "Some, but it's usually for supply trade agreements."

"Have you ever heard him mention rare artifacts or the *Dark Echo*?"

"What?" I frowned. My mind raced. I had rarely paid attention during those meetings. "What is the Dark Echo?"

"That building you were asking about—Merchant's Hall? The authorities found cracks throughout the floor, covered in drawn runes. Then there were miners secretively going in and out of the building. Finally today, the place was crawling with wizards. Word on the street is the Dark Echo is behind it."

"You found out about the building?" Freda asked in surprise, eyes darting to me.

"Yeah." I grimaced the weak apology. "Sorry, I forgot to mention it ... I was distracted by the teleportation circle."

Freda squinted back at me, opening her mouth to speak, but Alàn continued.

"My contact, the one who works in the Citadel of Light archive ... he's dead now." She looked down at the floor.

My eyes widened.

"It happened ... conveniently after he met your grandfather." Alàn looked back up at me. "I saw him yesterday before he was killed. He told me that the rare arcane knives that originally went missing were only in the Citadel of Light archives for one day. They had come in on a merchant's vessel—The Silver Sands."

The name sparked something in my mind. The Silver Sands ... I had heard my mother mention the ship to my grandfather before I entered his office that day. The day before I ran away ...

Alàn continued, "And the only ones who were supposed to know about the knives were the Council members. My contact spoke to them immediately after the knives turned up missing—and then he ran into your grandfather as he left the building."

My stomach twisted. That ... would have been yesterday. Grandfather was in Brunalin yesterday? Anxiety washed over my body like a thousand needles prickling along my spine. I had dismissed all chances I could even run into him in Brunalin. It was such a large city. But knowing he had been here only yesterday made it seem more likely.

"After that, he felt like he was being watched. We found a secure way to meet, and he told me everything. We were supposed to reconvene last night so I could help him get out of the city, but … " Alàn trailed off.

My hands were shaking thinking of his piercing, icy blue gaze across the desk. "I think I recall my mother and grandfather talking about The Silver Sands. My stepfather, Paul, was corresponding with their captain about something."

Alàn crossed her arms and cast a measured glare over me. "To be clear, I think your grandfather had my contact killed, and I wouldn't be surprised if he had something to do with the missing knife as well."

I glanced at Freda who offered me an empathetic look, but it was overshadowed by disappointment. I knew why. She was realizing how many details about my family I had never shared with her. I felt pain bloom in my chest again. Another betrayal.

I brought my attention back to Alàn. "Why are you telling me all this?"

"When we met a couple of days ago, I got the sense that your interests didn't align with your grandfather. Considering I saw you alone in a library in a major city, asking about devils and teleportation. I thought you might be someone who could help me work against him."

"Work against him, how?"

"It's rumored that the knives in question are capable of invoking rare arcana." Her lavender eyes sparkled slightly at the suggestion.

"Rare? Like what?" I glanced over at Freda—and immediately began cycling through every possibility in my mind.

"You're the wizards. You tell me." Alàn shrugged. "Either way it's a little unsettling. Arcane cultists serving the Dark Echo, rare arcane knives, and Lord Vendelfrey."

"And …" I paused, "you think my grandfather is behind all this?"

"Perhaps," Alàn replied. "Your grandfather is somehow tangled in parts. He clearly has an interest in the knives."

"You seem to know a lot about these knives," Freda pointed out with crossed arms. "What's the reason *you* are all tangled up in this?"

Alàn shot Freda a withering glare. "There are some things I can't tell you, but I can assure you that I do not want to see any of these powerful rare knives in the hands of someone who would attempt to actually use them—especially your grandfather, or whatever the hell the Dark Echo is." She adjusted her posture. "If we recovered the knives and determined them to be dangerous, I'd take them to Special Collections for protection."

I rubbed my face. "I'm open to helping you, Alàn. Especially where it's in my best interests to keep my grandfather from finding me. But more importantly, we haven't slept in over twenty-four hours. We need a safe place to sleep, and then we can make a plan."

"You can sleep here," Alàn said, with a bit more softness in her voice. "We should find a dark place for you away from the rest of us. It's one way we can keep whoever might *Scry* on you from guessing where you are." Alàn approached the adjoining rooms, looking for a suitable place.

Freda laughed. "That works?"

Alàn's voice rang from another room. "You can hide from anything if you are clever enough." I could hear the grin she was wearing in her voice.

Alàn helped me get set up in a small closet where on the floor we made a pallet of soft pillows and blankets. It worked well, actually—because I was a small person, but also because I didn't mind the confinement or warmth. I curled up inside, adjusting the blankets around me. Just as I closed my eyes, I felt something move under my shirt.

Emrys!

"Are you okay?" I sent the thought through the telepathic bond.

He climbed out of my shirt and curled up in a little kitten ball against my chest under the blankets with me, rubbing his head against my shoulder in reassurance. I snuggled in with him and closed my eyes again. I was about to drift into sleep when something tickled softly in my mind and I heard a deep, velvety voice hum through it like a caress.

"Do you like Emrys?" Leander purred to me through the *Mindtell* spell. The thread vibrated with his voice, vibrating me to my core. I hated how much I liked the way it rattled the thread between us. Were all devil's voices so ... alluring?

I contemplated not replying. He hadn't seemed to take any of my demands seriously when we first met. I glanced down at Emrys snuggled up against me.

Perhaps that wasn't totally true ... I would reply, but I wouldn't be wasting any spell materials on him with new *Mindtells*. I would only give him replies to his own and use each one to move the conversation to what I wanted.

"Yes." I replied through his spell. *"He's attentive to my needs and listens very well. He answers my questions directly and obeys."* I hoped he could sense the intentional aggravation I wove in.

"I'm sorry. I was not prepared to meet you earlier." He sounded wounded. At least he recognized why I was upset. It was a new *Mindtell* spell, so I was allowed another material-free reply.

"Why did you give me Emrys?"

"Because I ignored your first request for help and wanted to make up for it." His tone had shifted completely to something more serious. Nothing like when I'd spoken to him at the bar. When had I asked him for help before that? Had ... the plea for help I'd attempted to send to my father followed the thread instead?

"I was trying to ask my father for help, not you. Besides, don't I belong to you or something? Why haven't you taken me?"

I could taste the bitterness in my reply. I wondered if perhaps some of my anger towards Leander also came from the fact that until a couple of days ago, I hadn't even known he existed or was part of my contract—let alone my *soul mate.*

"My dear ... you do not belong to anyone."

I held my breath as if it might make me think more clearly. He was having an actual conversation with me. I needed to make my plea again while I had the chance.

"If you want to actually help me, will you contact my father?"

Silence steeped in the darkness of the closet. Was he going to reply at all? I felt the faint pull of the thread as I drifted closer to sleep. Despite the fact that a devil's voice in my head was now connected to it, it still felt as it always had—as a comfort. Then I heard his voice again, adding to that caress in my mind as sleep finally found me.

"I will try."

CHAPTER SEVENTEEN

I looked up at the devil sitting before me in my grandfather's study and tilted my head at him in curiosity.

"Are you my father?"

His expression shifted a little, and he nodded his head yes. He extended his hand, waited for me, and I felt an immediate sense of trust and safety. I placed my hand in his, and an orange-rimmed portal burned into existence like a ring of fire next to us. Heat and a warm pink light poured through the rippling mirror like surface from the other side.

"Do you want to see where we're from?" He smiled. He had fangs, like mine.

I glanced back at the door after my mother. It was closed. I turned to face him fully, nodded, and took a step closer. He held my hand gently, enclosing my fingers under his, and guided me towards the portal's edge, letting me take steps at my own pace. Not like how my mother gripped my arm and dragged me where she wanted.

We stepped through together, and I opened my eyes wide at what lay before me. Rust-colored clay roads wove between buildings made of tan stone in a sunrise-colored city. The sky was a pink hue as if it were cast in an eternal dawn, and the air was warm and dry. As he led me down the street of shops and dwellings, I saw a glittering lake beyond them. Not of water, but a rainbow of flames dancing and sparkling in infinite hues. We crossed a bridge over that lake of fire to a garden with unusual looking plants in shades of green and flowers of as many colors as the glittering lake.

Eventually, we stopped at a little cafe where he brought me a cup of yellow ice cream with tiny red sprinkles. It tasted both sour and sweet, and the sprinkles fizzed in my mouth as I ate it.

I finished my ice cream and looked up at him. "Can I live here with you?"

His face contorted in a pained expression and my hopes sank. "I'm sorry, but you cannot stay here with me. I was not supposed to meet with you like this."

I could feel tears welling in my eyes. I didn't want to go back. Back to my human family. Back to the house where I was pushed around and everything was controlled for me—my wardrobe, my playmates, my study times. The house where no one seemed to want me around or cared that I existed. Worst—worst of all—it was so lonely. I didn't want to be alone.

A tear rolled down his cheek. He opened his arms and pulled me in tight. He whispered into my ear. "I love you. Even if we cannot see each other for a long time, please do not forget how much I love you." He wiped tears from his eyes and pulled a small item from his pocket. "I have something for you."

He held it out in front of me. It was a plain looking, domed, brass button. He placed it in my open hand. I grasped the button and looked at it carefully.

"Whenever you feel alone, I want you to look at this button and think about us. We're special, and you are more powerful than you think. Always believe what you want is possible."

I held on to the button tightly.

"I love you so much," he said one last time, his voice *cracking.*

"I love you too, father."

I awoke from the dreamed memory of meeting my father to someone shaking my body.

"Reign?"

It was Freda's voice. I blinked my eyes open. Shafts of daylight cast through the cracked door and lit the edges of Freda's copper hair as she stared down at me, wide-eyed.

"Where did you get a kitten?" Freda squealed.

I sat up, sending Emrys to roll down the blanket between us. "Freda, this is Emrys. Emrys, this is Freda. He's my familiar," I said a bit sheepishly.

Emrys popped up from the folds of the blanket. He arched his back and flicked his thick, furry tail in the air as he rubbed his head against Freda's knee.

"He's so cute!" Freda picked him up and cuddled close to him, rubbing their noses together. Then she paused and I watched her considering my words. "Reign, there's a lot you are not telling me lately."

I peered beyond the open closet door. I didn't see Alàn around so I motioned her to come inside and shut the door. We sat cross-legged on the pile of blankets, Emrys between us. I snapped my fingers and my *Mage Lights* floated around us.

"I'm really sorry," I started. "I had always been afraid to talk about my grandfather. And the deeper we go into this—I'm just realizing more and more the risk and how I don't want anything to happen to you ..."

Freda petted Emrys's head. "We've known each other for fifteen years," she whispered. "You can always tell me anything, and ... I *want* to know—even if it's wild, embarrassing, or even dangerous. I want us to trust each other with anything."

"I do trust you—the most, actually! I'm just scared, Freda."
I exhaled. "I'm scared that the closer I lead you towards the
Nine Circles, the more likely you'll get hurt." I fiddled with
the blanket.

"We made a deal, remember?" Freda laughed. "I won't go
all the way there, but we have to communicate. Especially if
you want to keep me safe—maybe we can have more meetings
like this." She brought her hand under her chin in thought.
"We can even have a code phrase!"

I laughed. This is why I loved her.

"Like what?"

"Faizan's Tiny ..." she looked around, "Closet?"

I burst out laughing.

Faizan's Tiny Dome was a spell invented by the famous
wizard Faizan. It was used to make an invisible shelter that
was impenetrable to anyone you did not will to enter.

I started our first meeting of Faizan's Tiny Closet by telling
her everything I'd been holding back before. The *Mindtell* I
had tried to send to my father on her street several days ago
and how Leander had somehow received it instead. That we
had spoken through *Mindtell* a few hours ago and he agreed
to contact my father. The info about Merchant's Hall and the
Citadel of Light archives, outside of what Alàn had told us. I
gave her the details of Emrys's summoning, and that ... it had
been Emrys who had killed the two wizards.

"A tiny kitten killed two wizards?" Freda gawked at him
where he lay on the blanket between us in a dark swirl.

"You should have seen him, Freda ... he was the size of a
great hell beast! I think he's large enough in that state that we
could even ride him into battle!"

Emrys's ear flicked in affirmation at my statement.

"Well, let's go see what else Alàn wants to know." I scooped
up Emrys and crawled out of the closet.

We found Alàn in the leisure room sitting at the table, a large, brown leather square spread across it with many small contraptions, devices, and tools laid out. She pushed a small stone along the blade of the dagger she held, sharpening it.

"Alright," I announced to the room. "Rested enough to continue."

Alàn creased her eyebrows up at me. "I don't remember seeing a cat."

"This is my familiar, Emrys." I held the kitten out.

Emrys twitched his little black whiskers and stared at Alàn.

She blinked, then looked back down at her blade and smirked. "Cute name." She rolled up the leather with her blades and tools, then turned to me. Something dark flickered in her lavender eyes making her look other-worldly. "Tell me anything you can that would be an advantage against your grandfather."

"Alright ... On one condition. You tell us where else we can find information about what my grandfather might be doing, and more about the Nine Circles."

Alàn pressed her lips together. "Fine. Deal."

CHAPTER EIGHTEEN

I spent the next hour divulging anything of use I could think of. Alàn was precise in her questioning, asking in a way that elicited details as if she was practiced in conducting interrogation. It was a little unsettling. There was something about her I couldn't quite figure out, some sense of graveness that was concerning ... but there was a care to the way she spoke.

"Is this enough to help you?"

"I think so," Alàn mused, resting her chin on her fist. "It should be enough for me to blend in."

My eyes widened. "Blend in?"

"You can't learn everything from books," Alàn winked at me. "If the next time you see me is in an unexpected environment, I hope you won't blow my cover." A wry smile crossed her face.

Fear crept over me as I imagined the result of her implication. "Be careful," I said.

Alàn's face softened. "I'll be fine. Trust me." She looked down at the back of her slender hands, both covered in fingerless gloves. "I've suffered wraths worse than that of Lord Vendelfrey ..." Her eyes were dark for a moment, like she was trapped in some horrible memory. "I'm from Veldrasyl after all."

Not many elves who lived here in Novus hailed directly from the plane Veldrasyl. Centuries of war had driven many to our own plane over time. Was it as dangerous and brutal there as the Nine Circles of Hell?

Freda blurted what I was wondering, "Have you ever met a fae before?"

Alàn's gaze cut to Freda, sharp like a blade. Perhaps we shouldn't be asking her about this topic. I was sure what we'd both learned in a vocational class about Veldrasyl was hardly accurate.

"No." Alàn huffed. "And I'll be lucky if I never do."

I twisted awkwardly. "So, about the research?"

Alàn smirked and pulled a pouch no bigger than her fist from her belt. She opened the draw strings and then shoved her entire arm in down to the elbow.

I couldn't help but smile wide. I'd never seen an enchanted bottomless bag in person before. I watched in awe as she rooted around deep in the pocket dimension, then pulled a small notebook and a pen. She opened to a blank page near the back, ripped it out, and began writing.

"This is how to get to the Archive of Truth. It's private, but extensive. They have records that go back another thousand years over what we have in the Brunalin Library." She folded the paper and handed it to Freda. "I don't have a contact there—but I hope they can help."

"Thank you." I said as we all rose to pack our things.

Whatever it was my grandfather was plotting felt inevitable. He would figure out how to use whatever rare arcana he desired and there would be nothing I could do to stop him. If I meddled, he would simply apprehend me faster. I felt guilty for wanting to run away. I thought about Freda, her family, and innocent people like them who would be left to maybe survive my grandfather's machinations while I selfishly chased my happiness, and the guilt doubled—and tripled.

I glanced up at Freda.

She bent her eyebrows at me with concern.

"Well ..." Freda broke the silence between the three of us as Alàn finished her tasks. "We have another lead. And maybe we'll hear back from your boyfriend."

I narrowed a warning glare at Freda.

We left the apartment as we found it and made our way back to the street. We walked in silence for a while as dusk set in, then Alàn stopped us before a nondescript shadowed alley, turning to address us.

"I'm sure we'll cross paths again one day. Thanks ... for your help." She winked, bowing her head slightly as she backed down the shadowed alley.

"Good luck!" I called after her. I watched her slip into the overlapping shadows and I completely lost sight of her—as if she became a shadow herself.

Emrys rode in his new preferred spot, tucked in my shirt. When we found an affordable accommodation, we checked in and got settled. I immediately noticed the amenity that was a rarity among rooms this price—a tub. No hot water, sure, but what kind of wizard would I be if I couldn't heat a little water?

Freda slept on our bed while I slipped into the bath. Emrys sat on the counter nearby, like a little feline grotesque protecting me. I pulled some charcoal from my spell material pouch and sprinkled a bit into the bath. I dipped my hand into the cold water and it magically warmed till it was practically bubbling. I always liked very hot water—I wondered if it was a side effect of whatever I was. I swished in some soap from a basket to create bubbles, sank into the warm, bubbly brew, and closed my eyes. Not a few minutes later, I felt a tingle in my mind and heard—for the second time today—Leander's voice purr in my head.

"Enjoying your bath?" he whispered through the *Mindtell*.

I rolled my eyes and replied curtly, *"You're interrupting."*

"Oh apologies, my dear. I figured you'd want to know what Remodeus said." His tone was a playful lure, like a little cat toy.

Then suddenly, I realized. *"How did you know I was taking a bath?"* I quickly sunk further into the water to hide myself with the bubbles and looked around the bathroom.

A low laugh tickled my mind, then *"Emrys told me."*

I shot a daggered glance over to Emrys. He shook his small head in a panic. I sank further into the warmth of the water, concealed by the bubbles. Maybe he was here to play again instead of being serious.

"Tell me what he said," I replied.

I waited, watching a few bubbles pop at the surface of the water.

"He is ... willing to meet you, but he's a little preoccupied with another client."

"I'm not a client. I'm his daughter," I shot back in defense.

"What is it you want from him, exactly?"

A simple question, but upon hearing it, I was at a loss for words. What *did* I want from him? I wanted ... to feel the love I'd felt when he visited me as a child. I wanted to feel like I actually belonged to some kind of family.

Soul mate ...

My father had bound me to Leander. Perhaps ... I really was just a clause in a contract to Remodeus. Maybe he would never fill the empty space inside my heart. Or if he had never visited me, I would have learned to not want or need him. But then ... why had he claimed me as a daughter back then?

"I don't want to be alone anymore," I said. *"But I have questions too, and I want quick replies. No sassy remarks."*

"Mmhmm," he mused. *"Go on ..."*

"Did either of you ever plan on contacting me?"

I watched a few bubbles pop on the surface of the water as I waited.

"This contract was made without my consent. Your ... father stole a piece of my soul I had saved to bond with someone and instead used it to bind me to you. Seemed unfair to involve you further."

He had already broken the quick replies rule ... but what seemed like honesty made me feel he was being sincere. And the idea that my father had merely made this arrangement to be cruel to Leander made my stomach turn.

"He really did that?"

"You can't trust a devil," he replied with a playful canter.

I snorted at the irony. I pushed my hand through some of the foam, reorganizing the layer shielding me. *"What exactly does it mean to be soul mates through a contract?"*

A few moments later, his velvety voice tingled in my mind again. *"Two souls are split, and their fragments are swapped. When the two individuals are united in acts of love, the souls are connected to their missing piece—becoming one again. A soul mate,"* he said.

That sounded ... *nice*. How could it be that devils had crafted such a beautiful thing? Was that all there was to it? He continued.

"That aching tether you can feel between us is each of our soul fragments eternally vying to be connected with its other piece."

The thread. Was that why I had always felt the thread? I had assumed it was some lingering arcana from the contract and that it was attached to my father. This whole time my thread—my soul—had been pulling me unrelentingly towards ... Leander? Because a piece of my soul was inside him? And it wanted me to perform *acts of love* to be whole again? I felt a little betrayed by the thread. I suppose it made sense after what I had felt at the basement bar. How it had pulled me so forcefully towards him.

"Why would someone want to fragment their soul like that?"
After I said it, I realized I was asking why *he* would want that.

"I don't want to be alone anymore," he used my own words to reply.

I couldn't help but narrow my eyes even though I knew he couldn't see them.

"Some find it comforting. When they are alone. Even when it's the faintest, tingling tug, it's always there."

I stared into the rippling water of my bath. It *was* like that. Whenever I had been alone, sad, or scared, I would find the thread and its pull always brought me comfort. He ... felt that too? Did he find it as comforting as I did?

Then I pondered the idea that I didn't have a complete soul—that I had a piece of *his soul* inside me. A piece from a Prince of the Nine Circles and his, from a mortal. And this was somehow unfair to me? It seemed like it was more unfair to *him*. I was a mortal being, and he was ... not. I shuddered, imagining the pain of feeling the thread pull towards nowhere in particular, or not at all.

"What will happen to you when I inevitably die?" I had to ask. Exactly how cruel had my father's contract been to him?

"Are you concerned for me?"

When I didn't answer out of spite, he continued. *"When you ... or I die, each separated soul piece returns to its origin. Either way it's incredibly painful to have a soul ripped from you."* Leander's voice went a little ragged as he described it.

So it was inevitable that in the end, the small tugging comfort he had described would be taken away—likely from Leander. Devils suffering a true death—called the immortal's death in my textbooks—was hardly recorded. Leander was proof of that. He had been *killed* once before only to be returned to the Nine Circles where he reformed and regained his power. Enough power to get through the wards Alàn had described. Was the fact that he was bonded to a mortal what was keeping him from resuming the events of the Veiled Age?

But then, I began to feel sad for him. I had suffered the feeling of longing, and wanting for a real family, for a measly twenty-five years, but as for him ... I wondered how many centuries he'd lived trapped in that feeling. Wondered how or when he had decided he was ready for a bond—only for my father to bind his soul to a mortal whose soul comfort was only temporary as time and fragility moved to take it away.

My head swam with thoughts I couldn't push away. How I didn't want to lose this feeling of the thread I'd had my whole damn life. It *had* comforted me, had made the loneliness bearable. If I selfishly pursued what this bond offered, I could receive some of the fulfillment I had desired my entire life.

For Leander it would be a blink.

I swallowed and forced out my next words. *"Can you break the contract, then? And find someone who is immortal like you instead?"*

I glanced over at Emrys. He was asleep, curled up on the counter, his sides moving with his breath. I heard the sheets in the bedroom rustling as the water grew colder, and I figured I would not get an answer. I rose from the tub and flicked the water off my arms, then searched for a towel. I gave Emrys a little wet tap between his eyes. He shook his head and rubbed the water away with his paw. I dried myself and climbed back into my clothes. The tingle in my mind preceded another *Mindtell* and relief washed over me when I realized it was Leander.

"Because we haven't united yet, it's technically possible, but ..." I slowed my breath during his pause. *"I do not want to break it."*

My mind fluttered from one thought to the next. He didn't want to break it and find someone else? What about the other person his fragment had been intended for? Was there something he wanted from me? Something he ... liked about me?

I had to find out.

"Can I meet you again?" I said, nervous energy rattling every word. Maybe it was this thread manipulating my desire to go to him. I didn't care. The reward of following its pull had been fully gratifying, like the release of tension in an aching muscle.

And I was sore from waiting for answers.

"Tomorrow night." His voice said caressing me one more time. *"Come to the bar."*

CHAPTER NINETEEN

Sleep tormented me almost as much as the thread did.

I tossed around, my mind preoccupied with the anticipation of the next day. I was nervous, excited, and terrified all at once. Would it be like last time? He had toyed with me at the bar ... and though he had given me some answers, he had filled my head with even more questions. As my mind spiraled with what might happen, the undercurrent of the soft, steady tension of the thread quieted the churning thoughts and aching loneliness. It was like Leander had said, as I had always known.

The morning sun cast warm beams of golden light into our room. Freda set a plate of biscuits and jams between us on the bed where we discussed what to do next. I told her about how Leander suggested we meet again.

"He was watching you take a bath?" Freda, of course, picked up on an entirely different aspect to the story ...

"No!" I argued. "He said that Emrys told him I was in the bath." We both looked at Emrys.

Emrys looked back with wide eyes and tucked his feet closer under his body, perfectly positioned in one of the warm sunbeams.

"I don't think that's a thing, Reign ..." Freda said, her tone suspicious but playful. "Familiars are only supposed to communicate with their summoner."

"He's not a normal familiar though, remember?"

"You don't seem too bothered by the idea that he *might* have been watching you bathe." Freda's eyebrows arced up in a teasing expression.

My face heated. "I don't know, it's hard to tell!" I said. "Maybe it's the thread influencing me." I crossed my arms as I offered the weak explanation.

"I don't think it's the *thread* ..." Freda tilted her head in amusement as she plucked another biscuit from the tray, a suspicious smirk plastered on her face.

I had known this devil for barely a day and I was already developing what, a *crush?* The thread hummed against me and it was as if I could see that infernal glowing stare, feel that velvety voice curl along my spine—feel its arcane purr threatening to suck me in and consume me before I realized what was happening.

Oh hell, I did find him attractive, didn't I? I imagined shoving the dangerous thoughts into an imaginary bottomless bag and tying it shut.

"I just want to talk to him more," I answered, knowing my face was likely *somehow* visibly redder with how hot it felt. "Speaking of that—what if we temporarily split up? I'll drill Leander for more info, and you can check out that library Alàn recommended to us."

"Seriously?" Freda's green eyes narrowed. "Split the group?"

"I'm sure nothing bad will happen!" I laughed nervously.

A smile tugged the corners of her mouth. "Oh?"

Hell ... she could see right through me couldn't she? I picked at my black skirt pretending to see specks of dirt.

"Let me summarize. You want to go by yourself to meet this *hot Prince of Hell,*" she waved her biscuit in the air for emphasis, "who is sending you secret messages—especially when you are nude in the bath—and who shares a fragment of your soul which, by the way, makes you insanely magnetized towards each other."

She laid my feelings prone with each word.

"And," she went on, "remind me what the pull on the thread wants you to do? *Unite the souls.*" She raised her eyebrows and grinned at me, then made her coup de grâce. "I can see where this is going."

"What do you want me to say?" I said, shoulders sagging in defeat.

"I want you to be careful," Freda pleaded, "and honest with yourself."

She was right. I was intentionally distracting myself—searching for my father, avoiding my grandfather, worrying about the danger I'd put Freda in—to even properly acknowledge that I found the whole idea of relenting to the thread's pull appealing. I felt like a hypocrite. I had emotionally rejected the idea of being married off to some lord's son against my will, but here I was contractually bound to Leander and actually considering it.

Perhaps because he seemed interested in me exactly how I was. No *Modify Self* hiding the secrets of my origins. I didn't need to hide any of that from him. That acceptance was attractive to consider.

If I was honest with myself, *he* was physically attractive. Hell, and his voice ...

What would it feel like if more than his words touched me?

My heart sped at the thought and I wondered how much of it I could blame on the thread.

"I'll try to be ..." I dropped my gaze shyly to the floor. "When I go tonight—alone. I'll try to be honest with myself." All I really knew was that he didn't want to break the contract. I knew nothing of his motives. Could I really assume he was *actually* interested in me?

Freda sighed. "I guess I'll go check out the Archive of Truth while you go meet up with your boyfriend," she teased.

I leveled an unamused stare at her. "He's not my boyfriend."

"Yet," Freda added.

I raised a biscuit as if to throw it at her.

"Ha!" she laughed. "You really have a thing for throwing things at people you like."

My mind went back to the bar, and the piece of lapis lazuli chalk I had thrown at Leander. I winced. Would he hold that against me?

I put my hands together decisively. "So the priority is to grill Leander for info about the soul bond and the contract and to help me contact my father ... and you can research what you can about infernal soul bonds and anything that might help me with my father at the Archive of Truth. We'll regroup and compare notes!"

"I'll also see if I can find anything else about your grandfather and these ... creepy arcane knives."

I gave her a wry smile. "You want one don't you?"

A manic grin spread across her face. "Knives are cool, okay? Especially enchanted ones."

"What if they're cursed?" I teased.

She shrugged. "A problem for later."

We cleaned up and prepared for our missions. We shopped for spell materials, checked for spying with the *Scry* spell, and ate lunch. Freda left shortly after to find the address Alàn had given her. I sat across from Emrys and decided perhaps conversation would be a good distraction. I reached for our telepathic bond.

"Emrys ... how long have you known Leander?"

"Two-hundred years." The immaterial crackle of his voice scraped across my mind, like nails gently combing my scalp.

"Why would he want to have a mortal as his soul mate?"

Emrys tilted his head. *"I ... do not know."*

I rested my chin on my knees. I knew Emrys was not a normal familiar, and Leander had specifically said he had sent him to help me. *"What did you do for Leander before he sent you to serve me?"*

"I obeyed whatever commands he gave me."

I tapped my fingers on my knees. Killing time like this was getting me nowhere and making me anxious.

A thorough rearranging of literally all my personal belongings would fix that. I emptied my bag on the bed and heard tinging metal. I scooted my spell book to the side and found half rolled brown leather I'd never seen before.

Emrys's little onyx eyes flashed to it, then back up to me in curiosity. I lifted the soft leather and saw a bright dagger twisted in leather straps with metal rings attaching each piece. A harness? Then I realized, this is the dagger I'd seen Alàn sharpen. I held up the straps—indeed a thigh holster—and smiled at the gift. Guess she thought I'd needed it. I spent some time figuring out how to cross the straps and buckle them before showing it off to Emrys. If Freda had been here she would have begged me to let her have it. Especially after that enchanted knife comment.

The remaining daylight in the room waned with my patience. What would it hurt to go early? Perhaps he would arrive and the thread would surge when I was almost there. Yes, that was an efficient use of my time. I glanced over to Emrys asleep in a black swirl.

"Let's go!"

The route to the basement bar was pretty straightforward from the central district, and having Emrys at my side ... no one was going to mess with either of us. He trotted ahead, tail up and flicking in the air.

We arrived at the alleyway and I afforded a moment to look down the dark stretch of it. No light was on by the door. Just as

I sighed with disappointment, the red light flooded the alley and the thread yanked on me, tingling through my body.

Did he have any idea what his trips to this plane were doing to me? I rushed towards the door, but a heavy thud pulled my attention. I glanced over my shoulder to see the wizard that Emrys had decapitated. Only, he was looking a lot more *undead* than before.

Emrys growled, but then he cried out as arcane, violet-edged tendrils shot up from between cracks in the cobblestone and ensnared him.

I fumbled for my spell materials. Was it too late to cast *Nullify?* Just as my fingers hit the pouch Emrys phased out in the blink of an eye.

They ... had banished him. Back to the Nine Circles of Hell.

I stumbled backwards. My eyes scanned the alley and I caught sight of Cyrus perched on the rooftop. Glowing remnants of spell materials dimmed in his outstretched hand. The other wizard Emrys had killed slid towards the roof edge. I refocused on the one stumbling towards me when its putrid stench hit me. I extended my hand, a piece of amber now in my grasp, and focused on my concentration.

"*Slow down.*"

The pale green body slowed with the spell clinging to his movement. I was outnumbered, and this was my chance to flee.

I looked back to the door and rushed towards it. I gripped the handle and the lantern flicked off, sending the alley back into darkness.

No ... no! Not again!

Two more thuds sounded from behind me and I whirled back around.

Help me!

The three wizards advanced on me. Cyrus opened his palm and prepared to cast again.

Warmth like fire erupted beside me. For a moment I thought a spell had been cast but then there was a flash and my eyes went wide as thick, black smoke twisted in the air next to me. The dark swirls dispersed, and Leander towered at my side. The intense, magnetic draw of being so close to my soul fragment flooded me, the need to be closer to it practically vibrating through me. His scent—that smoked cinnamon aroma—enveloped me like a protective shield.

Leander's glowing fire eyes were narrowed at the three ahead. His expression was a calm, burning rage. For a moment I sensed the heavy weight of everything he was—power that eased around us, thick and hot and menacing, reminding me of the illustrated colossal hellhound that could easily wipe out this entire city with one swipe of its claw.

The two undead wizards advanced towards us and Leander's eyes blazed hot with hellfire. He sent a targeted glance at each assailant. Both crumpled to the ground, becoming a pile of bones and sagging flesh. My eyes went wide. He had unmade whatever necromantic spell had animated them. He snapped his fingers, and the corpses burst into flames.

Leander lifted his head, and cut his eyes towards Cyrus.

"Give her to me," Cyrus demanded, lurching forward, "and I will trouble you no further."

A dark, crooked smile spread across Leander's face. The points of his fangs shone.

Cyrus froze, as if he only now realized who he had made demands to.

"What will you give me in exchange?" Leander cocked his head with sinister playfulness. It had the arrogance of what he was baked into every word. This was not the same devil that found my demands amusing. Even from our brief interactions I recognized the undertone of wrath.

Cyrus scrunched his face. "What do you want?"

"You know souls are the most important thing to a devil." Leander answered smoothly. "What could you give me that would be worth trading such a *delicious* soul?"

I felt my cheeks heat at his words.

If he was seriously considering trading me I would throw *more* than just a piece of chalk at him.

"I don't have any souls to offer you," Cyrus replied. "And my own is already promised."

"How ... disappointing," Leander replied flatly.

"I serve a powerful—"

"This is boring." Leander flicked his finger towards Cyrus.

A dark energy flashed out from his outstretched finger. It slammed into Cyrus and pulsed over his body. It flickered out, and he slackened, collapsing to the ground—dead.

Was that the *Death Promise* spell?

A single finger that commanded death. I'd only ever read about it—so few had been able to cast such a spell.

Leander strolled toward Cyrus and leaned over his corpse with an open palm. A delicate silver wisp of light floated up from the body and swirled like twisting iridescent smoke into Leander's hand. He formed a tight fist and it vanished, as if he'd placed it somewhere for safekeeping.

I stared in awe. Not silver smoke—it had to be a *soul*. This was a soul collection. I thought of each time I had seen that wisp of light. Could I see the souls because I had part of Leander's soul inside me?

Leander finally turned to look at me. The wrath in his eyes was replaced with a soft gaze. He closed the distance between us and extended his hand, palm up, towards me.

"Do you trust me?"

He stood over me with his open hand looking like the biggest warning sign ever, from his spade-tipped tail all the way to his horns lit in what remained of the orange fire behind him.

"I barely know you," I answered. In fact, he had said himself that devils can't be trusted. But those eyes ... beautiful rings of molten fire floating in shadow. I swallowed around how much that glowing gaze and the proximity of our souls made me want to abandon all reason.

"*Will* you trust me?"

I caught the adjusted meaning. I didn't have to trust him wholly, but I could trust him, for right now.

Devils and their words ...

Somehow it felt odd not to trust him. The thread had been the constant in my life—always there—always a comfort. It had woven itself around me and kept me sane throughout my lonely childhood. And now I knew ... it had been *his* soul doing that for me.

I needed to know more. Trusting him in this moment felt worth it to take another step towards finding out everything I wished I understood. I moved towards him and slipped my hand into his till I felt the warmness of his palm embrace mine.

A thrumming current connected our palms and I gasped, fingers twitching as he gripped them tighter in reply.

Every sense in my body electrified as his soul inside me channeled a connection to its origin. I could feel something similar from his direction, a warm power struck towards me, missing remnants of myself meeting me for the first time. Like an arc of lightning, forming a current of energy.

It felt *exhilarating*.

He grasped my hand tighter and pulled me into his chest. His other hand slid around my waist, heat flaring as he squeezed me closer. The thread thrummed chaotically between us.

Was this what it was supposed to feel like when we touched?

Could he feel it too?

Black smoke rose around us obscuring the flickering fire in the alley. We were teleporting. Where to, I did not know.

But I would *trust* him.
For now.

CHAPTER TWENTY

Before, when I had used the teleportation portal, it had felt like I was adrift—spinning wildly—using every ounce of will and the guiding pull of the thread to arrive at my destination in a single piece.

This was different.

Because the source of the pull was right there—pressed warmly against me. It oriented me like a world orbiting a star.

Only a fraction of a second had passed, and then I felt a cool breeze shifting my hair. My eyes finally cracked open. We were standing on a long, shared balcony. The pink sandstone rails glowed faintly in the moonlight. I glanced in both directions down the night covered walkway and saw curtains hanging over patio doorways. They flowed softly in the humming evening wind.

Leander released me from that electrifying connection and walked a few steps to the stone rail, letting the cold air rush in where he'd once been. He rested his forearms on the rails and looked out into the darkness. I followed, doing the same. I listened to the roaring static as I took in the night shrouded seascape of jagged rocks and crashing waves glittered by the moonlight. No, not a roaring static. It was the ocean crashing against the beach. I'd never heard it before.

"Where are we?"

Leander looked a little surprised as he turned to me, moonlight absorbed by the obsidian of his horns. "Have you not been here?" My unamused expression must have said it all because he followed with a gesture towards the scene, "That is the Emerald Gulf. This is the Bon Mar."

My eyes widened. The Bon Mar. It was a popular destination on the Sapphire Coast—on the other side of the continent. I had only ever read about it. Traveling to The Bon Mar by airship would take five days from Brunalin. By train ... two weeks.

I had never traveled outside the estate grounds. I had seen more of Brunalin in the past few days than in the fifteen years of attending Midor's. And now, I was so far away. Anxiety settled in me as I considered that even this distance from grandfather may not be enough.

Leander looked me over curiously, assessing me with those infernal, glowing orange eyes. "Are you not afraid of me?" His voice was low and guttural, as if he were trying to test whether or not its predatory nature might cause me fear.

"Should I be afraid of you?" My caution, like the last time in his presence, was nowhere to be found under the reassuring vibration of the thread.

"Most mortals would be absolutely terrified that the most powerful devil in the Nine Circles abducted them to a far away location."

"Oh, I thought you asking me to trust you was me consenting to be abducted," I shot back, tilting my head at him.

He blinked slowly at me, adjusting his jaw. "Mmhmm ..."

Something in his gaze unnerved me, but once again the thread's pull swelled over me like a wave and I sighed into it. "It's hard to be afraid of you when all I feel is the pulling between our souls.

You were right about what you said. That feeling is probably the only thing I've ever found comfort in, even though I didn't know what it was."

He looked lost in a chaos of thoughts for a moment, his brows drawing lower as he faced the view beyond the balcony. I watched his eyes drift to that glittering moonlit sea before he changed the subject.

"Well, you wanted to meet again. Here I am," he said, throwing me a sidelong glance with that intense glowing stare.

I averted my gaze to study the shapes of the rocks below, barely defined in the moonlight. If I kept staring into those eyes, I wasn't sure I would be coherent. Whenever those two orange rings of flame narrowed on me it sent a fluttering of heat under my skin. I hadn't realized I had such a thing for infernal eyes like mine. I supposed it made sense—but I needed to stay focused. I had so many questions, I didn't know where to begin. Perhaps I should start by getting right to the point.

"Why don't you want to break the contract—so you can bond with an immortal like yourself?" I kept my sights fixed on the rocks.

"Does it matter why?" he replied curtly. I could sense a hint of annoyance in his tone.

I flipped my gaze back to him. "It matters because I'm also stuck in this contract."

He shifted at my tone. "Do *you* want to break it?" His eyes scanned me cautiously.

"I ... don't know." I stretched my arms out on the balcony railing. I took a moment to quiet my own annoyance by his tone. "Until a few days ago, I didn't know anyone else was part of the contract except my father. I figured I'd find him again, then he'd take me away from my family and I would finally be free."

"What makes you think Remodeus will do that?"

"I guess because ... he said it might be a while before we'd see each other again. He was the first person who actually loved me. Treated me as something other than a mistake ... So I figured that would still mean something." I lowered my cheek to rest on my folded arms at the balcony's edge and glanced up at Leander.

He had hidden whatever he was thinking well behind a neutral expression. Maybe I had annoyed him with my question. This conversation was not anywhere near as successful as the one we'd had while I was bathing—

"If you prefer to have conversations where you are in the bath, I can accommodate that," he said with a wicked grin, cutting off my thought.

I blinked. "Are you reading my thoughts?" I straightened and squared myself off against him.

"Most powerful devils can read thoughts," he replied, as if it were a commonly known fact.

"No," I said immediately, a stern command.

"No?" Leander's smile curled.

"Do not read my thoughts again."

The wicked grin persisted and his eyes blazed like fire as he teased, "You could read my thoughts too if you wanted."

"I can't cast any spells that let me read thoughts." I gave him an annoyed look.

"You don't need a spell. It works like you did to summon Emrys. Devils are granted magic through the primordial chaos, where our souls come from. And you," he glanced down at the center of my being, "have a rather large piece of my soul inside you."

I frowned. He hadn't agreed to not read my thoughts, but what he'd said about his soul fragment in me intrigued me.

He extended his hand for me again with an alluring, fanged smile. "I'll show you."

I squinted my eyes at him before reluctantly placing my hand in his. The feeling of our souls meeting again surged through me. Electrically drawn together, clawing to be closer to each other. My core fluttered and heat started rising to my cheeks.

"Close your eyes," he breathed.

I pressed my lips together in brief protest before letting my eyelids fall shut.

He pulled my hand, moving in closer, and I felt the heat radiating from him. Then he whispered in my ear, "You can sense me next to you, right? Even though you can't see me."

"Yes," I replied, holding back the shiver running down my spine from having him so close to me. I hated how much I loved the way it felt—loved how the thread reacted—despite how he'd annoyed me.

"Find my presence. Feel it around you, whatever it may be. A smoky shadow. A blazing flame. A scary dog." He chuckled and something low in my center clenched. "Then picture your hands reaching out to grab a hold of me, of my mind. I promise to let you in." His voice caressed my ear, throwing tingles along the thread and across my neck. "Then, if you listen, you'll hear what I'm thinking."

Surely this manner of seduction was the tactic devils used to convince people to sign away their souls. Despite my apprehension at the thought, I found myself following his instructions.

It was hard not to be so aware of him when I could feel the heat of his body along my skin and the sound of his breathing in my ear. Distinct, warm and ... the thrumming pull of the thread. Save for that, it reminded me of the sensations of choosing a destination for casting *Mindtell*. I focused on him. His hand enveloping mine, the thread thrumming between us and ... close to me—so close. I swallowed. Then, I pictured my two hands, glowing red in the dark, floating out and up towards his head—his mind. The arcana was different, it seemed to glitter at my imagined fingertips with warm steady power. As my metaphysical hands neared him, my fingertips sank into something dark and hot—and I froze.

"*Very* good," he purred into my ear.

I shivered—was he closer?

"Now, I'll let you in."

My heart started pounding. I sunk my metaphysical fingers in deeper. They hummed hot past the edge of his mind with no resistance. I kept my focus mostly on the thread—the connection between our souls—and it led me into the recesses of his mind. The thoughts poured in like a released dam. His velvety voice echoed in fragments, bouncing between here and there. I shifted my probing and brought it into focus. Then, the first clear thought ran through.

"*I much prefer ... the sight of you lounging in that bath ... hiding yourself from me under the bubbles. So ... many bubbles.*"

My eyelids flew open. He had used *Scry* on me! Freda was right—it wasn't a *thing* to be able to communicate with another's familiar. So much for placing a little trust in him. I turned my head, eyes darting around at the curtained doorways.

I yanked my hand away, severing the connection. "I assume one of these rooms is yours?"

"The one there ahead of you, dear," he replied, shifting his eyes in the direction of a white silk curtain.

I didn't think he was reading my thoughts anymore. If he was, he wouldn't have used the same soft, sensual voice he had before.

"Great." I said, my voice less restrained to hide my anger.

I marched to the door and flung the curtains out of the way before entering the room. On the inside there were two small twin doors to shut out the balcony. I flipped around to face him as he took steps towards me. I gripped the handles of each door. Giving him a final nasty look, I slammed the doors shut and quickly locked them. I knew it wouldn't keep him out, but at least it sent a message. I crossed my arms with my back to the door and observed the room. A single bed, a seating area with a small table, the edges of a bathing area beyond another doorway.

I heard a chuckle in my mind, followed by, *"I thought you wanted to talk more, my dear?"*

"I do, but you are not taking this seriously. Why reward bad behavior?" I moved and sat on the bed, crossing my arms. My heart ached as I thought about Emrys again. Banished. Could I bring him back? At least one infernal creature that helps me? Another *Mindtell* from Leander interrupted the thought.

"May I come in?" He had adjusted his tone to what I imagined was his attempt at being more serious. Why was he even asking? He could come in if he wanted with little effort ... Even through the locked doors I felt the thread dragging on me to walk to him. I squeezed my arms tighter, planting myself. The thread hummed at me, that comforting caress trying to sway me. I sighed.

"Fine."

The door clicked unlocked with arcana and the door creaked open. Leander floated through, unamused, and effortlessly lifted the chair from the seating area with a single hand and placed it right in front of me.

"Go on ... what do you want to talk about?" he said in a defeated tone as he sat and sprawled back in the chair.

"Don't you already know?" I asked flatly. "Just provide an answer."

He sighed. "No ... I don't know." His orange gaze narrowed on me, sending heat coursing back through my skin. "Because you said not to."

He could. And I would be absolutely powerless. I stared back at him in disbelief. I found it hard to believe I was being given so much autonomy from a devil. It quieted my anger a little though to see my boundary respected.

"Why did you start coming back to Novus a few months ago?" I thought of that night, when the thread violently shook me from sleep. "Before that, the thread was always so faint."

He held my stare for a moment, as if he needed the time to organize his thoughts. "I had not been to this plane since before Remodeus signed that contract. After a quarter of a century I became curious to feel the full expression of the pull." His words were slow and carefully chosen.

"The wards that the Temple of Lumoniel placed weren't an issue?"

He scrunched his face in a wickedly arrogant smile and laughed. "No."

"So why did you run when I came to the basement bar?"

He clenched his jaw, his infernal red skin flexing with the movement, and held my stare. I grew impatient and changed the subject.

"Can we get Emrys back before we continue?" I couldn't hide the sadness in my voice.

His expression softened. "Of course we can." He stood and extended his hand once again.

Rising, I took a step closer, eyeing his hand. The thread hummed louder, eager to make contact between our fragments. I inhaled deeply before I placed my own in his grasp. He pulled me into his chest and the black smoke of teleportation rose around us. Within a fraction of a second, the world stopped whirling by, and a dark cemetery flooded in around us. The cool air settled in my nostrils and the same moon I had seen on the balcony peeked through clouds in the sky. He slipped away from me and used his magic to raise a stone structure like a chair—no, a throne—out of the earth behind him. As he sat down, he gestured towards the setting as if to say *go ahead.*

I was still wearing my pack, so I retrieved my spell book and began drawing the runes in the soil. Dusting off my hands, I sat down across from the runes and pulled my button necklace out of my shirt to help me concentrate on the ritual.

"What's that?" Leander asked softly from across the graves, chin resting on his hand.

I looked down at the button and then held it out briefly so he could take a glance. "My father gave it to me to help focus my arcana."

Leander's eyes widened. "Remodeus gave *that* to you?" The confused look on his face almost made him look silly.

"You'll be surprised to learn he was actually pretty kind and sweet to me." I folded the button back into my hand and the warm tingle of arcana surged as I concentrated.

"I *do* find it surprising. Your experience with Remodeus is nothing like mine," Leander mused. "It makes me wonder if I really know him at all."

My concentration broke and the arcana I had focused melted away. I flicked my eyes to him. He was shrouded in night except for his two glowing orange eyes glued to me. The burning stare probably would have sent any other mortal off screaming between the headstones. But for me despite how much it annoyed me, that hellfire gaze flushed my skin with tingling heat.

"Are you going to keep talking to me while I do this? Because I have to start over each time, and this ritual took an hour last time." The interruptions annoyed me less than the ease in which I turned hot under his gaze.

The corner of his lips curled. "Apologies my dear, I'll give you some privacy." He shifted in his chair before adding with a devilish grin, "It won't take you an hour this time." Then he teleported away, leaving behind nothing but a dark mist cascading around the stone chair he had summoned.

The air felt colder after he'd left. A moment later, my heart sank with the loneliness of the faint pull. He must have returned to The Nine Circles. I had just wanted him to be quiet. I hadn't meant for him to ... leave me alone here.

Looking down at the runes, I reoriented myself to concentrate once again.

CHAPTER TWENTY-ONE

Leander had been annoyingly right of course. It only took thirty minutes to summon Emrys back. Perhaps because I had been practicing using *his soul* to wield the primordial magic. The light from the runes flashed violet and Emrys's feline form bubbled from the dirt once again.

"Emrys!" I extended my hands out.

He blinked as the light faded. The same black cat I had summoned before grinned up at me, needle teeth and all. He bounced up from his seat and started purring, crawling up to me. I scooped him up and hugged him, speaking through our telepathic bond.

"I'm so sorry, Emrys. I should have protected you!"

He simply purred in my arms.

The pull of the thread intensified and drew taut as Leander reappeared in his stone chair. I felt my lips turn in a small smile. I was relieved ... he came back.

"Hello, *Emrys.*" Leander's fiery glare targeted the familiar in my arms.

Emrys tensed up. He looked over my arms at that threatening infernal gaze, and jumped down and cowered behind me.

I gasped. "You're scaring him!"

Leander's brow twitched. "Good," he said sternly. "He should be scared. His only job was to protect you, which he failed *spectacularly.*"

Emrys made a high-pitched, meowing whine as if begging for mercy. I turned to him and scooped him back up.

"I won't let him hurt you," I said softly to Emrys.

He shook in my arms.

My eyes darted back to Leander. "Be nice to him!" I said with a scowl.

Leander rolled his eyes. "You have your *beloved* familiar back," he said sarcastically. "What else do you want from me?"

I stood up with Emrys in my arms and took a few steps towards him. Clearly, he was tired of my questions. Perhaps I should rephrase ...

"If you won't tell me why you don't want to break the contract—"

"It's because Remodeus made you look like *her.*" Leander cut me off in a pained tone. He leaned back into one corner of the chair and perched one elbow on the armrest, fingers pressed into his temple.

I stood there in shock at his direct and seemingly honest reply. The silence grew between us as he stared back at me and I waited for him to offer some kind of explanation. I held Emrys tighter. When he didn't speak further, I did.

"Was *she* also a mortal?"

"No." he replied quietly.

"So, my father," I began, not believing what I was hearing myself say, "made me look like someone you knew?" My stomach turned at the thought that I could have been made to look like someone else. "Who is she?"

He rubbed his temple in contemplation. His glowing eyes dimmed slightly with his thoughts, then he sighed whatever he was feeling away and said, "She was a devil. We were together for only a short time, but she ... changed my life. I was not in a good place a long time ago and she pulled me out of it. Made me reconsider how I was choosing to *live* my life."

So ... a lover? My father made me look like his former lover? Why?

"Was that after you had died here in Novus?" I continued.

Leander's eyes narrowed, the orange light behind them flickering, "You know about that?"

"Yes." I offered an innocent smile. He tapped his fingers on the stone armrest and I maintained my silence, waiting for him to be drawn back into the thousand year old memories.

"It's not just a blow emotionally or physically for someone as powerful as myself to be slain and returned to the Nine Circles. My status was put at risk and it took time for me to build back my power. I spent twenty years committing every sin I pleased to numb the dull drag of time while I was weak." He clenched his jaw, eyes glazed and lost in the vegetation and dirt around us. Did he not even want to look at me when he thought of *her*?

Emrys settled deeper into my arms and I stroked his head, waiting.

"Then she burned into my life like wildfire and challenged me. She helped me realize what I was doing to myself wouldn't make me truly powerful. Time would certainly grow my primordial magic and physical strength, but my mind—my will—would remain weak." His head weighed heavier into his palm. "In that dark dream, she was my salvation."

His salvation. I thought of my own situation that way. My father and the thread.

"She sounds wise," I said with sincere respect.

"She *was*." The fire in his eyes dimmed to embers, and I couldn't help but feel sad.

I wanted to ask so badly what had happened, but I didn't want to cause him further pain. Then I wondered what it meant that

I looked like her—if looking at me caused him the pain of losing her, or if he longed to relive those memories with me because of how I looked.

"Why did my father make me look like her?" I said instead.

Some of the orange fire returned to his eyes. "He and I have had many disagreements since I was slain, including his dislike of her. He's carried that resentment with him for centuries and decided to torture me for it at the first sign of opportunity."

"So even though it's torture, you still don't want to break the contract?" I asked again.

Leander's gaze went soft and warm as he finally looked at me. No ounce of the flirtatious twinkle was there. His gaze held a solemn reverence, as if he was seeing *her* again. "I didn't know you looked like her till I saw you for the first time. I thought you *were* her, then I felt your mortal soul attached to me and realized what Remodeus had done."

"Well, you didn't seem too bothered," I said, recalling our first interactions.

"I am *very* bothered." He rubbed the side of his head.

It was *honesty*. I could see it in how his infernal eyes blazed at me, as if telling me these truths might be the last things we ever say, and the last time he ever gazes upon the memory of her again. As if the truth was a vital material to keep this moment from ending—and her memory alive.

I shifted slightly. "Have you considered using me and the contract as a way of reliving these memories?"

"The temptation to do so is why I called it *torture*, my dear," he said flatly, his glowing eyes narrowing on me.

Why would he resist? Wasn't he supposed to be evil—like other devils? Why didn't he just do what he wanted?

"I'm not her," I said. "I'm a different person."

"You *are* a different person. But now and then you act a certain way, and I ... *see it*. I see *her*. Despite your mortal soul distinguishing you from her, you are too alike, and I couldn't treat you in a way that would dishonor her memory."

She must have been special to him. I supposed it explained why he was giving me so much agency. Earlier, I had contemplated the possibilities of this portion of the contract—to selfishly give in to our *soul mates* bond as one way to never again be lonely and gain that sense of belonging I'd desperately desired. I wondered what it would really be like if he always looked at me and saw another woman. Could I blame him for trying to see me as a different person, but then seeing *her* in me?

"I thought I looked like my father?"

"*She* happened to share his complexion too. It's not the most common, but our god gave us many different designs," he said softly before he examined me again. "Remodeus didn't only make you look like her—you sound like her too."

I had always thought my father made me look like himself—because he wanted me as his daughter. If it weren't true, it meant he'd changed me knowing how it would make my mother, my family, and even Leander look at me tinted by some pain.

I thought of the memory we shared together—it was so strong. I clung to believing the devil I saw that day as a child had done this for a reason—or it was a misunderstanding. But, for a moment, I entertained the notion he was as Leander described: a manipulative, punishing devil. One who used his power to transform what would have been a human baby into a specter to haunt Leander. The thought splintered something in my core.

Another thought was also making me queasy. Leander wouldn't break the contract, but he also didn't seem like he wanted to pursue it. Sure, he'd flirted with me, but it didn't seem like he had any genuine interest in the *soul mates* bond with me. I started to feel a little trapped. What if *neither* devil in this contract wanted anything to do with me? My stomach twisted, because I *did* find the whole thing appealing. And in the interest of remaining honest with myself, as Freda had pointed out, I also needed to admit ... I found *him* appealing.

There was one thing that was unclear. The bond draws us to bring our souls together through acts of love. He mentioned we could break this contract only until we *united*. Did *uniting* literally mean sealing the deal with *sex*?

"What happens if we unite our souls?"

Leander blinked at me, then shook his head. "Talking more was a mistake."

No—I was finally getting answers! "Why?"

He rubbed his face then stood up, towering over me. He extended his hand. "I'll take you back."

I backed away, my stomach dropping. This thread, even if placed out of cruelty, was special. How it thrummed to bring us near. How it warmed to touch him. I felt a little out of control, like I *needed* it. "What are you afraid of?" I said sharply.

"Afraid of?" He closed the distance I'd put between us with long strides. I swallowed hard under the gaze that still made me burn like fire. "It's not fear I feel, it's *torture*," he growled down to me. "The way you look at me—that I want to touch you—that I came to this plane *one time* out of curiosity. Then I felt the full expression of this pull, and I had to keep coming back—like a *drug*." His face inched closer and my own heated.

But ... he felt the pull too then. "It's only torture because you choose to see it that way," I snapped back. I was sure Emrys could feel my heart pounding through my blouse.

Leander pulled his head back and started laughing. "Are you serious? How would that be for you? When I'm fucking you and thinking about someone else?"

"I won't let you think about someone else." It was as if the confidence had been pulled from inside me, drawn along the connection in me to him.

He flashed a pained smile.

"Tell me what happens," I demanded.

"What happens," he ground out, "is the first time our souls are united, our fragments will become permanently split between us, and the only way to then break the soul bond ... is *death*." He glowered down at me. "There is no *break the contract* once that happens."

I refused to look away, taking the full force of his heated gaze. "To be clear, *uniting souls* means the first time we have *sex*?"

"Yes."

"Well, I'm not going to *fuck* you right now, so you can relax a little." I took a deep breath, pushing my fingers through Emrys's fur.

He gave me a measured stare, as if calculating what to do with me. I wouldn't give him the chance to decide.

"Take me back to the room. Not back to Brunalin," I pleaded.

He flexed his jaw, releasing some tension in his face. "Get your things."

I turned and marched to my bag and spell book, still sitting behind me where I had summoned Emrys. What bothered me the most was outright dismissing it all. The thread, the thing that brought me so much comfort. It had to be worth it to at least consider. I felt his eyes on me as I flipped my spell book closed with one hand and then set Emrys down to open my pack.

"Emrys, maybe you should go in here while we teleport."

He glanced up, searching the emotions on my face and then jumped in. I folded the flap loosely shut and lifted it to hang from my shoulder before I walked back over to Leander.

He extended his hand, and I placed my own in his. Our souls meeting again flooded my body like an electric current. As much as he annoyed me, feeling the thread churn electrically between us was entirely gratifying. I never wanted to tire of this feeling between our souls when I touch him. I now knew it felt just as good to him as it did to me. He pulled me into his chest and pressed his hand firmly into my lower back. My senses were flooded with his smoky cinnamon aroma and the warmth of his body as I melted closer. I waited for the black smoke to rise but instead he leaned in close to my ear.

"If you had said I *could* fuck you now, I don't think I could truly resist—no matter how brutal the torture," he purred, his voice deeper with desperate frustration in my ear.

I felt myself go molten and my hand tensed in his grasp. His neck and the warmth spilling from it was a breath away from me. *I wonder if ...*

"Would it be too much torture if you just ... kissed me?" I breathed under him. It was more than simply wanting to give the magnetism of our thread a chance. I wanted to know if the feeling would extend to when we kissed. If it would feel *right*.

He pulled away from my ear and dropped my hand to grasp my jaw, his warm fingers tilting it up towards him. My body went fluid at his firm touch. Before I knew it, I was clutching on to the lapels of his jacket. His eyes pierced me, beautiful rings of blazed hellfire, like the tips of a flame where the yellow-orange deepened into darkness. He assessed my helpless pleading expression. Still gripping my jaw, he melted closer agonizingly—torturously—slow until our lips met.

This was not lightning—it was a thunderstorm. The electric feeling surged between us, channeling down the thread and connecting our souls again. It flowed over me in waves that sent tingles over every inch of me. Soft and caressing, his lips moved gently—curiously, ardently—over mine. My knees wobbled and I leaned into him. I braced into how firmly he held my face—the hand at the center of my back.

Leander released my jaw and he slid his hand to join the one at my back, holding me upright with a squeeze. I sensed the light change as everything shifted around us. His lips continued to explore me more thoroughly until the surrounding space stilled into the room we'd been in before. Then he pulled away from our kiss. His eyes were soft glowing embers now.

"You are going to haunt me, my dear," he whispered, eyes wandering over my face. "You have been doing so ever since I started coming to this plane."

I stared up at him, barely lucid from how the kiss had melted me. I clutched his jacket, not wanting to let go.

"Goodnight," he said. His lips curled up ever so slightly. It confirmed the kiss had felt the same way for him, and it had been *everything*.

"Are you leaving me here?" I didn't want to sound desperate, but to be alone ...

He leaned in and pressed his forehead to mine, our horns tapping against each other's. "You will have to accept tormenting me from across the planes," he said playfully. His fingers on my lower back drew up my spine. My tail curled at the delicate touch. He continued, "So this is goodnight, and I'll be back in the morning."

I felt breathless, but I mustered a "Goodnight" in reply. He smirked and then teleported away. I set my bag gently on the floor before collapsing face first to the bed. Emrys crawled out and curled up in his signature black swirl next to me. I flipped to my back, staring at the glow on the ceiling from candles I didn't light, but he must have—with his magic as his lips devoured me. I sank into the undeniably amazing feeling of our souls connecting as I melted into his warm chest. All of it replayed over and over in my mind until I had etched it there.

Hell, it felt *incredible*. And despite how he had gotten on my nerves, I found myself *liking* him. I wondered if perhaps the reason I found myself trusting him so easily now was because his soul had always been a part of me. Perhaps it was why, despite the physical pull, I felt so drawn to him. It felt like I'd been laying there for ten minutes, and then my mind tingled with that familiar caress.

"Stop thinking about me and go to sleep."

"Stop watching me and I'll go to sleep," I answered.

I used the opportunity to practice using the primordial magic from his soul inside me. First, I cast *Unveil*—and as I suspected, I spotted a small glassy-looking orb about six feet above me. A scrying eye. It watched me for a few moments. I swear I felt him looking at me through the blue tinted sheen it held. A smile crept across my face and I cast *Dispel.* The orb dissipated into arcane dust.

I got ready for bed and found myself repetitively looking inward for his soul. Picturing it like I had Leander's mind, I tapped it with a metaphysical finger to feel the warm tingle of primordial magic that followed. I used it to tell Freda where I was and that I was safe across a *Mindtell.* Then to dispel the candles. Using this kind of magic felt hot, and a little volatile. I'd never really had anyone in my life who encouraged the part of me that was ... *devilish.* It had always been treated as something wrong with me. Never a strength or as an opportunity. Instead ... a deficiency, a red flag, a curse. It was another reason I found myself liking him. He seemed to accept me exactly how I was—even as a copy of *her.*

And I liked it.

CHAPTER TWENTY-TWO

I woke in the morning, not to that warm caress in my mind, but to a different voice.

"Reign?" Freda's voice echoed through a *Mindtell*.

I jolted up from the bed. *"I'm here! Is everything okay?"*

I waited nervously for a moment, then I realized ... I could save her spell materials by initiating the rest of the *Mindtells*. Oh, I was going to enjoy this new primordial magic.

"Did you find the Archive of Truth?" I said.

"I did ... but there is a problem. When can you come back?"

My stomach turned. I didn't want to leave just yet. Especially after last night. I wanted to talk to Leander one more time. If I sent him a *Mindtell* while he was on this plane, I had a feeling he'd answer me right away. I mean, he wouldn't kiss someone like that then not answer their *Mindtells,* right? Even with the torture of looking like *her,* I couldn't imagine him staying away from me. He had to be as drawn to following his end of the thread as I was mine. Finding and confronting my father was another matter, but at least I had found Leander and was sure that he would help me reach that goal.

"Later today?" I said sheepishly.

"The sooner the better."

I felt myself grow cold. It wasn't like her to be so serious. Something must really be wrong.

"I'll Mindtell you as soon as I'm back in Brunalin!"

I glanced at Emrys asleep on the bed and waited for her reply.

"Sorry, I needed to get outside to make sure no one could intercept this. When you come you can't bring Leander—I'll explain later."

A librarian would intercept a *Mindtell?* Where the hell was she? And ... I can't bring ... Leander? The questions boiled up my throat but I quieted the urge to send another *Mindtell.*

Instead, I stroked Emrys and stretched. Warm light poured in through the window at the seating area of the room, where I spotted clothing draped over one of the chairs. I rose and ran my fingers along the soft silk texture of the black material. Had Leander left it ... for me?

I couldn't help but smile as I undressed and slipped into it. It was one continuous piece, with pant legs and long sleeves—exactly my size. The majority of it was a translucent black fabric that was fitted in the bodice but the sleeves and pants puffed near my wrists and ankles where gold silk bands gathered the billowing fabric. Two other silk bands wrapped around my waist and neck. The sheer fabric was embroidered in black, the design swirled in the shape of fire down from my neck, across my breasts, and swirling around my hips. There was even a small hooded slit for my tail to fit through. It was as if I had been wrapped in a long black flame.

I used my *Mystic Hand* to close the silk covered buttons at my back, ankles, and wrists. When I turned in the light, I caught small shimmers of orange twisting among the embroidery.

I had seen nothing like it before ... It was as if it had been made for me. The button necklace tucked into the garment was barely visible through the fabric. It felt like a shame to hide who I was with *Modify Self* in such a well-suited garment, so I let my horns, eyes, and tail remain visible. I brought my tail up to my hands where I stroked it nervously. I realized I hadn't altered myself at all throughout my and Leander's interactions.

Emrys let out tired yawns as he stretched across the bed. I walked over and sat next to him scratching between his ears. Even though it was hard to read anything in his two tiny black eyes, his whiskers twitched as his eyes slid across me, admiring the clothing. *"Do you like it?"* I sent the question to him telepathically.

"It makes you look ... like home," his voice crackled.

A smile grew on my face.

Home.

Emrys had a home—the Nine Circles of Hell. That I reminded him of it made my heart melt. It stirred my desire for wanting a place that welcomed me—a home—that I could feel a strong longing for. It certainly wasn't the estate. Not even Midor's or Brunalin. I hoped it could be the Nine Circles.

"Emrys ... do you know the woman that Leander said I look like?"

Emrys blinked a few times. *"No ... She was before I came to serve him. He does not talk about her."*

My mind drifted back to the cemetery, and Leander's words.

She sounds wise.

She was.

Perhaps talking about her caused too much pain.

I passed the curtains to the balcony and mulled over whether or not to try to send Leander a *Mindtell*—if he was even on this plane. I hadn't actually sent him a message using *Mindtell* before, except by accident in front of Freda's house that day. I wondered if my new-found primordial magic would allow me to reach across the planes.

I propped my elbows on the pink stone rail, resting my chin in my hands as I looked over the edge. The rocks made a terrain of pitted charcoal that rose out of the white powdery sand upon the beach then stretched out into the water like jetties. Emerald waves crashed against the rocky formations, spraying a whitish-green sea mist in the air.

It was so beautiful. I'd never visited the ocean before. I had admired paintings but those places had been so far out of reach. Could I ... get closer?

It looked like I was only about three or four stories up, but the beach was maybe three or four hundred feet out. Maybe I could ... *Mystic Door* down there? I looked around and spotted Emrys stretching out in a sunbeam on the bed. I flicked my gaze back to the sand below. It was probably soft, right?

I backed away from the balcony and cast *Mystic Door.* When the glittering blue door appeared, I took a leap of faith through—and fell forward about ten feet onto the sand. I huffed out air and pushed my body up, but my hands sank into the sand. It *was* soft. I squeezed some of the powdery, white sand in my hands. It slid through my fingers and caught in the wind as it fell. Then, a roaring sound rumbled towards me. I looked up and an icy, salty wave slammed into me spinning me out on my back.

"Ack!!"

The wave slipped away gently, leaving me in a tumble of foam. I sat up again, soaking wet with sand clinging to me, my dignity absolutely scattered. I stumbled to my feet and gazed out into the ocean. As each wave advanced and retreated up the shore, I took steps towards the water, watching the bubbles and shells twirl as the foam-laced waves sank into the sand. I'd swum in pools at the estate once or twice, but never in nature. A few more steps and I was standing knee deep in the cresting waves. The beauty of the glittering light dancing on the water ahead of me had my mind drifting to sadness. There was so much of Novus I'd not seen. I had been so eager to leave it all behind that I hadn't considered what it offered. I still wanted a life in the Nine Circles, but I wondered if I should forsake Novus so quickly now.

The pull of the thread surged behind me, and I turned around to see Leander staring down at me from the balcony. He'd worn similar attire each time we'd met—a black jacket and white shirt, haphazardly half-open like he never bothered fully dressing himself. Seconds later, he was a puff of black smoke before appearing further up the beach.

"You look beautiful." His voice poured like honey in my mind.

My cheeks heated as I blinked at his stare. Should I reply? Should I—

Cold water slammed into my back and knocked me off my feet, catching me distracted. My eyes and nose burned in the cold churning water as it rolled over me. I had no idea which way was up, how far under I was—till the thread electrically thrummed with the connection of Leander gripping my arm and pulling me above the water.

I gasped for breath. I reached for anything to anchor me, and I quickly found myself clinging on to him. I wiped my eyes, and another wave rolled into us, attempting to peel me away. I squeezed tighter. He was so ... warm. The entirety of my back and sides prickled with chills, except for where our bodies met. He hummed a laugh at me and teleported us back to the beach. Water dripped off of me as I dragged myself free of him. I stood under him and his orange eyes glowed bright even under the blinding sun. His gaze fell to the wet clothing. It was plastered to me, leaving little to the imagination.

"If you knew how many souls that garment cost, you wouldn't be swimming in it," he purred. "Though after seeing that display, I cannot imagine a better way for it to be worn."

I looked down and cast *Spotless,* the hot tingle of using the primordial magic fluttered through me. The garment was cleaned and dried to its original state. "I don't know what you are talking about."

He smiled at me. Not the half smile or the devilish grin I had received before. A full fanged smile that stretched both corners of his lips. He took in every square inch of me, then he looked down at himself—and magic glittered his clothes clean and dry.

"Why did Remodeus pick you to torture me?" he said.

It was one of the many new questions I had myself for my father. Nervousness churned as the pile stacked higher.

"I don't know."

"You said you were lonely ..." he said softly.

I lowered my head and looked at the sand between us. "I thought he would come take me away from my family one day, and I'd go to a real one."

Leander's finger brushed under my chin and lifted my gaze to him. My body went hot at his touch, at the connection of our souls igniting between us.

"I suppose he's torturing you as well then."

"But ..." I fell silent as I contemplated the notion. How? How could he when he told me that he loved me? When he cried with me, and said that we wouldn't be able to see each other for a while. I couldn't imagine him acting so cruel. Even as a child, I knew it was love.

"Why haven't you asked me to take you directly to him?"

My eyes went wide. "You can do that?"

He flexed his jaw to a devilish grin. "I'm starting to think that you'll be impressed by absolutely anything I show you."

Despite the usual sensual cantor to his words, anxiety flooded me at the idea. Given what I knew and the questions I still had, suddenly the thought of confronting my father terrified me. What if it was all true? It would break me.

Leander seemed to lean closer, as if he could sense the fear that surged in me. "To be honest, I don't want to take you to him."

I blinked at him. "Why?"

"Because I have no idea what his motives are, and he holds all the advantage in this situation. He could destroy the contract and therefore destroy the thread you find so comforting. Our soul bond."

Right ... I supposed it was because we had not *united* and made it permanent. I started to feel lost, like I wasn't sure which direction to go—except for maybe the direction I had been following. The pull of the thread. To ... Leander.

I realized how little I knew of my father and his capabilities. I wondered if he could simply snap his fingers in the Nine Circles and the thread would be ripped from me, leaving me to unravel finally. "Then what can we do?" And the question I was afraid to ask: what did *he* want to do?

He dropped my chin, quieting the surge of the thread. "We make our own choices. Before Remodeus chooses for us." He moved in a little closer, close enough for me to feel the heat of him, but held back from touching me.

"I ..." I fell silent as I pondered it all. My grandfather and mother, Midor's, the idea that my father transformed me, then abandoned me. How he may not have cared one bit about me when it came to living this lonely cruel life and torturing another person with my image. So many things clinging to me to control me. "I want to be free."

He flexed his hand trailing at my side, pulling me into him, squeezing my lower back. The sensation of our bond flooded back into me and I tried to keep myself from melting into it.

"Do you know what I want?" Leander purred. I tried not to think of what he might possibly say, what a devil would want from a person whose touch is familiar and laced with the caress of a soul bond.

"What?" I said breathlessly in his embrace.

"For you to see something more beautiful than this beach."

"Show me." I demanded.

The matters here could wait a little longer. I imagined that if I was true to my feelings—let the pull of the thread, and allure of Leander, consume me—I would get swept so deep into it that by the time I realized it, I wouldn't want to turn back. Maybe I was a fool for letting it happen so quickly and letting my guard shatter, but that's exactly what I'd done.

And I didn't want to turn back.

CHAPTER TWENTY-THREE

After I'd gathered my things and collected Emrys, Leander once again extended his hand to me. Every time he squeezed me into his warm chest, the sensation of the thread connecting our souls sent me melting into him. He waved his hand and a large portal burned into the air beside us. Its edges were hot and orange like fire, and from its liquid, mirror-like surface, heat tinged with pink light poured off it. It looked so much like the portal my father had opened up for me as a child. Still holding me, he led me through the portal as if we were dancing.

I wrapped my fingers in the edges of his dark jacket as everything around us stretched and slowly rotated, some kind of dimensional air whipping around us. Then, abruptly, we emerged on the other side. I swayed, disoriented at the change. His grip tightened on my waist and held me upright. Once I seemed to have my balance he released me, taking a small step back. Emrys scrambled out of my pack, a bit wobbly as well.

I blinked, taking in the high ceilings of the surrounding room. Dark wood panels covered the walls, stopping at about head height where a decorative wallpaper with red and white flowers on branches with touches of gold accent continued. My eyes followed the branches upward to the ceiling, which arched into several points. Each alcove contained a painting depicting devils fighting in swirling dark clouds or flames. My eyes returned to Leander. He stood between one of the plush couches and dark side tables, and peeled his jacket off, leaving him in only the white, billowing half-buttoned shirt. I tried not to stare.

Suddenly, three impish-looking creatures burst through the doorway. None were taller than a few feet. Their leathery skin showed varying shades between a grayish purple and red, and their long pointed ears framed their fanged expressions. Then I noticed as they knocked into each other, whipping tails with points like a scorpion's flicked behind them. They did not wear clothing—how could they when a set of folded bat wings rested upon each of their backs? Bipedal, their claw-like feet scraped on the obsidian tile as they halted abruptly in front of Leander.

"Infernal Master, command us," they hissed in unison.

Leander dropped the jacket over their bobbing heads and reaching claws. *"Put this away."*

The imps squirmed with excitement. "A command! A command!" They lifted the jacket, wiggling about as they exited the room. There was something to their nature I could sense—something arcane, but I couldn't quite identify what it was. I watched the commotion, and it sunk in ... Was I really in the Nine Circles?

I turned my gaze around the room and saw no windows. My heart started racing as I ran past Leander in the direction the imps had left. I heard Leander call my name in confusion, but I ignored him and kept darting down the winding corridors, searching for a window—a door—anything. One more turn and there was a large door. I rushed to it, pulling—pushing—on the handles until it came free. The light from outside flooded my eyes as I emerged into a walkway that overlooked the surrounding landscape. First the arid, warm air hit me, then carried a smell I thought I had forgotten. Charcoal, pine, and anise. My eyes then focused on the familiar pink sky and the deep green of plant life that peppered the rust-colored dirt in patches.

This was it.

I was in *the Nine Circles of Hell.*

I was here again, after so many years. Tears started rolling down my face as all the sensations washed over me. I had wanted so badly to return here. I'd dreamed of it—practically dedicated my life to it. Then I felt a gentle caress of fingers down my back.

"When you said you wanted Remodeus to bring you to this plane, I didn't realize it meant this much to you," Leander consoled me softly.

"Thank you," I replied as I wiped the tears off my face. I turned to him and embraced him in a hug, squeezing him tightly. Perhaps he'd sensed it. How much I had wanted to come here—and this was the beautiful sight he'd wanted me to see.

His arms hovered for a moment before they enveloped me in return, and he rested his chin on the top of my head. His chest swelled as he breathed in and I leaned into it, listening to the beat of his heart.

"Are you ready to see the real attraction?" His voice vibrated through his throat, pressed against my head.

There was more? I sniffled and nodded.

A whirl of black smoke and we stood on a cobbled stone walkway. Before me was ... a lake.

This was the lake my father had taken me to.

It had been a dream like memory, but now I was seeing it again with open eyes in all of its glory. It was not a lake full of water, but of hellfire that stretched into the horizon. Heat rolled off it and into our walkway as the sea breeze by the ocean had. The flames of the lake glittered in infinite hues, a mirror to the light of the sun glittering on the ocean. It flared with flickers of purple before it shifted into blue and then orange, pink, teal, and yellow—and on and on in a beautiful chaotic dance. The further out my eyes traveled into the lake, the higher the flames rose, as if the fire there ran so deep that these flames needed height to lick the air and fuel them for eternity. The combination of colors and dancing silhouettes were like a siren's call to me—as if it knew I was just a mortal mesmerized by its beauty—and I wished I could walk out into it and become bathed in their dance.

Who knew what the other circles were like, but my father had brought me to this circle—The Fire Circle. I wondered if my father also lived on the Fire Circle, or perhaps he'd originally been from here as well.

"Reign, perhaps you'll indulge me with some questions of my own?"

Leander's voice gently broke my focus from the lake, and I realized I had been leaning towards it. I looked up at him and saw a slight smirk, as if the timing had been on purpose. I nodded to him. Of course he would have questions about me, and about my past. I had been the one asking all the questions, and if we were to make our own choices, we needed to learn more about each other.

His infernal eyes glittered at me, an orange-hued version of the lake to our right. He hooked my arm in his and strolled us alongside the lake of fire. The infernal creatures—devils and ... well I didn't really know what the others were—all scattered away leaving the path ahead deserted. We took a few steps in silence, both taking glances out at the dancing flames before he finally asked his first question.

"What made you want to learn to use arcana?"

I smiled. I hadn't been expecting a question like that. It seemed rather boring. "When I met my father for the first time, he encouraged me when he gave me the button I showed you." I brought my hand to my chest, touching the button hidden beneath my garment. I continued, "My grandfather is also a wizard, but I thought knowing arcana would help me when my father came back someday to take me away."

I could see Leander thinking for a few moments, his eyes scanning me softly, then he asked, "Why did you want to leave your human family so badly?"

I blinked. How long did we have? I didn't go into every detail, but I spent the next fifteen minutes summarizing the past twenty-five years of my life. I started with my mother signing the contract with Remodeus and her instant dismay upon my hellborn appearance at birth. Her prolonged dissociation from me, the disinterest of my stepfather, the emotional abuse of my half-sisters—the manipulation and exploitation from my grandfather. How I had met my father on my sixth birthday for the first time—the moment that had catalyzed all the following moments, leading me to think I would be worth something to him in the Nine Circles. Escaping to Midor's to build my own power, meeting Freda, all to follow my desire—to follow where I had thought fate was leading me, to actually belong somewhere with purpose. As I told my story, he gripped my linked arm tighter.

"You are resilient," Leander remarked. "In the same amount of time you spent training in arcana to build the world you wanted to live in, I'd only just finished destroying what was left of myself after being slain in Novus." He said it with a disappointed look on his face.

"You figured it out though, eventually." I smiled up at him, trying to provide some reassurance it had been worth it in the end.

He chuckled. "I suppose, though *I* had some help. *You* did it all on your own."

"Does it count as doing it on your own if you have someone who believes in you?" I thought of my father. Even if it turned out to all be false, he had offered me hope.

"Maybe not," he said with a devilish grin.

Looking up, I saw a familiar bridge over an edge of the lake. I realized that in our walking, I had guided us down the same paths I had walked with my father. I smiled as I led Leander up its obsidian steps. The bridge had no rails, only a simple walking platform which wove between the flames on either side. I was sure this looked like some kind of torture trial to humans, but I gazed into the glittering flames and felt peace. I enjoyed quietly reacquainting with the memories of doing this with Remodeus as we walked.

"When I figured out how to fragment my soul long ago," Leander said, "It was kept inside a crystal sphere. I thought one day I'd offer it to someone. Instead, about twenty-five years ago, I felt the thread snap tight and start pulling on me. That's when I realized Remodeus had stolen my soul fragment and signed a contract using it."

My face twisted. "Why would he hold on to a grudge for so long?"

"I barely got him to agree to help me bind my soul at all because of it. But he must have found something about your situation fitting enough to find a loophole in the deal we had made."

"Is that why you don't really speak to him much anymore?" I said.

He sighed. "Things have never been great between us."

I had demanded he take me to my father—help me contact him—without knowing what I was asking of him. But he had still tried to do it for me.

"Do you wish you had kept your soul fragment?" It was so clear this whole arrangement had been forced on both of us. We may have wanted to end our loneliness, but we hadn't chosen each other.

"I'm a selfish devil, Reign." He smirked at me with a teasing smile. "Maybe if I keep you I get to keep my soul fragment after all."

I laughed. "Is that why you are interviewing me? To see if I am a good fit for the position?" I imagined it was what an arranged marriage felt like. Someone matched a couple together and, maybe after they got to know each other a little bit, they found they could love each other, and it could work. As I warmed to the thought I felt a pang of irony remembering my grandfather had tried to do the same to me.

Leander returned a wicked grin at my questions. His blazing eyes narrowed down at me and the small hairs on my body rose under the weight of his open desire. I got the feeling he was choosing *not* to voice whatever perverse thought had entered his mind out loud. But ... was it *me* he was looking at?

I smiled nervously. "Do you still think about *her* when you look at me? Or have I become my own person in your mind?"

His lips twitched at the mention of *her*. Perhaps he had actually not been thinking of *her* at all till I brought it up.

"You have some similarities outside your appearance, but you had to fight for yourself and your power in this world. She, like all infernals, was born with power."

We reached the center of the walking bridge, both peering out into the glittering flames licking the air below.

He continued, "You and I are more similar in that way. After being slain in Novus, I had to start over when I was sent back here. I was so weak and vulnerable—like a mortal in many ways. It was a difficult journey back to my full strength, even after I decided my future was worth fighting for."

I wondered if the difference was really enough for him to see me as my own person. I'd felt so much empathy from him during our conversation, and no judgement at all. I had given him the same. In fact, I didn't think I'd ever had a conversation with anyone where we'd had such a mutual aim at understanding. Thinking about it made my heart and soul flutter. I'd known him for such a short time, but it didn't feel that way. It felt like I had known him for as long as his soul had existed inside me. I was so enraptured by him—wanting to be near him, talk to him—that the anxious thoughts about placing my trust in a devil I'd only just met steadily evaporated away.

We continued talking and sharing well past the bridge. My love of Transmutation, reading history and arcana books, and some misadventures Freda and I had gotten into. He told me about his Circle, and when I asked ... a little bit about my father. Remodeus sounded so different than I'd known him. I secretly hoped the difference had to do with how he'd treat a daughter over another devil like Leander.

Eventually, we neared the garden. He pointed it out to me, not knowing I had been there once before. We looked at the spiraling flowers, plants with stalks waving up in the air, and ornamental trees with sparking buds that were carefully cared for along the paths.

I told him about being summoned to my grandfather's study after arriving home and asking for my freedom. How I'd subsequently been running from him. The explosion in Brunalin and the stolen knives.

"I dislike the idea of you being so hotly pursued by these mortals."

"I don't like it either. Which is why Freda is researching the knives and what my grandfather might be up to."

"You could use me if you desired," he purred between us as if it was some dark pleasure he'd delight in doing.

I stared up into his eyes and watched those orange hellfire rings blaze hot. What had I said in the past hours to have him stare at me with such desire?

"You don't have to—" I started.

"What if I *want* to burn it all for you?" His tone lowered to a growl and his eyes searched mine. "I'd burn your mother and grandfather. I'd even burn Remodeus if you commanded it." His voice was a dark caress in my ear, as if begging me to allow him to do all the things he'd listed.

"I don't *want* you to burn it for me," I said with a half smile. "If I want it burned, I'd rather burn it myself."

"I've not had the pleasure of seeing you be violent yet," he purred, curling his lips mischievously and tracing his fingers up my forearms. "Do you promise to let me watch?" He leaned in over me.

I felt myself getting dizzy under the heat of his gaze.

"Only if you are on your best behavior," I teased.

The chuckle that erupted from him caused my face to heat and sent tingles running down my body. I felt like I was losing my mind. Was I moving things too fast? Whether it was the thread tying our souls together or two people who both wanted so badly not to be alone, I wondered if it mattered in the end. It felt worth growing closer, despite any potential threat of pain. We'd both felt enough of that and still pushed through. The pull of the thread had been there from the first breath of life I'd ever taken, followed by every inhale after. I felt it tingle electrically between us again, as if enforcing I was right—this was worth at least exploring.

I just needed time to think. Space to consider what it meant to pursue this bond. The question I wanted to ask next terrified me. Because the answer could send me one step closer to committing my life to something I had only just started to understand. Nonetheless, I felt drawn to the question, like I had been drawn to the glittering flames in the lake. Like I had been drawn to him. Like this was what I had always been meant for—dangerous, but filled with purpose.

"Since we've gotten to know each other better, would you consider ..." I focused on feeling the thread between us, "*thinking* about uniting our souls? To make the bond permanent?"

His eyes widened slightly. "Right now?" he asked with a wicked grin.

"No, not now!" I said, pushing against him. "I meant like, a *promise* to consider it—a verbal commitment that even though neither of us chose this, it's worth exploring. I want an opportunity to free myself from everything happening with my grandfather first, but maybe after ... we can formally make a decision."

He exhaled a laugh. "You are so particular in your wording. If I didn't know any better I'd say you were trying to make a deal with me."

My face blazed red hot. I had not meant at all for it to sound like a deal or a contract. He seemed amused—possibly even aroused by it.

"I don't need to think about it. I've waited a long, long time for a *soul mate*. The way this all manifested ... I don't want to believe it was merely chance."

"What ... made you change your mind?" My heart pounded as I asked the question. Last night he had seemed so resistant to suffering this brand of torture. However, after the entire day we'd spent together, he seemed so much more resolved to the fact that I was his *soul mate*.

"Last night I read the words of someone wiser than me. It reminded me the potential of pain is always worth enduring for love. It's the reason I'd split my soul in the first place." His fingers wrapped around mine and he pulled my hand closer to him. My heart melted at the romance of his words. "I ran away when you tried to find me because I was afraid of you—of that potential for nothing but pain. I knew after I felt this bond close enough to see you, I'd *want* you. Then I was resistant because I was afraid of how you'd undo me with the pull of our souls and looking like *her*. But the more I come to know you I find that I don't believe this was a mistake. I *do* want you."

I hadn't realized how deeply he'd craved a connection like this. To plan for it, and have my father betray him. If we made our own choices though, we could remake this into our own.

"So you *were* afraid then?" I smirked up at him.

His eyes narrowed on me, the embers inside them burning bright and hot. "Alright, I have a deal for *you,*" he said softly. He wrapped his hand along my neck and around the base of my head. His tight, claiming grip melted me. "Reign, *my dear,* I promise to unite our souls when you say you are ready. You may spend as much time as you like thinking about it." His fingers curled at the base of my skull, sending shivers down my spine. "I'll be yours as soon as you command it."

He pulled my head towards him till our lips pressed into a kiss. I slid my hands up around his neck, pulling him into me. The movement tightened his grip around the back of my neck. He spread his fingers, tilting me so he could more thoroughly taste me. His other hand grazed across my lower back, answering my pull with his own. The thread connecting our souls vibrated like an electric current, as if it knew what we'd committed to eventually doing, but whined wanting it now.

He pulled away from our kiss, eyes glowing hot with desire.

I sucked my breath in so I could get my next words out. "Deal."

He dove back into me kissing me again, like our lips might become the signature on that promise.

Oh gods, I must be insane.

CHAPTER TWENTY-FOUR

We teleported back to the palace so I could gather my things and Emrys before heading back to Brunalin. The imps followed not far behind us, waiting for commands.

"They are constructs," Leander said, catching me staring at them scattering ahead of us. "The Primordial Father created them to serve the plane."

I marveled at them. Constructs were a brief subject covered in the Conjuration courses during foundations at Midor's. They were neither biological nor truly living things, but artificial life defined by the arcana that created them. Wizards had used them in their towers to help organize and clean vast stores of research. I'd never seen one before, but I never pictured them so corporal. I had imagined them more ... spectral?

When I finally found Emrys curled up on a chaise in his signature black swirl, I smiled in relief. He had been fine without us.

Leander stood over him. "Why are you still a cat, for hell's sake?"

Emrys sat up, blinking at him, then looked at me. I opened my mouth to question what he meant, when the light reflecting off his fur shimmered. His form began to shift into an entirely different creature ...

My eyes widened as his limbs lengthened and formed into slender arms and legs. The fur of his body glittered away, revealing a torso—a *humanoid* torso. The glittering transformation sparkled over his face, leaving behind a humanoid nose, eyes, chin, and lips. He was only half-clothed, wearing black pants and exposing a bare, somewhat muscular chest. He shifted and his long, sleek black hair fell in wisps across his shoulders and down to the middle of his chest. He tucked his hair shyly behind a long pointed ear. An embarrassed smile spread across his handsome face, then his eyes rose to me. They were dark onyx gray, with the same small twinkles of starlight in them as his cat form, now framed by eyelashes. Of course ... not infernal eyes, but *drow*. Hell, he wasn't just handsome, he was beautiful.

"Em-mrys?" I stuttered in disbelief.

Leander shot a glance down at the imps wriggling behind him. "*Get him a shirt,*" he growled. They clawed over each other, scrambling for the requested object.

Emrys ... was definitely not a normal familiar. I tried not to gawk as my eyes got lost in the iridescent shimmer across his purple-rose quartz colored skin, and the alluring starlight in his eyes. I remembered learning in our vocational Veldrasyl class that the drow were called star blessed.

A white linen shirt flew at Emrys which he caught and pulled over his head, still stretched across the chaise

I snapped my gaze over to Leander. "You knew he was not a cat when you sent him to me? I took him in the bath with me and put him in my shirt!"

Leander smirked at me. "Oh my dear, Emrys will never make sexual advances on you." His eyes drifted towards Emrys, burning like red coals. "He knows if he did, it would be the last thing he ever does."

"It's true, Mistress." Emrys both cowered and assured me with an easy smile. His voice was sweet and cheerful now compared to the crackling hiss I was used to hearing in my head.

Mistress? Because he was still my familiar?

"But if you touched me or *Commanded* me to be close to you, I wouldn't mind," he added shyly, smiling softly as if he were also remembering the times I had literally sandwiched him between my breasts.

"Oh, you are not going in my shirt anymore!" I pointed at him. "In fact, I'm officially banning you from coming into the bathroom with me, and from sleeping in my bed!"

Emrys's eyes went wide in a panic that resembled the same look he'd made as a cat. It was ... eerie.

Leander began cackling.

Emrys pushed off the chaise and crawled to my feet. "Please Mistress, I didn't mean to upset you. Command me again!" he begged.

"I command you to change back into a cat!"

He let out a shuddered breath, as if receiving the command had been a vital requirement to survive. His body shifted back into the small black cat he was before, the pants and shirt disappearing with his drow form. Then he scuttled across my feet, rubbing his sides against my legs, purring for forgiveness. I hadn't actually used the spell *Command*, but he had obeyed all the same.

I found my pack and opened the flap. Emrys didn't wait for me to ask and jumped into it, nestling between the leather and my spell book.

"Are you ready to go back, my dear?" Leander purred, extending his hand.

I placed my hand in his, letting him pull me into him. "I'm still annoyed at you for not telling me Emrys was a person," I said flatly. The feeling of our souls touching quickly melted the annoyance away. He held me as another portal opened next to us and we moved through shifting light, darkness, and colors before coming to an abrupt stop. I recognized the dirty gray stone beneath my feet and heard the familiar rustling of people not far away. We had made it to Brunalin.

Leander leaned to place his lips to my ear. "When I get you back, I'll use whichever part of me you like to beg your forgiveness."

I could feel the wicked smile burning down my neck. My face heated again as he pulled away from me.

What the hell had Leander read the night before? And why did I like the attention *so much?* I pushed myself up on my toes and pulled his collar down, giving him a single kiss, then pulling away before the thread could surge and consume me whole.

"Will it make you unhappy if I keep an eye on you?" Leander said in a low tone.

I knew what he implied. The *Scry* spell.

"No," I said with a smile then glanced out to the busy streets. "I should go find Freda."

"Are you sure I can't come with you?"

I glanced back up at him. Hell, he was giving me the infernal equivalent of puppy eyes.

I swallowed. "Yes. But I promise I'll send you a *Mindtell* if I need you."

He flexed his jaw and the corners of his lips turned up. He refused to take his eyes from me.

The most powerful devil in the Nine Circles was just going to *wait around* for me to call upon him. What kind of power did I really have over him?

"Goodbye." I said sweetly and walked towards the busy street. I threw a glance back at him. He was leaning into a shadow, arms crossed, watching me walk away as if he needed to savor my view from behind. He gave me a little wave.

After turning a few blocks, I quickly found myself in one of the central districts. I slipped out of the open and used the primordial magic from Leander's soul to *Mindtell* Freda.

"I'm back in the city. In the central district." I glanced around. *"In front of a bakery."*

"Reign!" Freda replied immediately. *"I'm nearby. Meet me at the Light District Gate."*

"On it!"

I knelt to let Emrys out of my bag. He jumped to the ground and stretched out his legs, then looked up at me with the saddest eyes. Returning the pack over my back, I crouched down to him.

"Emrys ... I'm not upset with you. I was treating you like a pet and not a person. But now I know you are a person, and you deserve to be treated as one."

His eyes glittered. *"I enjoyed being your pet ... Mistress."*

His familiar crackling hiss had returned, but I could still imagine his cheery voice from before.

"Why do you like being treated that way?"

"That's how it is for all who serve devils."

I was starting to think I really didn't understand at all how the hierarchy in the Nine Circles of Hell worked. I knew souls were currency and provided power. And there was a system every creature had to work through to gain higher ranks. That usually involved serving devils. Then something warmed in my heart when I realized Emrys was implying *I* was like a devil to him.

"Setting that aside, what would make you happy?" I resisted the urge to pet him like a cat, knowing it was probably exactly what would make him happy.

"It makes me happy to make others happy." I watched the end of his tail wrap around his two front paws shyly, as he tilted his face to me. I suddenly felt so horrible for how I'd behaved. My anger should have never been directed at him.

"I'm sorry for how I reacted earlier ... I feel happy about having you as my familiar, so please forgive me."

I scooped him up and held him to my chest ... like I had before—even though it felt a little weird. Emrys purred the loudest I'd heard him yet. I petted his face as I walked and held him. Every block, I'd glance down at him and see how blissfully happy he looked to be held and accepted by me. I felt my eyes burn slightly at the thought. I supposed I knew something about that. The desperate desire to be wanted.

A ten-minute walk later and I saw a metallic gold gate glinting in the sunlight, Freda approaching from behind it. We locked eyes and she smiled before running towards me. I did the same.

"We have a problem!" We both blurted out at the same time when we met an arms distance away.

Freda blinked in surprise then surveyed my *distinct* garment. Her eyebrows creased up with an amused smile. "You first."

"Okay!" I began, dropping Emrys to the ground. "I feel like I'm going crazy. I've known this devil for a few days and he already has, like, a chokehold on my mind." I drew my fingers into my hair along my scalp for emphasis.

Freda flashed a confused look. "Do you mean an arcane one?"

I wheezed the laugh. Only a wizard would need specificity. "I meant figuratively."

"Somehow I'm not surprised," she teased.

"But I wonder if everything is moving too fast?"

Freda shrugged. "If you really want to dig into it we can, but there are more *important* things to discuss."

I narrowed my eyes at her. "Fine, tell me about *your* problem."

She pressed her lips together in a wince. "So ... the temple that killed your boyfriend. That's where the archive Alàn sent me to is."

My eyes went wide. "Lumoniel's Temple?"

Freda jerked her chin towards the gate and I flipped around.

Twelve-pointed suns with wavy beams lined the gate's gold design. I looked beyond it to small buildings plastered with white clay and more twelve-pointed suns. Almost everything around me supported the sun of Lumoniel. No wonder she hadn't wanted me to bring him. Would he seek revenge?

"And!" Freda said, breaking me from my observation. "The clerics think the knives your grandfather wants—are chronomantic."

"Time magic?" Why the hell would my grandfather want that?

"They said they had experience with the Dark Echo. Wizard cultists who want power over time," Freda laughed. "They were about to take me to meet the leader of the temple to discuss what to do."

Surely the members of Lumoniel's temple still hated devils. Was I safe here? I could feel myself leaning away slowly.

Freda's expression shifted to concern. "It's okay. I didn't tell them much but I did warn them that you are not to be harmed, and we'd cooperate when it comes to apprehending your grandfather."

"And you trust them?"

"Why not? They are holy people, they probably can't lie or they have to recite parables a hundred times."

I twisted my hands together. "They ... want to apprehend my grandfather?"

"Apparently they already didn't like him, and now that these knives are involved it took very little convincing." She rested her hands on my shoulders, squeezing a little tension from them. "Like hell I'm going to let these people hurt you, Reign. Let me protect you for once." She smirked. "One wrong move ... and blam! *Firebomb.*"

I smiled. The most misused Evocation spell known to wizards. The cause of more than a few forest fires and lost buildings.

"Okay ... let's go."

Maybe working with them was my way of setting myself free on my own. I could handle it. I could do this.

We turned into a courtyard and a fountain glittered with water arcs. The bronze-cast female figure in its center had thick curly hair that framed her face like a halo. I scanned the plaque near its base.

Her Light, Lumoniel.

Despite knowing she had been the one who had slain Leander, she had a kind face. Soft brows, relaxed eyes, and a gentle but confident smile curled her full lips. If she had gone to that length to protect the people of Brunalin, it was no wonder she had such a strong following. She was dressed in plate armor from neck to toe, and held a great staff tipped with a twelve-pointed sun.

With Leander's soul inside me, would she consider me an enemy?

Freda led me down a few more blocks till we reached a small, white clay-covered house. She pushed the creaking door open and we surveyed the inside. A thick layer of dust covered everything from the sills, tables, and chairs, to the floor.

"They said they would be sending someone to meet with us here." Freda offered as we both slipped inside.

"It seems abandoned." I looked between cobwebs in the corners, to the cracked dining table, to the foggy glass of the windows.

"Oh," Freda exhaled the word. "Because of your infernal origin I requested an unblessed house. Apparently this one is for refugees."

I cracked a silly smile at her. "What did you think would happen?"

"Well, what I don't want to happen is you step foot inside and the goddess thinks, *oh great that dastardly dog is back—time to smite.*"

I laughed and Emrys jumped to the table.

"It's true, Mistress." His voice crackled in my mind. *"Infernals are known to be frequently banished by the clerics of Lumoniel."*

A knock sounded at the door, and we looked at each other. Freda cracked it open.

I saw a woman peer past the threshold, her head visible over Freda's shoulder. Her piercing gaze caught on my infernal features, but she didn't seem scared by them. In fact, her overall demeanor was rather standoffish. She took a step inside, her brown hair neatly parted down the middle and pulled back behind her head. Everything about her was well kept, not a strand of hair or thread out of place. She was younger than I had expected a cleric to be. Probably a decade or so older than Freda and I.

"My name is Brin," she said flatly. "I am one of the five principle clerics for this temple." She gestured her slender hand to the table. "Sit, please."

I looked at Freda and she moved closer to me, and we sat on one side together. Brin gathered her brown and white-trimmed robes and sat across from us. She gave Emrys a brief, curious look before turning back to us, dismissing him. Her hazel eyes targeted me with a sharpness, as if she were passing judgement. She held that stare for more than enough time to make me feel totally awkward. Then her eyebrows creased.

"You didn't specify her infernal tie was a literal soul," she said, eyes flicking back to Freda.

"How—did you know?" Freda stuttered.

Brin tilted her head in a withering glare. "I can sense something as distinct as an infernal soul."

Maybe this was a mistake. Perhaps she could sense who it belonged to—and then—

"Okay, this is how it's going to work, " Brin said sternly. "Lumoniel's core tenet is truth. For us to truly bring your grandfather to justice," her gaze slid back to me, "we need to be honest with each other."

"We will be honest!" I said nervously. "What do you want to know?"

"Do you think I'm stupid?" Brin pulled a small pouch from somewhere in her robes, emptying an assortment of smooth polished gemstones. What was she—?

"Seriously?" Freda barked. "You are going to *Truth Cone* us?"

I blinked. *Truth Cone* was a Divination spell that prevented those inside its perimeter from lying. I whipped my head to Freda.

"How do you know what the materials for a *Truth Cone* are?" I muttered between us.

Freda gave me a sidelong glance. *"You've* never been sent to the dean's office for misconduct."

I looked back up and Brin had positioned the gems in a circle. She snapped a finger and they scattered out, forming a ring around us. Blue arcane currents zapped between them, and I felt a soft numbing sensation fall over my body.

"Let's start with the basics," Brin announced. "Where did you get the devil soul you harbor?"

"I was born with it." I spat back.

"How? Mortals are not just *born* with devil souls."

Wait—was this actually an interrogation?

"Is that relevant?" I squeezed my hands together in my lap as anxiety churned in my stomach.

"It is, actually," Brin said flatly.

I glanced over at Freda then down to the table. "My ... mom signed a contract with a powerful devil." I thought of my father. The apparent ruler of the Nine Circles. "I didn't get a choice in the matter." I added quietly.

Brin's eyebrows pressed together in sympathetic gaze. I didn't want to wait for her next onslaught of interrogation. I could use the *Truth Cone* to my advantage.

"Will the temple try to kill me because I have a devil soul inside me?"

Brin winced, but smiled. "No. We would never harm, let alone kill, an innocent mortal soul."

I held still to not reveal the relief.

"But," she continued, "we would like to *purify* your soul."

I could feel something deep and hot bubbling up inside me. Purify my soul? Purify *me?*

"What do you plan on doing to apprehend her grandfather?" Freda nudged in, surely sensing the anger rolling off me.

"We'll organize a trade. Saying we will return you to him for some kind of donation. When we have him, the clerics will restrain him, then he'll be placed in a secure holding."

It was my turn to frown. Were they prepared for my grand-father's power?

Brin faced me again and crossed her arms. "Do you or have you ever held any ill will or planned malicious action against the mortals of this plane?"

Freda's voice burst through my head. *"I'm about to plan some fucking malicious actions."*

"No! I don't want to hurt anyone, I just want to be free of my grandfather."

Brin's shoulders relaxed slightly at my response.

I sucked in a breath. "It's him you should be worried about! Not me, not devils. He's a horrible, deceitful, malicious man." I could feel the anxiety twisting and wringing my insides. I'd never said such things about him before. Never out loud.

Brin held my stare for a moment, then unfolded her arms. "Alright. You've gained my trust, temporarily." She snapped her fingers and the gems spun inwards towards the center of the table.

The numb feeling faded away and Emrys jumped on my lap.

"The Exalted Sun will share more details with you. We'll meet with him tomorrow," she said. Her entire demeanor had shifted from standoffish to neutral. "What questions do you have?"

I leaned in across the table. She trusted me, but could I trust her? "Why do you care about helping me? About taking my grandfather into custody?"

"You said it best yourself. He's a horrible man." The corner of her lip curled. "We've been watching him for a while. We wondered if we'd ever get a lead to seek justice." Her eyes shifted to Freda. "Then, as if divinely orchestrated, one walked right in."

Freda scoffed.

I held Brin's gaze. "He's cunning, very resourceful, and powerful. He'll see right through any simple traps."

Brin's eyebrows raised. "We'll place our best on the problem. I give it a week, and we'll have him in a cell."

There was no way. No way it could be that easy. I revisited everything I knew about him and what we'd learned in the past few days.

I straightened. "I think he might have some connection to the Brunalin Council. So whatever we do we have to be thorough." I held up a finger. "The arcane side, trapping him and physically containing him." I held up a second finger. "And preventing the Council from just letting him go—because he's bought them or threatened them."

Brin's eyes went wide with surprise. "Smart." She gathered her robes to elegantly stand from the table. "I'll take that into consideration."

Freda and I stood following her motion.

Brin dusted her robes flat, then folded her hands at her waist as if it was a resting position of the devout. "You'll want to avoid entering the main temple as long as you harbor that devil soul."

"Thank you." I positioned myself across from her as she went for the door. "I am very serious too about what I said. I don't want anyone to get hurt."

Brin slowed. She cast her eyes down to the floor before raising them to me. "I know ..." Her eyes shifted, holding some soft peaceful reverence as she gazed into mine. "It's your mortal soul. I will pray you never lose it."

We prepared the house for us to stay comfortably, bringing in new linens and stocking the pantry with some fruits and tea from a storage shack Brin pointed out to us. My mind wandered among the possibilities of what could come after.

What would my life be like after my grandfather was taken into custody? Would I then have my mother and stepfather, Paul, to deal with? What if the agreement with the Gisenwald's had some kind of legal weight that stipulated I follow through even after my grandfather was taken?

There was also the option that I could go back to Leander in the Nine Circles now. He would most definitely make good on his promise to unite our souls, forging an unbreakable bond except through death.

You are resilient.

Leander's words from earlier hummed in my mind. I never would have described myself like that before hearing him say it, but I was starting to believe it was possible. It made all the fear and anxiety about being in the same room with my grandfather feel more bearable. Doubts still clawed the edges of my thoughts, but I hoped it wouldn't be the same as when I had sat across his cherrywood desk, shaking in fear as I watched him *Deteriorate* that woman.

As it neared dusk, my mind reeled with everything I'd done in a single day. I mostly lingered on the pink skies. The glittering lake of fire. The fire that burned in Leander's infernal eyes when he had made his promise to me.

I would be resilient for that, too.

Chapter Twenty-Five

We had assembled a large futon of bedrolls and pillows on the floor in the single common room of the house like a nest. I allowed Emrys to stay with us in the bed-nest as well, despite the ban I had laid earlier. It seemed too cruel to force him away when he also desired to belong. I then spent the better part of the evening in *Faizan's Tiny Closet* telling Freda about everything—*everything*—that had happened. It surprised her to hear about how the Fire Circle actually was compared to the one fuzzy memory I had shared with her. Then we spent nearly an hour talking about Emrys alone—and I'm pretty sure he thrived on the attention.

Eventually, she fell asleep, leaving Emrys and I tucked into a large fluffy blanket. Emrys was asleep only inches away from my chest, snoring through a small triangular opening between his cat lips.

A familiar tickling caress entered my mind. My heart instantly quickened as I heard Leander's playful voice.

"I dislike even more you sleeping so close to the temple of my slayer. But I'm happy to return to you now if you want me to start a war."

I smiled, rolling away from Emrys. *"We're discussing using me as bait to apprehend my grandfather."*

"I heard."

"So you were watching me?" I tried to hide the smile sneaking in at the notion. I tried not to feel guilty for not casting *Unveil* as often as I should to check for the *Scry* spell, but ... I kind of liked the idea of not knowing when he was watching me. I imagined his infernal eyes glued to me in the most mundane situations.

"You were so angry when the cleric suggested she'd purify you. I would have liked to see you set her on fire," he purred.

I smiled, but my mind was more preoccupied with my grandfather.

"Leander ... ?"

"Yes, my dear?" his voice caressed my mind.

"Is there anything I could do with the power from your soul that could stand a chance against my grandfather?"

"I don't know what your grandfather's capable of, but you've already become quite good at using my soul to cast spells without those silly mortal spell materials."

My stomach tingled at the praise.

"You can command infernals like Emrys in your service. That is something those with purely mortal souls cannot do."

I pondered the explanation, *"But my grandfather has so many people who serve him. How is that different?"*

"When a devil takes a creature into their service, the primordial magic that fuels our souls enforces that devils will. The Primordial Father, the wise god he is," Leander added with a tone of sarcasm, *"designed the magic to instill a small growth in power so his creations would feel rewarded for executing their master's will. Then, over time—centuries—the creatures in service to devils become more powerful and may leave to serve more powerful creatures, or take other infernals into their service. And so infernals believe they can climb to the ranks of the princes."*

"But they can't?"

"I've never seen one that did. Though the Primordial Father has his ways of providing his own checks and balances."

I wondered what it meant that my father was now the ruler over the Nine Circles. What were his checks and balances like?

"Do you ... serve my father now?"

Leander laughed. *"Absolutely not. He is acting as a steward of the infernal plane, so he has social authority over me, but even with half of my soul he cannot use his primordial magic to command me. Fortunately for him, I couldn't care less about ruling the plane. Let him bore himself doing it."*

"You like ruling your own circle though?"

"It's my home. All the princes are descended from the Primordial Gods of the Nine Circles, with each their own circle to preside over."

"Is Remodeus also from the Fire Circle?"

"The Blood Circle, actually. It's why Remodeus has the most powerful contracts. They center on blood magic which can bind souls ..." There was a breath's pause, before he continued. *"My dear, I didn't start this conversation to give history lessons."*

I rolled my eyes. *"Okay, then why?"*

"I wanted to know what you are wearing under those blankets."

"Are you watching me now?"

"Of course I am."

I flicked a hand to cast *Unveil* and found the blue-tinted orb floating a few feet above me. I was wearing my usual silk night clothes under the blankets, so I thought he'd be disappointed. But ...

"I'll make you a deal ..."

"Oh?" The pure excitement in his voice bathed my mind like a drug.

"If you teach me more, I'll remove the blankets and show you what I'm wearing."

"It's a deal."

"I want to learn how to take a soul." I pulled the blankets down a little to expose one pale red shoulder and collarbone, little sanguine freckles sprinkled across them between the two thin straps of the night shirt. I'm sure he'd never seen these before.

"Oh ... I see." His voice caressed my mind, as if he were sliding his fingers along the skin I'd exposed.

I held in a shiver.

"There are two ways," he explained softly and slowly, treating each word as if it were those fingers, delicately drifting across my skin.

"The first way is to collect the soul when the body has died. You'll see it wisp up from the body. Your primordial magic from my soul will allow you to encase it and hold it as your property."

I recalled the wisps floating in my grandfather's study and the alley. Souls. So I could capture those. I wondered where they went.

"And the second way?" I lowered the blanket more, exposing my breasts. They were delicately draped by the thin, silk chemise top, held over my body by the two narrow straps across my shoulders. The cooler air touching my exposed skin caused it to prickle with goosebumps, and I felt my nipples peak under the silk. I hadn't meant for the game I was playing to be this erotic, but it was too late now. It didn't help that I was also getting aroused thinking about him watching me with desire, every piece of skin I'd so carefully hidden now exposed for him alone to enjoy.

"The second way ..." His voice sounded ragged.

I raised my brows in anticipation—and then realized I was unraveling him just with the sight of my body in silk.

"... *is reserved for only the most powerful devils. You bind another's soul to your service.*"

"*Like Emrys was in your service?*"

"*Reign ... let me bring you back now,*" Leander pleaded.

Who knew that an exposed shoulder and silk-covered breasts would be all it took to break him?

"*You can't wait a few days?*"

"*I've waited almost a millennium for you.*"

"*So a few days is nothing!*"

There was a pause that had my skin still heating before the heavy velvet caress re-entered my mind.

"*May I visit you in your dreams?*"

"*You can do that?*" I clutched the edges of my blanket.

"*You've surely heard tales about devils visiting poor, innocent mortals in their dreams and corrupting them.*"

I had actually, now that he mentioned it.

"*What are you going to do to me?*"

"*Everything.*"

The sound of need in that single word had tingles running down my body. I twisted my legs together, trying to quiet where that heat was rushing to. I was starting to care less about falling for him too fast. I wanted more than anything not to be *here*. Instead, I wanted to be wherever he wanted me—*however* he wanted me. Would touching him in a dream be enough? Would it be weird to be doing such things in a dream a few feet away from Freda and Emrys?

"*Knowing you might visit me is going to make it hard to fall asleep ...*"

"*Then I won't tell you when.*" I could hear the devilish smile in his voice.

"*Fine.*" I slid my hands down to pull the blanket back up.

"*What do you think you are doing?*"

"*It's cold.*" I rolled my eyes.

"You wouldn't be cold if you were with me."

"Are you going to keep begging or let me try to sleep?" I teased.

"I've never begged for anything so desperately in my life until now."

"Goodnight ..." I said back softly.

"Goodnight, my dear."

Chapter Twenty-Six

I awoke the next morning and my heart panged with the realization I had not received a dream visit from Leander. Even though I was instantly disappointed, I was a little relieved. I wouldn't have had to explain whatever state I woke up in to Freda. I glanced over and she shifted slightly, Emrys now tucked in her arms. Her eyes fluttered open and she glanced over to me.

"You know he's a fully grown drow man right?" I teased.

Freda laughed. "What am I supposed to do? He's such a cute wittle kitty." She pinched his cheeks and I watched his eyes roll back in his head, the little inner lid shifting up.

"You'll find out how awkward it is after you finally see him." I winked.

She rolled her eyes.

Soon after breakfast, two human clerics guided us to the inner courtyard to meet with the Exalted Sun. I fidgeted with my clothes. It wasn't that I was nervous or anything ... but I was expecting to be disliked. As we were led towards by the clerics, a pain started to twinge at my temples. Then we turned a corner and I saw it—the main temple. It loomed overhead, a beautiful white building with open, glassless windows along its sides. The closer we drew, the more my head started to pound. Oh gods, we were not going there, right?

We turned to the left and, when I saw the attached garden, I let out a sigh of relief. The clerics flanked either side of the entrance and resolutely gestured for me to enter. Freda went first and then looked back to me, watching for any sort of reaction. I could still feel that twinging pain, no doubt from the main temple building. Like a foreboding reminder that the goddess herself would squash Leander—or rather his soul inside me—with one wrong move. I shifted one, then two steps over the garden threshold. The pain seemed stabilized. No divine lightning strikes from above. I glanced back at Emrys. He stood outside of the threshold flicking his tail with a pained look on his face.

"It's okay, Emrys. Go back to where we slept and keep watch." I winked at him as the words traveled through our telepathic bond.

His eyes widened with the kind of pleasure that could only be created through receiving a command to fulfill. I think I understood it a bit more now. Every command, even though not arcane, made him feel good and made him more powerful. I was fulfilling a need. He scuttled back toward the house.

I rubbed the ache in my head and followed behind Freda.

Arches of flower-covered trellises shaded the walkway as the smell of sweet, star-shaped blossoms drifted in the air all around us. Despite the beauty of the canopy of flowers, I couldn't help but note the cautious looks from the plate-armored humans lining the walkway on either side as I passed. We reached the end of the covered walkway where I saw Brin, standing behind an older man seated at a small table, a single chair left open across from him.

The light pouring in from between the trellises overhead dappled his brown skin as if the goddess herself were shrouding him with her favor. Bits of gray twisted through the shoulder-length braids he wore, matching the braids in his beard. The braided cords at his temples were pulled back from his face and fastened at the back of his head with a gold sun relic. He actually smiled when he greeted me, unlike the walkway clerics who eyed me cautiously. One cleric pulled out the lone chair and I sat down. I extended my hand to greet the Exalted Sun, but froze halfway—would shaking his hand *literally* kill me? I saw his expression soften, acknowledging my worry.

"You can shake my hand with no harm," he said with a laugh, extending his own hand. There was a kindness in his walnut brown eyes—similar to the color I wore when I altered myself. It made me feel at ease. Safe. It was clear to me why he was the leader of this temple.

I resumed extending my hand and we shook, his fingers firm around mine. He was right—no instant pain or death.

He released my hand and said, "I am the Exalted Sun. It's a title given to the cleric that oversees this region's temples dedicated to *Her Light*, the goddess Lumoniel." He gestured around us.

"My name is Reign—well, you probably know me as Grace Vendelfrey, given my purpose in being here."

"Yes. Would you prefer to be called Reign?" he said.

I blinked in surprise at his consideration. Very few people who knew me by Grace ever bothered to ask me that question.

"If you don't mind." I smiled, still careful to hide my fangs out of habit. Though I realized at that moment he hadn't seemed put off by the rest of me—even my infernal eyes.

"So, Reign ... we have a bit of a problem."

The safety I had felt began to erode. I wrung my hands in my lap waiting to hear more.

"Your grandfather, as you know, is after some rare arcane knives. Our order has been searching for the same knives for centuries. They are rumored to invoke chronomancy."

I stilled. Yes, but why? What could he possibly want to do with them?

"As you know, all arcanum has a cost—a material, a spoken word, a gesture."

It felt as if Leander's soul was warming inside me in opposition to the statement, and I tried to suppress a smile.

"And," he leaned back in his chair, crossing his legs and resting his hands on his knee, "the cost in the practice of chronomancy is souls."

My eyes went wide. "Why souls?"

He shrugged. "In my whole lifetime I've never seen a person actually attempt chronomancy, but our archives record mention of the Dark Echo—one of the cults most interested in that particular craft. There's no telling if chronomancy is even possible, but we can't allow souls to be used this way, Reign."

"So what is the exact plan for how we entrap him then? Do you have the details for trading me to prevent him from using souls?"

"You misunderstand. The problem isn't the theoretical nature of chronomancy." He unfolded his legs and leaned forward on the table. He bent his eyebrows in genuine concern. "The problem is, you are a mortal vessel for both a mortal and an immortal soul."

The world began to shrink around me. I wrung my hands tighter. I didn't have any more time to process before he continued.

"So I imagine his true aim in taking you back is to use that infernal soul piece inside you. Souls," he looked off to the side as if recalling some scripture, "are delicate, precious things. Magic can't easily extract them, so in order for him to use either of yours, he'll have to kill you."

There it was.

I felt my body rattle as the truth began to weigh down on me. What if my grandfather knew about the contract as it was being made? And my father, Remodeus, subsequently added a soul bond just for this? Was being the expendable container for his spell material all I was? The only reason I was ever kept, not discarded when I was born? To be ... harvested?

"But I don't want you to worry—we're arranging a few things. Council Member Thrane is new to his position. He has ties with members of our temple and has an interest in eliminating corruption. He's setting up a meeting in one of their most secure chambers at the Citadel of Light. A chamber that has built-in anti-divination glyphs, as well as inlays for us to set up a binding circle."

"So ... do I have to go?" My voice shook. It was as if I was back in that chair in my grandfather's office.

"I think he's too smart, he'll know if you are not there. So yes. But you'll be heavily guarded, and your friend can stay by your side the entire time." He gestured to Freda. "Until then, would you mind if I asked you some questions?"

What more could they want to know about my grandfather? They seemed to know more than I did.

I clenched my hands nervously in my lap. "Sure ... I hope I can help."

"That's fantastic, exactly what I'd hoped you would say." The Exalted Sun lowered his head in contemplation before raising it again. "Can you tell me on which exact day you most recently saw Leander?"

"Leander?" I gulped. How did they even know my connection was specifically to Leander? Up to this point, we'd only ever discussed the fact that I had a devil's soul fragment inside me, not that it had anything to do with him. I caught Brin's expression over the Exalted Sun's head—she was just as shocked as I was.

"The Fire Prince of the Nine Circles of Hell. Have you witnessed any killing of innocents or soul harvesting?"

Brin leaned in towards him, "Exalted, how do you know it's his soul?"

"I knew it the moment I shook her hand. There is no mistaking such a violent and dangerous soul."

I shrank in my chair. Like hell I was going to say anything about him. "May I answer questions about anything else?" The possibility of taking my grandfather into custody was still appealing and I did not want to detract from that.

The Exalted Sun continued. "With your being *entrapped* by him, we have a unique opportunity to learn the mind of the enemy and prevent threats to the innocent people of Brunalin. So, what kind of violent acts are you both planning?"

What the hell? That fiery rage from earlier bubbled up from my core, as if it might shoot out my throat.

Brin turned around the table to face her leader. "Exalted, I already questioned her—her mortal soul is pure, and she doesn't wish—"

"You can't trust devils Brin, no matter what they tell you."

"He—we are not planning to do anything," I blurted. "In fact, if you want to protect innocent lives, you'll not harm me while I reside here." The sound of the bite in my tone surprised me. Because hell, I knew Leander would do something horrible if they hurt me.

The Exalted Sun's eyes narrowed. "Did your mother sell your soul to him?"

"No!" I shouted. "He doesn't *own* me." The way we were connected felt impossible for one soul to take priority over the other. I was so tired of the notion that someone had to own me. My grandfather, the Gisenwalds—now Leander being compared to them.

Nobody *fucking* owns me.

I flew up from the chair and glared down at the Exalted Sun. "I'll help apprehend my grandfather, but leave Leander out of this."

I turned, taking a few steps away and that hot energy raged inside me, burning and tearing under my skin. I fisted my hands and turned my head back towards him.

"If you don't leave him out of this, you won't need to worry about his threat, but mine." I stretched my fingers out, a strange tingling collecting at the tips. The hot energy crackled in my hands now, tingling back up my arm with sharp, heated pain. It was ... like nothing I'd ever felt before. Like Leander's soul was the one raging inside me.

The Exalted Sun did not flinch. He held my gaze.

I shook my hands out in surprise, trying to quiet the anger. I threw them forward and cast a *Mystic Door*, which I promptly stepped through and back into the house.

I collapsed on the bed rolls. That had never happened before ... I'd never been so angry that some kind of Evocation arcana had flowed out of me.

Emrys crawled over to rub against my arm. *"Mistress? Why are you angry?"* He was getting good at picking up on my emotions, something I was sure had both to do with being my familiar and ... an infernal? Drow?

"The Exalted Sun was asking questions about Leander," I groaned along our telepathic bond.

"I will make you happy again. Please allow me to kill him."

"No killing, Emrys. Don't kill any of the clerics either, even if they are mean ..." I picked my head up from the pillows. *"That's a command."*

The drow starlight in Emrys's eyes sparkled.

I heard footsteps approach and turned to see Freda come through the door.

"Okay, so like, when did you suddenly become an Evocation badass?" She laughed, sitting down on the bedrolls. "Those clerics looked terrified when you just walked out like that with whatever that was around your hands!"

"Sorry I left so quickly, I just had to get out of there." I buried my face into the pillows.

"It's fine." She shrugged. "I can't believe he knew it was Leander's soul from just a handshake."

"Never trust a cleric," I mumbled into the pillows.

"Brin seems nice. At least she stood up for you."

I pressed my lips together in a smile. Okay, maybe not *all* clerics.

"Well ... let's go on a walk and cool off before you start literally smoking," Freda teased.

"You are ridiculous," I said, but lifted myself from the bed rolls.

Emrys sprang up between us, flicking his tail in the air.

I smiled. "Yes, you can come too, Emrys."

CHAPTER TWENTY-SEVEN

The three of us walked the paths between buildings on the temple grounds till we found a little forest that butted up against the dwellings. Every corner of the place was so well-kept, with winding paths that curved around trees and sloped over hills, as if made to flow with the will of nature itself. Every now and again, we'd come across a lone stone statue, seemingly placed to inspire contemplation. Each one was unmarked, but appeared to wear temple clothing, so we gave them names and made up stories about them.

We had been walking for about ten minutes when we came upon another unmarked statue where a woman dressed in plain linen pants and a shirt crouched over its base. A canvas apron covered her front and she pushed a wet soapy tan cloth across the base of the gray statue. As we got closer, I realized that the woman scrubbing the stone was Brin. She looked exhausted, her clothes covered in sweat and dirt. She wiped her brow using the sleeve of her forearm as we approached. We made eye contact with her, but she said nothing, going back to vigorously scrubbing the stone base.

"I guess you are not allowed to use *Spotless?*" I said when we were close enough for conversation.

Brin smirked. *Smirked!*

That was probably the most friendly reaction I'd gotten out of her since we met.

"It's true. I'm not allowed to use arcana to fulfill my penance." Brin wrung out a cloth and draped it over a bowl of water next to her.

"Penance?"

"It's fine ..." she sighed. "It's what I have to do for questioning the Exalted like that." Brin looked down at the stone base, now cleaner and revealing small places to lay incense. I wondered how many statues there were total. We must have passed at least fifteen of them.

Freda leaned across the path, observing the statues just in this section. "Are we allowed to help you?"

"Penance is performed alone." Brin scanned our faces and then grimaced. "It's symbolic. Early followers of *Her Light* believed that when she eclipsed, she was taking in the pain and suffering of her worshipers and bearing it alone."

"Eclipsed?" Freda said curiously.

"Early followers thought she was literally the sun."

That certainly explained the twelve-pointed suns.

Brin scooped up the cloth she'd been using and soaked it in the water, then continued to scrub. "I didn't realize your other soul was *his.*"

"I kinda freaked out when the Exalted Sun started asking questions about Leander, but I still meant what I said when we first met. I don't want anyone hurt, and after what I learned today, my grandfather is the bigger threat."

"I know," she said solemnly as she scrubbed. "It's fair for you to be guarded about him—Leander. The Temple of Lumoniel would much prefer that your arrangement with him did not exist."

She was so blunt, but I found myself liking her for her honesty. Brin seemed like the kind of person who almost relished in forcing truth to the surface. I wondered if she had always been like that, or if it was because she was a cleric of Lumoniel. She seemed to catch my reaction to her words.

"The first tenet of *Her Light* is to make truth your gleaming blade by burning away all that might conceal or shroud it," Brin recited as she stood with the bowl and cloth in hand.

"What if the truth for me is this path?" I asked. "One that's with Leander."

"I know better than to question *Her Light*." She cast a sidelong look at me with a raised eyebrow. "If you could enter the temple, she might tell you herself what your truth is."

I shuddered. Could I really speak with a deity like that? The prospect was both terrifying and exciting. I hoped that what I was experiencing with the thread and our souls was our truth. Even if what my father had done to create the bond was to torture Leander or at the behest of my grandfather. If Lumoniel could lay bare the truth, I would know for certain ... but, would *her* truth need to be the same as *my* truth?

"I don't think I'm ready to be smote." I chuckled.

"Could be fun," Brin crooned. She glanced away in the direction of the next statue. "I have more statues to get to ..." She drifted down the path, squatting before another nameless stone figure.

We followed the path until it ended outside the main temple and the attached garden on the other side. From this angle I saw tall arching white stone, with enormous oak doors. A single, glassless window was hewn directly above the door near the point of the roof, and its top was fitted with a gold metal dome.

"What truths do you think *the goddess* has for you?" Freda teased as we stared at it.

"As interesting as it would be to find out, I have a feeling it will be the last thing I do," I said flatly.

Freda tilted her head at the doors, a crooked smile on her face. "What if I asked for you?"

"Freda ..." I gripped her arm tighter. Drawing the attention of a deity like Lumoniel seemed like a bad idea, especially on my behalf.

"I'm human, so I feel like it would be fine. She'll probably just try to possess me so she can come after you." Freda winked, pulling away from me and taking strides towards the doors.

The building's aura weighed heavier in the air as if already Lumoniel was turning her head towards me. I shifted a step away. "I don't know ..."

"I'll be back out before you know it. Besides, I'm really curious." She tucked her red hair behind an ear before she flew up the steps and pushed the door ajar, slipping in.

I held Emrys in my lap while I waited. I distracted myself by mulling over the plan to take my grandfather into custody.

What if he refuses to come?

What if he demands a different location that he has control over?

What if the restraints do not work on him?

What if he resists?

Will they kill him?

Could I ... collect his soul and hold it prisoner for everything he did?

Should I?

I sighed to myself. The truth was, that I was still terrified of him.

I heard a creak from the main temple door and stood as Freda slipped through the opening. She looked pale—all the blood drained from her complexion. She walked past me, eyes glazed over, arms crossed tight to her chest.

"Freda?" I trailed behind her. "What happened?"

"It didn't work. Let's head back." Her voice shook the words out. This wasn't like her.

"Okay, but something happened, right? Are you okay?" I trotted up the walkway to her side, bumping her shoulder gently with mine. I thought maybe I'd knock her loose from whatever shadow seemed to follow her.

"It's really nothing." She sighed, refusing to even make eye contact with me.

"Freda ... you can tell me anything. We ... we can visit *Faizan's Tiny Closet*," I pleaded. Anything to understand why she was so shaken by what had transpired inside the temple.

Her green eyes darted around for a moment. "I don't know. What I saw didn't really make sense. It wasn't about you. She ignored that request." Her expression was ... numb.

"Okay, so maybe it was your truth? What did you see?"

Freda scrunched her nose. "I saw snow. Wind. Strands of my hair whipping around in it."

I tilted my head. "That doesn't sound so bad. Maybe it's where you'll live or travel to?"

Her eyes shifted over to me, wide and lined with tears. Then she blinked them away. "I told you, it didn't really make sense."

I linked my arm through hers. "For it not really making sense, you don't seem okay," I observed.

"I guess I wasn't expecting to actually get a response." She withdrew from a far off thought and squeezed my arm into her. "I'll be fine though, I'm just a little shocked is all." She gave me a weak smile.

We rested at the small house for the remainder of the day. Freda finally went to sleep and I sank into the sprawling bedrolls, wondering if a good night's rest would disperse what plagued her.

The anxiety was building in me—in all of us—wrenching a pit in my gut. As I was on the edge of drifting away ... I remembered. Would Leander visit me in a dream tonight?

CHAPTER TWENTY-EIGHT

The air was warm, a sweet smell hanging in it. I stood on a night-covered balcony, facing a pair of ornate doors. Many branches of tiny white flowers spilled from pots and hung suspended between marble pillars. It had to be night jasmine—or some other sort of nocturnal flower—which only bloomed in darkness. Golden yellow light bled from the open crack of the door. Something else drifted through that opening with the light—the muffled sound of a piano and several stringed instruments.

Each step I took toward its melodic call had my dress swishing and dragging on the floor. I looked down at myself. I was draped in a beautiful, full-length beaded dress. It was a pale red—almost the same color as my skin—making me look like some kind of jeweled, forbidden fruit, waiting to be peeled. A slight breeze caressed my exposed arms and the length of my back, and my tail flicked through the diamond opening designed for it. Usually, I wore so much clothing, covered every inch I could, and this had me feeling practically naked.

The music surged. A delicate rain of clear tones descended as the piano hammers struck metal strings. The melody drifted an octave lower before making an abrupt transition to a dissonant minor key. The notes of that slow minor progression resonated in my chest, till it seemed to harmonize with my very existence. It was like the sound was a personification of my own self. Soft, delicate, and sad, but progressing with a slow, intentional momentum that built to a strong tension. Every few breaths, a single bright note mixed in, like a pulse, pulling against the low tones like the thread did in my soul. It drew me in, and I pushed the cracked door wider.

The golden light of the interior flooded my eyes with a grand ballroom. At the center, pairs of all manner of creatures floated across the glimmering gold floor in dance. Swaying and twirling, like leaves preserved in perpetual free fall. The walls stretched high and curved to arches holding up an ornately decorated ceiling. Hanging from its center was a grand black chandelier. Its multi-levels of candles were lit with red flame which seemed to burn in sync to the resonant swells of the music below. This was surely what it felt like to be trapped inside a blazing flame.

I took a few more steps in. No one seemed to notice I was standing there until I heard that familiar, velvety voice glide down my neck.

"Hello, my dear."

I turned and my smile went wide.

Leander's suit was well-fitted. A dark charcoal with embroidered black stitching that swirled like flames, covering the entirety of the design. The lapels and ruffles at the neck shone a brilliant gold color, as did his cufflinks and buttons. He looked like a true Prince of the Nine Circles of Hell.

"I don't think I've ever seen you smile like this." His orange, infernal eyes burned down towards me.

"Is this a dream?" I felt a little funny. I wasn't exactly sure what I had been doing before this, and the sounds and sights were cloaked in some kind of ethereal haze.

"It is." He extended his hand to me for a dance.

I placed my hand in his and he guided me among the gliding pairs. I realized that as our hands touched, it didn't feel the same as it had before.

"Why can't I feel you?" I tried not to sound desperate.

"Do you miss the rush of our souls touching?" He smiled down at me, tightening his grip on my hand.

"Yes," I pouted.

"Perhaps I should have abducted you ..." A devilish smirk crossed his face and his eyes trailed the skin of my neck and collarbone. "It's because I'm still in the Nine Circles, and, as we established, this is a dream."

My vision was hazy with a dream glow as we turned about the room. I watched pairs float by and searched their features, but I was sure I'd never seen any of them before. One devil prince with long white hair danced with another prince who had infernal, glowing green eyes. Another behind them had shadows trailing him as he moved, twirling a creature in a midnight gown that sparkled with red beads.

"Do you know all these devils?"

"Yes," he replied.

When my eyes returned to him, I realized he hadn't broken his gaze on me. I tilted my head back and narrowed my eyes at him. Then I whispered coyly, "Did you throw a ball in my dream to celebrate touching me again?" I felt his grip on my waist tighten.

"Our dream—not all of this is from my mind." He extended his arm and spun me slowly before greedily pulling me back into his grasp. "And yes, that's precisely why," he said in a low tone that melted me.

His hand returned to the bare skin of my back, fingers sliding gently down my spine. Tingles followed their path and the sensation continued on to pool between my legs. All I could do was hold on as I melted into his touch. His eyes glowed like soft embers as he looked at me with desire, but I could see he was restraining himself. I kept anticipating the surging electricity from the thread, but found it dulled, hazy with the physical distance of our bodies. It had me not really thinking about much else other than where he was touching me—and where I wanted him to touch me.

Perhaps I should unrestrain him ...

Or, perhaps I should torture him.

"You look delicious." He breathed into the space between our faces. The tone of his voice alone made it feel as if he'd released the first button at the back of my dress.

Who was I kidding? I was torturing myself by not letting him have me.

I swallowed, emboldened by the haze of the dream. "If I look so delicious ... then why don't you get on your knees and taste me?"

His eyes went wild a moment before his lips pressed into mine. His hand gripped the skin on my back so tightly that I could feel the sharp points of his nails clawing across me. He kissed me like he had an aching, desperate need, sending his tongue deep past my lips in exploration. He squeezed my body into his, and I could feel every inch of him—the firmness of his chest, the strength of his arm around me ... the long hard length of his cock straining against his slacks to be free.

He tilted me backward and I felt the room around us shift, then my head pressed back into something soft before he stood. We were on a velvet, black chaise in the center of the ballroom, which was now conveniently empty of all its guests.

He clumsily tore at the buttons on his jacket, striping it off and throwing it to the ground. The sight of him so mad with desire yet not touching me was making me writhe. He crawled across the chaise back to me, kissing me once again as he lay beside me. I felt a hand slide up the inside of my thigh, approaching the damning *evidence of how much I wanted him. I squirmed against the way the dress constricted my legs. His fingers slipped past the edge of the undergarment and explored delicately until he discovered the slick wetness that had been hidden. I let out a shuttered breath as a finger traced the soft opening between my legs, sinking in slightly with just how wet it was. My tail curled at the sensation.*

He broke away from our kiss and dropped his forehead against my neck, his horn pressing into my cheek. His finger traced small circles, slowly, as if savoring the feeling of my arousal.

I whimpered a voiced breath.

"Fuck ..." he groaned.

He rose and pulled at my dress skirt. I heard fabric ripping and beads clicking, bouncing across the floor. With the entirety of my legs and thighs exposed, he squeezed my hip in one hand and an ass cheek in the other as he pulled me down to the end of the chaise. Then he did exactly what I had dared him to do.

He lowered himself to his knees.

Whether it was because I willed it in the dream or that he had torn them off when he mangled the dress, there were no undergarments to further impede his efforts. He spread my thighs apart and started trailing kisses down them, letting his fangs gently scrape along my skin. My breath was already ragged, and he hadn't even touched my most sensitive parts yet. I squirmed for him as the heat between my legs grew. I couldn't form any thoughts—other than holy hell I've never felt like this before.

Finally, his kisses rose enough to find the sensitive nerve endings he'd been trailing towards. He spread me further and gave one long, luxurious lick along that one particular spot. It triggered a feeling of pleasure that tingled up my body in a rush before escaping through a devastating moan. He gripped me tighter at the sound.

My tail writhed, curling and gently stroking his shoulder. He released my thigh and wound my tail around his forearm—pin-

ning it to him to quiet it before gripping my thigh again. I squeezed his muscled arm tightly, and sent my hands down my body until my fingers ran through his hair between his horns, causing the groan from him to vibrate his licking tongue.

He increased the pressure of his movements, clutching my thighs firmly as he devoured me. He sucked in the sensitive area of nerves and I moaned at the wave of tingles it sent through me. He returned to licking, the strokes of his tongue intense with the desire to please me.

And it was pleasing.

I wiggled into him, shuddering with moans of pleasure in each movement. The tension of release was so close, but then another force appeared—a force that was pushing down on my chest. It was separate from the gripping rhythm Leander had on my body.

"Leander ..." I panted, pulling on his horns. "I think someone is trying to wake me up."

"I'm not letting you go until I've tasted your climax," he growled, repositioning my hips and thighs.

"I don't know if—I'll be able to in time—" I sucked in a hot breath as two of his fingers slid inside me. He went back to intensely worshiping that one particular spot with his tongue and began pumping into me with his fingers. My entire focus narrowed to how his touch sent rippling waves of pleasure though my body. The feeling alone of having something hard filling me was enough to start my release fluttering. He didn't yield a single second to allow whatever was trying to pull me into waking to succeed.

The fluttering pushed into release sending spasms of pleasure racing through my body. I gripped the chaise—gripped his arm with my tail—and he kept me spread wide despite it all to taste every second that transpired. My own loud moaning echoing in the ballroom was eventually replaced with rapid breathing as my *heart pounded in my chest. My body fell limp against the chaise and my legs trembled.*

I looked down to find him panting as well, running a few kisses up my thigh. I caught a fraction of a satisfied look from him before he crawled up onto me in a panic.

"Wait—!"

His voice echoed in the vast emptiness that was the space between dreams as consciousness rushed back into me. I blinked awake with a gasp.

Emrys was sitting on my chest and Freda was standing over him. Both wore concerned looks.

"Were you having a nightmare?" Freda looked me over with concern.

I sat up, lowering Emrys to my lap. I had soaked the bed roll in sweat. I pressed my hands to my cheeks and felt how warm and flushed they were.

"Uhm ..." My voice was still fluttering and my limbs were still shaking, as if I was back on that black chaise. "No! I'm okay."

Freda cocked her head. "Liar."

I looked around the room and realized how bright the light coming in through the window was.

"Did I sleep in?"

"You were ... Then you started squirming and sweating in your sleep."

My face heated again. "Uhm ... I had a dream ... and Leander visited me in it."

"You mean you had a dream *about him*?" Freda corrected.

"No ... we had a dream ... *together.*"

Freda blinked at me for a moment before shifting down to the bed rolls with me. "Okay—*Faizan's Tiny Closet*—tell me what happened right now!" Freda pulled the covers in, accidentally knocking Emrys out of my lap.

"He ... um ... orally—" I whispered, smiling.

Freda's eyes grew wide. "And? I'm assuming it was amazing!"

"Of course it was …" I muttered using my hands to cover whatever dark shade of red I was turning.

I peeked through my fingers and saw Emrys staring back. This was even more embarrassing to have him there. It was so easy to forget that he was actually not a cat.

"I'm going to go cool off." Yes. That's what I needed. Some cold water would help me reset from this whole embarrassing ordeal. I rose from the bedrolls.

"Reign, your back!" Freda pulled up the corner of my night shirt.

"What is it?" I asked, turning my head.

"Scratches?" she replied in a puzzled tone.

I brought my hands up to cover my face once again. That was from when we were dancing—he was—and then …

"It's fine!" I laughed nervously. "I'm going to rinse off …"

Every part of me was still on fire from the dream, but the bathroom of this small house had a tiny tub and only cold running water, thank the gods. I turned the water on and ran my hands under it to wash my face. Then Leander's voice erupted in my mind.

"Tell me which one of them woke you so I can kill them."

"Are you going to be in a bad mood now?" I said playfully as I continued cleaning my face with the cold water.

"No …" He somehow growled the pout. *"But I was not done with you."*

"Seems like you accomplished your task," I said, smiling.

I stood back from the tub faucet and flung the excess water from my hands. There was a long pause before I finally heard him again.

"I want to devour every inch of you."

I almost slipped at the sound of guttural need in his voice. It quickly resurged the sensations he had stimulated from inside the dream. The way he had licked and pushed his fingers into me ... like my pleasure was the last form of sustenance in existence and he had been starving for it. I tried to calm my racing heart and give a reply that didn't completely give away how his words melted me.

"I'll see you soon," I said sweetly in return.

Chapter Twenty-Nine

The next two days flew by. I showed Freda how I could cast spells without using materials. I could only do it for simple things. For the harder spells, like *Passage,* I still relied on my wizard training. She thought it was completely unfair and teased me that my primordial magic was akin to cheating on an exam.

We had met a few times with Brin and on the second day, we learned Council Member Thrane was ready. We would set out soon to meet at the Citadel of Light, in the secure chamber the Exalted Sun had mentioned. He would be present, along with Brin, Freda, and a dozen clerics and paladins. The Exalted Sun swore that the intel they had about my grandfather believing the ruse was sound, but anxiety still stirred in me.

I couldn't stop fidgeting the entire morning. This place was starting to get to me. I just needed some space—some fresh air. I commanded Emrys to stay behind, and checked for watchers as I snuck out of the house. I traced my steps back out of the temple grounds, past the statue of Lumoniel, and beyond the temple gates.

Crossing the threshold of the grounds immediately eased some of my anxiety. I took in a deep breath and looked for a quiet spot outside the crowds. Eventually, I found a little alley between buildings and slipped into the shadows there. I figured no one would dare bother a hellborn in a dark alley.

I placed my back against the wall and slid down to the cobblestone. The wall was cold against my back and relaxed the tension there. I thought about how in the next few hours I could be free or things could go horribly wrong. If my grandfather was taken into custody, what would happen to my mother and half sisters? Would they take over where he left off? Or would this also set them free? Then I remembered that moment with my mother when I was a child, she had sat in front of the fireplace late at night after being forced to do something for my grandfather.

If you are lucky, you won't have to do the things I've had to do.

What had he made her do? Would she be there this afternoon? The small part of me that still pathetically desired her love grew worried. Perhaps I should send her a *Mindtell*. I didn't know what I would say, but I wanted to believe that she had been relieved that I'd run away. Not just because I was gone from her life, but that I was free from *him*.

I wrung my hands and concentrated on my primordial magic. I felt it there beneath the surface, shimmering with an infernal heat. I'd never sent my mother a *Mindtell*, not once.

"Mom?" I sent the *Mindtell* into the ether, willing it to reach her.

A few moments went by, and then a few more. I wrapped my arms around my knees and stared into the cobblestone.

Her cold voice slipped into my mind. *"You shouldn't be contacting me, Grace."*

I froze. Should I reply? What should I say? The silence grew and before I could muster up the courage to decide on what to say, her voice sounded in my mind again.

"Don't let him find you alone."

She had spent a spell material on me. I felt pathetic again, because even that gesture warmed me. Not exactly affection, as she'd never given me any, but it seemed like some kind of desire to prevent the suffering that she felt under his watch.

"Did grandfather make you sign the contract? To change me like this?"

I had to know. Was all this part of his machinations towards chronomancy?

"I didn't tell him what I'd done till after you were born. Then he started demanding answers."

So ... it hadn't been at his request that I be implanted with a piece of an infernal soul? My father ... had only wanted to torture Leander?

Her voice seeped into my mind again. *"Don't let him find you alone."*

I glanced in both directions, and was met with the surrounding emptiness. The air felt colder with the realization that I really *was* alone. I imagined I could turn one corner and there my grandfather would be. I searched the thread. Its pull had been strong for days as Leander had resolved to stay on this plane in case I wanted to send him *Mindtells.* I concentrated on my primordial magic again.

"Leander? I'm alone ... and—"

I barely got the words out through my spell when I felt the thread tighten. Arcane smoke whirled in front of me—and there he was. I sprang up from my seat, feeling my body go weak as he took steps towards me. His eyes glowed bright in the alley's shadows as he pressed me into the cold stone wall. He slid his hand along my jawline till it reached my neck and his head lowered so that his eyes were inches from mine.

"You've been haunting me since that dream, my dear ..." he whispered desperately.

"Thank you for coming. I'm feeling nervous and I realized that in seeking solitude ... I did it too well, and then I got more nervous."

He pulled me into his chest and wrapped his other arm around me. It melted me to be in his embrace, like I could forget about everything that was happening for only a moment.

"You do not have to go to the meeting. If it doesn't feel right, we can find other ways to achieve what you wish." He rested his jaw on my head. "I dislike that the Temple of Lumoniel is involved, and I dislike that your grandfather plans on taking your souls from you. It would be very easy, you know." He gave me a squeeze. "Because you are mortal."

"That's why I'm so nervous ..." I sighed. "My grandfather is an intelligent man. I know when I see him in a few hours he'll likely be playing a different game than the one we are."

"Despite that, does it feel right to go? Or should I take you back home?"

Home.

Was the Fire Circle my home now? It made me a little teary-eyed thinking about it—my desire to have a home and be surrounded by people who love me. A place to long for. It didn't feel right to run away from this, though. How long would I have to run if I did? The rest of my life?

"I think I should go to the meeting ..." I said softly. "Running away will not set me free from him. I need to confront my fear. And I won't be alone. I'll have Emrys, Freda, and an entire temple of clerics and paladins. I know you don't trust any of them, but maybe you trust me?"

He pulled me away to look at my face, pushing my hair away from my eyes. "I do, and I don't want to keep you from where you believe fate drives you ... Although, I think that I'm allowed to not like it."

"Thank you," was all I said, gazing back up at him.

The devilish grin washed over his face. "Show me the smile you gave me in the dream." His words poured over me like warm honey.

"I can't smile on command." I intentionally gave my closed-mouth smile.

"Would you like to attempt resisting the magic of my *Command?*" he purred as his hands shifted down to my waist, where he started lightly pinching me.

"Hey!" I started laughing. I couldn't help it because of the absurdity of it. Here I was in a dark alley with a Prince of the Nine Circles, and he was tickling me to get me to smile instead of using an arcane *Command* to force me to do it.

"There it is ..." His voice was like velvet as I inevitably grinned, baring the fangs he so badly wanted to glimpse. He immediately closed the distance between us and brought his lips to mine.

I sank into the kiss, taking in his movements as the warm, caressing feel of him tore down all the walls of my anxiety. The thread surged between us, and I was sure it was a feeling I wanted to be lost in. Hells, I *needed* to be lost in it.

He pulled away abruptly, his glowing eyes flicking towards the temple grounds. "Someone is coming." He gave a wicked smile. "Should I hide in case it's one of those nasty clerics? They might never mentally recover if they were to see me in the flesh."

I could tell by the excitement in his voice that he would have loved to torment a poor innocent cleric with the mere sight of him, but no—not today!

"Yes! Hide yourself!" I gently pushed him away.

The wicked smile, along with his entire being, simply blinked out of view.

My eyes grew wide as I scanned the surrounding area for him. I could still feel the strong pull on the thread, so he was within reach. The *Invisibility* spell perhaps? Then, I heard the approaching footsteps. I watched a long shadow cast across the road outside the alley, then the figure turned as they caught my gaze.

I sighed in relief. It was Freda.

CHAPTER THIRTY

"Reign!" Freda called out to me. "I couldn't find you and some guards said you had left."

"Is this the one that woke you?" Leander's voice caressed my mind, and I felt his hand trail at my side.

I jabbed my elbow backwards to shut him up.

Freda cocked her head in a confused expression. "Are you okay?"

"I just wanted some space," I replied nervously, eyes shifting to the left and right of the *almost* empty alleyway.

"Well, I could have come with you—or Emrys. Who knows how many of your grandfather's guardsmen are crawling out here now that they know the temple has you." She began walking closer to me.

Oh hell, she was right. I didn't even think of that. I leaned into Leander and felt him there, warm and firm at my back.

"Did you not tell her you have a personal guard dog?"

I tried not to react, despite how my insides fluttered at Leander's words.

"Let's head back. We're leaving soon," Freda said, turning slightly to leave.

"Um ... I can't," I whispered.

Freda stopped. "What, are you giving up on the plan now?"

"No ... I—" I felt the warm arcana tingle up my back and I knew Leander had revealed himself.

Freda's eyes went wide. "Fuck!" She jolted back. Her heel caught on a crack and she started to fall.

I lunged for her, but I heard a snap behind me and some invisible force propped Freda back up on her own two feet.

"A little warning next time!" She bent over resting her hands on her knees taking deep breaths. "That scared the shit out of me."

"You *should* be afraid of me," Leander said in a low tone behind me.

Freda creased her brows and lifted her head, narrowing her eyes at him. "Oh not you, I thought you were a fucking guardsman. No, you," she pointed right at his face, "I'm still deciding whether or not you are good enough for her, so don't think you get any points by not letting me fall on my ass."

Leander breathed in to reply, but I jabbed him with my elbow again.

"She's my best friend, like my sister," I said through the *Mindtell.*

"Fine," Leander said out loud through gritted teeth.

"I'll make it easy for you." Freda crossed her arms. "Make her stressed out—negative points—make her cry—negative points—break her heart—so many negative points I'll find a way to get you killed all over again."

I could feel him tensing behind me. "And how do I accumulate *positive* points?"

I flipped around and faced Leander. "She's not being serious. She's just giving you a hard time because she loves me." I smiled the pretty fanged smile up at him.

"I take it you want me to guess as to what warrants a positive point?" He narrowed those infernal eyes on me with a slight curve of his smile.

I squeezed him and suppressed my running imagination. "You'll be fine. Freda will like you ... eventually!"

He looked up at her standing several feet away then back down to me. "Be safe, my dear." He kissed my head and then flipped me around. "Both of you." He nudged me towards Freda.

I curled my tail into my body at the loss of his heat. I looked back at him with a slight smile, then let out a sigh. I turned to Freda. "Come on, let's go back."

As soon as we arrived we scooped up Emrys, and Brin ushered us into a caravan with the Exalted Sun that brought us to the Citadel of Light. Inside, the pale fortress was eerily dark. The corridors were hewn from ancient stones and plastered over with modern adornments such as historic woven tapestries and wallpapers.

The other clerics, Brin, Freda, and I entered the secure chamber. I could feel the ancient, arcane runes warding the space—like a low hum in the back of your mind. I glanced at the Exalted Sun and the middle-aged man he spoke with. The man was plainly dressed in charcoal-colored wool, save for the silver pin on his lapel—a circle with his title etched in letters.

Council Member.

The man took a few steps forward and bowed his head slightly. A felt, black-rimmed hat obscured his loose brown hair pulled back into a bun at his nape for just a moment before his eyes flashed up again.

"Miss Vendelfrey, I am Rosin Thrane. Thank you for trusting me to help bring justice to everyone your grandfather has harmed." He rose and his warm, light brown eyes connected with mine. This was the man. The man who would stop my grandfather from exploiting his way out of containment.

"Not to sound cliche, but he tends to get away with everything," I said. "I'm glad another person in power is not content with letting him do so."

Rosin smiled. "That's exactly why I opened my bid to run for Chairman. I'm not interested in any of these old money families continuing to run this city like it's their own playground at the expense of common-folks."

Freda leaned forward. "You're not from one of the wealthy families?"

He tilted his head up with pride. "My father was a shoe cobbler and my mother volunteered as a primary education teacher."

Brin moved across the room and gestured to one side where we followed.

I looked back at Rosin. "It was nice meeting you."

"My pleasure, Miss Vendelfrey." He bowed his head slightly again.

When I turned back to Brin, she had pushed on a wall panel revealing a hidden door. We slipped inside a small octagonal parlor with a single window.

"Badass," Freda said as Brin closed the door behind us.

"This room is warded against other humans entering, so only Freda and I may enter," Brin said. "I will be guarding the outside. Ready?"

We nodded.

She turned and slipped back out the door, sealing it.

We waited, leaning against the wall. I could hear voices and my stomach turned in flips as I imagined my grandfather on the other side of the door.

I leaned away from my anxiety towards the small window, watching people push through the courtyard as if it were a normal day. Emrys jumped from my arms to the sill to watch with me and I petted him.

"I'm so glad this is going to be over," Freda said a bit nervously.

"Me too ... I feel like a vacation is in order." I laughed.

Freda cracked a small smile. "I think I'll stay in town and try to relax before going back to Midor's. Besides, unless you are paying there's not really anywhere I can go." She chuckled.

"Maybe I *will* take you somewhere nice for putting you through all this." I offered her a smile before refocusing on the trees outside.

Suddenly, I felt the hairs rise on the back of my neck. There was a poof of arcane smoke and I turned to the side.

Emrys was gone.

"Hello, Grace."

I spun to see a tall human man, about my age, and pale—with golden hair and hazel eyes.

What? I thought the wards—

He shifted closer, the sunlight casting a subtle sheen over his silk tunic under a navy-blue jacket. I tried to pull away, but I couldn't move. Not because I was afraid, but because something *arcane* was preventing me from moving. Just like before, with Cyrus. I glanced behind him and saw Freda, eyes panicked. He had done the same to her—we were both frozen still.

"I wasn't expecting you to look so much like him," he said, circling me from all angles.

I mentally pushed and fought, trying to break free of the arcana freezing me, but nothing surfaced.

He slipped a hand into his pocket and pulled out a velvet choker with gold threads in a swirling design woven into it, a small drop of blue crystal hanging from its front. He lifted it to my neck.

Everything was happening so fast, there were only seconds to react. That's right—I can cast a *Mindtell!*

"*Help—*" was all I got out to Leander when the choker snapped shut around my neck. The sensation of it clicking into place sent the world spinning. I'd have lost all balance if I was not being arcanely held in place. I tried to continue my words to

Leander, but there was nothing but blank coldness deep inside. My arcana—even the primordial magic—was completely cut off.

The man glanced at Freda then returned his gaze to me. "No one mentioned you had a friend with such beautiful, sanguine hair." He placed his hand on my shoulder and squeezed as the world slid out from below me. We were teleporting somewhere—the arcane winds blowing violently all around me as the world fragmented and reformed.

My mind raced. Wizards couldn't teleport people against their will. What the hell was going on?

When the world stabilized, we were inside of an ornate room, red wallpaper and gold furnishings around us. Tall walls stretched to vaulted ceilings. It reminded me of some manors my grandfather had taken me to so he could leverage the story he'd built around me to persuade other lords to make him better deals.

The man let go of my shoulder, but didn't release me from the arcana freezing me. My eyes pierced him like daggers.

"Don't worry about your servant. I dispelled him. He's likely waking up in the Nine Circles by now. I can't have him getting in the way." The man's hazel eyes flashed as he maneuvered around to face me.

A few human servants, all dressed in the typical black and white aproned attire, entered the room flanking him. He snapped his fingers and I fell to my knees. I started pulling at the choker, but it wouldn't budge.

"I think you'll find your magic no longer accessible," the man said in a bored tone. "That piece of jewelry also prevents *Scry* attempts, so don't count on that cute redhead finding you."

"Who are you? Why did you take me?" I shouted at him.

He stared at me for a moment then shook his head in disappointment. "I'm your betrothed, Heinrich Gisenwald."

I gaped at him. "I thought ... my grandfather was supposed to be the one to get me." My words rattled out.

"He's doing what he does—playing the game two steps ahead. My job is to keep you from getting yourself killed prematurely. Because," he leaned in slightly and I watched his jaw flex, "I hear you have part of a devil's soul in there ..." He peered at my center, then his eyes snapped back up to my face. "How interesting is that?" His voice went a bit monotone as he mused. He snapped his fingers to the waiting servants. "Get her changed for dinner."

The two servants took me by the arms and dragged me away. I fought their grip but they were stronger than they looked.

"See you tonight," he called after me.

CHAPTER THIRTY-ONE

The two servants dumped me into a guest room. They closed the door behind us and I pushed myself to stand. One's cold eyes watched me while the other began pulling clothing from a wardrobe.

"Master wants you to change before dinner." She threw several dresses on the bed.

I said nothing and maintained my glare between them. Their features seemed so angular, sharp to survive a place like this perhaps.

"If you don't change yourself, Master will come here and command you to change."

She closed the wardrobe and shot me an expectant glare as they both departed the room.

When the door clicked shut, I tore into my bag to see what I could employ to combat the situation. My spell book and materials were useless. The contract, though comforting, was also useless. Then I came across it—Alàn's dagger. If Heinrich wanted me to show up at this dinner all dressed up, I was going to add some accessories of my own.

I rummaged through the dress options, picking the one that would best conceal the dagger. The light blue color clashed with my pale red skin, but it was the most modest of the collection.

I put the dress over my head, hiking up the skirt to secure the dagger at my thigh. I drew the strings in at the back as best I could to fit it to me, then used the mirror in the room to examine the final look. The light blue satin was fitted in the bodice with a scooping neckline that had tiny white and green embroidered flowers lining it. Its overall style was ridiculously human—like something one of my step-sisters would wear. I hated it. However, the flow of the skirt perfectly concealed the dagger.

The door was locked, unsurprisingly, as was the window. I spent some time looking out the window at the grounds surrounding the manor, memorizing it. It was a similar design to my grandfather's estate—a geometric courtyard with stone fountains, retaining walls and topiary trees. Just beyond, I noticed the family cemetery. I marked its location in my mind, in case I gained access to my arcana and needed to re-summon Emrys.

I turned to scouting the room. It was mostly empty except for the wardrobe, which was stuffed with an overflow of garments. Thumbing through each piece, I noticed both women's and men's clothing, as well as some damaged pieces. I peered closer at the damaged bits of a sleeve. Its edges were peppered with cuts and bloodstains.

I straightened my back as I heard footsteps approaching down the hall. I closed the wardrobe and innocently took a seat on the bed. The same servants burst through the door and moved towards me, reaching for my arms again, but I pulled away.

"I can walk by myself," I snapped.

The two glared, but took a step back and extended a hand each in the direction of the door.

We turned down long corridors with wine-colored carpets and dark wood moldings till we entered a massive formal dining room.

There was an assortment of silver utensils, plates, and cups in setting places laid across the sixteen person table. Just as many servants lined the back wall, dressed in black and white matching uniforms, waiting to be called upon. The two that had been escorting me folded into the line with the rest.

Seated at the table were what I assumed to be the members of the Gisenwald family. Four women, three men, and Heinrich. To his left, at the head of the table, was Lord Gisenwald. I took a seat at the opposite head, placing many empty chairs and place settings between us. The lord's face was pale and gaunt with dark circles under his eyes—like he'd been sick or suffering from insomnia. The others looked similar. A bit more disheveled and sickly than I'd expected an upper-class family to appear. Heinrich, on the other hand, looked radiantly well. His face shone with a vitality and strength that was missing from the others.

A plate was set in front of me with food. It looked harmless enough, some sort of roasted bird with sides of vegetables. I kept my hands tucked in my lap and looked around the table. The other family members were silently staring either ahead or down at their food.

Lord Gisenwald raised his silver chalice and a servant approached with a decanter of wine, pouring a rather large amount into his cup. He took a few gulps before meeting my gaze across the table. "Welcome to my home, Grace." His voice was gravely and tired, exactly how I had expected him to sound.

"Yes, we've been waiting some time for you to arrive," Heinrich said with lackluster enthusiasm.

Lord Gisenwald took another full mouthful of wine.

One woman extended her trembling hand and lifted a fork to spear a bite of vegetables. They all began eating slowly, taking small sips of wine. No one looked at me. None except Lord Gisenwald whose gaze was locked on mine. Heinrich reclined in his chair, taking curious bites of the food and sips from his cup.

I stared down at my food, wondering what the consequences might be of refusing to eat. "Lord Gisenwald, am I a prisoner here?"

The gaunt lord's expression did not change.

Heinrich spoke instead. "You're not a prisoner here. We simply can't have you running away again." His eyes slid down to the choker fastened securely around my neck that cut off my access to my arcana.

"I can't get far without spell casting so you might as well let me roam where I please." My eyes shot back to Lord Gisenwald, looking for some sort of acknowledgement, but he did not react again.

"You may roam wherever you like," Heinrich said, eyes narrowed at me as he took another sip from his cup. The red liquid stuck to his lips, glistening.

"Then may I excuse myself and go back to my room? I'm not hungry, and it's been a long day."

Heinrich adjusted his jaw.

He looked ... displeased.

"Fine." He waved his hand, and a few servants approached, clearing my plates and cutlery.

As soon as they departed, I stood up from the table. I bowed my head towards Lord Gisenwald, turned, and hurried back to my room. Something about this whole situation did not sit right with me. Heinrich seemed to have more power in the family's dynamic than would be expected for a second son. Not to mention the obvious—everyone at the dinner had seemed dissociated—no, terrified—of something.

Everyone except for Heinrich ...

CHAPTER THIRTY-TWO

I waited for night to fall. I had planned to visit the family cemetery while everyone was asleep and at least attempt to smash the crystal on the choker so I could summon Emrys. If that didn't work, maybe I'd try to flee on foot till I found a settlement. We seemed to be out in the middle of nowhere. Such was how these residences of lords were—nested in privacy and seclusion.

I wondered if my initial *Mindtell* for help had reached Leander. Perhaps he was already tearing apart the temple or the city trying to find me. I hoped that he'd realized by now something had gone wrong since he couldn't *Scry* to find me. I had to at least try to get out of this situation myself. My stomach twisted as I realized this was likely always the intended outcome for me had I gone along with the betrothal. Even back then, my grandfather planned on spending me like a spell material. Holding me here till he was ready.

I watched the waning moon creep into the sky from my window. It had to be after midnight at this point. I dumped the hideous blue dress and changed into my original all-black garb. It would be better for slipping about in the shadows anyway. I kept the dagger strapped to my leg, and tucked all the important items I could fit in my pockets. Then, cracking the door open, I slipped into the dark corridors. Eventually, I found a door on the bottom level I could open, and I slipped quietly into the night.

I headed toward the cemetery, careful to use the topiaries as cover, then glided from tree to tree until I arrived.

It was a small cemetery, with only a few rows, but grave soil is grave soil. I spotted two rocks that I could use to crush the crystal and carried them towards the plots. Many of the graves were overgrown with grass, but then I noticed a plot near the end that looked disturbed. I moved in closer and saw a fresh mound of dirt. The soil covering the plot didn't even have weeds growing out of it yet. Only a wooden stake at the head of the grave marked it, a yellow ribbon tied to its top drifting in the night wind. I crept in closer to examine it. Blue embroidery—letters—ran down the ribbon. I stretched it out.

Heinrich

I dropped the ribbon and stumbled backwards. This grave was fresh, so who was the man I had met inside? Was ... there a body under this grave soil?

Then I remembered Lord Gisenwald's face. The family, all afraid and desperate.

"I see your roaming has gotten you into trouble."

I jolted at a disembodied voice that echoed through the cemetery, rattling the stones and shifting the earth with its vibration.

It sounded like the Heinrich I had met, but his voice was deeper—reverberating with arcana. My head spun as I looked around the cemetery, trying to locate him. I dropped the rocks and took off running. Heinrich appeared right in front of me, as if he had been hidden in the shadows. I couldn't stop in time and slammed into his chest. He grappled me, pinning both arms down to my sides. I tried to wiggle free, and then remembered the dagger. I flicked my tail out and wrapped it around the hilt of the blade, pulling it from its sheath. I continued to thrash in his grasp as a distraction while I brought the dagger up with my tail and plunged it deep into his leg.

"Fuck!" he growled, letting go of me.

I used my open right hand to yank the blade free as his stance wobbled from the wound. I pulled the dagger out, reoriented it up, and buried it deep in his throat. Warm red blood spilled out all over my hands, some spraying on my chest and across my face. I yanked the blade out and he grasped his throat, falling to the ground on one knee.

"*You fucking—!*" He gurgled through blood stained teeth. His eyes fluttered closed and he swayed. I thought he was about to collapse, then his eyes cracked open. He glared up at me with glowing red irises, the whites of his eyes an infernal black.

No ...

His skin shimmered from human pale to devil red, hair shifting from gold to black, and two reddish-black horns sprang from his hairline as he lost his concentration on his magical disguise. He removed his blood-covered hands from his throat and began coughing up more blood. The wound was still there, though it didn't seem to be anything other than painful for him.

Heinrich ... *was a devil?*

He stood upright and I backed away. He was massive as he towered over me, broader and more muscled than Leander. He lunged forward and grabbed my forearm, squeezing it so tightly that I thought it might break. The dagger in my hand slipped free and fell into the dark grass. Then the world shifted in a flash of colors and light, and arcane smoke settled around us as we landed in an entertaining room in the manor. He threw me down on the floor.

"*Servants, hold her!*" His *Command* cut like sharp teeth in the darkness of the room.

Servants teleported in, plumes of arcane smoke settling around them. They were no longer human, but infernal creatures of the

Nine Circles. They continued flashing in until there were ten surrounding me. One of them cast their magic towards me, and I felt a sharp pierce of pain in my mind. The coldness I'd felt when Cyrus had cast *Hold* on me chilled my skin again. I tried to writhe, but remained frozen on my knees, circled by the infernal servants. Arcane orbs of light burned in the space above us, casting a yellow light in the darkness of the room.

He commanded a nearby infernal with a growl of anger. *"Bring Lord Vendelfrey and the soul cage here. I'm tired of dealing with the body."*

The servant rushed out of sight, unquestioningly obeying his command the same way I had seen Emrys obey mine.

A few seconds later, I heard the familiar tap of heels on the hard stone floor. I knew the rhythm of that stride. My stomach dropped, and I immediately began shaking under the arcana freezing me. I shifted my eyes, the only thing I could move, until I found him.

His gray eyes pierced me like they always had.

Five human wizards followed behind him, their black leather coats, swaying with each stride. Two carried a twisted metal cage no larger than a loaf of bread between them. Blue runes carved into its edges glowed. I knew he would find more. More like Cyrus to do his bidding.

My grandfather stopped in front of the window opposite me and looked at the devil. "Take the collar off her so we can transfer the souls to the cage," he said icily.

The devil did not move for a moment, as if he was resistant to the very idea of being ordered to do anything by a human, but then snapped his fingers.

The collar clicked and dropped to the floor in front of me.

I felt my arcana rush hot through my body, down to my fingertips. I quickly sent a *Mindtell* to Leander. The primordial magic blazed through me, pushing against the icy spell griping my body till it burned it away.

I held my breath. I twitched my finger.

I could ... move.

I feigned that I was still held in place as the two wizards brought the twisted soul cage towards me and my grandfather and the devil advanced. I summoned every ounce of primordial magic I could reach to grant me success for the next spell. Then I whipped my hand out in their direction.

A point of light pulsed from my hand, a ray that shot across the room before a giant ball of fire exploded like a bomb in the space around the four of them. Heat blew back across my face as the flames swirled out, licking and crawling along the walls, curtains, and floor. I heard screams. Furniture, curtains, and wallpaper crackled as they caught fire. Smoke and cinder rose to collect under the ceiling above us. The *Firebomb* dissipated and my grandfather clutched his chest, scowling at me. Two charred bodies lay on the floor at his feet, the soul cage between them as they smoked.

The devil appeared untouched and had a vicious look of annoyance on his face. He bore his fangs in frustration and pushed his open hand out, fingers straining and curling, as if they were about to grab something. Then, an intense pressure closed in around my throat. I instantly started choking as the air and blood were constricted by the devil's arcane grip.

"I said to hold her!" he scolded at his servants. "Do it now!" he growled towards my grandfather. Other wizards rushed in to pick up the soul cage.

Time dragged on as I struggled for air. Was this it? This was how I would die? How my soul fragment would be torn from Leander's body? Not as intensely as it would have been when made permanent, but still ... I imagined the agony he would soon feel. That thought circled my mind, and for a split second I was glad that we'd not made it permanent. That when my vision darkened and my last thought trickled through my mind, he'd feel less pain than he could have felt.

My lips tingled. My head and the pulse in my face pounded as I failed to suck in a breath. I reached up around my neck, clawing, attempting to free his grasp, but there was nothing to pull away. I reached for my primordial magic, but its warmth fizzled away as my vision darkened and my body weakened. I didn't know what to do.

What do I do?

There was a sudden thunderous crack, and a tremor moved the earth below the house. Through what was left of my vision, I could make out new flames—flames that rose from fissures in the floor. The heat of them bathed my body as they spread like a wildfire, encircling the room.

Then I felt it.

Thrumming in my chest. The sweet feeling of the thread pulling taut.

He was here. He found me.

"Someone dispel her flames!" my grandfather shouted through the crackling of the fire.

The devil choking me stared into my half-shut eyes. They weren't my flames. I was on the verge of unconsciousness held in his grip. His eyes widened, as if he'd read my thoughts, and had seen what was coming.

My hands slipped down my body.

Fear and panic darkened his face. "Fuck!"

He released me and I fell to the floor, gasping for breath, head spinning.

The devil backed away. "You didn't say the soul was claimed by *him!*"

"What do you—"

The devil had teleported away before my grandfather could finish, leaving behind only a puff of arcane smoke.

"Never mind him, get the soul cage!" my grandfather shouted at the wizards.

The infernal servants began teleporting away, retreating after their master. The flames surged in a rumbling crackle before receding. When my eyes refocused, Leander was standing in front of me.

I watched him crush the crystal choker under his boot as he took a step towards my captors. The remaining wizards squared off in front of him. A wizard on the right pointed a finger at me to cast a spell. Leander tilted his head like he was simply cracking his neck, and the floor split in a chaotic rumbling rift under the wizard. Immolating hellfire erupted, bright, as if from the Fire Circle itself. When it dissipated, there was nothing left of the wizard that had targeted me. Not even ash.

The air in the room began to heat again as shadows bent around him.

"Point another hand at her, and I will incinerate this entire plane," he snarled with a low feral rage.

I glimpsed his eyes blazing wide as he glanced back at me, two glowing red coals suspended in black. Smoke poured from his nose and mouth which grew into a long snout. His lips peeled up to reveal rows of pointed teeth. His ears grew long as well, stretching out from his face. The rest of his body enlarged as black fur covered it, embers of hot coal glowing under the surface and tongues of flame crackling along his skin. As his size grew, he folded forward on all fours. His head pushed against the ceiling and bits of tile crumbled down around us. He was as I'd seen in the drawing in Special Collections—a black hellhound of both shadow and flame, bearing rows of sharp teeth and massive claws, a surging inferno in his wake.

He let out a deep, guttural growl that shook the room, and the flames surged chaotically in response. Those red coal eyes surged higher as he grew pushing through to the floor above us, till he seemed so far away from me. The wizards broke into a panic, dodging the falling ceiling, some shooting arcane spells at him. I lost sight of my grandfather, but readied myself in case he appeared.

Leander turned his hound face down towards me, his glowing eyes narrowing, and opened his jagged maw. A long, forked black tongue snaked out. It wrapped around my waist, yanking me into his mouth.

The sharp teeth clamped shut around me, protecting me like a cage. I clutched onto the tongue in the dark, warm wetness of his mouth.

I heard cracking and rumbling, and the space inside his mouth grew. I imagined him breaking through the top of the manor, until the inside of his mouth felt like it was the size of a train car—like the one I'd taken into Brunalin from Freda's. I could feel him thrashing around, despite being held tightly by his coiled tongue. A rumbling growl reverberated from his throat, shaking my whole body with it. There was a brief surge of what looked like flame deep in his throat, but it quickly faded. The sounds of explosions, crackling, and screams amidst the rumbling continued. I clutched the tongue and tried not to listen, tried not to imagine him being pummeled or hurt. Then I felt the transition between planes disorient me.

His maw opened and light flooded my eyes. The black tongue rolled me out on a grassy lawn. I looked up and saw the familiar pink sky of the Fire Circle. I wiped my face. When I sat up, I saw Emrys in his drow form running over from the garden doors of the palace.

"Mistress!" he shouted to me. Closer now, he slowed and froze, looking up at the massive hellhound towering protectively behind me.

I turned around to Leander as he shifted smaller and into his devil form. His eyes were still red coals when I threw myself into him, squeezing tightly as the transformation finished. Our souls lit up with warmth and electric current as we were wrapped in each other's embrace. The feeling began mending me after what I'd just experienced, comforting me just as the thread by itself had always done. He squeezed me, kissing my temple, and then rubbed the top of my head with his cheek.

"I couldn't scry on you to find you," he said, his voice tenuous, "until a few moments ago."

"I'm okay ..." I assured him. "Leander, there was another devil there." I pulled away slightly to look up at his face.

"I know ... I can see and smell his blood all over you ..." His concerned face shifted to one of pure delight. "Was that your doing?"

"I stabbed him in the throat."

Leander's smile curved into his devilish grin. "I want to hear in great detail all the violent things you did to Victus," he purred, fixing my slobber-wet hair out of my face.

"You know him?"

"I'll tell you about him. Let's go inside." He lowered himself slightly before lifting me into his chest. I wrapped my arms around his neck as he walked us into the palace, passing Emrys. He looked shattered, brows pinched in the disappointment of being sent away from me yet again. I reassured him with a smile that seemed to melt his anxiety slightly as his brows relaxed and he folded in behind us.

CHAPTER THIRTY-THREE

Despite the pink-lit skies of the Fire Circle, it was still the middle of the night for me. Apparently, Leander simply willed if he wanted it to be night or day on his Circle, with his preference for day. It seemed he didn't require sleep like mortals. My face warmed as I realized that meant he had only gone to sleep to visit me in the dream.

I was filthy, covered in slobber, dirt, and the blood of Heinrich—Victus—and minor cuts. I asked Leander if he had a bath I could use, and his smirk went wickedly devilish.

"The water on this Circle is not safe for mortals to bathe in, however, I can arrange a bath of Novus plane water *especially* for you." As he spoke, the imps rolled into view.

"Command us to make the Mistress a safe water bath! Command us!" The constructs wiggled and squirmed.

He kept his eyes on me and replied, "*Make her a bath of warm water from Novus.*" His voice was firm. "And ... if there is anything in or about her bath that harms mortals, I'll punish you with death."

I smiled at the silly punishment. A construct couldn't be killed.

"An important command! We will not fail you, Master!" They pushed each other, rushing out of the room.

"I will of course come to inspect your bath myself and make sure none of its elements will harm you."

"Please don't attempt to dispel them if the water is too hot," I said flatly.

His eyes slid down to my neck, and the smile vanished from his face. He ran his fingers and thumb delicately under my jaw.

"What?"

"You have bruises," he said sharply, not restraining the anger I could see bubbling up. For a second, his orange eyes flashed like the red coals I had seen before when he'd become a hellhound.

"I'm okay though." I raised my eyebrows in an attempt to pull him away from whatever darkness was on his mind.

Leander ground his teeth. "I want to go to the Blood Circle and kill him now." Then his eyes softened slightly. "But I will not leave your side again."

"Isn't the Blood Circle where my father is from?"

"Victus is Remodeus's son. He rules the Blood Circle since Remodeus oversees all the Circles in the absence of the Primordial Father."

"Wait, so he's my ... brother?" My eyes went wide.

My brother ... who wants to kill me, and is working with my grandfather. Did Remodeus know what Victus was doing?

"I would be happy to make you an only child," Leander smirked.

His touch was so soft along my jaw. Even though his words were sweetly spoken, I knew he was serious. I only had to show interest in the thought and he'd do it immediately.

"I don't want you to leave me alone again."

He sighed, surrendering, and rested his forehead against mine. "Very well."

My bath was completely normal and safe, warm water. I sent Leander away so I could soak off all the dirt and blood caking my body in solitude. He was disappointed that I wouldn't let him watch me, but I think the fact that I was here, in his palace—in his bath—helped him relent and leave me in peace.

My mind wandered among the bubbles. My grandfather and Victus had been working together ... For how long? To acquire my souls to do—well I had no clue what. Only that apparently it might involve chronomancy.

The dark spacious room that this tub quite literally seemed placed in just now for me, drew my mind to darker places ...

Why did my father make me like this?

Had Remodeus designed me to be used for some chronomantic plot? Had the visit when I was a child just been theater? A joke? Torture? If a chronomantic conspiracy had been the endgame for him, my grandfather, and Victus, what would it do to Leander when I died?

My eyes burned with tears as my thoughts drifted to the moments when Victus had been strangling the life from me. Leander and I had both waited so long for this kind of belonging. Even though it hadn't happened quite how he'd expected, he still wanted it.

Wanted ... me.

But if my souls were captured, and I died ... He might be okay with uniting our souls even though I was a mortal, but was *I* okay with it? I was not sure anymore ... especially after today. My feelings about him had not changed—I still felt like I'd fallen into a spell of madness with wanting for him. A new feeling rose. I was now afraid—afraid to take it, and then lose it all and inflict a terrible pain upon him.

I wanted to confront my father, as I had always wanted. I would demand answers despite my darkest fears, and hopefully he'd prove to be the devil I'd met all those years ago.

I sighed and left the tub. A black silk robe had been left out for me, so I slipped it on and tied it closed. I sifted through my dirty clothes and used *Spotless* to clean them, and brought them folded with me.

I opened the door to the hall and started tip-toeing around. Exhaustion was hitting me so hard I could feel sleep wanting to rush in. I sneaked from room to room till I finally found one with a bed. The room was expansive. The enormous bed pushed against one wall could easily fit a half dozen people. Accents decorated the walls that resembled flames. The room was bathed in the smell of cinnamon and smoke which told me it was Leander's room. If I slept here in his bed, would it be like inviting him to *unite our souls* immediately? I ... did not wish for that quite yet. I just want to sleep, and for my body not to ache.

I strolled around the room on my way to the large inviting bed. There was a desk that had books and papers spilled all over it. My eyes drifted over it when I noticed an unfolded letter, handwritten in glittering, gold and red ink—similar to my contract.

Hi again ...

She's probably not what you expected, but please believe me when I say that this is right. You'll probably push that thought away and resist what you feel deep in your soul. However, the more time you spend with her, you'll realize it. Maybe after you read this, you'll give in to her, completely. I really, truly hope you do.

Remember that she's not immortal, and while that scares you, it means she is more fragile than she might seem. She'll need to be protected, but she'll also need to be free to go where she feels her destiny leads her.

Should I be reading this? It seemed like a private letter written to Leander. The subject of the letter, though, sounded an awful lot like my current situation ... I couldn't stop my eyes from following the golden-red lines.

I know you ... you are asking yourself why it would be worth it to bond when it's between a mortal and an immortal soul. That it seems like unnecessary, inevitable pain. I want you to remember when we walked the ridge up the Crimson Mountain. You were miserable, and you hated it, but when we got to the top, I think you realized ...

Pain or suffering is absolutely worth enduring for love. The discomfort is what unlocks a new, refracted view. The pink skies you see every day are the same, but only now in this new context do you feel intensely, deeply, for them.

I'm not sure what you expected this to say when I handed it to you back then, but I'm glad that you are reading this now. It means you found her, and the purpose behind our meeting all those years ago was fulfilled. Maybe you are still hurt by it, but back then we were not meant to be together. You knew, too.

Regardless, I love you dearly.

I blinked as I flipped over the paper. Chills ran up my back and down my arms as I held it, reading the red-gold writing on the front.

Open this after you meet her.

My mind raced. Was this a letter from ... *her?* Was she talking about me? My hands shook as I set the paper back on the desk. She *was* wise. If she said things like this, no wonder she had changed his life. Had this been what he'd read that changed his mind about pursuing our bond? What had happened to *her?* Was there a way I could ask Leander about this without causing too much pain? As much as I wanted to find him now after the shock of reading the letter, my aching body and heavy eyelids begged for sleep.

I moved towards the bed and slid into the covers, tucking myself in. I laid there for a moment soaking in the smell of him in the linens, then suddenly it all came rushing in. Thoughts and feelings I'd been pushing away for the past few hours. Then, a single question cut through my mind, and it froze me like a stone.

If I close my eyes ... will they open again?
I struggled to keep my eyelids open as I contemplated my mortality. I kept my vision fixed on the edges of a maroon curtain as long as I could until the oblivion of sleep forced me into darkness.

CHAPTER THIRTY-FOUR

It felt warm and safe. I drifted into waking life to the lovely feeling of the thread. It blazed, just like when we touched—I sat up abruptly and looked to my side to find Leander curled up against me with his arm around my waist. I wasn't sure what time it was, but it felt like I'd been asleep for at least an entire night. Turning my head to look at him properly caused pain to blossom around my neck, where bruises had formed. I winced, and my body began to shake at the reminder.

Leander's eyes fluttered open. "Are you okay?" Concern flooded his face. His fingers trailed across my side.

As soon as he asked, I felt tears stream down my face.

"I don't understand." My voice trembled. "I was fine. Why is this happening again?" I looked down at my shaking hands and watched a few tear drops land on my skin. My entire being was unraveling, like a weak wind could completely end me. I recalled the memory of my mother sitting in front of the fireplace drinking, her hand shaking—was this what she had felt?

Leander sat up and pulled me into his chest. I wondered if the feeling of our souls touching like this could overshadow all the other things reeling through my body. Drown out the fear, panic, and anxiety. I burrowed my face into his warm chest as more tears brought on actual sobbing. He squeezed me and listened to me cry for a few moments before speaking. It was barely a whisper.

"Will you let me in? So I can hear your thoughts?"

I remembered now that I'd told him never to do that. But now ... I felt I knew his nature through my piece of his soul—I'd had it for my entire life, and it was the most trusted thing I knew.

I nodded my head, squeezing him.

My entire childhood of neglect and emotional manipulation rose to the surface. Everything churned violently around in me like a storm at sea. Hiding from everyone in the estate, and hiding myself from the world. The sounds—and stains of evidence in the estate of the cruelty of my grandfather. And now, to add to it, the disintegrated woman, the wizards chasing us—their decapitated bodies in the alley—and the dark purple bruises around my neck. Every heartbeat I had thought would be my last as that arcane hand had tightened around my neck. After each moment, I'd found a way to be fine.

I was fine.

I was strong enough to keep going. Why was it that when my life had been threatened this time it was different? I was stronger than ever in terms of what I could do with my arcana.

Why am I weak now?

Why can't I stop shaking?

Why won't it stop?

Leander kissed my forehead. I looked up at him, my face wet and puffy, and saw that he was crying, too. Could he feel everything I was feeling through my mind? The thought wounded me.

"My closest friend, a fellow prince that I grew up with, has always found himself in traumatic situations. Some were his own fault. Each thing, in isolation, was not very impactful. But time passed, and all of those experiences stacked up." He took a breath, pausing, brushing hair from my wet face. "Then he experienced something that didn't even happen directly to him. I was killed and my soul was returned to the Nine Circles. It finally broke him. So, he descended into the darkness with me when I returned. His reason for being there, though, was so much more complex. I couldn't make sense of which of the terrible things that had befallen him was the worst. It just filled him up until it was too much to bear any longer. And ... after each individual experience up to that point he'd been okay. Until he wasn't."

I sniffed. "What happened to him?"

"He's around. When I eventually found my way out of that darkness, I brought him with me. He does well most of the time, but there are moments now and then where I look at him and I can tell he's back there in that layered darkness, in the painful parts of every moment he experienced, for just a blink."

He pulled me away from his chest to see my face. "I'm telling you this because it doesn't matter that you were okay right after each thing you experienced. You may be okay or not be okay, at any time. Even if it's years from now. It doesn't make you weak to acknowledge your pain. It strengthens you when you see it, because if you see it, you can decide what happens next."

Leander wiped tears away from my cheeks with his thumb and continued. "My dear, there are no words, allegorical or arcane, that I can say that will make everything you are feeling vanish. And ... that is also okay. Time is a rather beautiful paradox of being both constant and changing. We know it endlessly moves us forward, but each moment alters us. You have so many more of those moments ahead of you where you can become different than you are now if you wish."

His words calmed me, and he was right—the fear and the physical agony my body had felt was still there rattling under the surface. I wasn't sure how to combat such things, but I felt something new at that moment. Before, when I'd felt this in small ways, I had been alone except for the thread. There had been no one to talk to, no one to hold me, no one to help me. I hadn't realized how grateful I'd be to have him be all of those things for me. He smiled softly as if he had heard the thought.

Ah, right ... he had.

"There is one thing I can do for you now ..." he purred.

I waited for some kind of lewd suggestion.

"I can bring a primordial cleric to heal your bruises."

I think he might have changed what he was going to say after I expected a lewd suggestion. This kind of teasing was going to take some getting used to, if he was always in my mind. Clearly, I needed to practice so I could return the torture.

He chuckled, dragging his fingers up my back.

"Okay," I said, "if the primordial cleric can heal a mortal, I'll take it." Then I'd figure out my next step.

"You can stay here as long as it makes you happy." He placed his finger gently under my chin, careful not to force me to bend my neck in a way that might trigger more pain. "This can be your home, if it makes you happy," he said. Then he leaned in close and kissed me softly.

The whirling connection between our souls swelled and over-powered everything. It was only me, him, and the glorious taste of his lips pressed to mine. I would never get used to this feeling between our souls. It was special. Worth protecting. If I ever needed a motivator to change in each moment time gave me, it would surely be to nurture this bond.

PART II

THE LOOP

Chapter Thirty-Five

The primordial cleric cupped my neck in her hands. Long, pale gray robes draped every part of her body. The only skin exposed was her face and hands. Multicolored threads were woven into the edges that brushed the top of her boots, circled her hands, and framed her face. Her skin was a shade of midnight blue so deep it stood in stark contrast with the robes. Her hands had barely visible black tattoos of runes and what looked like ancient Infernal. Horns curled out from her head covering which was also draped in beaded, linking chains, some wrapping to the tips of each horn. I watched, mesmerized, as her completely black, voided eyes scanned me curiously. Her hands lifted elegantly to my neck. I felt the arcane energy tingle, and the pain of the bruising subsided.

"I've never provided healing to a mortal before." Her voice was raspy and deep despite the youth that painted her face. Perhaps a side effect of being a cleric in the Nine Circles.

Leander stood nearby, watching as she performed her work.

"Perhaps," her voice now took on an otherworldly hiss, a reminder that though helping me, I should exercise some caution, "in exchange for continued healing services to your fragile mortal body, I could take your soul when you no longer require it?" Her smile revealed teeth that had sharp points. She glanced up at Leander, and my eyes followed.

Unamused, he stared back at her, with arms crossed, and a look in his eyes that provided the answer to her question. If the other inhabitants of the palace had questioned our relationship before, now the rumors would definitely spread.

She laughed nervously. "Will that be all, *Your Infernal Highness?*"

Leander remained silent, and sweat formed at her brow.

I rubbed my neck. I was so glad for the pain to be gone. Not that it had been particularly painful, but the soreness had been a reminder that triggered the panic to return.

"You may leave," Leander said flatly.

The primordial cleric bowed her head and backed slowly out of the room.

I stood up in front of Leander and smirked. "Should I call you *Your Infernal Highness* as well?"

"Only those below my rank call me that ... so any word that leaves your lips regarding me will be appropriate." His own lips curled up. "What sort of things should I call you?"

I simply shrugged with feigned ignorance, trying not to blush at his implying I was somehow as powerful as he was. "I like what you call me now."

He ran his fingers up my arm to my shoulder, looking over the work of the cleric. "Take your time to do whatever you need, *my dear.*"

"Thank you." I looked down at the floor to hide the anxiety I knew was creeping across my face. "I think I just need some time to distance myself from ... what happened."

Leander frowned slightly. "You should acknowledge it with words. To speak the trauma helps you take your power back."

His hand trailed back to mine and he squeezed it. "Trust me, I know something about that, having been slain."

If I said it out loud, it would surely shatter me. But I was not alone now. So it was okay if I shattered, right? Because he'd be here, to pick up the pieces and help me take form again.

I cleared my throat, feeling the knot that had developed there. "I need some time to distance myself from ..." My words choked off as if those arcane hands were wrapped around my neck. I could feel the trembling return. "From the inevitability that someday I will die. And I almost did." I couldn't stop my voice from shaking as my eyes burned. "And I won't get to start over." I stared into his chest, trying to find anything of interest to pull me away from this feeling.

Leander tugged me forward by my gripped hand, sending my fixed gaze to nestle into him. He squeezed me and rubbed his hands into my back. He held me silently, allowing me to sit in the space I'd just unearthed. We stayed like that until I was ready to venture out into the rest of the palace and find ways to occupy my time.

The next week passed quickly. The first thing I did was try to contact Freda and make sure she was okay. I wasn't practiced enough to cast *Mindtell* between planes like Leander could despite my devil soul fragment, so he brought her Calling Cards. Devils usually gave them to humans to coordinate soul deals across planes. They looked like small business cards, but were enchanted. When burned, each card sent whatever had been written to the mind of the devil who had given it to you.

The first thing Freda wrote back to me was a detailed description of how she almost knocked out my *sneaky boyfriend* with a book she'd thrown at him, and that he should be more careful unless he wants a Transmuter's Guide to Transfiguration textbook-sized chip in his horn. I hadn't laughed so hard since I'd left her.

Apparently, she and Leander had tried to find me after the kidnapping together, and, to Leander's credit, he had heeded Freda's repeated recommendation to *not* incinerate the entire city looking for me. She also wrote that my grandfather never showed up to the meeting. It had all been theater to allow for my abduction.

Now, she was back at Midor's to prepare for her classes starting in a few days. I asked if she'd be interested in coming to visit me here for a short time, but she said she had too much catching up to do on Transmutation, so perhaps in a few weeks. I decided not to force the issue after everything that happened. I would try to instead visit her as soon as I could. I was really, really starting to miss her.

Leander had been giving me plenty of space over the week. He even brought day and night cycles to the Circle to help me sleep and feel a sense of normalcy. I had thought for sure he would ravage me once I was here with him, but I think after he had seen how broken I'd been ... it led to him focusing on my recovery—which was a problem because I was terrible at initiating flirting and I still craved his attention. In the dream, there had been some kind of weird lifting of everything that weighed me down, and I had fearlessly demanded what I wanted. In waking life, things felt a little different.

Emrys could tell that I had been struggling as well. He had been very attached to me and shadowed me everywhere, trailing no closer than five paces away—which was taking some getting used to in his drow form. Despite that, I'd enjoyed his company the past week. We read together, he made me little snacks, and every time I looked at him he would smile. I wondered if other devils developed such relationships with those that served them.

Emrys had to make trips back to Novus to bring back safe food for me to eat. It was a good thing he was so eager to serve as we couldn't send imps. Leander had said imps, as constructs, couldn't leave the plane. It made me wonder if living here was as realistic of an idea as I'd originally thought.

Despite being a noble from Novus, I was not used to being *this* taken care of. The amount of accommodations I required to be here was making me feel uncomfortable. To get some solitude, I snuck away a few times so that Emrys, the imps, or Leander couldn't find me right away. Leander quickly realized what I was doing and let me be as I hid myself away in different parts of the palace—like I had in the estate. It was—perhaps sadly—a comfort to be alone like that.

My curiosity grew the more of the palace I saw. I would venture into a room and see a painting of one thing or another, then jot down my questions in an empty journal Leander had given me. At Midor's, I'd spent a lot of time in the library discovering new things. It had distracted me from heavier thoughts and opened my mind to possibilities—a feeling I enjoyed. A feeling that had been freeing. These moments felt a lot like that. Everything was new and unexplored. I still had not asked Leander about the letter I'd found my first night here—or for help to contact my father. With each day that passed I was waiting for the right moment.

Today was one such day where I snuck about the palace looking at the ceiling frescos, wall tapestries, and hanging paintings. Most depicted scenes—whether from mythology, text, or other places in the Nine Circles, I did not know, but they gave me a sense of wonder. I was met with one such tapestry in a large dining room.

It depicted a forest landscape shrouded in black mist. Jagged rocks swept up to a peak. A pale stone castle was carved from matching rock that glowed with a green light, like a haunted moon. Around it, the trees leaned in, spindly and petrified. At the base of the castle was a small shadowed doorway.

I was staring into the threads of that woven threshold when I heard someone behind me clear their throat. I whipped my head around in a panic.

A tall slender devil leaned against the threshold of the room, hands in his pockets. Something about the long, grayish-white hair spilling down his shoulders seemed familiar. It almost reached his hips, thin and straight behind the tilt of his lean. I froze as he looked me up and down. He pulled his hands from the pockets of his charcoal pants, and crossed his arms across the dark green vest he wore. The black voids and glowing, yellow irises of his eyes scanned me curiously.

I swallowed a lump in my throat and his infernal eyes narrowed.

"What ... *are you*?" he crooned.

A puff of arcane smoke and he was closer, towering over me. He lifted a piece of my hair towards him in examination.

My heart started thundering in my chest. Thoughts of Victus crept back into my mind with this unknown devil taking interest in me and getting too close.

"You are a mortal? Are you a *pet*?" He flashed an amused, fanged smile across his ashen bone-like face.

"D-don't touch me!" I pushed his hand away, and felt my body rattling again. I took in deep breaths trying to calm my fear.

He laughed. "Darling, you have the wrong idea," he said flatly, dropping my hair. "You're not *my* type, unfortunately."

"Silas." Leander's voice came from the threshold to the room.

The devil's eyebrows raised. He turned to look at Leander and smiled. "How did you work out getting a pet like this one?"

"She's not a pet," Leander answered. "Her name is Reign, and she's my *soul mate*."

Silas's eyes widened as he looked back down at me. Whatever amusement his face had held was completely gone and replaced with a deep sadness. His gaze shot back to Leander and he started walking towards him, completely ignoring me.

I exhaled in relief at the shift in attention.

"We need to talk about what the hell you've done," Silas muttered, and linked arms with Leander, pulling him away from the room.

Leander rolled his eyes, which comforted me. At least they seemed friendly. I followed them out to a parlor where we gathered at a small tea table and imps appeared around us. My anxiety lessened a little more as they started preparing kettles and filled teacups.

My gaze caught Leander's.

"It's okay," his voice caressed my mind. *"He's a dear friend."*

I smiled at Leander slightly as my chair was pulled out by an imp, and I took a seat at the table. Had this devil ... been one of those in my dream?

CHAPTER THIRTY-SIX

Silas tapped his fingers on the table, staring at me.

Leander broke the silence. "She knows she looks like her."

"Great, that makes this only *slightly* less awkward," Silas said curtly. "Why and exactly how did you manage to arrange this?"

"I didn't arrange it. Remodeus made her using the soul fragment I was saving." Leander paused, crossing his arms. "He's clearly trying to torture me."

Silas flicked his eyes between the two of us. "You don't *look* very tortured. In fact, I'd say you seem pretty content with the situation." His eyes stopped on me and widened with a saccharine-sweet smile. "Tell me darling, does he let you have your mortal sleep at all?"

I shifted and he chuckled.

"Silas ..." Leander warned. The red glint in his gaze made Silas roll his eyes and sip his tea.

I looked up at Silas. "Are you a prince too?"

He smiled and he set the cup back in its saucer. "Allow me to properly introduce myself. I am Prince Silas of the Ash Circle. I am also one of your ... *soul mate's* closest friends." He leaned back in his chair.

I examined him for any tell or distinction, that he might be the one Leander spoke of. The one filled to the brim with terrible experiences like I was. If it *was* him, he had masked it all under the playful cantor he continued with, despite the darkness that flickered between the glow of his eyes.

"Which is a rather important distinction because us princes definitely don't all get along." He stared at me for my reaction. "Am I the first prince you've met, besides Leander?"

"No ..." I replied. "I've met my father and, more recently, I met ... Victus, who I guess is kind of like my brother."

"Oh?" Silas replied as more tea arrived from the imps, poured from an onyx stoneware kettle. He lifted the cup to his lips. "How did that go?"

"He tried to kill me."

A smile curled across Silas's face. "Get used to it, darling. Playing games with *devils* often results in *someone's* death." He took a sip of the tea. "I'm surprised he didn't just drain you."

I blinked in confusion at how he'd used the word *drain*, and was still pondering when a squat imp placed tea in front of me. I smiled at the imp, but glared down at the cup. It couldn't possibly be safe.

"You can drink the tea, my dear."

I glanced up at Leander and then down at the teacup. Reaching out, I lifted it to my mouth. The tea was deep orange, aromatic, and filled with a citrus and spice flavor.

"Should I make him leave?" Leander purred in my mind.

I glanced up at his face again and saw the corner of his lip upturned slightly, exposing the small tip of a fang. Was he choosing now of all times to flirt with me?

"Yes," he replied to my thoughts, and I tried to hold back a smile. This was what I got for loosening my restrictions ...

I glanced over at Silas again to find he was watching us, a bored look on his face as he rested his chin on his palm.

"Primordial Father, spare me ..." he muttered. "I already regret coming here." He sighed, sending a knowing glare to Leander. He could clearly tell we were having a side conversation without him.

"Why did you come?" Leander said.

"I heard you transformed last week and now there are day and night cycles in the Fire Circle ... I was surprised." Silas swirled the remaining tea in his cup around. "Especially considering the last time you did both it was—oh, when was it?" Silas's tone shifted from dramatic to harsh as he continued, "Oh right, when you were *slain*. How could I forget?"

My stomach turned as I realized Leander had not transformed into the hellhound form he had used to save me since he had been slain by Lumoniel. How hard must that have been for him? I also hadn't considered how long this circle had been without night. I wondered how the other residents of this plane felt about the day-night cycles? Was my being here a burden?

Silas continued, "Though I suppose if Victus tried to kill your *dear mortal soul mate,* I can understand why ..."

"I will deal with Victus," Leander growled.

"I'd like to watch when you confront him. I'm sure it will be quite the spectacle," Silas crooned before finishing the rest of his tea. He turned to me and smiled. "Darling, if you'd ever like to visit the Ash Circle, simply command your soul mate to take you there. It's not much to look at, but we still have fun. I can show you my ash collection." His smile turned wicked.

Silas shot a glance back over at Leander and held his gaze for a few moments before he puffed away in a cloud of gray arcane smoke. I knew the look. A *Mindtell* exchange.

Leander took a sip of his tea before lifting his eyes to me. He narrowed his eyes like he was focusing on every edge of me he wanted to touch. The gaze he'd been using when we were alone.

"I didn't know you had not transformed since ..." I fidgeted with my cup.

He smiled. "I never had a reason, to be honest. It's quite a grotesque way to exist, and it's hard to get around when you are that *large*," he said playfully.

I smiled back, imagining a large hellhound trying to do something as mundane as drinking tea.

"I guess ... Silas also knew *her?*" I said timidly. I wanted to seize the opportunity to start the conversation about *her* and the letter.

"He met *her*, yes. She had stayed here a while during that dark time, as did Silas."

"I saw the note on your desk," I waited for his reaction.

He smiled softly. "When I realized I'd left it out, I was wondering if you did, but I didn't quite catch you thinking about it these past days. I've been trying not to abuse the power you've given me because I like to hear those divine little thoughts of yours come through your lips more."

"Can you tell me about the letter?" I looked up at him from my tea, trying to hide my coy smile at his remark.

"It was a letter she gave me over ..." he paused, tilting his head in thought, "nine and a half hundred years ago, give or take. She enchanted it so I could not open it until its conditions were met. Sort of like a contract." He rubbed the handle of his cup. "So ... the night after you and I first kissed, I tried to open it. It practically fell open and when I read what it said I ..." He swirled his cup as I watched some kind of memory move across his face.

"How did she know about me? And how did she know I was going to be mortal?" I leaned into the table. "And why did she write it in the common language?"

He laughed. "Was it in common for you? Guess you need to keep practicing your Infernal," he teased.

I gave him a playful scowl, narrowing my eyes.

He relented with a sweet look. "The enchantment allows it to be understood despite the reader's language."

I blinked. That was possible? Did she have a book I could read on primordial magic?

"To answer your first question," Leander continued, "she said nothing about you until the letter. So it was a surprise to me as well that it seemed so specific. By all physical appearances she was a devil, but her primordial magic felt as if it were dipped straight from the well of cosmic chaos. Like the divine. Perhaps she had been keeping herself secret, and with the Primordial Father and Mother both absent, she felt safe to come out of hiding. But I'd seen what she could do, and if she was divine, then maybe it was foresight."

I looked at him, tilting my head. "So you're telling me you were in love with a *goddess*?"

"I never said I was in love with her ..." he muttered.

"It seems pretty obvious to me."

Leander narrowed his eyes at me, the devilish smile creeping across his face. "Are you jealous?"

I smiled, setting my teacup down and resting my chin on my hands. Perhaps I should try to read his mind and learn what he was really thinking. I stared into his glowing, infernal eyes and stretched out my metaphysical fingers. His grin turned even more wicked as I touched the outside of his consciousness. Primordial magic glittered at my fingertips, then my hands sunk in as he opened himself to me. The hot feeling of thoughts rushed into me, flooding my mind. Through all the chaotic and unfiltered words, the general theme I could put together became clear.

Let me show you why you shouldn't be jealous—let me worship you—let me taste you—let me devour you—

I quickly retreated into my own mind as my body heated. His wicked smile remained. I needed to change the subject before I forgot why I had wanted to bring this up. "There is something else I wanted to talk to you about."

His expression softened. "Yes, my dear?"

"When we made the promise to unite our souls ... I didn't know my grandfather wanted to kill me and use your soul as a spell material in Chronomancy."

"What does the threat of your grandfather have to do with whether or not I give you the ultimate pleasure of uniting our souls?" The velvety words rolled out like it was a divine directive given to him.

My non-rational mind questioned if it really did have anything to do with the topic. Especially since the thought of it ... my cheeks burned again, the heat from a few moments ago swirling in my body, funneling to rest between my legs.

"Well ..." I began, adjusting my seat and trying to push down the desire building that was working to dissuade me from this conversation. "I think it increases the possibility my soul will be torn from you and you'll suffer unimaginable pain."

"Would you hesitate if your life was not in danger?"

"Not really ..." I mumbled.

His eyebrows turned up, and he flashed a fanged smile. "I've already felt unimaginable pain. I can accept the risk that you could be a future cause, but at present you are my cure." His infernal eyes slid across me. "You are an unusual mortal."

I raised my eyebrows. "Care to explain why?"

"Mortals tend to be fixated on the short term, on how they might take and enjoy life immediately, because ... their lives are so short and fragile. They don't know how much time there is before they enter eternal oblivion."

What a poetic way to describe death.

He continued, "But you seem to acknowledge a sense of how much time you may have with this threat, and yet with that urgency you are hesitant to take anything."

I stared down at my now empty teacup. "I'm hesitant because our fate, even if everything goes right, is that one day I'll be in that *eternal oblivion.* It'll be the blink of an eye for you." My heart broke as I spoke the words.

Leander observed the place setting silently as if searching for the right words himself. "When I had my soul split," he said, "I didn't imagine my soul bond would be with a mortal. I just imagined what having a soul mate would *feel like.* To look at another and know with every piece of me, that I was for them and they were for me. I wondered how it would work, though. How do you just decide to have a bond like that and it works out? I *stopped* wondering about it ... the first time I saw you."

I felt my heart beat faster in my chest.

His burning orange gaze locked on to me as he continued, his voice caressing me. "In the end I didn't get to choose, but I couldn't ignore that it felt exactly how I thought it would. You were standing there, only six feet away, and I couldn't explain why ... but I felt like I *belonged* to you. Once I stopped denying what I was feeling, I realized these moments—*the blink*—it's more than worth it. It's everything I exist for. Even if you refused to unite with me, and death came to break the weaker form of our bond, it wouldn't have kept me away from you. I would have found a way to bring you back to me or followed you into that eternal oblivion."

My entire life I'd felt the pull of the thread. Despite all the theories on why and what it was, one thing had always been a certainty. How the thread had made me feel. How his *soul* had made me feel.

"I understand what you mean," I started. "Understanding and embracing how this connection felt and where it drew me has always been guiding me, as long as I can remember. I thought it was going to be my father I found at the end of the thread, but it was really *you* I found. I'd built up this plan and these fantasies around what I'd do when I reached the end of this relentless tug, assuming it was my father. But ever since I found you, you are all

I can think about ... all I want to think about." I blinked, looking down at my lap, before lifting my gaze back to him. "Now there is so much happening, trying to tear me away from what I've found with you. I wish ..." I trailed off, head tilted down to the place setting.

Leander stood up from the tea table and walked around it to my side. "Tell me what you wish for," he encouraged in a tone that said whatever answer I provided, he would find a way to do it for me.

"I just want to be free," my voice cracked.

I felt his finger drift delicately under my chin as he lifted my gaze to meet his. His orange, glowing irises blazed at me, with more than just the usual desire to touch me. They held something deeper.

Pure, burning devotion.

"You will free yourself." Leander's voice was deep like when he commanded those in his service, but for me it lacked that arcane lacing and delivered more like a promise—for a future he would help me fight for.

He shifted his fingers to slide along my throat, his hand turning to grip my jaw, just like he had the first time we'd kissed. He pulled me up to stand against him, his other hand sliding around my waist and gripping me tightly. I couldn't help but let my eyelids fall slightly and my mouth part open as his fingers tightened around my chin. When he touched me like this, the thread between our souls was like a wild arch of energy. Pressed against his warm body, I looked up at him, silently begging. He licked his lips and spoke again.

"Will you command me to be your weapon? I would be delighted to be your means of liberation," he purred into my face.

I melted into him. My heart pounded as I clutched onto his white linen shirt and savored how wonderful it felt to be so close to him—intoxicated by his smoky cinnamon scent, pressed tightly against his warm, hard body, the thread thrumming chaotically between us.

A smug, devilish smile curved across his face as he narrowed his burning eyes at me. "You can't even form a thought when I touch you like this, can you?"

I laughed, grinning.

His eyes drifted down to my mouth. "I enjoy seeing your cute, little fangs. I wonder what they'd feel like pressed around my cock."

My cheeks burned as I tried to hold back a smile. "Right now?" My voice was dry, like my body was starving for him.

He smiled, acknowledging I had just given him his own words back from when we promised to unite our souls. He leaned closer—but a heartbeat later, footsteps sounded, entering the room from the passageway behind me.

"Mistress!" Emrys raced into the room. "I found the sugary confection you wanted! The one with rare pink strawberries and cheesecake!"

I turned around and saw Emrys grinning, holding up a platter with a slightly yellow cheesecake crowned by a ring of alternating red and pink strawberries. I had commanded him to find it in Novus as something to do, because he had been feeling useless lately.

"*Get out,*" Leander growled.

The guttural vibration of the *Command* made me a little wobbly as it resonated through my body. I turned swiftly back to Leander. "Be nice to him! He did what I asked him to! Besides, he's not *yours* to command anymore."

Leander's expression was that of agony, the kind that comes from being edged away from indulging a desire so many times.

I shot him an empathetic look before flipping back around to Emrys.

He looked terrified, clutching the cake platter.

"Thank you, Emrys! This is the exact cake! How did you find it?"

I extracted myself from Leander reluctantly and began walking towards Emrys. He led me to one of the dining rooms, chattering about his endeavors. I could feel Leander following closely behind me, his eyes burning holes into my backside. The story about how Emrys had acquired the cake was quickly drowned out by Leander's velvety, caressing voice.

"I'm not finished with you ..."

I turned my head slightly, side-eyeing him with a devious smirk. "I know ..."

"You can make it up to me by letting me eat this cake off any setting of my choosing," he purred back.

I stared hard at the back of my familiar's head. I didn't want Leander to see the expression on my face. One which said I was imagining where he'd choose, and it was making me burn hotter.

CHAPTER THIRTY-SEVEN

We took seats in a small dining room brightly lit from large windows on one side. Emrys placed the cake at the center of the table, transferring it to a gold-colored serving plate. Excited, I sliced a few triangles and eagerly passed one each to Leander and Emrys. Then I sat back down and pulled my slice in closer. I must have been nine or ten when I last tasted a cake like this one.

My grandfather had been hosting a reception for a few dignitaries, and there had been a buffet table of desserts. After they had paraded me around, I was ushered out. But, when one guest saw me eyeing the cake, he had made a comment. My grandfather only had to nod his head, and a servant had prepared a large slice for me to take to my room.

I took a bite of the cake in front of me now and closed my eyes as the flavor melted in my mouth. Both sweet and slightly savory—creamy.

I opened my eyes and caught Leander plucking one of the pink strawberries off his slice. He held it in his hand, examining it, eyes shifting between it and me. I laughed, realizing the pink strawberry was similar in color to my skin. Of course, I was not actually pink, but my pale red fit more closely with his strawberry than it did the ripe red ones.

His eyes shot over to me and the corner of his mouth tilted up. He lifted the pink strawberry to his lips. His tongue slipped out and licked the strawberry in a pattern strikingly similar to the one I recalled feeling from that dream. He took a sensual bite of the strawberry next, letting his lips push out against the flesh.

Two could play at this game. I plucked the red strawberry from my slice, the mate to his pink one. He watched as I lifted the strawberry with careful precision to my lips. I paused for a moment, flicking my eyes over at him. He was wholly still, as if he didn't want to breathe until he saw what I was going to do. I swirled it in the air before taking a huge bite, bearing my fangs as I sank my teeth into it.

He chuckled low as he lifted a bite of cake to his mouth.

Emrys didn't seem to notice our secret game. He was so captivated by the slice I'd given him that he had almost finished it already.

After swallowing, Leander spoke. "So, my dear, what shall we do first to set you free?" He grinned slyly as I took a full bite of the cake.

I finished another bite of my slice and lowered my fork to the table.

"I'd like to talk to my brother."

"Just talk?" Leander asked in a somewhat disappointed tone.

"No ..." I smirked back.

His own amusement curled across his face.

We finished our slices and placed a dining room chair in the center of the drawing room. I shook my hands, trying to steady my nerves. Leander noticed and took a few steps into me, cupping his hands around my own.

"You can do whatever you like to him. He won't think of trying to harm you." I felt him bring his lips to my forehead and kiss it.

The comforting feeling of connection between our souls melted some of the anxiety. I blinked slowly, looking up at him.

"I'll be right back," he whispered excitedly, before vanishing into a cloud of arcane smoke.

Several seconds passed, then a puff and swirl of smoke settled to reveal Victus with Leander behind him, gripping his arms. He forced the struggling devil into the chair and snapped his fingers. Victus strained against the magic, but he was completely immobilized by what Leander had cast on him. I looked him over properly in the room's light. Victus's eyes glowed red—like mine—though his complexion was a little more red than our father's.

I trembled under his gaze—then I noticed a scar at the base of his neck. The place I had stabbed him.

Leander took a few steps around the chair and stood at my back. The delicate touch of his fingers ran up my arms protectively till I felt him drop a kiss on the side of my head.

"Does he need to speak, my dear?"

"Yes," I replied softly.

Leander flicked his finger at Victus's face, and the spell he had cast fell enough to allow the movement of his mouth.

"Leander, I didn't know!" Victus shouted desperately. "Please, release me!" There was sweat beaded at his brows. He was terrified. Properly terrified.

The nervousness I had held before faded away completely. My memory of my father was gentle and kind. Perhaps if Victus was anything like him—how I hoped he really was—he would be too.

Victus began pleading again. "I didn't know she belonged to you! I would have never agreed—"

"Oh, you've only got it half right, I'm afraid ..." Leander took a few predator-like steps around me, placing himself behind Victus again. He lowered his mouth to Victus's ear. "You see, *I* also belong to her. All she needs to do is tell me she desires your head to be separated from your body, and I will do it to please her." Leander's finger scraped across Victus's neck, marking where he'd slice.

Victus twisted his face in a panic. He quickly re-focused his red infernal eyes back on me. "Look, I'm sorry. I thought you were just some mortal who made a pact with my father and was cursed to look like him. When they told me you had part of a devil's soul, I thought it was unusual, but I didn't really question where it came from." He whipped his head back, trying to look at Leander. "And I definitely didn't know you had some kind of *thing* with Leander."

I hadn't realized before, but his deep voice—it sounded so much like my father's.

"It's a little more than a *thing*," Leander replied, the deadly edge in his voice deepening. "You put your hands around my *soul mate's* neck." He pressed on Victus's neck again as a reminder.

Victus's eyes went wide with realization.

I stared at him, saying nothing.

Leander waited, eyeing Victus's neckline closely in anticipation of my command.

"What do you want from me?" Victus pleaded, eyes searching mine.

"You work for me now."

"What?" A confused and concerned look flashed across his face.

Leander's amused smile turned positively wicked in approval.

"*I, Victus,*" I recited, "*son of Remodeus, hereby recognize Reign, daughter of Remodeus, as my true sister. In fact, I will address her as 'Sister' henceforth.*"

As I spoke the terms, Leander summoned an enchanted parchment. It hovered in the air next to me. Each word I had spoken wrote itself on the tan surface in golden, arcane ink. Leander's infernal eyes blazed at me as he hung on to every word I uttered, continuing to outline the terms of the contract.

"I, Victus, from the moment of signing, grant my total and complete servitude to my true sister, Reign."

Victus's eyes bulged as I continued with more details.

I used every bit of my knowledge to architect an unexploitable contract. At the Midor's library, I had read hundreds of them when researching my own. I'd also heard my grandfather negotiate countless contracts and trade agreements to his benefit. I even included sections defining terms, outlining contingencies as well as exclusivity.

Victus seemed caught off guard by the level of detail I laid out in our contract. The way he leaned back in the chair and let his face go slack said everything. All of my excellence in academia and arcana came together as if I had been meant for doing this. I glanced up at Leander a few times as the length of the contract grew. His infernal eyes were blazing with awe and desire.

"Finally, servitude will terminate upon the death of Sir Bernard Vendelfrey the Third." I opened my hand and Leander, on cue, summoned an enchanted pen that fell into my palm.

I recognized it from a drawing I'd seen. These pens had been designed specifically to sign arcane contracts. The edges of the nib were intentionally razor sharp so that the signer's blood could be easily extracted. I took a step towards Victus and ran the nib's sharp edge against his forearm. He took in a sharp breath, acknowledging the pain. The clean cut quickly pooled blood that flowed arcanely through the opening in the nib, filling the ink well inside the barrel. Leander leaned forward slightly and released part of his spell's hold on Victus's hands. Then, I extended the pen towards Victus.

"You can't expect me to actually sign this!" he argued.

Leander growled behind him.

Victus jumped slightly. "I mean, what are you going to do if I don't sign it?" His eyes darted as far as they could to look at Leander.

"Oh ... I don't know," I crooned. Might as well continue on the vein of intimidating him. "If you won't sign it, I suppose that makes you useless to me. I never had a brother to begin with, so I can't say I'll miss you terribly."

Leander's sinister chuckle came from behind Victus before his sweet caress entered my mind. *"I love watching you behave so deviously sexy."*

I smiled, welcoming the tingles that his praise sent across my body.

"If I kill your grandfather, I am free from this contract?" Victus said.

I pointed out a paragraph on the parchment. "Section eight, sub article four dash A. The death of Sir Bernard Vendelfrey the Third must be the result of Reign's command. This includes executions by Victus's body, mind, arcana, manipulation, or will, regardless of intentionality or pre-meditation—with exception made for Reign's life being in immediate danger as defined in section four, sub articles one through five." I looked back at Victus. "And for now, I don't want you to kill him. I want you to continue working with him and tell me what he's planning."

He shook his head. "This is fucking ridiculous." He grabbed the pen from me, but grimaced as the contract floated down into his reach. His eyes darted across the words again and again, searching for some kind of loophole or misjudgment on my part. Resignation washed over his face as he realized it was airtight. His glowing red eyes shot back up to me. "I want to add an addendum."

I tilted my head at him.

"I want you to include language that specifies that the contract will terminate upon your death as well."

I scrunched my eyebrows at him.

"I know perfectly well why you excluded it. Don't forget that in the Blood Circle we're known for our contracts."

He was right. For devils, dying meant returning to the Nine Circles, which meant that as it stood now, the contract would hold to my soul, even in the eternal oblivion. The request seemed reasonable ... I glanced at Leander.

"It's not too late," Leander purred in response. "It's a lot less complicated to just kill him."

I pulled the contract back to me and added the addendum with my own wording. My death would need to be an act of the gods, and not anything Victus could convolutedly construct. Victus took a moment to look it over before sighing in defeat. He signed the bottom of the contract in his own blood, arcanely binding himself to its terms.

CHAPTER THIRTY-EIGHT

Leander sighed, listening to Victus explain that the Dark Echo was what wizard cultists called the Primordial Father. "What a ridiculous name."

Victus crossed muscled arms over the black silken tunic he wore. "I was confused when I was first recruited. I think they expected me to know him by that name."

We'd since released him and moved to more comfortable seating on the chaise and couches, forming a triangle as a group. Despite his sour demeanor, Victus carried the same dark aura and handsomeness all devil princes did, though he dressed more casually. Something about the way he carried himself made me feel like he was from a younger generation. He did resemble my father a lot—especially in the way his horns curled and the color of his glowing eyes. His hair was shoulder-length though, pulled back in a messy knot behind his head. Watching him sit there shifting on the couch, I noted how much bulkier he was than Leander.

Victus continued, "He speaks to your grandfather mind to mind across the planes, giving instructions. I don't know for how long."

"Mortal minds are weak," Leander commented. "He's likely an indentured drone, bent to do the Primordial Father's bidding."

"Do you know what his bidding is exactly?" I asked.

Victus gave me a withering glare, still clearly annoyed by this entire arrangement with me as his *Mistress*. "I was promised the Gisenwald family to drain in exchange for posing as Heinrich to hold you. I was told you had a fragment of a devil's soul that he needed, and infernal muscle was required just in case there were disputes about who would get that soul." He pulled his crossed arms tighter, and then said in a flat tone, "Which would have been no problem at all, had the fragment been claimed by any *other* devil." His eyes drifted to Leander seated across from me.

"Why does my grandfather even want to work with the Primordial Father? And why does he need my souls, and chronomantic knives?"

"He probably promised your grandfather some kind of wicked power as a reward. Typical tactics for mortal coercion," Victus mused as his eyes darted across the floor in thought. "I never saw arcane knives. I don't know what that has to do with anything. And I didn't really care what he wanted the souls for so I never asked. I was going to get what I wanted."

I blinked at Victus. "Wait, what does *drain* mean?" My eyes darted to Leander, who's lips began to curl in a devious smile.

The corner of Victus's mouth turned up. "I drink their blood. Human blood has a somewhat mild, intoxicating effect. However, the opportunity to slowly drain them while adjusting the flavor with the food they ingest and no interference, is a rare and pleasant experience."

I stared back in shock. He was going to *harvest* them? I looked back at Leander and he elaborated in my mind.

"It's a common practice of the Blood Circle. If you would like to try it, I would offer you my own blood." His eyes blazed orange at me.

Hell, despite how disgusted I was, when he said it like that ...

Victus seemed to catch our private moment and cleared his throat.

I flicked my eyes back to him.

"Are you going to explain to me now, *Sister*, why you have a soul bond with Leander, given there hasn't been a soul bonding made since before the Primordial Father's banishment?"

"Our father did this. I didn't know until recently."

Victus scrunched his face in disbelief. "No ... Father can't split devil souls. Only a god can do that." Victus shook his head, arms still tightly crossed. He glanced over at Leander. "What did you do?"

I glanced at him. Had *she* split his soul for him?

Leander tilted his head. "I met someone a long time ago that said they could split my soul for me. We were not sure if it would work. Clearly, it did."

"Are they still around splitting *more* devil souls?" Victus said in a concerned tone.

"No. She's gone," Leander said flatly, crossing his arms. "Nowhere on this plane, or any other accessible by our primordial magic. Trust me, *I tried.*"

Sitting between the two powerful devils meant their tension pressed in on me even though I was the one calling the shots. I shifted.

Leander offered me a concerned look. *"I'll tell you more when we're alone ..."*

Victus sighed. "So what is it you want me to say when I go back? I haven't seen your grandfather since I left him to deal with—that," Victus gestured at Leander, who responded with a sly smile.

"Say whatever will bring you back into his service," I replied. "Something about how you are so much weaker than Leander so you had to flee," I heard Leander chuckle, "but you knew you couldn't return unless you had something of use for him, which is the knowledge of where I am."

Victus raised his eyebrows, angling his face to the side in surprise. "You want me to tell him you're here? At Leander's palace?"

I shrugged. "He can't do anything about it. If he comes to this plane, Leander will kill him."

Victus turned to Leander. "Speaking of which, why didn't you just kill him when you had the chance?"

Leander narrowed his eyes. "Because my dear *soul mate* was choked half to death and I needed to bring her to safety first." His growled answer was a warning.

Victus looked back at me. "How long do you want me to stay with him?"

"Come back or send me a *Mindtell* when you know something worth sharing," I replied.

Victus rolled his eyes as he stood. He extended his hand and a gold-rimmed portal spun up right next to him. "Till we meet again, *Sister*." He gazed back at me for a moment before stepping through.

I sank into the plush velvet sofa, letting my head fall back. A sense of calm finally washed over me, and I breathed a sigh of relief. *It worked* ... Forcing Victus to sign a contract to serve me. I took in the ceiling frescoes depicting a variety of devils and whispered, "I guess I should learn more about the Primordial Father ..." My gaze jumped between the devil faces in the fresco and I wondered if any of them were the Primordial Father.

"That was very impressive what you did," Leander said, his voice velvety with sensual praise.

I sat up straight and Leander's eyes narrowed at me across the space between the seating.

The thread between us tightened, the pull from his direction willing me to come closer to him.

He continued, "I could hardly control myself. I found it very arousing to see you be such a dark, devilish Mistress."

Almost in tandem with the increased force of the thread pulling on me, I popped up from the sofa and took a few steps closer, till I was standing at arm's reach right in front of him. He stared at me with a lustful half smile, fangs just barely visible.

"You don't look very aroused. Maybe I should have tried harder," I teased.

His smile turned dark. "Don't take my word for it. Investigate for yourself." Leander shifted on the couch, spreading his legs slightly and leaning back, inviting me into his lap. This all day flirting ... I felt consumed by the need to touch him—to taste him—and quiet the undying ache that had formed inside me. Would it really be bad to just give in to all of it? I wasn't sure how much more we could endure before the tension ripped us apart.

I lifted a leg over each side of him, wrapping my arms around his neck and straddling him on the sofa. When I lowered my body down onto him, I felt the outline of his hard cock, restrained only by his trousers, pressing into me and the heat between my legs ignited. I leaned my chest closer to his and whispered into his face.

"Why do you keep telling everyone we're soul mates when we haven't united our souls yet? Isn't it a little premature?"

His hands slid up my thighs and along my hips, and, finding the edge of my blouse, his fingers pushed past the hem, caressing the bare skin of my back.

"Because ..." He ran those teasing fingers up my sides, deeper under my blouse. "It's inevitable."

I leaned into his heat and kissed him. Hell, I wanted to taste him—I opened my mouth wider and the thread surged at the way he immediately slid his tongue inside me. Tingles tricked up my back at his fingers dragging along my skin. I wanted more of him, but I had more questions.

"So," I said, panting, "are you going to tell me how *she* split your soul?" I nudged his nose with my own.

Leander looked off to the side, away from me. "I was not planning on going into detail on that part," he mumbled.

I didn't have to read his mind to guess what he was avoiding. I gave a sly smile. "You had sex with her, didn't you?"

He searched my face and then I felt him reach for my mind. So, I gave him a thought to hear.

It must have been great if you searched across all the planes for her.

Leander adjusted his jaw and flashed a pained smile before he offered weakly, "I'm sure you can understand, if uniting requires sex ... so can splitting."

"So, when the Primordial Father created soul bonds before he was banished, you all had to have sex with him?" I said with feigned innocence.

Leander blinked. "No ..."

"Ah, I see." I raised my eyebrows. I was teasing him more than anything. He had had a millennia to be with others before me. Being jealous of *her* felt weird. It was not like the mere possibility of me had even existed over 950 years ago. Besides ... she was gone, and had not wanted to stay with him.

"She didn't know if she could do it," he said in a low tone. "She had never split a soul before. But she had experience in soul mating because she had one herself."

"And she still had sex with you to help you split your own soul?"

"She said her soul mate had died, and she was trying to find a way to be with him again. To follow him into that eternal oblivion."

I could feel my eyes welling up, thinking about what it would feel like. To lose Leander, and have to continue on without him. It made sense why she'd said they couldn't be together in her letter. Putting myself in that position, I wouldn't have given up on finding Leander either—just like Leander had said of me. It made me wonder, was *her* soul mate relationship like mine and Leander's? Except she was the immortal one who lingered on after her *soul mate* had passed?

"If no one else could split souls except for the Primordial Father, when you realized she might be able to do it, you seized the opportunity," I summarized. Not really a question, but I was still so curious about his relationship with *her*, especially since she'd had accurate predictions about me.

"Sort of ... but there is a lot you have to learn about the Primordial Father's cruelty," Leander said softly, tucking a loose strand of hair behind my ear. He pulled me into his chest.

I nestled my body against his warmth, pressing my forehead into his cheek, and listened.

"I had not wanted the soul bond before I met *her*. Very few devils desired it. The Primordial Father would allow bonds to be made for love—like Silas had—but generally that emotion was considered a defect."

I stiffened at the thought of Silas suffering the loss of a soul mate. "Why create soul mates at all?" I blurted out.

Leander winced a laugh. "The Primordial Father constantly manipulated the chaos of the universe, trying to bring order to it. Primordial chaos is the god's well of power that we insignificant infernals scratch the surface of and call magic. He wanted to create the perfect being—perfect for killing and soul collecting—and he discovered creating the soul mates bond was a key to that.

"So, he forced soul bonds on princes when he wanted to craft a new powerful tool, free from the defects of their parents. It was like that for my father.

"My father was a First Prince, like Remodeus, the direct creation of the Primordial Father and Primordial Mother. But the Primordial Father observed emotional defects in him he did not like. So he decided he would breed my father, and then send him to conquer the Flame Rift, an elemental plane, to enslave its fire sprites to further wars in soul-carrying planes. Since the Flame Rift is a soulless plane, if he were slain there his soul would not be able to return to the Nine Circles. It would be an *immortal's death*.

"At the time, the Primordial Father had been rounding up all the powerful, resistant females for use in his machinations, and holding them in cells till they were of use. Other, more submissive females of power were allowed to roam ... for the time being. My father was given a choice between three female infernals—two devils and one great, feral hound of shadow—all selected for their magnitude of power and potential to produce offspring that could succeed the parents in ability. My father realized the hound was the only one to be formally imprisoned and chose her to at least give her freedom from her prison. The Primordial Father transformed her into a devil, created a soul mate's bond for them, and it was done. When I was born, the Primordial Father sensed my power and knew he had succeeded. But ... the Primordial Father was paranoid. He decided my mother would influence me against him, just like he blamed the defects in his creations to come from the Primordial Mother.

"So, after my father failed his conquest and suffered the immortal's death in the Flame Rift, my mother was kept around for only a few more years before he claimed her soul, returning it to the primordial chaos and giving her the immortal's death as well."

I stilled at the thought—for his mother to be taken from him so young. I pushed my ear against his chest and listened to his next words vibrate through.

"That cruelty permeates this entire plane. His manipulations of the primordial chaos hold it all together as its creator. But all power granted here is merely a manipulation of his, part of his goal to tightly control and contain his play things.

"When I returned to the Nine Circles after being slain in Novus, I was so bitter—having died, having both my parents taken from me, forced to be a toy—a weapon for whatever the Primordial Father desired. Then I met *her* ... She told me she also had a soul bond of love. She made me believe that seeking a soul bond for love would make the pain worth it. After we severed my soul, I'd hoped for a future that might have that kind of power to heal."

Listening to Leander's story made me realize how little I had known about him or even this plane. He'd spent so much of existence without me and had so much in his past. I found myself craving to know more.

I was about to ask when he tightened his grip on my body, squeezing me in. "I am worried ... about what it could mean that your grandfather is receiving communications from the Primordial Father. After a thousand years of quasi freedom, his return would be catastrophic. The Primordial Father can *Command* all of us. Force us to do his bidding. The moment he returns he'll likely want to resume using me as his weapon. He'll probably also break our bond. If he couldn't will it with half a thought, he'd kill you to do it." Leander's voice was raw as he said the last part.

I nestled my head into him to comfort him. "If the Primordial Father is banished to Abyssus, what about the Primordial Mother? Where is she imprisoned?"

"At the core of the Nine Circles there is a dungeon. It's where all the females with power who resisted the Primordial Father are imprisoned—where my mother was originally imprisoned."

"Can she do anything about it?"

Leander pressed his lips together. "She's a god just like the Primordial Father, but few, including the Primordial Father himself, treated her that way. Her only purpose to him was as a tool to produce the infernals of this plane, including the first princes. Even before she was imprisoned she lived a very isolated life."

"That's so sad ..." I whispered quietly. "No one will worship her?"

"Some do. Even if you did now, I'm not sure she'd want to answer you. Not after an eternity of solitude and abuse." Leander sighed. "We need to do something about your grandfather and sever the connection to the Primordial Father before this progresses too far. I don't know if Remodeus is involved in this as well, but he's able to nullify the contract until we ... *unite*. He may use that against us."

"What are you suggesting?" I sat up and looked at him.

His eyes narrowed on me, lips curling into that devilish grin. "First, I want to make you mine," he purred, leaning into my face.

Feeling the heat in his breath and the thread thrumming between us re-liquified me in his lap.

"After that ..." his fingers returned to the edge of my blouse where they curled around to my sides, gently caressing, "if you are satisfied ... we'll finish setting you free." Leander rested his forehead against mine, as his fingers splayed higher and around my back, drawing circles and dragging along my skin.

"So ..." I bit my lip, surfacing the words I wanted to use, "how do devils prevent the ... *breeding* part of all this?" I felt bad asking, wondering if I had completely killed the sexual tension between us.

Leander still caressed my back with his fingers.

I held my breath, leaning into that caress.

"There are never accidental offspring for devils. We use our primordial magic to prevent or ensure conception. It's why you've heard of the debauchery of devils, but only rarely seen their offspring. A leftover tool of the Primordial Father's control over his creations." Leander sighed. "If the Primordial Father did return, any male child of ours would be taken from us since we have a bond between souls." He paused for a moment, taking the seconds to continue gently caressing my back. "If it was a girl, then he'd give her the immortal's death or imprison her."

How horrifying ... Though I let out a little sigh in relief. "Okay, because there is kind of a lot going on right now and I could use fewer things to worry about. So ... please use your arcane birth control."

Leander's eyes erupted with heat, burning into me like flames. "Does that mean I can take you to bed?"

"Ye—" I barely got out the affirmation before the world slid out from beneath me and we teleported.

CHAPTER THIRTY-NINE

The familiar scent of Leander's room rushed in around me, and I gripped his chest—still perched on his lap—as my vision settled. We'd been teleported directly to his bed.

I heard him snap his fingers and arcane candles appeared, floating in the air around us. The yellow light brought warmth to the darkness of the room and I relaxed a little. I watched the embers of lust in his eyes, like the glow of a flame's tip before it deepened into a void of darkness, burn hotter as his hands under my blouse unfastened my bra. My heart started pounding, heat rushing to every sensitive area of my body. His hard cock pressed against me between our clothing, triggering my pooling warmth to tighten as he slipped my blouse and bra over my head.

Leander looked down at my exposed breasts in delight as his hands trailed closer to them, fingers running along the curve of each one. He leaned in and his guttural voice spilled over me, "Let me taste you."

The sheer power of desire in his words caused my skin to prickle, sending both of my nipples into stiff peaks. He let out a half-ragged breath at the sight of them. Before he could act, I started carefully unbuttoning his silk shirt. He pulled me closer at the brush of my fingers against his skin. Once I had his shirt open my eyes fell to the full expanse of his broad, sculpted red chest. A chest I felt the urge to stroke, lick, and—

Leander scooped me up by my rear, pushing me up to my knees, higher on his chest, where my breasts just so happened to align perfectly with his face.

He kissed the skin between my breasts, slowly working his way up one curve. My thoughts fluttered with sensations of the thread's pull, the weight of it increasing as it thrummed electrically inside me. I felt his lips wrap around my right nipple. And then his tongue dragged over it before his lips came together in a soft kiss. He left it bare for a breath, then closed his mouth over it again. Each kiss and lick sent a pulse down the thread, vibrating me to my core.

"Can you feel it too?" I shuddered. My entire body felt like it had tightened while I struggled to do anything more than just breathe.

Leander didn't stop kissing and licking, instead I heard his gentle reply in my mind, *"Yes ... I don't want to let go of you."* Even his mental voice sounded completely unraveled. *"I only want to exist like this."*

I replied with my own message to his mind. *"Stop teasing me ... I've been drenched all day thinking about you."*

He chuckled against the skin of my breast, and threw me down on my back in the center of the bed. "Is that so?" He grinned at me as his hands tore away my skirt and undergarments—and any other remaining articles of clothing—until I lay on the bed before him completely naked.

I curled my legs and tail at the sudden exposure to the air, writhing in wanting for the sensation to be replaced by his warm body instead.

Leander pushed off the bed, standing beyond my feet, and pulled off his unbuttoned shirt. He jerked his chin towards me with a wicked smile as his hands unfastened his trousers. "Touch yourself."

There was nothing arcane about it, but hearing him say the words stirred my insides with a burning desire to please him.

So I obeyed, sending my hand over my hip and between my legs. I spread them open slowly for him so he could see exactly what I was doing. I brushed my fingers over that *one particular spot*—where my nerves tingled at my touch. Everything heated as I swirled my fingers around that swelling knot of nerves. I moved my fingers lower, till my tips grazed the sleek wetness waiting for him. I glanced up at him, struggling to control my breathing, and watched his infernal eyes track up with my fingers swirling.

Leander clumsily fussed with the two buttons left restraining the hard evidence of his desire for me—what I ached to have fill me. He'd leaned forward slightly, slowed and drunken by the sight of my legs spread for him, doing as he commanded. His eyes were lit like two orange rings blazing in the dim room. I writhed again, tilting my hips toward him, silently begging.

I reached metaphysical fingers for his mind. I barely had to push before I was inside—he must truly be at my mercy.

"Do I slow down so I can watch her pleasure herself, or do I rip this off so I can fuck her senseless?"

I was about to give an answer when another thought floated to the forefront.

"Or do I want to feast on her first?"

He finally removed his trousers, setting free the thick length of what I'd felt pressing hard against me more than once today. My body quivered in response to the sight of it. I had expected a size that matched what I'd felt through his trousers, but now, seeing it ridged before me ... my mind was taken over by imagining what it would feel like to be stretched and filled by him. The heat from those imagined sensations rushed directly between my legs in anticipation. I felt the thread tighten and surge between us. So close to giving it what it wanted—what we wanted.

Leander crawled across the bed and my legs spread further to accommodate his body as the warmth of him poured over me. His head settled between them, one of his hands sliding down my inner thigh as he began trailing kisses across my knee. He slid his other hand exactly where he'd been staring before, and a finger circled before gliding into me just enough to feel how absolutely drenched I was.

"Fuck," Leander breathed into my knee. "Have you been aching for me like this all day?" The kisses trailed further and further up my leg as he pulled out the finger and then pressed back into me with two.

It was so much more intense than the dream as I felt myself stretch, flexing and wet, my body welcoming him in. This feeling alone had me moaning and arching towards him. It wouldn't take much more of this and I would come on those two fingers. I pulled my hand away, opening up the space for him to do what he pleased. I writhed in agony as the kisses never quite touched the spot I wanted them to. His eyes flashed up to me and his other hand trailed down my tail, as if he were recalling our dream together. He planted more kisses across my thigh as he twirled his hand, wrapping my tail around his forearm. I squeezed against him, and he pinned my hips into the bed. Then he descended, his hot tongue finally pressed into me, caressing the spot I'd been circling before.

I moaned, practically begging as he brought me closer to the edge. I gasped in air—could hardly breathe. I reached for his mind—or maybe he'd been listening already.

"Leander, please ... I want to come with you inside me."

"I am inside you," he purred back, unrelenting in his worship of me, fingers curling in and out.

"Please ... I want you ..."

"You seem to think I'm only going to make you climax once."
As he said it, he pushed the side of one of his fangs against the thoroughly swollen little spot he'd been licking, using it to apply pressure as he continued his ravenous swirling and sucking. I pulled at the sheets, trying to find something to hold onto as I arched myself against him. I could feel it, my body ratcheting closer and closer, that glittering edge of climax looming over me—

He kept me firmly pinned to the bed as my release tore through me. The room echoed with the sound of my satisfaction as wave after wave hit me. When the swell finally ebbed, I laid there panting, still deliciously tormented by the feeling of the thread dancing chaotically between us, not quite having what it wanted—what it craved.

He sat up, licking his lips, savoring the taste of me. He gripped my hips and pulled me down closer to him. I was still panting when I felt the tip of him pressing into me.

"Please ..." I begged again. *"Make me yours."*

He pushed slowly into me, leaning over to watch my face. Inch by inch he filled me, my body needing to stretch more to accommodate the size of him.

As I took him deeper, I felt the thread between us fall in on itself like a loop. It was like ... a circle, a closed ring of electric energy. Our souls flowed into each other and swelled at the wholeness of each being with its severed part. It felt incredible, like the meaning and purpose that each of us had existed for was to close this eternal ring and bring our souls together.

He pushed in till the thick base of his cock stretched me fully. I ran my fingers up his back, gently clawing. His voice—or maybe his thought—slid between the sensations.

"Make me ... yours, Reign." His words poured through my mind, bathing it in their caress.

"You *are* mine," I breathed into his ear.

He groaned, pulling himself out slowly to the tip, and then thrusted back into me.

I breathed out moans with each thrust.

"Summon your *Mystic Hand*," he purred into my neck. "I want you to climax so hard I can feel you clenched around me."

I obeyed again, using my practiced primordial magic to will the arcane hand into existence. It floated between us, sliding down my stomach until its spectral fingers went to work on the spot he'd just fully worshiped. What had been a chaotic dance of the thread before was now a wild current of energy wheeling between us.

I panted. "Leander ..."

He kissed the side of my face and neck with ferocity.

"Make ... me yours," I breathed between his kissing and thrusting. His fangs scraped along my neck as his claiming kisses became sloppy.

"You *are* mine," he growled over my skin. Then he continued in my mind, his mouth prioritizing kissing my neck. *"You are mine and I'll spend every second of my existence worshiping you."* He started thrusting harder and I clutched onto his back. I could feel the second release he promised me surging, each thrust filling me closer to one drop away from spilling over.

"Leander," I breathed, squeezing onto him. The loop between our souls blurred the lines between everything—our bodies, souls, and even our minds were one. I could hear his thoughts, *feel* his pleasure. My release teetered on the edge again, and I *felt* his own approaching release pouring into my mind. His cock throbbed as I enveloped him warmly. He felt on the edge of erupting, the tension building in him, his aching need to spill all of himself inside me, growing.

Feeling his pleasure pushed me right over the edge. I gripped him tighter, clinging to him, trying to get more and more of his cock to fill me. I came exactly as he said I would, *hard* and clenched onto him, bathing us both in waves of pleasure. I held on for dear life as the euphoria of the release slammed into me, each thrust amplifying the pleasure of it. My orgasm flooding his mind dragged him over the edge, and his shuddering moans spilled hot across my neck. I held him, enjoying the feeling his own euphoria in my mind, not wishing to let a single moan spill anywhere else but into my ear, my face, my thoughts.

He collapsed half on me, being careful not to crush me with his size. He nestled his nose into my neck, draping his own tired limbs across me. We breathed and panted almost in unison, trying to catch our breath. Everything felt so right, like this was how it was always meant to be. I rolled into his chest, pushing him onto his side. I didn't want this feeling to end.

Leander placed kisses on the top of my head. "Are you satisfied, my dear?"

I smiled, still panting. "For now ..." I teased.

"Oh, I see ..." His fingers trailed down my side before stopping at my hips and pushing me onto my back.

He leaned over me and started trailing kisses across my collar bones to my breasts. I couldn't do anything but be a blissful, shaking puddle underneath him. His hands pinned my hips and slid back down between my weak legs. I arched to the sensitivity his touch provided. My breath came in quickening pants as he kissed and touched all the places that were already at peak stimulation. A tingling heat rushed back into the space between my legs as he lingered there, soaking his fingers in what he'd just done to me. I still felt every part of him in my mind, his hungry desire to turn that *for now* into something that had me completely ravaged. Leander hummed across the skin of my breast in approval at what I knew was the feeling of arousal coursing through my mind and into his.

He pulled me on top of him so that I was straddling him. I could feel him, already hard again, pushing against me between my legs. His hands trailed caressingly up my thighs and to my waist. He stared up at me with blazing eyes.

"Do anything you desire to me," he said, his velvety voice spilling into the air between us. He drew circles on my bare skin as I sat perched atop him.

I smirked and leaned down to his chest, placing my face right in front of his. "Anything? What if it's boring?"

The devilish smile curved across his face, and his hands squeezed me. "Whatever you desire is my greatest interest, and therefore cannot possibly be boring."

The thread between us felt different now, less chaotic and more constant. It had me feeling glued to him, wanting to close that loop again, and again, and again. I lifted myself up, then lowered onto him, inch by inch, filling myself again. That loop between our souls wheeled with the pleasure of uniting with each other's fragment. I shuddered. It was like being poured over with a warm, electrifying liquid.

I placed my hands on his chest and rode him. Each bounce and movement I made had him gripping my hips tighter, brows furrowing, and he groaned underneath me. I re-summoned my *Mystic Hand* and returned it to that *particular spot* between my legs. It was so sensitive now that I barely had to touch it before I could feel my muscles tighten around him.

I felt his arousal pour into my mind. Me warmly wrapped around him, the tingling stimulation and pressure he felt with his cock being pulled and pushed inside of me with my movements. Though our shared pleasure began to blend, I could feel how deeply enraptured he was by what I was doing, how he wanted to still me with his grip and pound into me himself. How much he desired to hear and feel me climax on him. My core went molten in response to it.

I rode him harder trying to give him what he wanted. The combined feelings of everything between us sent us both tumbling into that abyss of ecstasy once again. I shuddered as the wave of my third orgasm rang through me. Then he did exactly as he desired, gripping my hips and taking over the percussion of our movements, grunting with each pound into me. I took each euphoric thrust deeper as it dragged out my spasming release, until he came again, spilling himself inside me with each slowed thrust.

I collapsed on his chest, panting, exhausted. Not even bothering to let his twitching cock exit my body. Our sweaty skin stuck to each other as I resigned to just breathing and melted into his chest. His hands roamed up my back, caressing the muscles.

It had been so simple—nothing adventurous or edgy—and yet the way it stimulated us both had been beyond understanding. No wonder it took the gods to fragment souls and create bonds like this. No wonder it threatened such total devastation upon separation.

Even now, with our soul mate bond permanent, and the potential threat of heartache later still looming, I did not regret it one bit.

CHAPTER FORTY

"We should probably leave the bedroom at some point." I snuggled my head against the side of Leander's chest as we laid across the sheets.

He ran a hand down my side in response.

Not only had we not left this room in three days, but we had foregone clothing for just as long. Leander would let me sleep, resting beside me. Then, as soon as I roused, his hands were trailing up my body and he started kissing every part of me. He commanded food to be brought to the bedroom and we routinely cast *Spotless* to clean ourselves. We explored each other's bodies and found several ways to invoke pleasure.

"As soon as we leave this room, I'll have to vie for your attention," Leander purred as he continued trailing those fingers down my hips to my thighs.

With every ounce of my being, it felt like I belonged to him and he belonged to me. As if the soul bond and constant sex were not enough, we also professed our love to each other verbally, spilling sweet words that I imagined would make the poets in the romance section of the Midor's Library cringe. I felt so many things with him that I'd never truly felt before. I felt desired, loved, and safe with him. I realized that growing up I had always been on edge at the estate. At Midor's, I was always the odd one out, rarely in a moment where I felt fully comfortable. Here with him, I felt like I could finally exist without any of those things weighing me down. I finally felt a sense of belonging and peace within our now unbreakable bond.

"All you have to do is look at me and I won't be able to resist," I said sweetly back, dragging my finger across his chest.

Leander shot me a sultry glance, the exact look I imagined he would use to unravel me. "You are right," he said. "Though ... there are a few things we should take care of while we wait to hear from Victus. For example, I think you should learn to use more of the primordial magic my soul provides."

I popped my head up. "Really? You think there is more I could learn?"

"We can certainly try," he said, amused by my excitement.

I lowered my chin to his chest and curled my lips, looking seductively at him from under my brows. "Will you be my teacher?"

His devilish grin smeared across his face. "I'll give you private lessons—but I must warn you that my instruction methods are very hands on." I felt his hands on me again, tracing the curves of my body, nearing my inner thighs.

"What spells should I learn first?" I said excitedly. Learning new spells had always been my favorite part of my schooling at Midor's.

"I could teach you *Command*, so you can arcanely command me to do whatever you'd like me to do to you," he purred, eyes blazing at me.

"Would you like it if I gave you *Commands?*" I raised an eyebrow, smiling at him. "Even though my arcane *Commands* are not powerful enough to actually affect you?"

"It doesn't matter if you use arcana or not. From your lips could come the destruction or the salvation of worlds and I would delight in seeing it done." Leander trailed his thumb across my lips as if he could see his waiting commands just behind them. He licked his lips, eager to taste them.

"Even *without* arcana, huh?" I lifted myself from his chest and crawled up his body. I thought about the many times I had made demands of him. Had he seen those as arcane *Commands?* Had it aroused him? "Tell me the first time that, when I ordered you like a command, it made you hard ... and aching for me." My words dragged with temptation, fully intending the statement itself to sound like a *Command,* despite the fact I had cast nothing. The way his eyes ignited told me he noticed.

"You licentious, devilish creature ..." His tone was purely wicked. He lifted his upper body to meet mine and his mouth drifted onto my neck.

I only grinned, waiting to hear his answer.

"My favorite was when we were in the dream, and you gave me the *Command* to dine on you ..."

I hadn't even used arcana to *Command* him, and yet it seemed to have ignited him. Would he survive me attempting to use my arcana to cast *Command?* I knew the spell already. It was a pretty common spell at Midor's. I knew he would not actually be bound by it as powerful as he was, but maybe he could feel it the way Emrys felt the intention of my commands as his Mistress.

"*Teach me to Scry,*" I said with arcana-laced words, casting the *Command* spell.

Leander pulled his head back from my neck, his eyebrows raised in amusement. A wicked grin plastered across his face as his eyes burned into me. "Of course, my dear ... What else would you *Command* me to teach you?"

I pondered a bit more. "When ... I met with the Exalted Sun, I got angry, and these little sparks appeared around my fingers. Do you think it's supposed to be lightning?"

"It could be. Lightning is not my style, but I could still help you learn to summon it." His hand moved lower and lower, down to my backside.

I tapped my fingers across his hard pectoral in excitement. "So, when can we go practice?"

"Hmm ... I'm not sure if I like all these *questions*," he purred.

I grinned wide, showing my fangs—something I knew he couldn't resist—and used arcane words again to *Command* him. *"Take ... me ... to ... practice."*

Leander's eyes drifted down to my mouth as he pushed me backwards and pinned me to the bed. Having his strong naked body holding me to the mattress sent my head spinning and my core melting. He smiled in satisfaction, acknowledging the effect he had on me and leaned in to kiss me.

"Change into whatever you like, including nothing." He brushed his lips over my nose and then back to my mouth again. "Then we will find a nice secluded place for you to practice your spells."

I squirmed out from under him, receiving small kisses of opportunity as I rolled off the bed. I quickly gathered my clothes to make myself at least decent enough to leave the room. Leander resigned himself to finally leaving the bed and began donning his own clothing. I noticed he intentionally left his shirt unbuttoned—and untucked—giving me a full view of his red, sculpted chest.

Maintaining my concentration was going to be a challenge, that was for damn sure.

CHAPTER FORTY-ONE

Thick, charcoal-colored trunks stretched up around us, branches arching to support foliage. Under the canopy, the forest floor looked dark-teal in the shadows. It was similar to a forest one might find in Novus, only everything was cast in that blueish-green hue. I looked up for a moment and admired the beauty in the contrast between those deep teals and the pink skies.

Leander had taken me into the forest outside the palace where we had been practicing for nearly two hours. I'd almost gotten the hang of *Scry*. I tried to learn to *Teleport*, but it felt just outside my grasp, the spell fizzling out just before completion. Finally, it came down to the one I had been the most curious about.

Lightning.

Leander lifted my hand, examining my fingers sensually by splaying them wide in his grasp. "What was the trigger that led your fingers to sparkle, as you said?" His lips curled as if he already knew the answer and simply wanted to hear me speak it.

"I was mad," I replied, teasing him with a curt response.

"But it doesn't happen every time you are mad?" He kissed my fingers before letting my hand fall. "I want to hear every detail. What did it feel like?"

I pondered the question for a moment. What had it felt like? It had felt wild, protective ... "I suppose it was more than just anger ... it was rage. It felt like a malevolent fire. Vital, like a heartbeat." I paused letting the solitude of the forest provide me courage. "The Exalted Sun was asking me questions about ... you. He wanted to know about your whereabouts, your soul collecting, your intentions."

Leander's infernal eyes glowed like orange embers as he closed the space between us. His hand slid around the back of my neck and he pulled me into his warm, bare chest. His face hovered oh-so close to mine, and his lips curled fully into that devilish grin. "And that sent you into a rage? So beautiful and deadly that you would have made him a martyr with your lightning?"

"I might have ..." I whispered.

"Why didn't you?" he purred. He tightened his grip around the base of my head, fingers curling and dragging across my scalp. The warmth of him spilled over me as he stroked the hairline at my neck with his thumb. I was doing everything I could not to give up on the lesson and beg him to take me in the woods.

I breathed deep. "Because ... they are just trying to protect their people, and the innocents of Brunalin. Should I have killed them for that?"

Leander held my stare in silence for a moment, then spoke softly into the breath between us, "Do you think if they were met with the innocent residents of the Fire Circle that they would make the same choice?"

I scrunched my face, finding stray leaves across the forest floor to hide the terrible thoughts that surfaced. They wouldn't spare any infernal creature. Even if they'd never left this plane, or collected a single soul. They would wipe them out without hesitation. I lifted my gaze back to Leander's. His eyes glowed at me, and I knew he'd heard the thought.

"That's why you are better than all of us, my dear ..." He kissed my cheek and spun me around so that he was behind me. His body pressed against my back, and he lifted my right hand in front of me. He splayed my fingers wide.

Ahead of me was mostly open area except for a few trees peppering a stream. Leander's lips lowered to my ear, and I stared at the large, gray tree growing on the bank of a stream as he instructed softly.

"First, think about how it felt physically when the sparkles appeared around your fingers. Not the rage, but the tingling in your fingertips. The slight sting of pain when the current arced from one finger to the next. The way the hair on your body stood on end."

I'd never tried to learn arcana like this. In my studies at Midor's we had to copy spells, outline rituals, acquire material, and practice. Over, and over, and over, until it was second nature. There was no emotion or feeling to it—that was more the domain of wild magic—a rare innate ability for channeling arcana through feeling instead of study. I wondered if wild magic and primordial magic were related in some way.

I concentrated, picturing what I'd experienced before at my fingertips. Then I thought of a storm. The air seconds before a strike—a sense of tension—energy waiting to discharge itself.

A spark popped between my fingers and it startled me.

I felt Leander's hands around my shoulders, squeezing me with praise. "Good ..." He waved his hand in the space in front of us and an illusion of Cyrus appeared, just in front of the stream. "Wait for the spark, then pull that rage from within, and throw it towards him. Think of it like a physical thing—a deadly arrow."

I stared at Cyrus. I would have used my lightning against Cyrus, but Cyrus was already dead. He was no longer a threat. I concentrated for a moment, trying to bring myself back to our last encounter. How he'd banished Emrys, how—

"Perhaps something more real ..." He waved his hand in front of us again and the illusion of Cyrus rippled, the arcane mist reforming into ... my grandfather.

I flinched backwards into Leander.

"It's okay, my dear," he breathed. "This illusion can help you overcome your fear, and practice defending yourself."

It was hard to control my shaking as I stared at the illusion of my grandfather across the clearing. He looked like he had that night Victus had strangled me. From how he shifted in place down to how he turned his head to scowl at me. I felt frozen. Every thought and feeling I had just practiced to summon the sparks felt miles away.

Leander's hands drifted from my shoulders closer to my spine. He gently rubbed there, releasing tension I didn't realize I had been holding in my state of fear. My muscles gave in to the warmth and pressure of his fingers. The man near the river was an illusion. I was safe. As my body loosened, I brought my hand out in front of me, pointing it towards the illusion. I started with the feeling of the sparks between my fingers and the raw elemental nature of it. Then, once a few crackles of the energy arced between my fingers, I dug down for the emotions, bringing everything to the surface.

The years of being forced into the shadows of the estate, only brought into the light as a demeaning focus of pity. The screams through the walls from servants who disappointed him. Watching my mother waste away in his service. His complete control and power over my life. I felt stings of pain and glanced at my extended fingers.

The energy was crackling out from my fingers now in erratic arcs.

Leander's voice caressed my mind. *"Set yourself free, my dear."*

I inhaled and then let go. I threw the rage like it were a physical object, hurled it towards that illusion. I kept my eyes wide so I could see it as it flashed out so fast. A single arc of white light bolted from my fingertips across the clearing and straight through the illusion, splintering a tree behind it and chaining out to the surrounding trees. A fraction of a second later, a thunderous boom rattled the forest, jolting me. I gripped the pain surging up my forearm, staring in shock at the pieces of tree and singed leaves falling to the ground. I turned my head back to look at Leander. That devilish grin was plastered across his face.

"Very good ..." he purred, lifting my chin upwards. "You seem to have an affinity for lightning."

I pondered for a moment. "I don't know why. Is lightning a common element in primordial magic?"

Leander shrugged. "I wouldn't say it's common, but some devils favor it." He leaned in closer and his eyes blazed on mine. "Would you like to receive your reward for doing so well?"

I felt my lips curl into the little fanged smile I knew aroused him in answer.

CHAPTER FORTY-TWO

I filled my days with practicing my primordial magic, translating and reading every book I could find about the Primordial Father, and memorizing random facts about the other Circles of Hell. For example, I learned that Silas's circle—the Ash Circle—was infamous for curses.

After finally getting a report from Victus, we set a meeting for the end of the week to discuss our plan. That meant I had one day left to occupy myself, and, if I was being honest, I was exhausted from all the arcana training, reading, and *bedroom activity* over the past week.

Emrys had been feeling neglected as my familiar—or was he my infernal servant? So this seemed like the perfect opportunity to spend time with him and give him *Commands* as he craved. I wasn't sure if the way I treated him was normal, but it was the way that felt right to make him happy.

The two of us set out to the shops by the lake to do some exploring. On the path there, we were met with the bustling crowd of infernal creatures—devils, mortals carrying an aura that made them seem somehow *other,* like Emrys, and creatures that looked as if they might have been bred from nightmares—who poured down the sidewalks and in and out of shops. No one paid us special notice as we walked between the clay-stuccoed buildings. I led Emrys along until a shop with a pretty black and red banner caught my eye. We slipped inside. Arcane lights dimly lit rows of glass cabinets and walls filled with baubles and trinkets.

Emrys and I turned down either side of a row of tall, four-sided curio cabinets. We caught glimpses of each other through the glass, smiling as our eyes moved from gemstones, to jewelry, to small metal statues.

I glanced up to the counter across the room, and my eyes went wide on a female devil reclined against a wall on a stool. I thought of how few female devils I had seen and remembered what I had only recently learned about the Primordial Father. How dangerous it must have been for them to even exist.

Her infernal yellow eyes flicked up at me from the book she was reading. She slanted her head, her shoulder length straight black hair swaying along her red face. "Can I help you find something?"

"I—" I whipped my head around looking for Emrys. "Nothing in particular, but I'm sure I'll know it when I see it." I smiled nervously.

Her eyebrows raised in amusement. "You like *games of fate?*" She closed the book and set it on the counter. "Want to play a game?"

My stomach sank as I observed her sinister grin. I couldn't forget—a devil was a devil after all. "What sort of game?"

She shoved her hands under the counter and brought out a red, velvet-lined tray. She snapped a finger and three objects appeared.

I turned my head again, looking for Emrys, and spotted him across the shop eyeing a table of herbs. I took a step closer to the counter.

The first object was a bone knife. Plain, save for the sharp end of it, which held an unsettling sanguine tint. The second object was a gold-chained necklace threaded through an amber pendant.

A shadow flashed within the amber, but as soon as I blinked it was gone. The last object was a polished oval fire opal with a simple carving of a single eye on the top.

I looked back up at her and her sinister smile melted into a softer one. I imagined she might use it to lure mortals into a false sense of security.

"The game," she tucked her hair behind one of her long pointed red ears, sweeping it around her short black horns, "is that one of these objects costs nothing. You may keep it, if you can figure out which one it is. You get one guess, but if you answer wrong," she narrowed her glowing eyes on me like a predator, "your soul is forfeit."

"Sounds like the game is actually knowledge, not fate." I tried not to shudder under her gaze as that soft smile melted to a frown. "So you are already lying about the terms?"

"Fine. It requires knowledge to play." She huffed. "Since you don't have such knowledge, go on *mortal*—make a guess."

She's not going to even have me agree to the terms first? I looked between the objects. I could sense they were all magical and wondered what they could possibly be. She hadn't said I couldn't ask questions.

"What does the bone knife do?"

"Is that your answer?" she crooned.

"A question is explicitly *not* an answer."

She scowled then pointed over each item impatiently. "The knife is a sacrificial implement of the Bone Prince, the amulet traps souls, and the stone is a sacred beacon of the goddess."

Goddess? I knew of two now associated with this plane. Which was it for?

She leaned over the counter. "Now, give an answer."

Was it a riddle? Why hadn't she said it was *free* instead of that it costs nothing. Was *nothing* actually something of meaning in the Nine Circles?

"Ooh!" Emrys came in from behind me, snatching up the eye-inscribed fire opal. "Someone gave me one of these at a festival one time!"

Okay ... so literally costs nothing then.

"The fuck is your problem, *Turned?*" the devil growled.

I watched the cheery nature in Emrys crack as his eyebrows turned up in a self-conscious pain.

"It's the sacred beacon of the goddess," I said shortly, turning back to the devil.

She huffed out a breath. "Take the rock, cheater. Maybe if you wish hard enough on it the goddess will transform your companion into a *real* infernal."

"You didn't specify that I couldn't receive help. Maybe *you* should have wished on it to be better at writing deals," I shot back. Seriously, a mortal walked into her shop and she used just about the weakest logic possible to try and entrap my soul. *I* could have written a better deal than that. In fact, I *had.*

I pulled Emrys out of the shop by the arm. Anything to put distance between us and her. We stepped into the warm light of the main street, and Emrys lifted my hand to slip the fire opal into my palm.

"It's pretty right?" He smiled weakly.

There was something in Emrys's eyes that told me the devil's reaction to him cut deep—really deep.

"Are you okay?" I tugged at his tunic.

His face softened, and he looped his arm with mine as we walked in the direction of the garden. "She reminded me of the life I had before, in Veldrasyl. Elves and drow harbor similar blind hatred towards each other."

It was hard to imagine such constant mistreatment of a kind soul like Emrys. The revelation broke my heart. "Is that why you left them?"

Emrys pressed his lips together in a half smile. "No ... I died."

My eyes widened. "What do you mean you died?"

"I may look like a drow, but when I died, so did that part of me. Leander found me after and bound my soul to him. It resurrected me, but while I looked the same as I did before on the outside, on the inside I became an infernal, bound to this plane in immortality. That's why she called me *Turned*. It's what they call infernals who were not originally creations of the Primordial Father."

She had said it with such vitriol, like she saw Emrys as lesser for what he was. It must be so isolating. "Does your family know you are alive?"

"No ... but it doesn't matter," he said a little solemnly. "I can't go back to how I was, so I belong here now."

I squeezed his arm, the fire opal in my palm. "I'm your Mistress now, and I'll do anything to make sure you are happy. Even if that were setting you free to return to your family in Veldrasyl."

"Being here makes me happy," he said with a smile.

I held the fire opal up in front of one of my eyes. "If I was the goddess, I wouldn't need to fulfill any wishes about you." I pulled the stone away to see him properly. "You are already perfect as you are."

Tears laced his eyes, then he smiled again. "As you command, *goddess*." He bent down to squeeze me in a hug before lifting me in the air.

I laughed clutching his neck. "After the garden, we should go back to the palace before I get into more trouble."

We strolled through the garden, then made our way back. After returning, I found my way to the library. The fire opal eye was stuck in my mind. I wondered if the goddess it's about, was *her*. I pulled a few books off the shelves, searching for the symbol among the words. I found plenty of references to wishes and the Primordial Mother, but came up short on any mention of another goddess or a fire opal eye.

After a few hours, I felt Leander's warm presence behind me as I pushed the books back onto the shelves. His hands slid immediately around my waist, and his sensual voice filled the space around us.

"Already bored of the outside world and here to study your Infernal?"

"Sort of ... Emrys and I went to a shop, and I was given a stone." I turned around in his arms to face him. I pulled the engraved, fiery opal out of my pocket and held it between us. I watched Leander's expression carefully. He definitely seemed to withdraw at the sight of the stone. I turned it over in my hands and continued, "The shopkeep said it was a religious beacon of the goddess." I looked up to find his playful expression gone. "I was trying to find out if it was tied to *her* by matching the symbol to ones in these books."

His hands felt a little cold as his thumb trailed my palm. "When she was here, she performed many acts of a divine nature—besides splitting my soul—that some saw. They made up stories about her over millennia to the point where a few small cults even worship her." He closed my hands around the opal, covering it. "It's why you won't see anything about her in this library. Things like this opal are a bastardization of what she was. The infernals who made this did not know her."

"What kinds of acts?"

Leander stared at me silently, squeezing my hands.

Did these memories cause him too much pain?

"Transformation, healing ..." he said quietly. "She was very powerful. More than Remodeus, who at the time would have had the greatest power. Because of my freshly-slain state."

"How ... could she know about me?"

Leander's expression softened a little as he held me there. "I am afraid we may never uncover the answer to your question." He let out a sigh. "If I am being honest, I do not care why. I do not want to think about the past, about her, or how she knew enough about you to write that letter. All I want to think about is the present, and you. Knowing how will not change anything for me."

Would knowing change anything for me? I'd never been involved with deities or religion ... it was all uncharted territory for me. I couldn't help but be curious.

I leaned into him. "I don't suppose it changes anything for me, either. Will you tell me what happened to her, though?"

He tucked hair gently behind my ear. "She left this plane behind to chase her own bond. If she really was a goddess, she might not even be among creatures like us in the Physical Planes. Or perhaps she found a way to reach that eternal oblivion."

"And you tried to find her?"

Leander looked down to the space between us. "I did. After 500 years I was strong enough to leave the Nine Circles again, so I traveled to different planes to see if perhaps she was there. I never found any evidence of her on any other plane. That was how I found Emrys, though."

"Emrys told me he had died." My voice broke a little as I recalled the conversation from earlier.

"I saw him die, actually. Elves cornered him and killed him. Likely internal quarrels between the courts of Veldrasyl. I did not ask. I had just arrived there and I thought perhaps having a guide might be helpful. So, I turned him to my service. It made no difference. I found no evidence of her there either." He tilted my head up towards him. "What else do you wish to know?"

"It feels a little weird considering your past with her ... but I wish I could thank her, I suppose. She split your soul, and she wrote to you about me ... She is the reason we have what we have now," I said, gazing up at him.

Leander kissed my forehead. "If she *was* a goddess, I do not want to question her will. You could try to pray to her if you feel compelled to."

I leaned in to squeeze him. I didn't want to question her will either. If she had the power to split devil souls and predict the future, she could likely undo it all on a whim. I'd never prayed to a deity before, but I closed my eyes for a moment and sent the thought out.

Thank you.

CHAPTER FORTY-THREE

Waking up every morning to the humming of the thread between us as Leander held me in bed, was a feeling I never wanted to take for granted. I'd spent too many nights and mornings before waking up with the leftover anxiety of the previous day. I'd sit with the silence of being alone, and with the fear of leaving my room.

So I'd spent the better part of the morning snuggled up with Leander. I had told Leander about the devil I'd met. He wanted to take me back and watch me torment her and other less powerful devils. I had hated how she treated Emrys, but the whole encounter had me feeling a little more hopeful this was a place I could find my own way in. There were still a few things that didn't work. I needed sleep and food, and Leander was more than willing to disrupt the entire order of the circle to give me things like day and night cycles.

By the afternoon, Victus arrived and we met in a large room with vaulted ceilings and an entire wall of made of stained glass windows. Bright light filtered in through the glass design—white flowers between long orange flames. Something about the scattered orange, yellow, and white light from the window brought a sense of excitement and hope to the room. A large table had been set up in the open space there where I sat with Leander and Emrys at my side. Victus sat across from me, slightly less sour than our last meeting where I had become his Mistress.

"I had to help your grandfather modify the instructions from the Primordial Father," Victus said. "He wants him to construct a portal, and your grandfather thinks he can use these ancient lodestones to do so."

I crossed my arms on the table. "And how do you feel about the potential of the Primordial Father returning? Is it worth a single, drained human family?"

He narrowed his glowing red eyes at me. "Can I actually tell you, or will you punish me?"

I straightened a little, pushing my hands into my lap. "I won't ever punish you for telling me the truth."

Victus stared back at me in surprise.

Was it common for those who served devils to receive just as many punishments as they did *Commands?*

He looked down and to the side before answering. "I never knew what it was like to live under his power, but I wonder if our plane has become weak without the guidance of a deity for the past millennium."

Leander cleared his throat. "Surely your father has told you about how it was when the Primordial Father ruled." Leander's stare across the table was sharp like a knife, as if to combat those awful memories.

"Not really," Victus scoffed. "It's not like we sit down and have story time."

"Well, allow me to stress, you do not want what you think he will provide," Leander said with a venom, eyes glowing hotter. "When the Primordial Father ruled this plane, we had no free will. We were all expendable, and he did expend us."

Victus lowered his head again slightly, signaling he understood Leander's meaning.

"Is it possible to destroy the lodestones?" I offered, changing the subject. "Prevent the portal?"

"I suppose it could be, if we can locate them," Victus mused. "Your grandfather was rather secretive about that part."

"How much time do we have before my grandfather is ready?" If I could just find a hidden detail, a loophole to exploit ...

"The last thing your grandfather mentioned was attuning a lodestone in his possession to the location of the Primordial Father in Abyssus. After that, they would collect the other lodestones to arrange around it, acting as an amplification to target him." Victus locked eyes with me. "That's why he wants your souls. As a mortal you are easy to sacrifice, and he will use your devil soul fragment to help attune the lodestone."

"The Lumoniel clerics thought he might want to use my soul fragment in a chronomantic ritual," I pondered. "But this sounds like a summoning ritual."

"Oh, that's the other thing ..." Victus grimaced. "Your grandfather formed an alliance with the Lumoniel Temple. He's got them all scared shitless that Leander will return, and they must prepare for some kind of brutal battle to keep him at bay."

Leander chuckled at the remark. I watched the devilish grin curl across his face, savoring the potential opportunity to reduce the temple to cinders.

Victus glared at Leander. "He's likely manipulating them so he has a force to distract you, to snatch her somehow."

The grin faded from Leander's face and was replaced by a dark, burning malice. "They will not touch her, or—"

"Yes, I know," Victus said flatly. "You'll incinerate the entire plane of Novus—or something else overly dramatic."

My mind worked. We needed a plan that was less likely to provoke any of these deadly outcomes. Could we really get close enough to the lodestone to destroy it? And where would he get the others?

"Do we know where the lodestone my grandfather wants to attune is?" I said to Victus. "Can we destroy it?"

Victus brought his hand to his chin to ponder. "I didn't realize that's what it was at the time, but a while back we destroyed ancient arcane glyphs in one of those human buildings. The lodestone was buried below the foundation and they had to dig for it after the glyphs were dispelled."

"Do you mean Merchant's Hall?" The building Freda and I had seen the smoke rise from upon returning to Brunalin. That meant the attack we thought had been simply a distraction to steal the chronomantic knife, had contained a dual purpose.

"Yes, that is the one," he confirmed. "My guess is it was always there and the building just happened to be built over it. Like I said, these stones are ancient." Victus's eyes caught mine. "It's not like one of your mortal lodestones you can fit in your palm. These are massive, weighing at least twenty tons and occupying the space of an entire room. Last I heard, your grandfather was still trying to work out a way to move it."

I pondered for a moment how one could destroy a large arcane stone, then I glanced at Leander. His eyes were wide and unfocused. He blinked and looked at Victus before turning to me. With a snap, a small scroll of paper with writing on it appeared between his fingers.

"Freda just sent a Calling Card," Leander started in a worried tone—but I snatched the parchment before he finished.

Reign
Someone following me
Help
Oh no ...

I stared back at 'n' in my name that trailed off as if she'd barely been able to write it. So few words. So few words like she'd been running—or hiding just long enough so she could burn the card. We had to go. Had to do something now.

"Where is she?" I demanded of Leander.

"I don't know. And I don't know her well enough to find her with *Scry*." He looked down at me. "But you could."

I turned to Victus. "Did you know they were planning to take Freda?"

Victus raised his eyebrow. "Who?"

"She's my friend—the human with me when you abducted me." I set the paper on the table. How could this be happening?

Victus's eyes lit up. "The one with the sanguine hair?"

I leveled a flat stare at him.

He shifted in his seat before continuing. "I didn't know she was part of this, and if they spoke of her I didn't realize ... I *can* tell you it's likely a trap to lure you in for the sacrifice."

"And it's going to work, because we can't leave her with them!" I had raised my voice, but I was more angry at myself. Why hadn't I seen this coming? How stupid could I be to think nothing would happen to Freda while I selfishly hid away on another plane?

I felt Leander's voice caress in my mind, *"This is not your fault, my dear."*

I turned to face him and felt the tears welling up in my eyes. My closest friend, who didn't deserve to be wrapped up in this at all, was being harmed—used simply as bait—to capture me. My grandfather had made threats before, alluding to the life of my friend being optional. Had this been his plan all along? I pushed the thoughts down and began picking through the possibilities. I *would* get her out of this.

"We will not outsmart my grandfather if it is a trap," I said. "I think whatever plan we come up with, we have to use it to play right into his hand, and win by overpowering him with sheer strength."

Emrys, who had been quiet until this point, finally spoke. "Mistress, please allow me to go rescue her. I will kill anyone who brings harm to her."

I sighed. "I would, Emrys, but they will just banish you here like they've done before."

Leander leaned forward. "Actually, if we open a portal between planes with Emrys in his current form, he will be just as difficult to banish as any infernal creature of the Nine Circles."

"It's true," Victus confirmed. "The only reason I could send him back was because you summoned him using the familiar spell. It's a weaker form, with many limitations. As a true infernal, he can do much more."

My heart melted at *true infernal*. Victus did not share the perspective of the devil in the shop. Somehow I trusted him more for it, to know Victus didn't think of Emrys as any lesser despite being Turned.

"We will go together then," I said. "We can go through the portal, and then I'll scry on Freda—then find her, rescue her, and teleport away. Two devils, one infernal, and one wizard. Surely that's enough to save one human?" I laughed nervously.

"Honestly, with him," Victus shot a glance at Leander, "it's probably overkill. But your grandfather has not spoken to anyone about what other things the Primordial Father whispers to him from across the planes. While he hasn't asked me to do anything specific, he is surely planning multiple scenarios in which he claims your soul fragment."

"Then we don't give him time to think any longer." There had to be a way to Freda quickly. Had to be a way to catch him off guard.

Leander looked at Victus. "What does your father think about all this?"

"He's not interfering unless the plot becomes too viable. He hates dealing with humans and traveling away from the Nine

Circles. I'm sure once he realizes my role in this, he'll find some way to make my life a living nightmare."

Was our father really like that? I hadn't considered confronting my father or trying to enlist his help in all this. I'd become so enraptured with Leander, and the true meaning of the pull of the thread, that I'd not thought about him. If he really disliked leaving the Nine Circles, perhaps the reason behind our one past encounter was as simple as that. Still, anxiety fluttered through me, and I realized I had developed a growing fear of meeting him and discovering the truth.

I looked back at Leander. "You said you'd be a weapon for me. I don't want you to *burn the plane*, but I need your help to save her. Please." The truth was, as a target and as a mortal being, I couldn't do this on my own—or at all really. I would try, but I needed these great, immortal infernals. Without them, it would be hopeless.

At my request, Leander's eyes flickered like molten rock ready to erupt. It said everything. He would do anything, including lay waste to an entire plane, for me. His next words were soft and reassuring. "We will go tomorrow, my dear. There are some things we must do today to prepare." Leander stood from the table and approached me.

"But what if they are hurting her now?" Every minute that went by felt like I was being ripped from the inside out.

"I will send her a *Mindtell* now, and we'll make sure she's okay. If this is a trap, we need to be prepared. I must make sure you will be safe," he said softly.

"Say it out loud so I can hear it." Please, please let her be okay.

Leander closed his eyes. *"Hello, Freda. Reign has received your message and would like to know if they are hurting you—"*

I poked at his sides, "Ask her where she is!"

"—and where they have taken you." He opened his eyes and leveled a flat stare across the room.

I leaned forward. "What did she say?"

Leander sighed. "She says she was dragged to a holding cell."

I blinked slowly in suspicion. "And that alone made you make that face?"

His eyes slid to me. "She also told me to be a *good dog* and get her the fuck out of there."

Victus broke down into chuckles before I could. I was relieved though. She wouldn't be making jokes like that if she was not okay.

"Alright ..." Victus drummed his fingers on the table. "What commands do you have left for me, *Sister?*"

I knew I'd made it part of the contract to call me that, but I couldn't help but smile. "Stay here in the Nine Circles, and tomorrow we'll leave together. You can go home or stay at the palace, if Leander allows it." I glanced up at Leander.

"I don't want to hear what goes on here at night, so I'll be returning to the Blood Circle," Victus said with a sigh.

Emrys faced Victus. "It's not really that bad! In fact, most nights it feels lonely and unsettling if you can't hear Mistress in the throes of ecstasy."

My hands flew to my face as it heated.

Leander pulled me up and into him, as if trying to shield me from the embarrassment. His dark voice dripped like honey over my mind, the heat of the embarrassment swiftly shifting to arousal, *"I enjoy knowing that how much I pleasure you is heard through these walls. I want everyone to know I've made you mine."*

"Hell ..." Victus complained as he stood and teleported away, leaving behind only a puff of gray arcane smoke.

CHAPTER FORTY-FOUR

I waited in one of the sitting rooms for Leander the next day after doing all I could to prepare myself. We would be meeting the others soon to return to Novus, but he'd said he had something he wanted to give me first. I waited on the soft black chaise alone for a few moments, looking at my button. I wished I'd asked Victus if he knew what it was. I tucked it back under my shirt on its necklace, when Leander slipped through the doors and shut them behind him again.

"It took longer for me to prepare it than expected," Leander sighed. "How are you feeling, my dear?" He sat next to me on the chaise. Every time we were close like this, every anxiety melted away—anything that would get in the way of simply feeling our souls swirl closer to each other.

"Maybe just a little nervous," I answered, wringing my hands. I had to shake these nerves away so that I could focus on rescuing Freda. "But if I am with you, I'm sure I will be fine." My eyes flicked to a box in his hands. "What's that?"

"This is what I wanted to give you." He pulled a chain link bracelet from a box.

It was made of gold metal, and it had a single black stone laid in a gold band set between two links. The black was absolute, but its glossy surface reflected light. It was beautiful.

"This is obsidian mined from my circle. It's been enchanted with shielding arcana. If you wear it, you can shield both physical and arcane attacks against you."

I leaned closer to look at the sleek stone. "I didn't know something like this was possible."

"Well ..." He pressed his lips together into a smile, "It only absorbs some of the attacks. Too much, and it will break. Then it must be returned here to be repaired and re-enchanted. Will you wear it?" He unclasped the chain, holding it open for me.

"Of course." I extended my wrist and he clasped the bracelet around it. I let him turn my hand over to see the obsidian resting against my wrist when he was done.

He stroked my skin round the bracelet. "It should only be used as a last resort."

"I hope you are not worried about me and that's why you are giving me this." I laughed nervously.

He looked down for a moment, then back up at me. "I *am* worried." His hand trailed up my forearm as he continued to speak. "I've never wanted, needed, or loved someone as much as I do you." His eyes searched mine. "If you are resolved to come and not stay here, then this may help if I fail you."

"You won't fail me." I grasped the hand caressing me and clenched it. I'd never seen him like this. Never seen him look worried, or frightened.

"Mortals are fragile, my dear. All it will take is for me to be distracted for one second. One second and your life can be taken." He said the words with a finality that only came from experience—the experience of taking mortal lives. The experience of dying.

"And you're still okay with me coming?"

"Part of aiding in setting you free is letting nothing else hold you, including me." The bite to his tone told me it was something he'd avoided acknowledging out aloud. It would be so easy for him to *Command* me to stay here. But I would gain my freedom from one individual just to have it transferred to another. And he knew it. This way ... He truly wanted me to be free.

"That's why I love you." I squeezed his hand and leaned in to kiss him softly. "I've never felt more free than in the time we've spent together. Soon, I'll be entirely free. I know it." I smiled, trying to reassure his anxiety. "And you will have helped me do it."

His expression softened slightly in response before something dark resurfaced. "If you find yourself on your own when we go, do not let death take you. I do not care what the consequence is," he said with a grave seriousness.

"The same goes for you!" I narrowed my eyes at him. "If you die, I'll find a way to return to the Nine Circles and kill you again myself." I smirked.

Leander started chuckling in that low tone that usually meant he was imagining how whatever I'd said could be turned sexual.

I brought the conversation back to the task at hand. "I suppose the next part is the hardest ... waiting for Victus to get here so we can leave."

That devilish smile I loved curled across his face. "I can offer you a distraction," he purred. His hand drifted to my knee and trailed up my thigh.

I shifted nervously. "But we're in a public room! What if someone comes in?" My body turned molten regardless of my words, thinking about his hands on my bare skin instead of over my clothing.

"This is my palace. Every room is mine to do whatever I wish." He leaned in and flooded me with his scent and heat. "But if it helps you feel more at ease when I fuck you over this chaise ..."

His other hand lifted, snapping his fingers, and I heard the lock on the single door to the room click.

I stared into his infernal eyes, waiting for him to act. He held my stare as I melted in front of him in anticipation. Was he waiting for me to act first? I gave him a wide-fanged grin and summoned my primordial magic.

"Make me orgasm."

His expression quickly shifted to pure, wicked delight. He stood and unfastened his trousers.

"As you *Command,* my dear."

CHAPTER FORTY-FIVE

"Ready?" I asked the group.

Leander, Emrys, and Victus nodded. Leander extended his hand and brought a fire-rimmed portal burning into existence. Through it, we could see the part of town we'd targeted—a central spot just outside the merchant district. The mirror-like surface rippled like water with humans bustling by, tall buildings, and the shadows stretching across alleys. One by one we stepped through, Emrys going first in his drow form, then Victus and I followed. But as soon as Leander set foot on the stones of Brunalin, high pitched horns sounded in alarm. Their steady, arcane warble screeched down at us, emanating from all directions.

Leander, Emrys, and Victus all doubled over, covering their ears in pain. The sound annoyed me for sure, but it seemed specifically designed to repel infernals. I looked around frantically for a place to slip into to draw less attention. People who had been occupied with midday shopping looked around at the sound of the alarm, then began running and pushing past each other. We linked our arms and I pulled each of them into an alley—only the sound seemed to follow the three of them wherever we went. Between the focused alarm and our combined appearance, we drew attention quickly. Everyone who spotted us shouted and scurried faster.

Not good—not good!

I pulled them towards a different quarter in an attempt to lessen the sound as they continued to cover their ears, faces set in grimaces. When we approached a four-sided courtyard, the horns silenced. I watched the three of them rub their heads and re-orient themselves. The relief was short-lived as I glanced back and saw the Exalted Sun emerge across the courtyard. Clutched in his grasp was—Freda! She was bound and gagged, struggling as he dragged her over the cobblestone towards us.

I ran towards her. "Freda!"

"Don't! Reign!" Leander had followed me, grabbing for my shoulder, stopping me twenty feet from the Exalted Sun. "It's an illusion."

He snapped his fingers and what I had seen as Freda glittered away, revealing an equally scared young woman I'd never seen before. A stand in.

I turned back and saw Emrys right behind me, and Victus still at the courtyard's edge. Had the Exalted Sun seen him? I sent him a *Mindtell*, *"If you are not joining us, then hide before your cover is blown!"*

Victus slipped into the shadows.

Leander growled beside me. "I'm surprised the righteous take so much pleasure in binding and gagging a scared mortal woman." There was something about being in the presence of Lumoniel clerics that darkened his aura. It made him look like an infernal monster. "You'd fit right in at the Nine Circles of Hell."

The Exalted Sun said nothing and held his stare.

Something wasn't right.

Leander's eyes flared wide in a sudden realization, his focus darting around the courtyard.

Runes flashed with a blue arcane light across the stones beneath us. They ignited in glowing lines that looked carved into the stonework. My eyes darted around, tracking their path—and then I realized as well. It was a binding circle. A massive binding circle taking up almost the entire courtyard. It looked ancient, like the lines had been drawn here a thousand years ago, waiting for the threat of devils to return.

"You seriously think this can hold me?" Leander's voice erupted in anger. There was a deep rumbling from underground, as if he were trying to summon the Nine Circles themselves.

Seconds later, a half a dozen paladins turned a corner and entered the binding circle. They carried something between them wrapped in purple velvet. They stopped behind the Exalted Sun and whipped off the velvet to reveal a gleaming sword. At the tip of its hilt was a shining, palm-sized gold ball, and etched up the length of its blade were gold rays woven with runes that emitted a soft yellow light. When Leander caught sight of it, he seethed, baring his fangs in a snarl. The earth rumbled violently, dropping me to my knees. Emrys dropped beside me, steading himself like a shield next to me.

"You can't be *fucking serious.*" Leander's words deepened to an arcane pitch. *"Brandishing that blade against me is the worst thing you could have done!"* His voice boomed across the courtyard in a feral anger as his eyes flared wide, the pupils sharpening to the red coals of the hellhound.

Chaos broke around us.

The paladins and clerics in the square scattered frantically. The ground continued rumbling, cracks forming across the cobblestone—only to be halted by the arcana of each glowing rune. The circle flared as the cracks smacked into the runes, struggling to contain the fracturing of the earth. Leander's dark aura rippled from his growing form. I felt the weight of it like a dark, suffocating blanket around us, like the size of what he would become already occupied this space.

Emrys picked me up and carried me to the edge of the circle, wincing as he approached its edge. Victus emerged from his hiding place behind a stone archway as we approached. He was already outside the binding circle and came to a stop inches from the outer ring. Emrys placed me on my feet.

"Go with Victus," Emrys said with urgency I'd never heard him use. "Your mortal soul will let you pass."

The stones cracked behind me and I glanced back.

Leander was beginning to look more like a colossal monster of the Nine Circles than he did my soul mate. His hound head stretched high, cresting the tops of the square archways and growing. The maw he'd once protected me with glowed with deadly potential. Shadowed hackles rose along his back, and flames cracked beneath the breaks in his fur. As every part of him took on the quality of a deadly weapon, I realized whoever had drawn that ink sketch of him had likely never seen *this*.

Emrys pushed me over the circle's edge into Victus's arms. Victus half-lifted me, attempting to lead me away from the square.

"But Leander—!" I turned my head back towards him.

The hound's height now reached the tops of the two-story buildings. Rubble fell as he thrashed and knocked arches and stone walls. I could barely stand with how much the ground shook from the successive impacts.

"That was the sword that killed him," Victus shouted. "He *will* level everything now that he's seen it. We can still get Freda while he distracts them, but first we need to get out of here—Now!"

I spared Leander a worried look. No wonder he'd become this after seeing that blade. Then I tore my gaze from him, and we began our retreat.

"Be careful, Emrys!" I shouted as Victus pulled me along. "That's a *Command!*"

Emrys gave me a soft smile before he transformed himself into a version of the hellcat that seemed more panther-like without the restrictions of being a familiar. He would be okay too. I had to believe he would be.

I cast *Mindtell* to Leander as I ran beside Victus. *"Leander—I love you. Please don't get lost in this wrath. Be careful. I'll be okay. Just protect yourself."*

"Do not come back here."

I shuddered as the deep, infernal growl, tinted with his horror form of the Nine Circles, sank like a heavy brick in my mind. It was a *Command*. The arcana of it would prevent me from disobeying. If he had used *Command* like that on me he must be terrified ...

A thunderous boom echoed behind me, followed by the crackling of fire. A quick glance back and I saw my soul mate, a hellhound of shadow and flame looming over the highest building.

The flames erupting from his neck licked against the blue of the sky. His eyes glowed with infernal fire as arcane spells and arrows flew through the air towards him. He opened his sharp-toothed maw and the air marbled as heat poured out before a glowing, orange light surged.

He was trying to break free.

"Victus!" I shouted.

My brother whipped his head around and looked up at Leander. His eyes widened, and he pulled me swiftly into an alleyway. He covered my body with his as a loud boom cut through the air, shaking the buildings around us. Wind gusted violently down the streets. Then the orange glow lit everything—the street, the stone walls, the windows—and an inferno of flames rushed past like flood water. I peeked around Victus. Hot fire licked up his back, but came no closer. I re-tucked myself against him.

Whatever Leander was doing had to be on par with what had happened during the Veiled Ages. Was he lost in the memory of the monster the Primordial Father had forced him to be? Triggered by seeing that sword? How many innocent people would die because of this? Would Lumoniel return?

"I love you," I sent again, hoping it reached him—that he had not completely succumbed to the creature he was now.

The flames dispersed as the rumbling continued.

Victus dragged me back onto the street as I looked back, trying to catch sight of Leander.

Leander's hell hound eyes glowed like bright red coals as his head descended back into the square, teeth bared and dripping with orange flame.

I turned my focus ahead and followed Victus's pull into a run.

Something hot slammed into my back. The sputtering sounds of sparks and embers glittered into nothing as the bracelet Leander had given me hummed around my wrist. I whipped my head around just in time to see another—a bolt of fire—whizzing overhead. It sputtered with sparks until it slammed into a building ahead of us. I had been hit by that first bolt of fire ... and unharmed. The bracelet had worked.

We looked back as five wizards emerged from the surrounding alleys. Victus pulled me faster. A crumbling sounded overhead as large cracks spread along the side the building that had been hit. Chunks of wall and rubble fell into the path before us, filling up the space fast—too fast—it threatened to trap us!

"Fuck," Victus muttered. Bearing his fangs, he jerked his head back to the wizards and pointed a finger. An orange-yellow ball of flame surged and erupted in the space around them. Its sizzle was followed by the echo of their screams.

A *Firebomb!*

I whipped my hands in front of us, pushing my primordial power into it. *"A door!"*

My *Mystic Door* appeared, its glittering, blue opening shifting into place, and we ran through, exiting the other side just past the collapsing building. The door dissipated and the ground shook again as the falling building scattered against the ground, a plume of dust billowing out from the impact.

I scrambled to keep my footing. "I need to find a place to *Scry* to find Freda," I huffed as we ran.

As we entered the next block, we saw more and more people fleeing as the chaos in the city descended swiftly upon us. People shouted and bumped into us as we pushed towards the building. Then Victus pulled me into an alcove away from the crowd.

"Hurry!" he said, looking back out into the rushing people.

I closed my eyes.

When wizards used *Scry*, they needed expensive materials and items—but I had been practicing using the fragment of Leander's soul, and he'd made good on my *Command* to teach me *Scry*.

Light rushed in behind my closed lids, revealing a clouded sky and a dusty cityscape below. I focused on Freda and my view blurred with motion. Colors blazed by, then it slowed and focused, sweeping towards the ground. I saw the roof of a building—the same architecture as Merchants Hall—in front of the courtyard Freda and I had passed by. The scrying eye sank through the rooftop, dropping me past floor after floor after floor till it slowed to a stop. I made out the blurred edges of a dark, stone cell. The scrying eye sharpened focus again, this time on a figure curled in a ball, arms hugging her legs to her chest from her seat on the stone floor.

Freda.

I opened my eyes, and I blinked as the light of the alcove rushed back into place. "She's at Merchant's Hall—far underground in some kind of cell."

Victus looped his arm in mine. "I can teleport us nearby to see what were up against. Freda won't be alone."

A whirl and a flash of arcane smoke and we were in that courtyard I saw in the *Scry*. We unlinked and I had hardly registered a step when I realized four wizards were ahead bearing the same black leathers all my grandfather's guardsmen wore. They had positioned metal bars across the large doors, and now turned to us, hands stretched wide as they summoned spell materials. I could feel a familiar eerie hum from ahead, a glyph I knew all too well—the Palisade glyph. We'd need to navigate through the building physically.

Knowing Freda was in there sent the anger burning inside me. How dare they touch her and bring her into this? It shouldn't be her under threat, it should be me.

Crackling energy glittered across my fingers.

The four wizards squared off, spell materials flashing in their hands—but I was faster. I didn't need to summon anything other than what was already thrumming inside me. The energy in me spilled over and I threw my arms towards them, curling my fingers as if I was pulling raw energy from the air itself. The crackling intensified as I gritted my teeth and unleashed myself upon them—and the large doors.

A solid white arc of lightning erupted from my fingertips. It hit the nearest wizard, then chained between the others—jumping from body to body—before terminating on the doors. The fingers of white lightning were followed by a cracking, thunderous boom that shook the entire quarter. The four wizards fell to the ground, and the door hung in smoking shambles, blown open.

"Hell, Sister ..." Victus remarked. I'd say he looked rather impressed.

We raced past the bodies and pushed through the threshold. As soon as I stepped through though, a flash of metal swung towards me and a force knocked me down to the floor. The bracelet hummed at my wrist as a large brute of a man with a broadsword towered over me. He sneered at me through the helm covering part of his face.

"I won't miss this time." He raised the broadsword again.

Victus rushed in and punched the man clean across the face. I watched him grab the man's arms, twisting him to the ground. There was a snapping noise at the guards neck, then Victus rose to assess me.

I looked down at the bracelet. The stone was cracked. He ... had not missed me. Had that been the last shield?

Other servants of my grandfather rushed into the small hall. I scanned each of them, wizards and fighters, till my eyes landed on a tawny elf with dark green hair.

Alàn?

She was wearing the same leathers that matched them, but her lavender eyes flared on me in recognition. As Victus made to push his hand out at the guardsmen at the front of the pack I sent him a *Mindtell*.

"Don't hurt the elf. She's with us."

"What elf?" he replied.

I blinked. Alàn was gone.

Victus twisted his wrist. A flowing wave of necrotic energy raced towards the servant. They moved too late and it barreled into them, causing their form to fly back as it withered to nothing.

The one closest to me, another wizard, summoned a maroon braided cord to his palm. My eyes widened. There was only one spell that required that specific material. This asshole was going to cast the Transmutation spell *Polyform* on me. Just as it glowed with the arcana of spell casting, I pointed a finger at it with *Nullify*.

"How *dare* you use Transmutation against me!" I shouted at him.

I let the anger continue to flow out like the lightning, but this time I focused on my Transmutation specialty. I had become so familiar with accessing my primordial magic that I thought with enough motivation and willpower I could cast a theoretical spell

I'd always been curious about. I lifted an open palm towards the wizard and I willed the arcana to take shape.

A green pulse of light flew from my hand with a surprising ease and familiarity. He stiffened, spine inching towards being straight as a board. His entire form clicked with the sound of cold, heavy stone. It worked ... it worked! *Petrify*, a brutal Transmutation spell I'd only ever read about, had flown out of me as if it had been waiting for me to harness its potential.

Victus made quick work of the others nearest to him, using either his fists or his magic to end each of them. The last opponent was another fighter, shifting around the stonework I'd just transmuted. His eyes fixed on me. He had a long, large blade he'd unsheathed from his side. I quaked, moving back slightly. Without my bracelet, and in a melee fight, I would be done for. Just as he was about to lunge, I saw a flash from the shadows and he halted with a sharp grunt. His hilt slipped from between his fingers, then he collapsed forward to the ground. Three short blades were sunk into his back.

Shining, lavender eyes blinked into view from the shadows as Alàn took a step forward.

I sighed, stumbling a little in relief.

"Are you okay?" She rushed to my side.

"Yes! How did you do that? You just vanished!" I looked around the hall. It was small and somewhat dark, but had no obvious place to hide.

"Being sneaky is kinda my thing." Alàn winked a sparkling eye at me. She glanced up briefly at Victus and then back at me. "Your friend is in a cell at the bottom level. I can take you there." She began moving down the hall silently and swiftly.

We followed her to the main spiral staircase where she descended first. After several turns, she halted abruptly. Her hand flew out to signal us to stop. We plastered our backs to the staircase wall. She crouched and peeked around the corner of the opening just ahead. A *Mindtell* sounded in my mind—I'd forgotten she had trained herself in arcana like me.

"There are two ahead. I'll lure them to the stairs, and when they pass the corner, take them out. I'll tell your devil companion the same."

I nodded and looked over at Victus as he received the same message. He nodded as well. Alàn stood silently and rolled her neck. She inhaled and exhaled quickly, and then pushed herself around the corner as if she'd been sprinting down the stairs. "Quick! They're here. We need support on the main level!"

Her shout was so convincing I took a step back in surprise.

"Upstairs now!" one man growled. "You, stay with the prisoner."

"Yes sir," Alàn's voice called back.

The heavy footfalls of the men came closer as they ran for the stairs. One passed the threshold into the stairwell. Victus reached around me and grabbed the first, silently twisting his neck. Just as I lifted my hands to cast toward the second man, I heard two wet thumps. He tripped and fell forward, two knives jutting out from his back. Alàn rushed to the body, retrieving her knives and rummaging in his pockets.

"Remind me never to turn my back on you," I chuckled.

She let out a short laugh.

We rushed down the corridor, and Alàn led us straight to the cell where Freda was being held. She was filthy, still sitting on the ground of the cell exactly where I had seen in the *Scry*.

"Freda!" I shoved my arms through the iron bars towards her.

She jerked her head up. When her eyes landed on me, she let out a cry and ran over to me, hugging me through the bars.

"I'm so sorry," I cried. "This is all my fault!"

I pulled away to hear Alàn rifling through a ring of keys I hadn't noticed her acquire. She snatched up a particular one and the door clicked open for it. Freda ran through and we flew into each other's arms.

"It's not your fault!" Freda squeezed me. "Thanks for the rescue. It sounds like a war out there!"

"There *is* a war out there," Victus said flatly, scanning her red hair.

"Right ... Freda, this is my ... brother, Victus." I tilted my head with a smile.

I heard Victus sigh, and had no doubt he was rolling his eyes behind me.

"There is a Palisade glyph on the building. We have to get outside, then Victus can teleport us somewhere else," I said.

"Right ... okay. Let's go then."

I turned to lead us out, but paused as the thought pierced my mind.

This can't be it.

What if the lodestone was here? What if I could destroy it now? My lightning had destroyed those large barred doors. Maybe it could destroy an ancient stone. I needed to try ... I needed to take my freedom into my hands. To fight this with everything I had, like Leander back in the courtyard, bound in that circle.

I turned back. "Alàn, have you seen a large lodestone here? Or the knife we talked about?"

Her eyes darted about as she considered. "I haven't been in the room at the end of this hall. They won't let anyone outside the inner circle in there. Those two down here were actually supposed to be guarding it."

"Victus, take Freda outside and teleport her somewhere safe," I said, looking up at him, "as far away as you can. Then come back here for me."

"Are you seriously going to send me away?" Freda argued.

"Yes!" I said. "I'm not letting you end up as a bargaining chip again!"

Footsteps padded up the hall and we all turned our heads in the direction of two more guards. Victus began a step towards them, but a flash of arcana lit the hallway and Freda's *Mystic Hand* slapped the guard so hard he spun out into the wall, then slid to the ground, unconscious. The other guard halted, looked over the four of us, then started running in the opposite direction.

"Yeah, you better run!" Freda shouted after him.

"See? I need you to clear the way out." I winked.

Freda sighed. "Fine. Come on," she said looking up at Victus.

He bent his eyebrows up together.

"Oh right." I turned to him. "Victus I *Command* you to protect Freda at all costs, get her to somewhere safe, then come back for me! And don't let her come back with you!"

"Be careful, Reign!" Freda said as she started running down the hall.

I watched the two of them disappear, then turned to Alàn. "Can you lead me to the room? If we find the lodestone, will you help me destroy it?"

She smiled. "Let's go fuck up a stone." She grabbed my arm and we sprinted deeper down the corridor.

CHAPTER FORTY-SIX

We slipped through the corridor before slowing at a big steel door that was slightly ajar. We looked at each other, then Alàn slipped into the opening. I followed and was met with narrow and steep descending stairs. They had been dug out carefully from stone and curved tightly in a spiral deep into the darkness.

We looped around again and again. Keeping up with Alàn was difficult—she was so fast down the dark steps. When we reached the landing at the bottom, we practically collapsed on the floor. Alàn let me heave a few breaths before she pulled me upright and I studied the softly lit expanse.

It was a massive excavated room, the walls and floors dug out from gray stone and dirt. Levels rose and fell around me like a quarry. Large stone pillars seemed untouched, holding the ceiling above us in place. Stray arcane lights had been left active in the musty room, casting a dim yellow light on dirt ramps and paths.

We spread out at a careful, stealthy pace. Alàn circled away from me down the longest side, searching as well. I slid down an incline into one of the deeper excavated areas. The wide open pit looked like it had been recently dug, a strange, dusty smell still hanging in the area all around it.

A few seconds later, the hairs on my body stood on end. I whirled my head around and realized I had lost sight of Alàn. I heard a click on stone, then a second, then a third. I knew that sound. I started trembling as I frantically searched the room for him and any place I could hide.

Fingers snapped.

The icy tingle of arcana flowed over me. I tried to move—tried to do anything—but my body was frozen. He had cast the spell on me before I could react, before I could do anything to defend myself.

My grandfather lowered his hand, standing at the edge of the pit. He took measured steps down to my level, using carved out steps I had not noticed, heels clicking as he descended.

"The lodestone is not here," he said smugly. "Neither is the knife, Grace. It's all at the estate."

Even though I couldn't move, I could feel my body shaking against the arcana holding me. I tried to send a *Mindtell* out hoping that, despite how far underground we were and whatever arcana protected this place, it would be delivered to Leander.

"Help. I'm alone with him. I'm under Merchants Hall."

I heard swift footfalls into the room and my mother appeared where my grandfather had been standing. She wore clothing similar to what the guardsmen had worn but fresher and more femininely cut. Her eyes widened as they met mine down in the pit. She descended to join us and a nearby floating light illuminated her face. It had only been a little over a month since I'd last seen her, but she looked dreadful. Dark circles hung under her eyes, which were a dull gray now instead of their usual blue. I tried to scrunch my eyebrows up at her, pleading for mercy and understanding.

She stopped ten feet from him. Both looked at me from the other side of the pit. She turned to face my grandfather.

"Lydia ..." He tilted his head towards my mother. His tone was the same as when he'd ordered anyone in his service. "Kill her."

My mother clenched her jaw. She glared at him before her eyes shifted back to me. I remembered the only time I'd seen her cast arcana, the simple magic of *Spotless* to clean her blood-stained hands before the fireplace. Could she cast something powerful enough to kill? Or would she cover those hands in blood again? How could she even do such a thing to ... her firstborn?

But then I saw tears well in her eyes, and a white, crackling energy sparked between her fingers.

Lightning?

The realization hit me like lead weights. The overwhelming sadness that I did belong to her—even though she'd never wanted me like this. That despite how I had been transformed to be a copy of another devil, I was still her daughter, and she'd given me my affinity for lightning.

The way my mother's hands danced delicately through the air told me she was *much* more practiced. The lightning coiled out around her, snapping in the air. I felt the surrounding air charge with potential. She didn't break her stare with me until the very last second—when her eyes flicked to my grandfather like daggers.

A flash and a thunderous, cracking boom jolted me.

I fell to the ground—and everything went hazy.

My ears rang and my chest shook. I stretched my rattling fingers across the dirt stabilizing myself. Finally, my eyes focused as I rushed to push myself up, head spinning. My grandfather had been blown back, splayed across the floor against a dirt wall, spots on his chest smoking. I turned.

My mother looked over her shoulder at me, hands trembling and tears streaming down her face. "Grace—" Her voice wavered, then her pupils flared wide, and the the dull color in her eyes dimmed. Her body slackened as she fell forward, collapsing to the floor.

"Mom?" I scrambled to her, throwing myself down next to her. I looked beyond her and saw my grandfather wincing against the wall, still holding out a pointed finger.

Death Promise.

I couldn't think about how he'd become so powerful he could master such a spell. Instead, tears pushed down my face as I trembled, pushing my mother's body to her back, clutching her leathers.

Then I saw it. The small silvery essence of her soul pooled at her chest. I heard my grandfather grunting, trying to lift himself from the floor. If I got up now, I could attack him—try to kill him.

But, I couldn't. I couldn't let her soul go. I couldn't let him try to take it—to use it in a way she wouldn't want.

Or let her pass into some unknown, *eternal oblivion.*

Even though she hadn't known the consequences, she'd tried to choose me when she signed the contract. She wouldn't accept my death as a price to be paid then, and she hadn't accepted it now.

I stretched my hand across the silver essence and drove all my will, my primordial magic—everything—into a single claiming *Command.*

This soul is mine.

I felt the silver essence flow out from her body like a warm liquid and weave through my fingers into my palm. Pulling it into my body, I squeezed it till I felt it vanish into my grasp. Though it had disappeared, I could still feel its presence, like I had placed it somewhere eternally bound to me, safe and secure.

There was a distant boom outside, and dust fell from the ceilings.

My grandfather pushed away from the wall. "Enough—"

"This has gone too far!"

I clutched my head, the piercing new voice split through my mind and clanged louder than any bell. I fell across the floor only a few feet from my mother. I heard a groan and forced my eyes over to see my grandfather had also collapsed, clutching his head. The dirt under me glittered with a red arcane light. My arms and legs tingled as they began sinking into that glittering floor as if it were liquid—and suddenly, I was free-falling.

After a short distance I landed on a cold, polished, yellow stone floor. I sat up. The voice was gone, but a new anxiety settled in as I realized I was encased in a cylindrical, glass chamber—as if I was some kind of specimen. I looked beyond the glass at what appeared to be a throne room I'd never seen before. My eyes darted around the unfamiliar pillars, high stone arches pushing above to sharp points, until I saw a fire-rimmed portal flash to my right, its mirrored surface facing the floor. Leander was thrown from it—in his devil form—and he pushed himself up weakly.

He looked wounded, covered in blood, burns, and cuts ... I shouted for him, but my voice seemed to echo and reverberate within the glass. I banged my fists against the barrier. He looked forward towards the empty, obsidian throne, then his eyes slowly chartered around the room till he finally saw me.

"Reign!" His voice was muffled through the chamber as he jumped to his feet and ran towards me. He pressed his forehead and hands against the glass in an effort to touch me.

The same mind-splitting voice from before, now audible and also muffled, drew our attention.

"The likeness is impressive, is it not?" the voice crooned.

I turned away from Leander, my eyes drifting towards the voice.

My father—Remodeus—had taken a seat in the empty throne. My mind raced. He looked exactly as I had remembered him, except here he wore midnight blue, silk robes, and held a gold scepter tightly by the armrest.

"Release her!" Leander growled.

"Please humor me and tell me how close it is to the real thing," Remodeus said instead, smiling and shifting his gaze to me.

My father was acting so differently from how I remembered him. Why did he have me trapped here? Why was he not even addressing me? The questions I had been harboring in fear burned up my throat.

"Why did you make me?" I banged my fists on the glass. "Why did you visit me and make me think you loved me—that there was a future for me here?" I shouted through my shaking voice. I ripped the button necklace from inside my shirt and slammed it against the glass. "Why did you give me this?"

Leander looked between me and my father. "What did she say?"

"She wants to know why I made her, and ..." A confused look formed across Remodeus's face. "I never visited you, girl."

What? I felt like I couldn't breath.

Leander's head twisted to Remodeus. "You are seriously going to play games with her right now?"

"I haven't stepped foot in Novus since the day the contract was signed," Remodeus belted across the expanse of the throne room.

Leander seethed. "You gave her one of my father's buttons ... how else would she get that if you didn't give it to her as a part of whatever this twisted game to torture me was?"

My button ... belonged to Leander's father? My fingers trembled, clasped tightly around it.

"Twisted game ..." Remodeus laughed. "The twisted game was waiting so long just so I could see what it did to you when you found her and learned her *name*." He lowered his voice to a more theatrical tone. "I made you," Remodeus's infernal eyes—my eyes—focused on me, "because when that sniveling human woman cried and cried over the prospect of losing you or her lover, she told me she'd already picked out a name for you ... *Grace*."

Leander's head whipped back towards me. His eyes widened, revealing more of that black void around the orange rings than I'd ever seen before. Like he'd seen a ghost.

"Your given name was *Grace?*" Leander's voice wavered with the question. His eyes darted frantically over me, trying to understand.

That's right, I had never told him. Why would I? When it was everything I was trying to escape from.

He was ... trembling now.

Remodeus continued, "So, when I found out she was going to have the same name as that whore goddess, I couldn't resist the opportunity to give you what you wanted all those years ago." His laugh sounded again.

Her name had been Grace, too?

"But now," Remodeus sighed, "you've both made a mess of Novus—one I will need to clean up so we don't have another holy war with Lumoniel." His eyes went back to me. "I know what your grandfather is trying to do, and why he needs you for it. Frankly, I don't want the Primordial Father to return either. So until this is resolved, I'm going to hold on to you so he can't take your souls." Remodeus snapped his fingers.

The glass sang with a chime as if a metal object had struck it. The floor once again turned to a cold liquid that began swallowing me.

"Wait!" Leander shouted down at me.

The last thing I saw before the darkness swallowed me whole was my soul mate's face—eyebrows turned in the first true expression of fear I'd ever seen him wear—as the hands of some guard grappled him away from the glass.

CHAPTER FORTY-SEVEN

I descended through the darkness for what felt like ages until a cold, wet, stone floor pushed up under me. It was completely dark. I couldn't see anything at all, and I was utterly alone.

I didn't want to try to light the area. I didn't want to know how large the room was—what was the point? I had gone from cage to cage. What difference was one to the other?

It was so quiet I could hear my heart beating in my ears, and each breath that entered and retreated from my lungs. Every now and then, the silence was broken by a low rumble in the distance with some sort of associated shriek. Then it returned to silence. I breathed in just a little too deeply, and it felt like something cracked in me. *In my soul.*

In the dark recesses of my mind, I heard my mother's voice echo to me, brittle and fragile, crackling through me like her own lightning.

"Grace—"

The last word she had spoken before she was murdered. I wondered if she had been as much a prisoner as I was now. All of her choices bound in her father's will—and yet ... From the beginning, she had wanted the idea of me—the chance that I would live and that she would love me. She had paid the price of hope for me with her happiness. When asked to end me again, she'd chosen for me to live—a choice she'd paid for with her life.

"*Grace—*"

Remodeus had used my mother—all because of the coincidence of my given name and *hers*. All so he could torture Leander. Had he ... ever loved me? It had to be a lie. Some part of it had to be. How could he forget about when he'd visited me and gave me Leander's father's button? It was him. *He* visited me. I know it. I saw him with my own eyes—but something had clearly changed him ... changed how he looked at me.

"*Grace—?*"

Leander's wavering question when he learned my given name. When we'd first met, Leander had seemed to sense the incomplete truth of my name. I wondered if he couldn't read it in my mind because I'd buried it so deeply. Grace was not me. *Grace* was the child dragged around the estate. *Grace* was the tool used in trade negotiations. *Grace* was a means to an end, a material in executing the spell of my grandfather's will. *Grace* was a prisoner.

Grace was also apparently the one Leander had loved before me.

Victus knew my birth name. So did Emrys. Why had it never come up with Leander? Why had he looked at me like *that* when he'd heard it? Like a corpse resurrected. Like a phantom from a dream. Not like me—Reign. His soul mate. *His everything.*

The tears began rolling down my face as the nothingness of the cell filled with the weight of it all. Everything I was—did—am. All the pain of being made to never belong—being used to serve the purpose of others. The sadness from my lack of utter control over anything in my life. And being lonely—so lonely—simply from wanting a family. To be loved. The reality pressed down heavy around me until it had nowhere else to go except squeezed through the tears from my eyes, till I collapsed on the ground and wailed. I longed to feel anything, even physical pain, instead of this. Anything to distract me from *this*. I pounded my fists into the stone. Sharp pangs shot up my arms as each impact increased, but it did nothing to numb that tearing feeling inside.

I was utterly alone.

A true orphan.

Abandoned.

An imitation of a former lover.

Then the tiniest whisper formed, almost indiscernible amidst the crying and pounding.

"So alone ..."

I paused, sniffling. Had I said that? Or heard it? I took deep breaths through my mouth, trying to be quiet to see if it would happen again. Several minutes passed in silence with just my sniffling and breathing.

"You are abandoned like me."

"Who's there?" I said aloud, scooting across the floor till my back pressed against a wall.

"Tell me about those who abandoned you." The voice had left my head now. It was disembodied, echoing around the room with me. It was the voice of a woman, smooth as glass, and close—as if she were right next to me. All *around* me.

"Tell me who you are and maybe I will," I replied, wiping my nose. I knew better than to give details to mysterious devils or monsters locked down here with me.

"My name ... is Erebell," she replied.

"And what are you, Erebell?"

"I am like you," she replied. "A tool to be used, a material for a spell, a prisoner."

It hurt hearing the words in my mind played back to me. If she could read my thoughts through these stone cell walls, she must be powerful. Perhaps she was one of the female creatures imprisoned here—like Leander's mother had been.

She continued. "I can't remember the last time I had a conversation ... It's been so long. I've answered two of your questions. Please. Answer some of mine?" There was a melancholy tilt to her voice. Was this my fate as well? To forget the sound of conversation? To be kept arcanely alive in this dungeon until Remodeus could resolve the mess in Novus?

"Alright ..." Why not? At this point, I had become everything I'd tried so very hard to avoid. I was utterly alone. Abandoned, orphaned. There was a small hope that if I saw Leander again I could find that love and belonging, but the way he had looked at me ... Would he ever be able to see me as Reign again? Or would I forever remain a cheap copy? The thread pulled gently against my soul. So, so far away.

"Who abandoned you?"

"The ... first person to abandon me was my mother. Then my father." I could feel my eyes burn with tears as I said it out loud. There was no taking it back. It was too real now.

"Why does that make you sad?"

I blinked. At first it seemed like an obvious answer to a simple question. But the more I contemplated it, I realized it was anything but that. I thought about the letter. The advice that the goddess had given to Leander.

"It makes me sad because what's the point of all this pain and suffering if there can't be love?"

There was silence. I wondered if she'd left, then her voice trickled back into the air around me.

"Love ..." Erebell sounded pained. "I am a mother. I loved all my children, but they abandoned me."

"I'm so sorry." I didn't know what else to say. No one deserved to be abandoned. In the end, my mother redeemed herself, but all those years of cold neglect had still hurt. This creature had another side of that pain, and it made me sad to think about her here alone, wishing to see them. "Did your children visit you before ... ?"

"I am not allowed to be with them."

Oh. I sniffed into the darkness, and felt the cold of the floor seep into me.

"The father of my children was cruel," Erebell continued. "He forced me to bear him only sons. I wanted more than anything to have a daughter—another like me."

I didn't want to think about what he might have done to the babies had they been born female, but I imagined it was awful.

"I am sad to hear that your parents abandoned you," she said. "I would have adopted you as a daughter if I could have."

"That's kind of you to say," I replied with a half smile.

I curled up on the cold, wet floor. The thought that in a cell nearby was another prisoner who had absolutely no ties—biological, contractual, or otherwise—to accept or want me, and yet they did. It didn't seem like such a dangerous fantasy to slip into while I was down here.

"I wish ..." I trailed off.

"Yes?"

"I wish I could be my own person," I said, "not a pawn or a thing that was created for torture or to be a sacrifice. I wish I could be your child who visits you and shows you how having a daughter is different than having sons."

Erebell laughed. It was scratchy, as if rusty from disuse. "I would like that."

I smiled.

"I can never leave this place. But if I set you free, do you promise to visit me?"

I uncurled and sat up straight at the question. "Can you help me escape this dungeon?"

"No. But I can set you free." While her words were vague, they were soft with the genuine promise of love, not deception.

"You don't have to do anything. Eventually they'll come down to retrieve me ... and I'll come back and visit you, like a daughter."

"My own children never showed me such kindness ..." she said sadly. "If you visit me as my daughter, I'll be a mother to you." Her voice was sweet and I could hear it in her words—the same deep desires as mine. To be accepted and loved—to be bonded.

"Deal," I said back with a soft smile.

As soon as I spoke the word, there was a twinge in my chest. I sat up straighter at the feeling. I inhaled deeply, but the pain became worse. Then, the twinge grew to a full-blown, searing pain.

"What's happening?" I called out to Erebell. I coughed. It was hard to breathe, let alone speak with the pain radiating across my body.

"You are being born, my child," she said lovingly.

"What?" I gasped for breath, writhing on the ground.

What had started as a burning pain in my chest now surged through my body like currents of wild electricity. I struggled to grasp something—anything—to center me. I thought of the thread. The thing that had always comforted me and grounded me. I searched deep inside myself for it and grabbed it—only for it to slip through my hands like sand.

"Wait!" I screamed.

I searched wildly for the thread, finding it and then losing it again and again. My entire body started burning, and the smell of singed hair and skin filled my nostrils. I refused to let it go—the thread—so I turned completely inward. I sent my mind deeper than I'd ever gone to the center of myself—and found the warm energy of my souls. Frantic, I looked for Leander's soul.

"No, no!" My mortal soul shuddered as the pain sizzled and erupted in a wave across me. The silver essence of me sputtered and bubbled like boiling water. Everything I was—that mortal girl, transformed and abandoned—*burned* from my body. Then, Leander's soul was pulled across the now vacant space deep inside me—where my soul should have been. I screamed again.

"Wait! Please!"

My eyes flew open to the darkness where the invisible flames that burned me raged on, and the curl of silver caught my eye. I reached my hands out for the stream of Leander's soul as it floated away from me like a glittering dust carried on the wind. I *couldn't* let go of it. I didn't care if I had no soul of my own, I couldn't let go of him.

I had no soul to call upon, no primordial magic. So I threw my hope after it—my will—my desire to keep it with me—not to let it leave me. My hands grasped at the darkness until the last speckles of the silvery dust of Leander's soul drifted away.

"No, no, no!" I begged and reached out, trying anything to follow the remnants of him.

Something in my core snapped. There was a breath, and then I felt death. I was void of all warmth, movement, life. I was nothing, with no pain and no purpose. Just ... essence, like a breath of air drifting over the edge of eternal oblivion.

CHAPTER FORTY-EIGHT

LEANDER

Indescribable pain.

Worse than the bites, stabs, and attacks I'd suffered as a hell-hound.

Worse than watching my mother die—at the hands of the Primordial Father.

Worse than that killing blow from the celestial blade of Lumoniel impaling me then decapitating me.

It lanced through my chest, driving all other thoughts away. I rolled to my side on the stone floor of the prison cell and clutched at my chest, sucking in whatever air I could. I could do nothing else but succumb to it. I screamed until reality was peeled away from me and replaced only with blackness.

Where is she?

I floated through the dark in chaotic circles like a ship caught in a current with a broken rudder. Before, it had been her steadying me. Her at the other end of the thread to my soul, binding us more surely than time itself. There was nothing to hold on to now. No guiding sense of direction. Just the cold and vast emptiness of eternal oblivion stretching before me. This was my fate without her. To be alone. To face immortality without her. I would rather be wherever she was. I would rather be nothing than spinning in this endless oblivion ...

I cracked open my eyes.

The intense pain was replaced with an ache that sharpened with each inhale. There was nothing of her left inside me. No gentle, caressing pull. No light by my side in the darkness. No soul fragment pulling me towards her. In its place was a long-forgotten remnant of my own soul, the fragment I had given up for her.

She was dead.

I couldn't move ... moving would acknowledge that this was real. I felt absolutely empty so quickly—too quickly. I'd gone from feeling full of her—her warm, tender soul—to this gut-wrenching emptiness. I reached for her, but it was like I had been trapped inside glass. I could feel nothing. The only means of escape was breaking the glass, but on the other side was only the pain of moving forward without her—alone.

I felt tears roll down the sides of my face as I lay on the cold stone of the cell Remodeus had put me in to keep me from interfering, but it didn't matter now if I stayed frozen here for the rest of my immortality.

My soulmate ... my love ... my dear Reign ... is dead.

Suddenly, I heard footsteps approach my cell. My utter despair shifted to anger. These cells were typically enchanted against a devil's magic, but I had never been this enraged before. And now I had the full wrath of my complete soul at my disposal. If I couldn't make whoever approached open the door, I would *break* it open.

Victus caught my gaze as he turned a corner across the bars of my cell doors. His eyes widened and he ran up, his expression panicked. "What happened? I can't find her!"

He should have better calculated putting himself in my presence. I stood and approached the bars. He followed my movements, unafraid—until I shoved my arm through the space of a gap and grasped his neck with my hand. Victus instantly started choking. I squeezed harder. His muscles strained against my fingers, and his arteries throbbed desperately. I yanked him against the bars.

"*Open this cell,*" I growled.

Victus's eyes bulged at the *Command*. He reached frantically for the mechanism that locked the door. I watched his face turn a purple hue as I squeezed his neck tighter. Good. He should know what it feels like to have the life wrung out of him—like what he had done to my Reign. He'd had one fucking job to do when he escorted her to Freda. One simple job.

Protect her.

The cell clicked open.

I threw Victus down to the ground and shoved the door open. He scrambled across the floor, backing away from me as I surveyed the hall.

"Victus," my voice boomed down at him.

He remained on the floor in submission and merely nodded, awaiting my next words.

"If you place yourself in my presence again, I *will* kill you. I don't care how your father punishes me for it." I turned away from him and teleported.

A moment later, I appeared in the throne room.

"How did you manage to get out?" Remodeus called from behind me.

I turned and found him emerging from the connected room.

Once he saw my face, his expression changed from curious to cautious.

"I want her body. *Bring the cell she's in up here,*" I Commanded. He would feel the magical demand behind the words. The power of my complete soul.

Remodeus blinked at me in shock before using his hands to cast towards the tiled floor of the room. The chairs and tables rattled as a ten-foot, rectangular, stone-walled chamber surfaced.

I rushed over to the metal door and ripped it from its hinges. Leaning inside to look around revealed it was empty.

Remodeus pushed forward and surveyed it himself. When he turned to face me his eyes were wide. "I do not understand," he said, backing away. "There is no way in or out of that dungeon. Not even for us."

I took note of the burn marks seared across the stones of the walls, floors, and ceiling of the cell.

Remodeus followed my gaze. "She's a mortal. This was bound to happen eventually. You can't be upset at me for the fragility of their kind."

No body? Fine. I'd go retrieve her soul.

I did not acknowledge Remodeus before I teleported again. This time to the Shadow Circle.

Chapter Forty-Nine

REIGN

I was nothing. Then hot fire ignited in that space made barren of both souls. Its power grew and filled the space, pressing to the very edges of my being. I didn't care. I didn't want to be filled with anything other than us—*him*. Whatever had replaced my soul burned hot and angry, like a raging inferno. I arched as it unfurled within me, struggling to bear it. It didn't matter that I couldn't see his soul anymore. I'd known it for my entire life. I could sense it somewhere out there. I would follow it.

The darkness of the cell now glowed with a bright, glittering fire that crept up around me. It was a rainbow of colors, flashing and blinding. It bathed my skin until all I knew were strobing lights and those chromatic flames licking at every inch of my body.

Time seemed to slow. Minutes felt both like eons and milliseconds as I floated there. The pure glittering inferno held my vision in chaotic, dancing patterns till the weight of consciousness flooded me.

I was no longer burning.

I twisted and rose, the flames bathing my back, pushing till I surfaced to the cool air of a dark, starless expanse stretched above me. Was I looking into the *eternal oblivion*? If I left the warmth of this inferno, would I be letting myself pass on? The fingers of flames licked up into the black, and I turned my head to look across their surface to a rusty-red shore. Shadows and small lights danced across it, and my heart warmed. I wasn't alone? Something besides me existed on the edge of nothing? I turned and adjusted my arms and legs as I swam closer through fire. Perhaps, despite whatever Erebell had done to claim me as her child, I had survived. I was alive. And perhaps she had helped me escape—but to where?

I felt the ground brush against my toes and took step after step, emerging from the glittering inferno. The flames licked at my body as I advanced, as if giving me one last caress before I left them. On the shore were devils, imps, and all manner of hellish creatures, all staring wide-eyed at me. I looked behind me.

The lake.

The glittering lake of the Fire Circle flickered a familiar rainbow of hues behind me. I must have awoken at the deepest part. I looked down at my body, and my hands flew to cover my breasts as I crouched to the ground. The flames had completely burned my clothes away. Everything had been burned out of me, in fact. My contract, my button—even the bracelet that Leander had given me. It was all gone.

The crowd parted, and a small imp approached with the lack of fear only a construct could have—and folded clothing. It extended grayish-purple arms with its offering. I accepted the clothing and stood, unfolding it. It was a shimmering, black silk dress. Long and slinky, it was semi-translucent and supported by two thin shoulder straps. I tilted the material through my fingers. It looked like the edge of a dark metal blade with how it refracted in the light.

"Thank you," I said to the imp, then slipped the dress on over my head. It was far less modest than what I was used to, but I was grateful.

The imp waited there, staring up at me with wide, solid black eyes as the dress fluttered into place around me.

No others in the growing crowd dared approach me, but they stared and whispered to each other under a thin layer of silence. I looked past them toward the palace. The night was so dark I could hardly make out the towers usually visible from here. I tried searching for the feeling of the thread, but it was completely gone. I closed my eyes to feel Leander's soul—what I thought I could sense despite it being ripped from me.

I felt ... empty. So empty still. I opened my eyes and looked back towards the palace.

If it was night, something had to be wrong. Leander had only ever made it night because I'd needed to sleep. Before that, it had not been night since he'd first been killed and returned to the Nine Circles of Hell. Dreadful thoughts plagued my mind. Had he made it night here now because he thought I was dead? How long had I been floating in that lake? My heart started breaking, the pain radiating across my chest. I needed to find him, prove that I was okay. I reached for my new soul, and felt it burn hot as I cast *Mindtell* to him, searching for his familiar presence on this plane.

"Leander? I'm here! Where are you?" My heart pounded as the seconds went by. Please, please find him.

"Such a pretty voice. If I tell you where I am ... will you show me who it belongs to?"

My stomach turned as the voice dragged across my mind like a sharpened claw. It was him, but ... he sounded sinister. Wild, like an actual monster of hell. Was this what feeling our bond break had done to him?

If my *Mindtell* had reached Leander, we had to be on the same plane. I hoped he was in the palace. The last time we'd come down to the lake, Emrys had led the way back and I, admittedly, had not been paying attention. Not to mention it was so dark now. Everything looked so different.

I glanced back down at the imp. *"Please help guide me to the palace."* Something hot and sharp surged through me.

The imp's eyes flared. It appeared to be trembling. "A ... command," it said, voice shaking.

I hadn't intended to *Command* it, but I must have used this new magic on accident. I'd never felt it this way before. Even when I had purposely cast *Command*, it had not felt like this. This felt old and endless. Like reaching into the expanse of the sky. Ancient in comparison to myself by all comprehension, and unknowably vast.

When Erebell had claimed me as her daughter, had it made me an *infernal?*

The imp gestured excitedly for me to follow and led me away from the shore. The crowd parted as we passed. Some fell to their knees. Some scattered and ran. I heard muttering and whispers among them increase as we moved. I thought they were calling me 'Mistress' at first. Then every hair on my body stood when I finally heard it clearer as we exited the crowd, as if they were calling it out to me.

Goddess.

CHAPTER FIFTY

Winding pathways twisted off through streets and we climbed in elevation until we reached the edge of the palace grounds. There, a single road sloped up towards the palace gates, and I saw a group of three ahead of us moving in the same direction. They peered back at me and slowed as they reached the first gate, enough that I could catch up to them.

It was three female devils dressed in revealing leathers with straps, buckles, and leather laces. They glared at me, and one standing in the middle stepped in front of the pack. Her twisting black horns curved around the sides of her head, framing her fanged smile.

"Are you here to see *His Infernal Highness* as well?"

I frowned at her. "Yes."

Her tail flicked behind her as she clicked her tongue. "He has a thing for leather ..." Her red-lit infernal eyes slid over the practically see-through slip of a dress the imp had given me. "In case you want to change."

I pushed down the rising anger and decided to press for more details. "Is this your first time at the palace?"

The devil to her right flashed a pretty, fanged smile. "We traveled here from the Poison Circle when we heard about the invitation to the Palace of Flames."

I'd never heard anyone call it that before.

"Invitation?" I said, crossing my arms. I thought briefly of my sisters and wondered if these three also sought to torture me by avoiding answering simple questions.

"If you don't have one, they probably won't let you in," the last devil answered. Her glowing, yellow eyes narrowed to me.

Something was weird about this. "What's the invitation for?"

"You must be living in a cave if you don't know," the first devil responded.

The anger finally flared in me, and I could feel something hot bubbling behind my eyes in warning. I wondered if she could see it.

The devil's face went slacken and she sighed. "Every year since His Infernal Highness was ... *returned* to the Nine Circles, he's thrown a massive, multi-month party at the palace. It features debauchery, sin, torture—the most exciting things." Her voice ticked up at the end into a friendly tone.

The devil to her left tucked a braid behind her ear and added, "Someone always dies. It's so entertaining!"

I froze. Was she implying that his *returning* meant when he was slain on Novus? That was almost a thousand years ago ...

The first devil tilted her head. "You know what we're talking about, right?"

I tightened my crossed arms. "Of course, I know about *His Infernal Highness* being slain."

"Shhh! Quiet!" The devil to the right hissed, looking around in a panic. She continued in a cautious whisper, "He can hear everything that is said in his Circle, and it does not please him when anyone refers to it as anything other than *returning.*"

I rolled my eyes. Was this a dream? Or the afterlife? Maybe I had really died, and this was my own personal hell where I had to endure Leander at his worst.

I pushed between them and the gates, and started marching up the steps to the door that led into the palace through the garden. It wasn't the main door, but it was the nearest. Perhaps the whole *invite* thing wouldn't be an issue. The imp trailed behind me, and the three devils followed behind it. I twisted the handle.

Locked.

Impatience grew in me and I cast *Enter*. A loud click sounded and the door floated open.

The group behind me gasped.

I looked down at the imp. "I'll be fine here now. Go do whatever you like for as long as you like."

The imp fidgeted.

I pressed my lips together, realizing what it really wanted. *"Go find me more dresses, ones that cover more skin."* I felt the primordial power weave through me again.

The imp's eyes widened with the pleasure of receiving the *Command*. It skittered off down the path, back towards the lake.

As I took a step through the threshold and looked around, I realized the palace was nothing like I remembered. It was dark and dimly lit here and there by flickering arcane lights. Dirt, dust, and cobwebs were everywhere, and the air was musty, as if the halls had not been cleaned in decades. Faint music floated down the passages. A dissonant, macabre sound that carried an uneasiness in the stale air.

I advanced down the hall, stepping around piles of who-knew-what, dust and crumbs pressing against my bare feet. The three devils huddled tightly behind me as they followed me. They seemed a little unnerved, their excitement from earlier dampened by the atmosphere. The further down the hallway I strode, the darker it became. I brought *Mage Lights* to life and spread them carefully out ahead of us. The palace felt so much more maze-like in this unkempt state. I traced through the halls, counting entryways in my head. Finally, I made it to the archway of one of the larger rooms, one I recognized. It had the same high, vaulted ceilings, and an entire wall that was nothing but stained glass.

My lights shifted closer and I froze. The depiction on the glass was different. When I'd met Victus there, it had been white flowers and flames. Now, it was a horrifying depiction of colossal devils fighting in a burning hellscape of orange and red.

My foot slid on something wet as I reached the center of the room. I looked down and saw a streak of dark liquid spilled across the ground. The *Mage Lights* floated down closer to it.

Blood?

I whirled my head around, looking for the source.

The three devils halted near the threshold of the room. They looked to me as if *I* was the one that might protect them.

"It must be from one of the beasts!" the first devil said.

My eyes snagged on blood-soaked reptilian footprints leading across the room. They were enormous. One would completely engulf my own foot ...

A growl sounded and one of the devils screamed. I turned back around—but only two remained inside the threshold. A shadow scurried across the ceiling, and I felt something wet rain down from above. It was hot, the drops speckling across my face. I wiped my hand on my cheek. More blood. There was a wet crack, and an object fell from the ceiling hitting the floor with a loud smack. My *Mage Lights* shifted, and the head of the female devil lit in my view. Another shower of warm liquid—I assumed blood— splattered across me.

The two devils fled screaming down the hall.

I looked up in the direction of the dripping blood.

Two, slitted, gold eyes blinked from the darkness of the ceiling. I shifted my *Mage Lights* till blue light illuminated a scaled maw with long, pointed teeth bathed in blood. The creature turned its head in a predatory motion before crawling across the ceiling and down the wall. Its eyes never left mine, but I realized there was no trembling in my body. I was not afraid. Something warm stirred that deep, magic well inside me. I felt drawn to the creature, as if we were one of the same kind. The lights shifted and glistened on its scales.

"Are you a drake?"

It halted across the room, tilting its head at me. It dropped the decapitated body on the floor, then a male voice hissed, "You can speak Drakon?"

I blinked. Was I? The language of drakes and dragons was studied by many masters students at Midor's, but I'd never learned it. The new magic warmed inside me again, stirring me to take a step closer.

"Answer the question," I insisted softly, drifting towards him.

"I ... am," he hissed, closing in. "What are *you*?"

The word that the lakeshore crowd had spoken clanged in my head.

Goddess.

"I'm your new Mistress," I said in an arcana-laced *Command.* I didn't care to actually be his Mistress, but it seemed like the easiest way to avoid becoming dessert.

"You ..." He circled me, sizing me up cautiously. "I've never met a devil more powerful than *His Infernal Highness.*"

I stilled at the comment. Was I? What Erebell had done to me, was more powerful than *him?*

The beast took a few steps from the shadows, revealing himself to be a metallic, golden-scaled drake. He moved closer on four limbs, and a tail curled twenty feet beyond his snout. Light glided across his beautiful scales and the spiked rows down his back, to two bony protrusions extending from his shoulder blades. A sense of loss rose from deep in my heart at the sight of them.

"What happened to your wings?" I couldn't keep the hurt from my voice.

"The Primordial Father cut them. He made me burrow under the earth like a wyrm to kill."

How utterly cruel. Not all drakes had wings, but to make one that had been born to soar in the skies instead live a life of service underground ... How many of his own infernal creatures had the Primordial Father maimed like this during his rule?

I drifted forward gently, reaching out till my hand touched his neck. He flinched at first, then relaxed as my fingers trailed over his smooth scales. He eyed me with caution, but I drew closer and rested my head against his neck. I ran my hand up his back and touched the nearest bony protrusion gently with my fingertips.

I used to be one of the most gifted students of Transmutation at Midor's. I had always been most interested in transmuting living creatures, like how my father had transformed me from human to the likeness of a devil—and, I suppose, like how I had been turned into whatever I was now. Something more ... with a hand dipped into that glittering, primordial chaos.

I closed my eyes and the flames sparkled beneath my lids, already licking my fingertips. There was an ancient hum to it, an undertone of ... something unknown. I thought of the Transmutation spells that restored, like *Spotless, Renew,* even *Manipulate Rock.* Why couldn't I manipulate magic to renew his wings? I focused on the feeling of my new magic first, then the longing, desire, and wish to be free and fly—to summon it like how Leander had taught me to cast *Lightning.*

The ancient, unknown magic that stirred inside me now surged into the drake. He hissed a breath, but stilled as if he knew. I called for that which had been lost to be reformed. I visualized it—two great wings, vast and just as beautiful as the rest of the golden drake. Air rushed in around my face. Only after the warmth of my magic had settled and the drake gusted a breath over my hair did I open my eyes.

A pair of giant, leather wings stretched out beyond and above the drake, fanning the air. His new scales glittered a shiny gold under the *Mage Lights,* each wing tipped at the joints with a single, brown claw talon.

"You ... are *not* a devil." His eyes were wide on me, and he looked over my form again. "A devil could not bless me like this. You ... are like *me.*"

I didn't know what he meant by that. Perhaps he felt what I had felt too. A connection that drew us closer, perhaps not too unlike the arcane connection between souls.

He shifted his feet and eyed me in anticipation. I knew what he wanted.

"My first *Command* for you ..."

The drake held its breath.

"... is to fly."

The drake inhaled sharply. He charged past me, his claws scraping and gripping against the tiled floor as he angled towards the ceiling-high, stained glass wall. He burst through, sending shards of colored glass out into the night and across the floor. I ran to the gaping opening and watched the drake flare his wings, sweeping up into the night sky. He let out a triumphant, guttural cry that sounded like it echoed for miles. Wind flooded in through the gap, buffeting me as if I were flying too.

I smiled till I could no longer see him against the dark sky, then turned around to a gigantic mess. Glass, blood, a severed head ... I tiptoed across the glass shards and began to wonder. If I was really here so soon after Leander had been killed on Novus, did that mean ... did that mean that I would see *her?*

The question rang hollow with denial in my mind. Then I remembered her name, and the truth flickered deep in my soul.

I ... think I am her.

But how had being set free from that dungeon send me back in time? The last moment that I remembered before I woke in the glittering flames was not wanting to let go of Leander's soul. So I'd thrown myself after him, hopelessly following that familiar caress of his soul. I guessed that had brought me to the lake but ... whatever was powering me now was different. A new fire—a new power—a *new soul*. I wondered if in my desperation, and this new power, I'd somehow overshot. I had followed Leander's soul, but not *my* Leander. Not the one that remembers me.

CHAPTER FIFTY-ONE

I peeked around the corner of a threshold that the dissonant music flowed from and found a banquet room.

The walls were draped in black, velvet curtains, dimly lit by half-melted candles, and populated by dark wood furniture for sitting and, by the looks of it, *fornication*. It was exactly what I would imagine a hellish brothel looked like. Latticed wood carved in flame-like designs separated open space where devils and infernal creatures were tucked into their activities. I peered across the crowd and through the open spaces in the dividers, hoping to catch a glimpse of him. I squeezed between infernals until I bumped into a long refreshment table. I peered down, eyes jumping over bon-bons, mysterious meat skewers, and a number of tinted, glass bottles.

I pushed away from the table and worked my way around the outside of the room. I turned near a corner and finally, through a parting in the crowd, I caught a glimpse of him and my heart skipped.

Leander reclined across a velvet chaise, his overall posture and build more slender than I remembered. His hair was long, and flowed down his shoulders past his chest, as if he had not cut it in decades. He had that familiar devilish grin plastered across his face, though it was much more feral—more sinister looking—as he slid the fingers of a naked succubus seated in his lap into his mouth.

I wanted to snap her neck—I wanted to snap *his* neck. But ... I didn't think it would have the desired impact considering he probably didn't actually know who I was. Still, seeing him again warmed my heart despite the building jealousy and anger.

Leander's glowing, orange eyes flicked up and caught my stare. I bolted.

This was a mistake. I didn't know how I could talk to him—how I could face him when he wouldn't know who I was—or, I suppose, who I *would* be.

The entrance came into view as I pushed through the crowd. I rushed through it and down the corridor till I reached a bathroom. I slinked inside and pushed the door shut behind me.

Arcane flames lit the sconces on the walls as if enchanted to detect a presence. I ignored the hall connecting to toilets and instead looked through the cabinets. I pulled a few towels of cloth and surveyed myself in the mirror, then tried to wipe off the blood. There was plumbing with water, but I recalled how the water here was not safe for mortals. Would it be safe for me now?

The flames lighting the bathroom flickered. The floor creaked and I saw a hazy shadow bubble on the floor behind me in the mirror. I turned around to face it and heard Leander's disembodied voice precede his materializing form.

"Are you the pretty voice I heard?" The shadow bubbled up, rising to form horns and a silhouette, then it hardened. The black mist trailed down his disheveled, half-buttoned black clothing as he towered over me, just a few inches away. I didn't feel the same presence I had felt the first time I'd met him.

No ... this Leander was ... diminished. I felt so far from him, despite only being inches away. Then his scent filled the space around me—that same cinnamon and smoke—and I almost reflexively swayed into him. There was something about him and his unhinged demeanor that heated my cheeks. It made me want to run my fingers along every inch of him. But ... this Leander was not mine. Not yet. And despite his proximity setting my insides molten, I was still angry. Angry that I was here, that there was no bond between us—that moments ago a *fucking succubus* had her fingers in his mouth.

"Your palace is filthy," I said sharply. "You should clean it."

"Ah, it *is* you, pretty voice ..." he responded in a sinister caress.

I almost went weak at that tone.

He brought his hand to my face. The touch was not the soft delicateness I knew but a sharp, talon-like scratch. "You are pretty dirty yourself. Look at all this blood." He smiled crookedly, as if he enjoyed the sight of me covered in blood.

I didn't have to wonder. It was exactly the kind of thing he liked.

He wobbled a little. "Are you telling me you have higher standards for the state of the palace than *His Infernal Highness* himself does?"

Hell ... was he drunk? Or high? Or both?

"Are you telling me that your standards died with you on Novus?" I replied, hoarse with anger.

He cracked his jaw and narrowed his glowing eyes at me. "What should I call you, pretty voice?"

I could tell I'd struck a chord by the edge in his tone. As for what he should call me ... I said what felt right. "Grace."

"*Grace* ... why have I never seen you before?" His sharp nails slid down and around my neck, gripping against my skin. The shadows around him licked up his back like the flames of the hellhound. Was he trying to intimidate me?

"I'm not afraid of you, Leander," I said instead of answering.

"That's a fatal mistake ..." he growled, tightening his fingers around my neck and squeezing.

For a split second, my memory flashed to Victus—to when he had choked me. Perhaps Leander expected me to scream or beg, but I'd meant what I'd said. I could never be afraid of him. So I stared into those blazing, hellfire eyes and waited, watching for that shift in his eyes I knew would come.

When he saw that there was not a single ounce of fear in my eyes, he let go of my neck.

"You are amusing, Grace," he said flatly, wiping sweat from his face with his sleeve. "Stay as long as you like. Clean up things if it's too filthy for you." He dematerialized into black smoke and shadow, gone just as swiftly as he had come.

CHAPTER FIFTY-TWO

All I knew about *Grace* was that she had helped him. In the short time I'd spent with him so far, he definitely seemed like he needed help. He was driving himself and this circle further into despair. The thoughts of how I could stop it weighed on me as I crept down the familiar—albeit ill-kept—halls, till I found a guest room and lounged on the bed. I wasn't really sure what I was doing here or how I could get back.

I slept only a few hours, waking up constantly as if sleep didn't quite work the same as it used to for me. Was I really not a mortal anymore? The thought made me a little sad, but I tried to remain focused on why I was here, now, in this time. I would try to help Leander—even if it tortured me.

Eventually, after a sustained thirty minutes without dozing off again, I rose from my bed. I felt a tingle in my mind, and I cracked open the door to see the imp. I blinked at it in surprise, realizing I could sense its presence.

"Goddess!" The imp rushed up excitedly, a basket balanced on its head. "I have clothing for you." It offered me the basket.

The fabrics slid smoothly under my fingers. These were such fine clothes, as nice as the one Leander had given me at Bon Mar—the one that had cost many souls.

"How did you get these, exactly?" I said, a little concerned. "Do I owe you anything?"

"No, Goddess. They were given to worship you." The imp's lips peeled back in a wide, pointy-toothed grin.

Oh. Great. Maybe I should keep a lower profile before this entire circle started erecting temples. I recalled the opal, and the female devil shopkeeper who knew about ... me? No, no, no—this was too confusing to think about. *Focus on Leander.*

"Thank you. Don't mention to anyone else I am here, okay? I want to have a vacation where I may move about freely—unrecognized." I winked at the imp.

The imp's black voids widened. "Yes, Goddess. I will keep your presence here discreet!"

"I'm not really sure how to have you help me next, to be honest. But I will call upon you when I think of something."

"Yes, Goddess! I will remain nearby unseen, awaiting your next command!" The imp hardly finished before backing away and glittering out of sight with invisibility.

"Thanks!" I took the basket to my bed and looked through the options.

I changed into the first item, a high-collared, black velvet dress. Its fitted sleeves had cutouts exposing my shoulders, and at my wrists a triangle of it extended down the back of my hand to a band at the base of my middle finger. The skirt edge swished around my shins softly. Gold embroidered swirls lined the buttons from the waist to collar, circling around my neck and meeting. After I fastened the buttons, I dawned soft, black leather, knee high boots. This felt so much more comfortable than that practically see-through dress from the night before.

I poked around the palace and heard the same music playing as the previous day—or what I guessed was the previous day. It was hard to tell how much time had actually passed with the sky constantly dark. I drifted into the banquet hall and found the devils were easily recognizable—it looked like they had never left. The refreshments table had been restocked, and I eyed the little trays of food. Should I be eating? Surely if I needed to eat, I would feel hungry. I surveyed the bottles and finally poured myself a red-tinted drink. I couldn't try things like this before. Perhaps I could now.

I lifted the glass to my nose and sniffed.

"It's not poison, trust me," a familiar voice crooned next to me.

I looked over at the owner of the voice.

It was Silas. He was covered in sweat and had dark circles under his eyes. The sides of his mouth were stained a pink color, probably from drinking blood, if I had to imagine.

I took a sip from the drink in my hands. It had an interesting sour flavor but was also sweet with cherries and anise.

"I've never seen you before, and I know everyone," Silas declared.

I shrugged and feigned a half smile.

"Which circle are you from?" he pressed.

"I'm not from this plane," I replied.

Silas bent his eyebrows up in confusion. "You have such a distinct aura to you, it's very Nine Circles."

I took another sip of the drink.

"Who is your father?"

My throat burned as I choked.

Like I could even begin explain the true answer to that question.

"He's dead." I raised my glass to him. "Enjoy the party."

He narrowed his eyes, but he raised his half-empty glass in return.

I slipped away between others till I couldn't see him any-more.

Maneuvering through the crowd, I looked around to see if I could spot Leander. I found him unsurprisingly on the same chaise and in the same clothes as the day before. He was sprawled with his arm draped across his eyes, a variety of half-drunk, stemmed goblets littered around him, a few broken. He looked dreadful. The sight of him in pain pulled at my heart. I just couldn't stay away from him. I didn't even know what I was going to do when I had his attention again, but at least this time he was alone ...

I moved in closer and stood over him, casting a shadow across his form as I stared down over the rim of my own goblet. He must have sensed the shift in light because he lifted his arm slightly and squinted at me. Dark circles hung under his eyes from the abuse he was inflicting on himself. His eyes flicked up and down, and then he covered them again.

"Why are you wearing so much clothing?" he droned.

"Why are you alone at your own party?" I cut back. I didn't want to be so mean to him, but it bothered me to see him like this when I knew what he could be—would be.

"Because I have a splitting headache, *thanks to you*," he growled.

I laughed.

His eyes peeked through his arm to see it.

"You have a headache because you are intentionally hurting yourself," I answered back.

His silence told me this was exactly how he saw the par-ties—a compilation of ways masquerading pleasure to punish himself for being so weak. How many years had he already suffered like this? Would *her* efforts—or rather *my* efforts—be able to course correct? Or would it take much longer to wake him up from this pretense of prison?

I felt that ancient primordial magic inside me stir as if in support. It was bolstering me with a growing confidence. Perhaps there was something I could do to make him feel better in the short term.

I leaned down towards him and brushed his hair away from his forehead, channeling a thread of my glittering magic into him to erase whatever pain plagued his head. I'd never tried using magic to heal like this before, but the tingling under my skin told me I could.

He removed his arm fully, staring up at me in surprise with burning orange eyes. "My ... headache is gone."

I curled the corner of my lip up and said, "You're welcome."

He sat up on the chaise as I turned to walk away. I didn't want to sit around at this party and watch him abuse himself.

I refused to.

"You are leaving?" He sounded disappointed.

"Just the party," I said, giving the room another appraising look before glancing back at him. "Try *not* to get another headache." I felt a tinge of my new magic slip between the words, like I was giving a *Command*.

His infernal eyes lit up at the words.

CHAPTER FIFTY-THREE

I found the library easily. It was dusty, mostly from neglect. Probably because going to the library was not high on the list of fun party activities for anyone, except me. I spent the next few hours casting *Spotless* on the shelves, floors, tables, and chairs, till it was pristine. I lit the candles in the chandelier and the sconces with a white arcane light, as it was better for reading—which I fully intended to do.

I selected a few interesting texts I had not read yet—*Histories of the Nine Circles*, *Primordial Creatures: An Anthology*, and even some works of fiction—then curled up in one of the now clean, red velvet chairs. Reading and understanding the infernal came so much easier to me now, and I spent the next few hours devouring the new information. Eventually, I came across a large, religious tome I'd never seen. I wondered if Leander had gotten rid of it.

It spoke of the Primordial Father and Mother. They did apparently have their own names outside the titles given by their infernal creations. His name, Erethor, was easiest to find next to his title. My eyes floated further down the page where they snagged on her name.

Erebell.

I froze, gripping the book. Given everything I had experienced in the last forty-eight hours, I'd had my suspicions. Now I knew for certain.

Knowing made me sad, however. That meant that the Primordial Father—Erethor—was the one who had refused to allow her to have a daughter. He was the one who had locked her up, and her direct descendants—the First Princes—who'd never visited her. Remodeus was one such First Prince. How could they ignore their mother? A goddess with that much power ... It made me wonder how much like her she'd made me. I knew Leander suspected *Grace* of being a goddess based on what he'd told me. But I wasn't sure if I was one. Wouldn't I be a First Princess?

I re-summoned the imp to find a blanket, which I wrapped myself in and spent the next several hours reading. The freshly cleaned library provided a warm and comfortable air. I wondered if it would be weird to just attempt my sleep in here. I felt cradled, grounded in familiarly—especially now that I didn't have the thread to comfort me. I fought back tears thinking about the loss of that connection.

The lights flickered again as the floor creaked, and then Leander was standing in the center of the library, looking around.

"Are you trying to make yourself difficult to find?" he huffed.

"Is *Scry* too hard for you now?" I teased.

He had an annoyed expression on his face, but he smiled around it.

Did he like it when I was mean to him?

"I couldn't *Scry* on you for some reason ... care to tell me why?" His voice cut like a razor's edge.

Then I felt him in my mind—or rather, that he was attempting to enter my mind, but his metaphysical fingers kept bouncing off me. His smile faded. I raised my eyebrows, acknowledging his failed attempts.

"What are you?" he growled. "Are you here to depose me?" When I didn't answer, he took a few steps closer and the shadows flickered up his back like hackles, the flames of the candles bowing before him. "Magic will prevent you from killing me on palace grounds. But I will kill *you* if I have to, despite how *pretty* that voice is."

I knew it was an empty threat. I had already sensed his diminished aura, like Silas could sense my amplified one. A lot of the things he was doing—flickering the lights, becoming shadow—seemed more like simple illusions meant to intimidate by feigning more power than he had.

I didn't want to be mean anymore. I wanted to hold him, comfort him. Tell him it was all going to be okay. That one day we'd meet and this would all be worth it in the end—that we could finally begin. A dark thought entered my mind ...

What if for me, it ends here? And I never make it back to my time, with my Leander?

"Actually," I said, "I'm stranded here. And I want more than anything to go home."

Leander's infernal gaze softened and the shadows leaned back. "I'm stranded too ..." he said quietly.

I looked up at him in surprise. The gentle caress in his tone. It was his voice, the one I knew.

"I wont be able to leave this plane for another 480 years."

He'd been slain in Novus only *twenty years ago*? That was nothing to an immortal—practically yesterday. I instantly regretted being so mean to him.

"Nor, as I said, leave the palace either," he continued with disgust. "A devil with a *pretty-voice* may try to kill me again to take my seat as ruler of the Fire Circle while I'm weak."

"You are not weak," I said, leaning up in my chair, adjusting the soft blanket around me.

"How would you know?"

I couldn't help but laugh, my fangs flashing. "I've heard plenty about you, Leander," I said teasingly. I began listing his strengths. "You are devastatingly devious, and quick-thinking, not to mention rather thoughtful and—"

"Did you *read* those things about me?" he said with curiosity.

"No." I grinned. "Tell me, *Your Infernal Highness*, would you like to leave the palace tomorrow? Don't worry. If any scary devils come to usurp you, I'll see that they meet a tragic, awful end." I could feel that primordial magic burning behind my eyes—proof that I was serious.

"If you desire to be violent, I can arrange something here for you to kill." His voice was a sinister caress as the shadows flared again in the room. "I would love to watch you become bathed in blood again."

"I think you need to get out of the palace." I refused to let him distract me from the subject, despite how his words sent tingles down my spine.

He frowned slightly. "Very well. We'll have breakfast on the verandah."

I laughed a breath. "I suppose that is technically outside the palace ... Do you promise to clean yourself up?"

He narrowed his glowing orange eyes at me, though there was a slight tug at the corner of his lips. "I'm beginning to think you *like* me," his voice once again that smooth, caressing velvet I knew.

Heat rushed my cheeks as I remembered the things he had done to me while speaking with that heavy, smooth tone, and I couldn't help but shift in my seat.

His eyes, burning with that beautiful hellfire, flicked over my face as if he could feel how hot my skin was. "Mm-hmm," he hummed the acknowledgment. "Do you promise to wear *less* clothing?" He placed a hand on each arm of my chair and leaned into the space above me.

If I had to use my body to lure him out of this state, I would. Selfishly, I *wanted* his attention on my body. And if that's what would work ...

"I'll make a deal with you," I said sweetly.

His eyes widened and his lips curled into that familiar, devilish smile. He didn't know how well I knew his nature. He wouldn't be prepared for how I could *torment* him.

My stomach fluttered with the excitement.

I leaned forward myself, keeping my eyes on his. "If you send everyone home, end the un-ending party, and clean the entire palace ... I won't wear *any clothing* for our breakfast tomorrow."

His devilish smile turned positively wicked and he leaned in closer. "You seem to think highly of yourself, that I would do all that just to see you nude."

"Do we have a deal?" I smiled up at him, letting my fangs peek through.

I watched his eyes drift down to them.

He never stood a chance.

"It's a deal."

CHAPTER FIFTY-FOUR

I thought about Leander as I tried to will myself to get some sleep. Flirting with him like we used to had felt so gratifying. I think it was the only reason I could relax enough to truly drift off this time. It felt so *normal,* despite the empty pit in my soul where our bond had been—would be.

After a little bit of sleep, I cracked my guest room door open to peek out and was met with the sweet aroma of night blooming jasmine filling the hallway. I glanced down the hall in both directions. It was *pristinely* clean. The dust, cobwebs, and dirt that had layered the hall were all gone. Heat rushed to my cheeks.

Did he really clean the entire palace because of our deal?

I pulled a silk robe from the imp's basket and wrapped it around me, hiding my nude body underneath. Then I stepped out of my room and began checking his work.

The banquet hall was quiet, the refreshments table, furniture, and lattice dividers all gone. The room had been reset as a simple meeting room, with a few tables and chairs, no trace that a party had ever occurred there. Not even the floors betrayed the previous day's activities with a speck of a lingering spill. The room where the drake had killed the female devil and scattered broken glass was returned to an orderly state. Even the stained glass had been meticulously replaced, but now ... My eyes widened as I gazed up at the white flowers and flames. It was as I remembered. This had to mean I was doing the right things.

I kept walking and couldn't help but smile at how beautiful the palace looked now—not to mention how much more quiet it was.

I finally made my way to two large doors that opened out to a verandah. Leander was seated there, waiting for me. There were candles set up on the table and the posts outside to provide lighting in the darkness. I saw tea, chocolates, little sandwiches, and pastries stacked on confection stands all over the table. I took a few steps closer and stopped just shy of the other chair when he turned his head to me. He had cleaned himself up and changed into a black silk, button-down tunic that looked so soft I wanted to touch it.

"Are you pleased now with the state of the palace?" he said in a low purr. His eyes drifted up and down my form, eyeing the edges of the robe.

I didn't reply. Instead, I untied my robe and let it fall to the ground to show my approval of the new state of the palace. His orange eyes burned hotter, re-examining me from head to toe. The arrogant, satisfied grin that plastered his face told me he was pleased with his view as well. I left the robe on the ground and placed myself in the chair across from him. His eyes were glued to me, taking in every bit of exposed skin I had to offer.

"I noticed my drake is missing," he said, eyes still drifting over me. "You wouldn't know anything about that, would you?"

"I set it free," I said, as I poured some tea for myself.

"It won't survive long on its own since it can no longer fly."

I cracked a devious smile. "Something tells me the drake will be just fine." I poured tea for him and leaned in to slide it across the table.

He hardly glanced at it.

Just as I took my first sips, I felt warmth pour into the right side of my body. A purple hue had been cast over us. I looked out over what would have been the ground gardens and watched as the sky bloomed into a violet, and then a magenta, slowly blushing towards that pastel pink I knew. My smile grew so big I could hardly control it.

I looked back at him. "Why did you bring day to your eternal night?"

His eyes, still sliding over my skin, trailed up to my face. "Because the candlelight was insufficient." His voice was like the caress I had always known.

I felt my skin heat as the light bathed my features for him to see. He'd kept this circle in darkness for two decades. Then, just to see me better, he'd made it day again. I'd hardly been here for two days. It gave me hope I could do more.

I just smiled at him and sipped my tea, reclining in my chair to give his eyes access to all he wanted. This Leander was not mine ... but I would do anything to get back to my Leander.

Chapter Fifty-Five

Over the next week, Leander joined me in the library to read. Now and then we'd be interrupted by Silas coming in and out, but it was mostly just the two of us. I focused my reading on books about devils and soul binding. The ones I found outlined how the contractual magic worked between masters and mistresses and those who served them, as well as how the Primordial Father's magic was used in the soul mate bond. I studied the pages for any clues as to a ritual I knew I would have to perform. Of course, Leander had told me they—*we*—had sex to split his soul, but how exactly did I—would I—do that? Eventually, the topic would have to be surfaced.

I looked up at Leander, who had been reading a book about the architect of the Circle Transporter—the method most infernals used to travel between the circles.

"Have you ever thought about binding your soul to someone, like a soul mate?" I lifted the book slightly, showing the title.

He looked at it with a pained expression. "I am not sure why anyone would willingly do that," he replied.

I recalled the story he had told me about his parents. About how the Primordial Father had forced matches for his personal gain.

"I don't mean like what the Primordial Father does ... for power, to be a pawn—but to choose a soul mate for love. Because you see them, and you know deep down with every ounce of your being that you belong to them, and they belong to you."

He stared at me pensively. There was a look on his face, like the concept I'd just described was completely foreign to him and he was struggling to wrap his head around it. "You have felt that way?"

"I *had* a soul mate ..." I replied, and it was impossible not to hide the sadness.

"So, it ended badly for you. My first statement stands. I cannot understand why anyone would willingly do that." He lowered his head and stared down into his book.

"I would do it again, a million times over, even if the outcome was always the same."

He set his book down in his lap. "Why? Why would you cause yourself that much pain and grief all over again? It cannot be worth it."

"It was worth it—it *is* worth it. Every single second of it." I looked into his eyes. The eyes that had made me feel all of those seconds. "The pain I'm feeling now reminds me of how much I love him. How much I value him. How I belong to him—with him. I never want to stop feeling that, even if there is pain laced in there."

"What happened to him?" he said, eyes still on mine.

"He's gone... and our bond was broken. But even though we are no longer tethered together ... I'll keep following his soul even if it takes me to the *eternal oblivion*."

"What if you never find him?"

"Then I'll have died or wasted away to whatever is at the end of immortality. Because I refuse to stop till I do." The space that held my soul ached thinking about what it had felt like to have Leander sitting across from me much like this, but with our souls relentlessly pulling towards each other. The sad thought re-entered my mind. That all I had *was* the memories. That I'd never find him again after whatever I did here.

"Silas was the last devil to choose a soul mate before the Primordial Father was banished," Leander said. "He loved another prince ... Florian of the Poison Circle."

Ah. Leander had mentioned before that Silas had once chosen a soul mate's bond for love—a bond that hadn't ended well. I didn't realize it was with another prince.

I cleared my throat, almost afraid to hear what I knew had to be tragic. "What happened?"

"They are still connected because they made it permanent. If I had to guess, the break up seems mostly on Silas's end. I don't think Florian realized just how broken Silas was. Silas separated from him shortly before I was ... *returned* here."

"Is that also why you never considered it? You saw what it was like for Silas?"

"It doesn't matter. The Primordial Father is banished." Leander picked up his book once again.

"The Primordial Father is not the only one who can split devil souls." The words spilled out of me automatically. I had no idea how to do it yet, other than having sex with Leander, but I knew I would figure it out. "The Primordial Father wasn't involved in creating my soul mate bond," I clarified.

He said nothing further, merely offering me a side eye, then he stared back into his book.

I sighed. "Sorry for bringing it up ..." I stood, stretching my back. "I'm going to walk a little before I pick a new book."

His infernal eyes flicked up at me briefly. "I'll be here," he said flatly.

Right ... I hadn't realized bringing up the topic of soul mates would make him so grouchy. I made it only halfway down the corridor when I sensed someone following behind me. I smiled, thinking it was Leander, but when I turned—

"Hello, Silas," I said in surprise.

He didn't offer me a kind look. In fact, he seemed rather frigid as he trailed silently up to me. When he did speak, he cut straight to the chase.

"Why are you filling his head with nonsense about the soul mate bond?"

I scrunched my face and continued walking.

Silas followed beside me.

"Surely, you know, right?" I said curtly. "How much agony does it cause you to be apart from your soul mate?"

There was silent tension in the air as we walked.

"My mother and father also chose to be soul mates for love," Silas said with pain in his voice. "Want to know how that went for them?"

I slowed and gave him my attention, looking into his glowing, yellow eyes.

"My father murdered my mother, giving her the *immortal's death*, and then he gifted it to himself."

I froze. I knew I wasn't hiding my look of horror.

His expression changed to recognition. He knew that kind of horror all too well.

"Why would he do that?"

Silas stiffened. "Now, that is something I have not told anyone, including Leander."

I knew a warning when I heard one by now. It wouldn't be fair to insist he tell me. I supposed it didn't matter anyway, considering the pain Silas must have suffered.

"And you still asked for your own soul mate bond for love?" I said instead.

He looked ahead of us to where the halls forked. "I was naive." He split from me, walking down the hallway that retreated deeper into the palace till I saw him turn out of view.

CHAPTER FIFTY-SIX

"It just so happens I've been invited to a formal event in the Prime Circle. Would you accompany me as my guest?" Leander's eyes narrowed on me, as if he realized I would finally get my wish to see him leave the palace.

It had been a over a week, and I knew there had to be a moment coming when I'd see Remodeus. As much as I didn't want to see him, *his* seeing *me* was how he would know to create me ... These mental backflips were becoming too hard to keep track of. Despite that, thinking of going to a formal event with Leander reminded me of the ball in my dream, and the thought of it sent tingles down my spine.

I smiled. "Of course, I will."

"May I choose your clothing?" he said in a sinister tone.

The desire to please him outweighed the uncomfortable feeling I usually got when I showed a lot of skin. It didn't matter whether it was this Leander or my Leander, I trusted him completely. Besides, I was curious to see what *this* Leander would pick out for me.

"I suppose I can reward your good behavior ..." I replied in feigned disinterest.

His lips curled. "I'll have something sent to your room."

Later, when I laid eyes on the dress he had picked out for me, my heart melted. It was sleeveless and high-collared, a band of white silk circling my neck like a choker. Sheer black fabric under the white strip clung to me down to the waistline. Black, opaque threads were embroidered in that frame, and swirled like smoke around my breasts, as if holding them each in their own shadowed swirl. I liked to imagine those two black swirls of shadow belonged to Leander as they hugged my body. The shadow-smoke flowed up from a black silk band at my waist. The black tulle skirt of the dress had tiny, white silk flowers sewn in the shape of night jasmine. Each flower had a transparent yellow crystal in their center. The flowers were peppered more densely down towards the hem of the skirt as if caught in a wind and free falling into drifts. It was breathtaking.

I met Leander in the foyer. He looked equally stunning in a black tuxedo with a matching white silk pocket square, embroidered with the same flowers. The coat had just the faintest threads of gold woven into it. His hair was pulled back neatly in a bun at the nape of his neck. Despite how devastatingly handsome he looked dressed so formally, I found my myself missing his usual attire, the half-buttoned white shirt and jacket.

As I approached, he extended his hand to me as he used to—arm low, muscles relaxed, and posture open. I placed my hand in his and was struck with the missing feeling of our bond. I tried not to let the disappointment show. He held my hand tightly and spun me around so he could see every angle of me.

"You look delicious." His voice was the new sinister purr I'd gotten used to.

"You look nice, too," I replied, trying and failing to not think about what he did to me the last time he uttered those words.

He pulled me into him and squeezed a hand to my back, still holding my hand out, swaying.

"Are you dancing with me?" I remarked in surprise.

"I have to now ... before everyone in the Prime Circle tries to steal you away."

"For someone who doesn't see the value of bonding for love, you are quite the romantic."

His face shifted slightly at the comment, as if he'd never considered himself romantic.

I laid my head on his chest as we swayed. "What do you wish for? If you could do anything, or be anything," I said, staring at the walls of the foyer shift by as we turned.

"I'm not sure," he said at first. "Before I was returned here, I simply wanted to keep my power and resist the commands of the Primordial Father. But I didn't have any goals ... I still don't have goals other than to exist until I regain my previous primordial power. So, I suppose what I want is to be more powerful."

"Power is not just this primordial magic. There's power in your mind. The power to feed it whatever knowledge you desire. There is also power in your will—to resist what you do not desire. The Primordial Father only has primordial power. If he had the other kinds, he probably wouldn't be floating in Abyssus right now." I squeezed him tighter. "You have a gift that many creatures in existence squander—time. Time is the only constant that you can rely on, but it's also the greatest changer. It brings you to moment after moment, and you can use your power to be the thing that changes. You can have your power *now* if you decide to."

"I did not realize you were such a philosopher," he said softly. "Is that what you believe?"

"Yes."

"That must be easy for you to say. You appear to have a deep well of primordial magic."

I pulled my head away from his chest to look into his eyes, glassy and peering down at me. "I don't really use my magic much unless you make me angry," I teased. I couldn't tell him about my past.

About why I truly believed what I said. That they had been the very words he'd said to me. I wondered if this was where he'd gotten them to begin with.

"Are you ready to go?" he said.

I nodded.

He looked around the foyer and back at me, his expression leaning into embarrassment. "Have you been to the Prime Palace before?"

I blinked. I had—once—when Remodeus captured me. Assuming that had been the Prime Palace. Had *Grace* been there, though?

"The problem," Leander began, "is that I can't teleport that far in my current state."

I smiled, realizing what he was implying. "Do you have a painting of it?"

His eyebrow raised. "You are quite clever."

He led me to one of the smaller meeting rooms. Hung across its wall was a large painting of the front of the Prime Palace. Its spires rose from a manicured garden like a golden sculpture, gleaming in the light. Small topiary trees peppered the surrounding landscape among marble pathways. My eyes narrowed in on a group of trees set aside from the entrance in the painting.

"What about there?" I pointed out the trees.

He nodded.

I grinned wildly, extending my hand before him, and couldn't help saying, "Are you ready, *my dear?*"

He looked at me, more confused than anything, but a similar smile spread across his face. He placed his hand in mine and I pulled us together, squeezing him against me.

I pictured the place just like I'd picture a person I was sending a *Mindtell* to. I probably should have told him I'd never actually done this—but that primordial magic burned inside me as if it needed to be spent—that it knew what to do. The world slid out from under us, and I felt him press a hand into my back. He glided his fingers across it—not in feral scratches, but in a gentle caress as he once had, and would again.

The trees tilted into place behind us and we turned. Braziers with red flames lined the walkway to the palace. Devils and infernal creatures in beautiful silks, beaded jackets, feathered gowns, and sewn leather accessories drifted towards the entrance ahead of us.

Leander linked my arm and led me closer, bringing me inside.

The room we entered was as large as a ballroom. Infernals strummed instruments in a corner, and guests drank from glass goblets as they conversed. My eyes scanned the crowd when another devil—who seemed familiar—caught my eye. He appeared to focus more on Leander as he walked elegantly over to us, straightening his dark velvet jacket. His ebony skin was adorned with the faint shimmer of glittering powder spread across his cheeks and eyelids—even his horns—giving him a regal and otherworldly glow. It matched the shifting cream and green stitching down his dark lapels. His hair was short and cut close to his head, his face framed by the shadow of neat stubble. His friendly eyes shifted between the two of us, voids of black with glowing pale emerald irises, which finally settled on me. I realized then that he was one of the devils I had seen in my dream with Leander.

"I don't believe we've had the pleasure of meeting ..." His voice was deep, rich, and smooth. "I am Prince Florian."

"I'm ... Grace."

"Just Grace?" he said with a slight smile. "You look like you'd be a princess, or perhaps even a queen." He chuckled.

There was something just under the surface of his cordial mask, a sadness. It had only been two decades since he and Silas had fallen apart. My heart twisted for them as I thought of how awful it felt to be far away from that comforting tug ... Did Silas and Florian feel that, too?

"Apologies, Leander, for not coming to ... your parties," Florian said. It made sense with how much I'd seen Silas there.

Leander shrugged. He was distracted, constantly surveying his surroundings.

"Is this the first time you've left the palace?" Florian's question was directed to Leander, but his eyes flashed down to me.

"Is it that obvious?" Leander said under his breath.

I'd never seen him like this before. So uncomfortable and self-conscious. Would devils here really attack him for a chance at the Fire Circle? If anyone tried to harm him ... we would see just how powerful this ancient magic Erebell gave me was.

"Is Julian here?" Leander's voice was quiet with anger. He gripped my arm hooked in his, tighter.

Florian turned his head to look around. "I saw him moments ago. I'm not sure where he got off to. Probably best to avoid him." He grimaced and placed his hand on Leander's shoulder.

I wondered ... The tapestry I had been looking at when Silas had first found me—had he been there because he wanted to see it? "Excuse me, Prince Florian?"

He smiled at me. "Yes, Miss Grace?"

"Is your castle, a glowing green stone? Like a pale, haunted moon?"

Florian laughed. "I'd never thought to describe it that way, but now that I've heard it, I think it's quite beautiful and poetic." He bowed his head slightly. "Perhaps I could convince you to come to the Castle of Poison where you are welcome to write all the beautiful poetry you like."

I smiled back, but something in my heart broke for him. "Thank you. I'll think about it." Did he know Silas visited that tapestry and looked at his castle almost a thousand years later? My eyes shifted up to Leander.

He was looking through the crowd, gaze jumping erratically.

I tugged on Leander's arm. "Let's go get a drink," I whispered to him.

He gripped my arm tighter, but pulled me along.

I waved goodbye to Florian, and he waved back in response.

We watched the party while enjoying our drinks. Some began to float along to the music, and Leander shifted behind me, leaning to put his lips near to my ear.

"Will you dance with me again?" he purred.

"Of course."

The dance here was much more energetic. We bounced across the floor and swung in and out between pairs of couples in syncopation with the music. After a while, the music slowed. He pulled me into him again and we swayed. I rested my head on his chest and closed my eyes, reaching out for every bit of him. His warmth, his heart beating, his breath ... It was easy to picture this was my Leander with my eyes closed.

"I'm glad you invited me here," I hummed against his chest. "It's so important."

"What do you mean?"

"You could have decided not to come. This was one of those moments, where you used your power to choose."

"It's just another party," he protested.

"This *choice* was the important part." I finally looked up at him. I wanted him to believe that he had all the power he already needed to be the person he wanted to be. He didn't need to wait another 500 years wallowing in that palace. He could be that devil now.

I must have been staring too intensely because his eyes lowered.

"Can I show you something?" he whispered, pulling me away from the dance floor.

I followed.

CHAPTER FIFTY-SEVEN

He led me away from the party and down a hall to a small study. More than books adorned the shelves here. Between the texts were ceramic jars, porcelain creatures, and jewelry-draped, glass figurines. I was instantly drawn to the books and released Leander's arm to approach them, thinking there was something among them he wanted me to see. I ran my fingers down their spines, examining each title. The door lock clicked shut behind me, and then I felt Leander's breath by my ear—hot—his hands clawing up my waist like a predator's.

I whipped around and he pinned me back against the bookshelf. Every sense in my body heightened at his touch. I arched against him, reaching for him automatically. *What am I doing? Is this going to mess everything up? Would I—*

Before I could finish the thought, his hand slipped behind my neck and he pulled me in to his mouth.

I melted.

He was not gentle like when I had been a mortal. He devoured my mouth like a wild creature, demanding—claiming. When he felt my hands slide up his back, it unlocked something in him. His hand shifted down to my skirt, frantically pulling it up until he found my bare leg. He pushed me harder against the bookshelf, then I felt his hand slip into my undergarments. I didn't protest—I couldn't. It was everything I wanted. Every touch was like a drug. Every scrape of his claw-like nails against my thigh further drenched me for him.

I felt him tear at my undergarments, then himself. Without breaking the connection of our lips he lifted me against the bookshelf, shifting me to a panel between shelves where it was flatter against my back. I wrapped my arms around his neck and parted my knees, automatically making space for him. Then I felt him, hard against my entrance, and I whimpered into his mouth. I was so wet he was met with little friction as he pushed into me, stretching me fully. I wrapped my legs around him instinctually. He groaned in an approving tone. His hands were gripped around my ass, holding me up and pushing me against the books as the shelves creaked behind us. My mind went blank at the feeling of him, solid and thick, filling me. He tore away from my mouth and pressed his face against my neckline.

"Fucking collar," he growled. He snagged the white silk with his fangs and tore it, baring my skin for him to taste.

I moaned at how rough he was. Each plunge in and out of me sent objects falling off the shelves, some breaking on the floor. I entangled my hands behind his head, unraveling his bun. I was so desperate to be with him again that I was already so close to release. My hands clutched around him as each thrust pushed deeper, filling me so completely with him, sending me closer to that edge.

"Leander," I panted to him, trying to tell him I was so utterly close to shattering.

He let out a sinister groan, pinning me harder against the books, and unleashed the full force of himself against me. A few more thrusts and I was coming—hard. He pushed his mouth against mine, drinking the sound of my ecstasy.

He slowed a little while I rode the waves of pleasure. He had just quickened the pace of his thrusts again when a pounding sounded on the door. His growl vibrated my skin, one that said he would willingly kill whatever was on the other side of that door for interrupting. He didn't slow his pace, but the pounding at the door sounded again. His mouth drifted to my ear.

"Had I known you'd be this wet for me, we would have had some more fun before we left the palace," he purred. He pulled out of me and set me down, righting his pants and jacket before walking to the door.

I stood there for a moment, in awe at what I'd let him do to me, fully acknowledging that I would let him do it again and again. I would ... try to be a little more guarded. At least this will make things less weird when I have sex with him to split his soul.

I looked around and saw books and trinkets scattered all over the floor. Picking up a few, I cast *Renew* on them and returned them to their spots on the bookshelf. I felt Leander behind me again.

He whispered in my ear. "What are you doing?"

"Fixing what we broke?" I said, confused.

"These are Remodeus's things. Fuck him," Leander growled.

I gave a half smile and dropped the item I was holding. The red-brown ceramic depiction of a devil cracked again as it hit the floor.

Leander let out a deep chuckle. "You are such a cheeky devil." He steered me around towards the door. "The dinner with every Circle's prince is starting and I—we—are requested."

My fingers felt the ripped edge of my dress collar. I cast *Renew* spell again, and the frayed threads began to weave anew. He frowned at my fingers and I raised my eyebrows. "What?"

"I liked the idea of everyone at dinner seeing what I've done to you." He smiled sinisterly as his eyes blazed like fire at me.

This version of Leander ... he was going to undo me completely.

I stopped an inch from the edge of the collar and left that bit torn.

He leaned his head closer to mine and the smile transformed to the devilish grin I knew. "You've become rather obedient."

"Don't get used to it. I'm just rewarding you for leaving the palace."

When we arrived at the table, Leander pulled my chair out for me. I had been placed between Florian and a ghostly pale, brown-haired devil I'd never met to my right. Leander strode across the room to sit opposite me. Somehow he'd fixed his hair back into a bun and made his clothes look neat, like we hadn't just fucked against a shelf in the study. He caught me looking at him and his lips curled. I glanced away at the head of the table and immediately spied Remodeus.

He was staring right at me.

Florian leaned in and spoke in a whispered tone. "That is Remodeus. Best to avoid him in my opinion."

"Thanks," I breathed into the space between us. I wondered if this conversation could be heard.

"That one there," Florian's eyes flicked to the devil to Remodeus's left, "is the Bone Prince."

He was massive, easily the tallest, and physically strongest devil in this room. He was similar to the ceramic devil I'd seen in the study—his skin the same earthen-red tone set with stark, gray horns curling up and out from his black hair.

"Definitely avoid him," Florian continued. "He'll lock you up as breeding stock."

I squeezed my fists into my lap. He could certainly *try*.

Imps passed behind us with refreshments, and a glass of what looked like wine was placed in front of me. I took a sip as the pale devil to my right spoke.

"How long ago was it?" His voice was gravely and low.

I glanced over at him. There was something familiar about him. I knew he had to be a prince—they were all devastatingly handsome. Devastating ... and dangerous.

He almost looked human, given his slightly rugged and un-kempt appearance. He didn't wear formal clothing like the rest of us. Instead, he bore leather armor over a black tunic that covered him from his jawline all the way to his wrists. His black horns contrasted sharply with his ghostly complexion, and his fangs were longer than other devils I'd seen, the tips peeking out even when his mouth was closed. But his eyes ... they were haunting, icy blue rings on that infernal black sclera that made me feel a little on edge. There was something about the way he looked at me that made the air around him seem cold. His attention sent an uneasy feeling over my skin that pulled at my instinct to hide.

"How long ago was what?" I said, distracting myself with the wine. I hoped he couldn't sense how off-put I was by his unsettling presence. I tried to ignore how he studied me intently, as if trying to answer his cryptic question through my appearance or my expression.

"How long ago did you die?"

I choked on the wine. When my souls had been burned away and replaced with what Erebell had given me, had I *actually died?* It surfaced that horrible thought I'd been dreading. If I *had* died, it meant that Leander had felt it. He had felt the worst kind of soul bond breaking—the kind only death can bring. That meant that back home, my Leander was moving through his immortal existence as if he had *lost me.* How was it possible that I could die and break our bond, but still live? My interest in convincing the Leander in front of me that creating a soul bond lessened a little, knowing the pain I had caused the future him. I knew deep down it was still worth it, but right now, the thought of the pain and despair he was surely feeling was too much to bear.

The devil replied for me after seeing the look on my face. "Ah, I guess it's still a little fresh for you ... my apologies."

"It's just not what I was expecting to be asked," I replied, attempting to adjust my tone to hide how my voice was breaking.

"Is he making you feel uncomfortable?" Leander said from across the table. He looked displeased by whatever interaction he'd just witnessed.

The devil shot a glance across the table at Leander. "I apologized, didn't I?" he growled.

Leander's expression shifted slightly to a half smile. When he spoke next it was to me. "You will have to excuse him. He does not get out much, so his manners are dreadful. Well, does not get out much with creatures like us." Leander shifted his gaze back to the devil. "How is work, *Amias*?"

"Boring, thanks to you." Amias sat back in his chair and took a sip of wine.

"I'm Grace," I said, turning to Amias. "What do you do for work?"

He scrunched his face in pained smile. "Maybe I should be grateful that you don't seem to know, considering ..." He set his goblet down, then his infernal blue eyes glowed at me. "I am the Prince of *Death*. The only prince that has a *job* to do." Amias picked up a dark brown roll from a basket at the center of the table like he hadn't just admitted to being a real life reaper. "I exist so that when life yields to death, I can guide souls that are supposed to pass on to this plane."

"Devils can take souls though," I pointed out. "Why is your job different?"

"I don't *take* them. Reaping for most gods is about guiding beloved souls to an afterlife with other believers. For this plane, it's sort of a permissible loophole that creates a constant stream of soul revenue. It generates a lot more souls than devils could take, even in an immortal lifetime, and it's a lot less conspicuous to the pantheon of gods than just *taking*."

"Do you ever reap souls that belong to another deity?"

He laughed, amused at my questions. "These days it's quite orderly. There are no attachments to particular souls, it's just a numbers game. If a reaper of another god or goddess expresses interest, they claim that soul. Then, next time I claim a soul. Of course I also reap all the contracted souls between devils and other creatures if the devil is not present at the time of death. When a reaper lays claim on a soul, it's greater than any other's as an extension of their deity."

I began to pity Amias. It seemed he was eternally enslaved to the order of the plane with no freedom to do what he wanted. I wondered what the consequences of him not doing this job could mean for the Nine Circles, or even for others if the volume of souls shifted drastically.

"If you are so curious about what I do, I can take you with me the next time I'm called away." He glanced over at Leander raising his eyebrows. "I can think of several tasks you could assist me with." The smirk on his face suggested the lewd nature of those tasks.

Leander narrowed his eyes at Amias. "Would you like to find out who will reap *your* soul, Amias?"

Amias chuckled. "I had to try." He threw me a sidelong glance. "Let me know when you get tired of him. Having a reaper *claim* you more than once is a rare delicacy."

I laughed at what he implied. I wanted to be disgusted by him, but something about the arrogant smirk he gave me was endearing.

The atmosphere changed swiftly as another prince, probably Julian by the scowls he drew, sat down next to Leander. He was just as handsome as the others, but there was a sour purse to his lips as he glanced over at Leander. He appeared the complete opposite to Leander with a blueish-purple skin tone and short, combed back hair that was almost white between two gray horns. It was as if winter sat next to summer. He seemed to intentionally ignore Leander, frostily avoiding making eye contact. Leander did the same.

Dinner plates were brought and placed in front of us, bearing some kind of meat-based roast with brightly colored vegetables and flowers. A fork and knife appeared next to my plate, and then Remodeus raised his glass.

"It's rare that so many princes come together like this." He leveled a glare at Leander. "Fortunately, we've been graced by Leander for the first time in twenty years. It's too bad Silas didn't have the stomach to show, otherwise we would be a complete set."

Florian shifted slightly at the comment.

Remodeus swirled the wine in his glass. "The Primordial Father used to rule the Prime Circle. Since his banishment, my circle has remained ungoverned. So, I have started looking for a female to bear me a son to take over the rule of the Blood Circle while I remain steward here." He glanced around the table. "It's not been done like this before, but do I have your support in this change to tradition?"

The group was silent. I looked around at all their faces, trying to discern their attitude towards the declaration.

"No opinions?" Remodeus's voice boomed. "Perhaps our guests have opinions that would be interesting to hear."

Several of the Princes had also brought guests, but of course Remodeus's gaze landed on me.

"You, who came with Leander? Tell us your opinion."

Here we go ...

I already knew the eventual outcome of his proposal—my brother, Victus. But what had *Grace* said back then to influence it?

413

Best speak from the heart.

I cleared my throat. "The Primordial Father was a cruel and abusive ruler who forced you to bend to his whims of pairing so he could gain more powerful toys. I think if any of you have the desire to seek companionship, love, or family outside his corruption, you should embrace it."

They all stared at me, eyes wide or covering coughs. Leander's eyes blazed at me from across the table.

"Such a *blasphemous* opinion." Remodeus chuckled, taking a sip, "Though, I find I agree. Any other opinions?"

Amias's voice next to me cut through the silence like a knife. "No one cares who you fuck, Remodeus." He stabbed a slice of roast with his fork.

The rest at the table remained silent.

"Great." Remodeus narrowed his eyes and took a long sip of his wine.

Chapter Fifty-Eight

We began dining on the food as some conversation finally floated around the table. I was about halfway through my vegetable roast and Florian's account of the talented troupe of devils he'd hosted just last week, when I heard aggressive muttering between Leander and Julian across the table from me.

"Fucking pathetic," I heard from Leander as he tore into a baked roll with his fangs.

Julian's eyes swung back to Leander. Then, in the blink of an eye, he lifted his plate and smashed it over Leander's head. Then he grabbed Leander by the throat, pulling him to stand.

Glittering rage flowed through me so quickly I hardly had a chance to exert control over it. I stood just as swiftly as Julian had, my chair clattering over behind me. The room flashed with white light and then rattled as thunder cracked somewhere nearby. My skin tingled as if I had discharged it. I felt the energy that preceded the lightning everywhere—buzzing in the air around me, fizzing around my fingers—just waiting for me to harness it and strike the prince who had his hands around Leander's neck.

"Let go of him," I warned, rage filling my tone, eyes burning with that primordial flame on Julian.

"Or else what?" He sneered in a sour tone. His blue hands tightened around Leander's neck in challenge, pulling a choking noise from him.

The rage in me boiled over. Static began sparking around my fingers, arcing across the table as another loud boom sounded outside. When I raised my hand to unleash the lightning, I heard Amias's voice at my side.

"Grace ..."

I glanced down at him and he was shaking his head as if to say, *stop*. Was ... this not what I was suppose to do? I retracted my fingers, and the lightning fizzled away, the energy dissipating into the room.

From down the table, I heard Remodeus say, "Go ahead and put him in his place so we can finish our dinner."

I had been prepared to kill Julian to protect Leander. My eyes flicked between each of the devils. All were focused on me. I may be *Grace* right now, but I knew exactly what *Reign* would do. I snapped my fingers.

A puff of blue smoke rose up around Prince Julian, engulfing him as he shrank and *Polyformed*. I used my *Mystic Hand* to lift his tiny new form and bring him to me. He was a rather cute, periwinkle blue chick. I held him in one of my hands and he screeched, pecking my fingers with his tiny, black beak. I wished Emrys were here as a cat. I would send him chasing the Julian-chick around. Instead, I downed the rest of my wine in one gulp and dropped him into the glass. He chirped and slid down the walls of the glass, attempting to escape.

We left Julian chirping in the glass and conversation resumed. I knew the entire dinner party was staring at me, including Leander—except his gaze on me was hungry. After the course completed, I excused myself to get some fresh air. I walked around the palace a little before I came upon a lounge, lit with arcane, glowing stones on side tables and chaises scattered between them.

A red one caught my eye and I collapsed on it, closing my eyes. All my actions were becoming difficult to keep track of. Was I saying the right things? Was I doing the right things? More importantly, how would I get home?

I felt a shadow cast over me. I opened my eyes and saw Amias standing over me like a specter.

"What are you?" he said, infernal blue eyes glaring down at me.

I sat up, raising my eyebrows. "I'm sorry?"

"You shouldn't exist."

It felt as if all my blood had drained from my body. "I do exist ..." I replied warily.

"Because of what I am, I can sense when a creature is near death—if it's the true moment they are fated to die, or merely a close call. It's always precisely one or the other, like a coin flip landing when fate is decided." Amias's eyes drifted down me as if to observe some hidden nature. "When you began casting that lightning ... it was a paradox. Prince Julian was not fated to die, but he also was. The decision dangled between your fingers, not in the chaos that controls creation and destruction. Only gods can choose a thread of fate." He inhaled deeply, slowly. "So I ask again, what are you?"

I was speechless. I suspected I was something like a goddess or like what the princes were, but an *actual* goddess? Despite his direct manner of questioning, Amias was tense, holding his breath in nervous anticipation for what I might do. How had things shifted so quickly? Instead of me being the one trembling around these powerful devils, they were now the ones who feared me. What could it hurt to tell a partial truth?

"Amias ... I don't know exactly what I am. This is just how I exist. No one told me what I was." I lowered my face. "I won't be on this plane much longer, so you don't have to worry about me interfering with fate. Actually, I would appreciate it if you kept your suspicions between us. I don't really want to attract a lot of attention."

"Good luck, after the show you just put on with Julian."

"I didn't mean for it to go that far ... I just got furious when I saw his hands around Leander's neck."

Amias smirked and raised his eyebrows. "I wish I had a feisty lover willing to kill devil royalty to protect me." His eyes dropped to the torn collar at my neck. "There's something else. When we first met, I could sense death around you. That's why I asked about your death. I didn't think a *probably* goddess could even die. Care to explain what's going on there?"

"And remove all elements of mystery?" I smiled weakly, silently pleading for him to not pry any further.

He frowned.

"I'll admit there are things I'm withholding, but what I can be honest about is I didn't mean to come here—it was an accident. All I want is to go home."

Amias assessed me, focusing on my face, and his demeanor softened slightly. "How did you get here?"

"I woke up in the lake ... the glittering lake in the Fire Circle," I said softly.

Amias scratched his head. "That lake is an ancient shrine to the Primordial Mother. Perhaps since it has a connection to our gods, it acted as a pathway for you."

I had come through the lake, so perhaps I could return through the lake. Then I realized what he'd said first. "It was made for the Primordial Mother?"

Amias chuckled. "I doubt anyone remembers." He lowered his gaze to the floor. "I was the first ... First Prince. Back then, the Primordial Mother was valued because she was needed to bear more princes, and populate the plane. So, her first—and last—worshipers made the lake for her. Only her own primordial chaos fills it now."

It warmed my heart to know it had been intended for Erebell, but I also felt sadness—that others had forgotten about the lake as well as her. I had always thought the lake so beautiful ... had always been drawn to it. Perhaps this was why.

"If you were the first," I said, "why aren't you the steward of the Prime Circle?"

"Ha—!" He let out an exasperated laugh. "I *have* a job, remember? Reaping souls gives our plane more power. While I have my circle to preside over like the other princes, its design is also to support that purpose." He adjusted his posture, straightening his shoulders. "All souls pass through The Shadow Circle's soul gate. Our lakes aren't flames, but deep, glowing pools of souls. The Primordial Father didn't want me to get distracted, so he gave me these to control me."

Amias dragged his sleeves up from his wrists one at a time, revealing rows of infernal tattoo lettering, black iridescent stains scaring his flesh. They wrapped in one continuous command around his wrists, spiraling up his forearm. I then noticed the peaks of infernal lettering at his collar, and I wondered if the tattoos might cover his whole body.

He continued, "One of those mandates is *not* ruling over the Prime Circle."

"And what's the reason you never visited the Primordial Mother?"

Amias froze, a look of hurt and sadness on his face. "Why would you ask that?"

I'd clearly touched on a sensitive subject. I tried to recover the little trust we'd developed. "She's your mother, right?" I tried to convey my empathy through my question.

"She is ..." his eyes darted around in thought. "Even though the Primordial Father is banished, his original will holds as the creator of this plane. He willed for her to be imprisoned." He straightened his cuffs again. "Many assume it was the mortal clerics who imprisoned her, but it was *him*. He saw the possibility he would be banished, and he hated the idea that her primordial chaos could take over the Nine Circles when it happened. So the last thing he did was imprison her. The will of his primordial power also prevents us from seeking her out."

"Oh." My heart broke for her. Did she ever consider the reason why her sons never visited her was because they had been arcanely prevented? "I'm so sorry."

A thought steeled into my mind. The princes were prevented from seeking her out, but I was not. Everything I had learned so far about the Primordial Father made me hate him. He was yet another male using his power to control and manipulate others to his favor. I had more than a few ideas about what I'd do about that when I could return to my time.

"Amias." I stood up from the lounge to hold his gaze more directly—which was difficult, considering how much taller he was than me. "Please keep this between us—what you've sensed about me. Please."

He smirked. "I wasn't going to say anything, but now you've got me wondering if I should have bargained silence since you are begging."

I rolled my eyes.

His expression shifted, and his ice blue eyes focused on me with a serious stillness to them. "I wouldn't mind being owed a favor by a goddess."

I wondered what I could even do for him, if the power I had gained could really grant him a worthy favor. I thought about how much he had suffered under the Primordial Father's limitations. The ancient primordial magic of the Primordial Mother—her chaos—stirred in reply. I would try to help him if I could for her sake.

"Alright," I agreed. "I owe you a favor. But ... being the wise creature I am, I will ultimately get to choose when it's time to grant the favor—and what it is." I felt like a fraud for the last bit, but I needed to play the part of a goddess.

He chuckled. "It's a deal. I wouldn't expect a goddess to make one that didn't benefit her."

"Okay, since we are in agreement, quit calling me that." I jabbed a finger at him.

"Yes, of course, *Grace*," he said sarcastically.

"Are you going back to the party?"

"No. I have work to do." He gave me a wry smile. "It's not too late if you want to come." His infernal blue eyes flashed at me.

This devil ... he might give Leander a run for his money in charisma and charm.

"Maybe next time." I winked and smoothed wrinkles from my dress. I walked for the door, pausing before exiting. "Thanks, Amias. Happy ... reaping?"

Amias chucked. "I like you, Grace."

I smiled before slipping back out to the party.

The sky darkened to a bruised plum color. I realized there were little stars beginning to take form. I wondered why—when Leander's Circle did not have them. I would have liked to explore the Circle more, but I knew I wouldn't be able to convince Leander to come along. So I resolved myself to navigating the party.

It was different than observing from the shadows as I had before. I had always dreaded being seen, but I found some of the discussion rather engaging, particularly when Florian brought up the shared histories between the princes. The night carried on as I chatted with Florian and met a few of the other princes. I avoided Remodeus, though I knew I would probably have to talk to him more at some point to set my existence in motion. No one paid much mind to the Julian-chick in the wine glass, and eventually he fluffed up and sank against the bottom, glaring at me for the rest of the night.

At some point, I stopped trying to contribute to the conversation and just nodded. I discovered none of the other princes had soul mates or even a partner they'd been in a long term relationship with. I figured it was likely an after effect of how the Primordial Father used them. He'd only been banished for a measly two decades—not very much time to consider forming bonds or seeking true romantic connection for the immortal infernals. I wondered if they were still just as lonely in my own time.

When the exhaustion finally got to me, Leander leaned into my ear. "Should we leave?" he said in a sinister purr. Having his voice in my ear like this warmed my soul—my new soul.

I looped my arm in his and grinned. "Let's go!"

The air whipped around us as I teleported us back to the foyer of the Palace of Flames. I moved to unlink our arms, but Leander pulled me into him.

"We didn't get to finish what we started in the study." His eyes burned bright on me.

I wanted to say *he* was the only one who didn't finish. I wanted to flirt back. I wanted to strip off the dress right here and give him anything he wanted. But I was holding a growing concern. I was starting to realize how deeply I had affected my Leander as Grace. I'd suspected he loved her, or rather they had a thing, but I never imagined it was this intense. Was this ... right? Was I going to jeopardize everything by giving in to my desires too fully now?

"I can't stay here forever. What if it's just easier to save you the pain now by not finishing what we started?" My body revolted at the words. They completely opposed everything I believed.

He frowned slightly. "That doesn't really sound like you." There was still an undertone of seduction in his voice when he spoke again. "You would tell me whatever is between us is worth the pain." I felt his fingers sweeping up my spine as he spoke.

I turned slightly. "Tomorrow we're going on a trip. No objections or sassy remarks."

"Does this trip affect whether or not I can enjoy you?"

"It might ..." I crooned to him.

I knew if I let him keep talking I'd eventually end up in his bed. It was so hard to withdraw further, to pull myself away from his grasp and let that achingly cool air rush in.

"I have some things I need to take care of ..." I gave him a soft smile.

He let me retreat from his grasp. His face downcast with my rejection. "I'll see you tomorrow then ..." he said lingering, watching me walk down the hall.

I headed to the library. I needed to plan a hike.

CHAPTER FIFTY-NINE

LEANDER

I hated coming here. It was dark, cold, and desolate. Not like the warmth of the Fire Circle. By nature, everything here was dead. Except for Amias. It hadn't always been that way, not when shadow wolves like my mother roamed it.

I moved deeper into the cavern, the wet gray clay floors curving up and over me to low ceilings. A combination of stalactites and stalagmites made it feel as if I were walking through the mouth of some legendary, primordial creature that had yet to swallow me. The tunnels were so shadowed and dull, that when I finally sighted the largest pool of souls, it was a relief.

The pool for mortal souls from Novus was massive, and completely misnamed because it was the size of a great sea. An ethereal, blue-green light glowed out from the liquid surface, but was swallowed by the grayish clay cavern that opened to a larger cave. The sheer size of the cavern made it easy to forget this was all still underground.

I walked the shoreline of the pool, watching streams of glowing silver lights swirling below the blue-green glow of the water. It was difficult to assess how deep the pool really went. Souls spun and swirled downward with no end, until all the silvery soul light faded into the murky depths. I'd heard rumors that it was bottomless.

I stopped by the edge. How did summoning souls from these pools work again? I had just extended my hand over the pool's edge when I heard him clear his throat behind me, right on cue.

I turned my head to look at him. "Amias, tell me how to find her soul."

He stood there staring at me, his long, brown hair pulled back over his work clothes, a typical mix of black cloth and leather armor. The blue-green light from the pool lit the angles of his face.

"Who?" Amias said gruffly.

"My soul mate." I whispered over the water, as if the mention of it would surface her delicate soul. I looked at my hand outstretched over the glowing waters. The red was cancelled out in the contrasting blue-green light. It was the most unnatural thing I'd ever seen. The air above the surface was cold and still, despite how I willed for her soul to appear.

"When did this happen?" Amias crossed his arms.

"Which? Her binding herself to me, or her death?" I said shortly, shifting my gaze to the souls below in case I saw hers flutter by.

"The death, Leander," he answered flatly.

"Not very long ago. Perhaps in the past twenty-four hours."

Amias sighed and moved in closer to the pools, searching my face. I could feel the way his glowing blue eyes assessed me. He knew better than to try to convince me to do something other than what I wanted.

"What's her name?" he droned.

"Reign," I said solemnly, lowering my hand. Saying her name out loud was almost enough to shatter me—to lean forward and allow myself to fall into the vast pool of souls and be forgotten.

Amias raised his own hand over the pool. The surface swelled towards him. The glowing, blue-green light pulsed at him brightly, sliding along his features in a way that enhanced his presence. "No soul by the name of Reign in the past twenty-four hours—not even the last week."

I clenched my jaw. She had another name ... "*Grace ...*" I said quietly.

Amias turned to me, his eyes wide.

"Grace Vendelfrey."

Amias trembled as he raised his hand over the pool once again.

Now *that* was unusual for a reaper.

"Leander, there is no Grace Vendelfrey either, only a Lydia Vendelfrey in the vaults," he said, staring into the pool. "What do you mean her name was *Grace*?"

"Remodeus took my soul fragment and bound it to a mortal yet to be born whose name was to be Grace. A mortal that he also decided to transform to look like Grace—the *Grace* that *we* knew," I clarified. How could her soul not be here? This was where mortal souls that died in the Nine Circles should go.

"And this *Grace*, your soul mate, she died on this plane? Did you see how she died?" Amias said warily.

"No. Remodeus locked her in the dungeon below the Prime Circle. I was placed in a cell in the palace. Then, some time later, I felt her soul ripped from my body and my own fragment return. Which would not be possible except in death. There was no body in her cell though." I looked up at Amias. "And apparently no *soul*. How is that possible? Where else could she go?"

Amias's infernal eyes flicked all over as if he were weighing the possibilities. Then, he turned his head to me slowly. His expression was grave, lips pressed so tight together it strained his face.

"What?"

"Leander," he said, tone apologetic, "I made a promise not to say anything."

No. He would not withhold any information about her. I didn't care what it was. I would not allow him. I took a step closer, feeling every ounce of fire in me blaze, and pushed him to retreat against the edge, inches from the pool of souls. It wouldn't kill him if he fell in, but it would be a while before he got out, and he would not be happy about it.

"Leander—"

"I *will not* give up trying to find her," I seethed. "So, decide whether you want to keep your promise, or keep from falling to however far down this wretched pool goes."

"Pretty fucking far, actually." Amias squared himself off with me. He had never balked at any of my threats. He knew me too well. Under regular circumstances, I considered him a friend and ally.

Then Amias sighed. "When I first met *Grace*—you know, the one I'm talking about—I sensed it all around her. She had *died* just before we met her." Amias took a step forward, shifting the two of us away from the pool's edge.

"What?" I could barely get the breath out. *Grace* had died just before we'd met? And ... this Grace, the mortal Grace, was nowhere to be found, body or soul. "Are you suggesting—"

"I'm not suggesting anything," Amias cut me off. "All I know is that she had died. I never make a mistake with that sense. At the dinner, there were moments where I could sense Julian's fate dangling between her fingers, undecided. You know how it works. There is always a decision, a flip of the coin. Not with her. She could have chosen."

My mind raced, replaying every interaction, every moment, every touch. There had been so many reasons I'd thought they were similar. So many things she'd say, and it sounded exactly how *Grace* would say it. I'd told her things that *Grace* told to me first. Could it really be that they were the same? If that was true, then of course there was no body—no soul—because she was *there*. There ... a thousand years ago. She had said she was stranded—and wanted nothing more than to go home—

"Leander?" Amias's voice jolted me from my racing thoughts. "What are you going to do?"

If she was in the past ... well, the past had already happened. I had *watched* her leave. I'd searched *every* plane I could for her. I'd never found her again. What if she never made it back here? What if she was stuck somewhere?

"I'm going to find her."

"You can't change *time*, Leander," Amias huffed.

I could *try*. With one of those knives and that lodestone. And I would kill as many as I needed to gain the souls to power it.

CHAPTER SIXTY

REIGN

"Do I get to find out where we're going now?" Leander sighed. He was grumpy, probably because of how I had denied him after the party.

"Nope." I smiled at him, trying to bring his mood back up. I extended my hand towards him.

He placed his hand in mine and pulled me in. The ground shifted below us as I teleported us to my secret location.

Tall, leafy trees pushed up all around us, gray bark and branches stretching out into the canopy. I grinned as I found the ground in front of us was starting to slope up. I had brought us to just the right place. Good.

"Isn't it beautiful here?" I gazed up at the canopy, my eyes dancing between the patches of pink sky and the dark green of the leaves.

Leander glanced up. "Beautiful," he said flatly. "Why are we here?"

"We're going to hike to the top of Crimson Peak." I grinned at him, making sure I exposed my fangs, knowing how irresistible it was to him.

He narrowed his eyes. "Are we?" he said with an unamused smile.

"Remember, no objections or sassy remarks." I wagged my finger to warn him.

He let out a defeated laugh and turned me around to face the mountain, then gave me a gentle push forward.

Not thirty minutes into hiking up the slope he broke the silence.

"How long will this take, exactly?"

"By my calculations, I think we could make it to the summit in ... five or six hours?"

"Are you serious?"

Yep, he definitely sounded annoyed. In the letter that Grace wrote—that I will write—she said that Leander had hated this hike.

"I am," I replied.

"And why can we not just teleport to the summit instead of doing this?"

We? I was the only one who *could* teleport us that far. "Don't you want to spend time with me? If we teleport, it will be over too fast!" I teased.

"We could have spent time at the palace doing much more enjoyable things together," he muttered.

I stopped, and he caught up with me. Then I grabbed his hand and resumed my pace, pulling him along.

We slowly gained up the increasing incline, then turned the opposite direction at a switchback and cut along the side of the ridge to climb higher. We stopped about three hours in and took a break.

"Would you like a snack?" I said excitedly.

In our resting spot were giant stone boulders and rock shoring the mountainside. I thought about the spell I had used at Midor's to help that young boy crushed by the side of the stone building.

My heart warmed at the thought of casting in Transmutation. It made me feel like the old me. I cast *Manipulate Rock*, feeling the primordial magic glitter through me, moving and shifting the stone into two small stumps and a low table between us. A flick of my hands, and two stone cups wobbled up out of the table, then two stone plates.

I smiled wide and rushed in to sit down. Leander joined me reluctantly, eyeing the tableware. He looked miserable sitting there. I felt a little bad, but I knew this was important.

I pulled at the power of my new primordial magic. Could I perhaps dabble in the Conjuration school of magic? I twirled my finger in the air and water materialized and flowed in each of our cups, then two blueberry muffins plopped onto each of our plates. I cackled softly. I was grateful that these simple spells seemed to come so easily.

"Do you have a fondness for food from Novus?" Leander asked, eyebrows raised at the muffin.

"Have you never eaten a muffin?" I plucked the muffin up from the plate and deflected.

"I have not, though I have had other food from Novus before I was ... returned."

I chewed a bite of my muffin, thinking about the time my Leander had encouraged me to speak about the trauma I had experienced. "Leander, can I ask you a question?"

"Only if I can ask you a question," he said as he lifted the muffin for a sniff.

"Alright. Why do you avoid acknowledging or saying outright that you were slain?"

He loosened his jaw, leveling his gaze at me. Buying time before having to answer, he took a bite of the muffin. Then finally, "Because ... it's evidence that I am weak. So I prefer not to acknowledge it."

"I guess being powerful is the most important thing to you," I said sarcastically. I was just about tired of this explanation.

"It is when I am the next most powerful thing on the plane to the gods themselves, and yet even that is not enough to be free."

My heart sank. I'd never heard him talk about being trapped and controlled like I was.

"Were you not free when you fought in the war with Remodeus? Or before that?" I said softly.

"No. I've never been free until now. The Primordial Father used us to do his every bidding. I couldn't stop him from killing my mother or forcing me to spend decades as that hell-forsaken hound, trolling about killing and looking for creatures for him to take into his custody to mutilate." His hand clenched around the muffin, crumbs bouncing to the tabletop. "Then, when he decided that he wanted more souls for our plane, Remodeus and I were sent to wage war and collect. I wondered if his greed would ever end. If he would be satisfied and I'd finally be free. Little did I know that all it would take," his eyes shot back up at me, glowing hot in challenge, "was *dying* for it to all come toppling down."

My heart broke for him. No wonder he'd been so caring and supportive to me when I'd said I wanted to be free. How he'd do anything, including become my weapon, to help me do it. It had come from a place of knowing what it felt like to live a life that was not his own.

"But you are free now," I offered. "Does that give you relief? You can finally do what you'd like."

"I don't know what I like. Or what I want. It all feels pointless," he huffed.

I stared down into my water. I wanted to hold him and tell him that things would be different 980 years from now.

Not yet ...

"What's your question for me?" I said, taking a sip of water.

He paused, staring at me as if he was debating what to ask. "Why do you care about helping me?"

"Because you deserve—"

"No—that's what you think about me. Why do you *care* about me?"

"Leander ..." I leaned across the small stone table. "There is no reason that would make you less worthy of being loved. Caring about you doesn't need justification."

Leander sighed. "You asked three questions. I want to ask two more."

"Go ahead ..." I finished the muffin and downed the rest of my water, then refilled it with a snap.

"What was it like ... when your soul was bound with another?" His eyes were like soft embers on me.

My eyes widened. He was asking me about the soul mate bond? On his own? I hadn't been trying terribly hard to steer him that way. I had just wanted to help him realize his true power.

"It was like a tight thread connecting us, always pulling us together. And when we *were* together, it was like living with the ultimate purpose. Every touch, every kiss, every—*you know.*" I smiled softly. "It would bring our fragmented souls together again like that thread had woven into a closed loop. We were two complete souls, existing in a harmony that only acts of love can create." I stopped for a moment, feeling the tear slide down my cheek. I missed him and our bond so desperately.

"It felt so good—so right—that you are willing to experience losing that all over again if only to feel it one more time?" The look on his face, a mix of curiosity and concern, made it seem like he might understand now how special the soul mate bond could be.

"Without hesitation." I could feel the fire blazing behind my eyes. "I would even take *more* pain, more *grief,* to have it again."

Leander was silent. He sipped from his cup, then stood up from the stump. "Let's keep going," he said, beginning to make his way up the incline.

I returned the stones to nature and followed him.

We spent the next few hours mostly in silence as the trees thinned. There was an odd quietness to the thinning woods around us, and a current of wind pushed at our backs as if guiding us on. Eventually, the tree line broke and I could see that the ridgeline continued upwards, barely covered in brush and trees. I smiled and checked on Leander who was covered in sweat. We picked up our pace, climbing up and up the ridgeline until it leveled out to a stone bald. I panted, out of breath from the last bit of steep ground, and looked out. Leander stood next to me.

I could see how the mountain edge sheared down into a slope of hills and forest, a small glimmer of gold on the higher elevated area where I knew the palace was, and then it swept down further into the city by the lake. Each building looked like tiny daubs of pink, brown, orange, and tan paint, the surrounding air a wavy haze from the heat of the glittering lake behind it. The deep green of the forest surrounding the area rustled in a wind, domed by that beautiful pink sky. I grinned widely, drinking all of it in, letting the view burn into my memory. Then I turned to look at Leander.

He was staring at me.

"If we had teleported up here, it would not look this beautiful," I said before turning back to the glittering majesty. "Time and pain have given us this version to view. Isn't it more beautiful?"

He watched me for just a breath longer. "It is," he replied.

We hardly spoke the entire way back. I was grateful the rest of the way home was downhill, though it reminded me that there were many muscles in my body that I'd not been using until now. Somehow the return felt faster, though I'm sure it took just as long. I could feel my body turn to jelly in relief as we arrived at the place I had teleported us to. I was exhausted, aches tightening my limbs and bowing my shoulders. I guess whatever immortality and magic were granted to me by Erebell didn't extend to my body's physical fitness. It was a relief, to be honest. I wouldn't mind working harder to get stronger.

Leander looked out in the direction of the palace. "What if we just walked the entire way back to the palace?" he suggested.

I laughed. "I appreciate you taking to heart the hike, but my body is screaming. I don't think I can make it the whole walk back to the palace."

He took a step closer to me. "I can carry you."

"It's at least a few more hours and we've already been out here for so long."

"I'll carry you as far as I can, then we can teleport," he amended.

I would be lying if I said I wasn't craving for him to hold me, even for the hours-long walk back. "Okay, fine—"

He scooped me up and held me close to him, one arm behind my back and the other under my legs. I rested my head against his chest, gathering my hands in my lap. He was so warm ... I could hear his heart beating against my cheek as he went on. I inhaled deeply, the smell of smoke and cinnamon still detectable under his sweat. I smiled to myself. For anyone else, this would probably be disgusting. But for me, the scent called back good memories—moments where he had been sweaty and holding me. I let myself feel the comfort of those memories for just a moment before I fell asleep in his arms from exhaustion.

CHAPTER SIXTY-ONE

I cracked my eyes open and the ceiling of the guest room came into focus. Leander must have carried me the entire way here and left me to rest. I was filthy, sweat soaking my clothes and dirt clinging to my legs. I used *Spotless* to clean my body, clothes, and the part of the bed I'd been sleeping on.

I wonder where he went ...

I walked the halls, eventually coming upon the mess I'd left in the library. I sighed and began gathering up the cartography scrolls, history books, and spare parchments I'd used to calculate the distance and time for our trip. I could have easily used my magic to put away all the books, but I liked feeling like I was in the library at Midor's and doing things the manual way. So I searched for the original location of each book before sliding it back in place. I had a few scrolls and books left when I heard steps behind me.

"I've figured out what I want," Leander said in a divisive tone.

I shot a half-glance back toward him as I slid a scroll into place. "That's good!" I smiled, looking for the next empty spot to place the next scroll. *Perhaps the hike did work after all.*

He narrowed the distance, coming in closer behind me, then I felt the burning heat of his body as he leaned into my ear. "I want you to split my soul." His voice was demanding, almost ragged.

I turned around to face him.

He pushed me gently against the shelves. A similar position to one we'd been in recently ...

"You do?" I said in disbelief. I thought I would have to plead with him to even consider it. Yet here he was demanding it of me.

"Because what I want," he leaned in and rested his forehead on mine, sliding his hands around my waist and lower back, "is you."

My body froze, objecting to what I knew I had to say.

Not yet ...

"Leander, I can't stay here with you ..." My voice shook as words I hated left my mouth.

"I'll follow you wherever you need to go."

I almost melted completely at his words. "You can't leave this plane for another four hundred and eighty years," I whispered.

"Then stay here with me," he pleaded in a desperate tone. "Everything ... every fiber of my being is screaming that I belong to you. That we're supposed to be together."

My heart pounded. He had felt it, even now, that we were going to be together. I didn't want to keep going ... I wanted to stop right here and hold him, kiss him, and tell him how I so desperately felt the same. But ...

"I have a soul mate that I need to follow ... to try to find." My eyes welled with tears.

His hands ran up my back. "If he's dead, and had the immortal's death ... there is no getting him back." Leander said it carefully, as if he were trying to protect me from the truth of such a statement. I would have been hurt by it had my Leander truly been gone. However, I knew he was waiting for me ... in my own time.

"I have to believe I can find him. I won't give up." The words felt hollow in this moment between us.

Leander let out a sigh and pulled away from me, so he could see my face. "What are you going to tell him if you get him back? How is he going to react to learning you've not only fucked another, but have driven that one so utterly insane that he's begging you to bind his soul to yours? Will he still want you after that?"

"If you were him, would you still want me after all that?" He didn't know that we were talking about him. *My Leander ...*

Leander let out a defeated laugh. He lifted his eyes to me, blazing with agony, want, and need. "Absolutely." He lifted his hand to my cheek. "I will always want you. Even after you leave me for him, I'll want you."

I knew what awaited him. We *would* be together, and this would be the catalyst to start the flame.

"I want you to find your soul mate. I know you will. I can feel it," I said, bringing my hand to his face. "And now you'll be open to it when your paths cross. You'll see her and know it."

"I wish it could be you," he whispered.

"I know," I whispered back. "I can still do it. I can split your soul and place it in a vessel. You can save it for her." I breathed the words gently into the space between us.

"What do I need to do?" he breathed back.

"Me."

He exhaled a pained laugh and slid his fingers into the opening between the buttons of my blouse. "I am starting to think you like torturing me." He ripped the shirt open. "Or that I am a pathetic masochist."

I lifted my body, placed my arms around him, and fell into his kisses. They were wild and rough, devouring my lips and tongue, and then burning down my neck. It was as if he needed to feel and taste me like he needed to breathe, no matter that I would break his heart.

I found my hands tearing at his shirt, his pants—running up and down the skin of his chest. I felt his hands swoop lower, picking me up and carrying me away. Glancing down, I saw a fur rug between the two reading chairs. I motioned towards it and he lowered me to it. The soft fur pressing against my back as he undressed me made me feel like he was unwrapping a gift as more and more skin became exposed to the air. I pulled at his remaining clothes as well till we were both completely naked. His mouth dove straight into my collarbone, kissing and biting greedily before moving down to my breast.

I moaned, wanting even more of him. Despite the painful conversation, I was more than ready to have him.

He spread my legs and his fingers trailed up my thighs. Two of his fingers slid into me, the sensation had me panting and spilling delicate moans into the surrounding air. I arched instinctually into his touch, trying to take more of those two fingers inside me.

"You poor thing ..." His velvety voice rolled over my skin, causing it to prickle. His fingers retreated slowly and then pushed back into me. "You're writhing."

I melted into the floor, his touch reassuring me. I could do it. I could split his soul and find my way back to my own time. I could return to him. I could do it for us ... so I could feel this love between us that appeared to supersede time itself, for the rest of eternity.

He broke away from his kissing and sucking at my breast. "How are you going to concentrate on the job when I have this effect on you?" He grinned arrogantly into my skin.

I bobbed my head up. "You lay down," I panted.

His grin turned wicked and devilish. "Are you *Commanding* me?" His eyes glanced up over me, practically begging for it.

"Maybe," I purred. *"On your back."* I was not strictly using *Command*, but I could feel the warm primordial magic woven in the words.

He gave me a look of lustful awe, like it was a wonder I knew exactly what unraveled him. Then he did exactly as he was told.

I crawled on top, straddling him, and folded myself over into his chest. His hands immediately went to my waist and then my hips, gently trailing with his fingers. I gave him a few kisses before I sat back up, working the hard length of him into position before lowering myself, inch by inch, driving him into me. His groan at stretching and filling me was maddening. I felt ravenous to have my movements be the thing that sent him over the edge.

I placed my palms on his chest, coiling my fingers against his hard pectorals. I lifted my hips, gazing down at his face as I rose and fell, savoring the feeling of how incredible it was to have him inside me. He glanced down at me riding him, and I saw his eyes flash as he cast a floating spectral hand—a *Mystic Hand*—that slid delicately down my stomach until it reached between my legs.

I drew in a tight breath as the fingers of that hand applied pressure and started circling that *one particular spot.*

I squeezed my hands against his chest as my legs spread wider, wanting more of him. He grinned in approval and pulled me down to collapse on his chest. He held my hips firmly as he lifted his own, bending his knees and thrusting up into me. Each thrust had me spilling jagged moans against his neck.

"Are you doing it?" Leander said, his voice completely ragged.

I couldn't reply. Each thrust combined with the *Mystic Hand* aggressively circling that spot between my legs had my mind completely blank and at the mercy of the sensations in my body. All I knew was the pleasure building up inside of me, desperately aching to spill all over him.

His dark chuckle caressed my ear. "You need to finish or you won't be able to concentrate ... and I can't have you messing up my soul."

His grip tightened around my hips. He thrust into me harder, the *Mystic Hand* driving me closer and closer to that sweet release. The tension rose so high before finally flooding over the edge and giving way to waves of spasms that ripped through my body. Each thrust between the waves intensified the sensation, and I couldn't control my moans.

After the waves passed, I melted across his chest, my cheek pressing into his collarbone as I panted.

"You are so easy to please," he purred against the top of my head.

No ... it's you. Any movement you make, every touch you give me, sends me spinning.

He was still hard inside me as he ran his hands up my sides. I sat up, wiggling him deeper into me, still panting hard. His hands trailed back down to my hips.

I smiled. "Are you ready?" I ran my fingers up his chest.

"I am at your mercy." His eyes glowed hot as his voice caressed me.

I locked my gaze with his as I rode him again, hips tilting. Then, I closed my eyes and gripped his chest. Between the ultra-sensitive tingles rolling through me as I brought him deeper within me, I tried to surface the feeling of that internal place I'd experienced when our souls had united. I couldn't follow a thread because there was none, but I reached out with my metaphysical fingers, my new primordial magic, looking for that familiarity of his warm soul. There, so close, right at my fingertips, was that essence of him. The one I'd known my entire life. I followed that feeling of him until I could just see it in my mind—the silvery wisp of a soul. Being so close to it again, was bittersweet.

I manipulated my metaphysical fingers around it. One part of it leaned out to me, but it seemed hesitant to split from itself—likely a form of self-preservation.

"You are concentrating too hard," I said, keeping my eyes closed and my focus on that silvery soul. Then I smiled. "Maybe I need to break that concentration."

He squeezed my hips in response.

I picked up my pace, lifting myself till I felt the tip of him, then rammed myself back down. I could hear his groans and feel the twitching of his hands on my hips.

"I want you to erupt," I begged, riding him hard.

His hands squeezed me tightly as his body shuddered under me. "I ... am," he groaned, pulling in sharp breaths. He tensed under me and began bucking, grunting in the pleasure his own climax brought.

The soul calmed. My opportunity at last. I slid my metaphysical hands around the soul and separated it gently. I took the fragment into my custody, cupping it close to myself. It was so warm, and wavering from side to side in my grasp like it wanted to continue on to me—to be with my own soul.

I slowed from the deep thrusts while his cock was still twitching inside me. Then I finally cracked open my eyes again.

He rubbed at the center of his chest where my hands had been.

"Did it hurt?" I looked him over for any signs of bruising or damage.

"No ..." He caressed my legs. "It just tingles," he breathed.

I snapped my fingers, and a small crystal globe fell into my palm, its curves gentle against my hand. It glowed slightly with a silver light, and I could see movement within its hollow center. A center that now held a fragment of soul.

He looked at the globe in awe as I placed it in his hand. I lifted myself off of him and slid in next to him on the floor, watching as he held it up in the air. The light in the room refracted through it, small bits of orange from the candlelight mixing with the silver glow of the soul fragment. The crystal was clear, and I could see the wispy edges of the soul as it swirled around.

"That is all there is to it?" he said, as he peered through the crystal.

"Excuse me?" I glared at him, rolling to my side to face him. "I put in a lot of work to extract that from you."

"Mhmm." His gaze shot over to me, smirking. "Let me think of how I'll repay you ..." he trailed off. "Perhaps I can allow you to perform some more extractions from me." The devilish grin crept across his face.

I leveled my eyes at him and he rolled to his side, his free hand tucking my hair behind my ear and then stroking my cheek.

"Thank you."

CHAPTER SIXTY-TWO

LEANDER

Merchant's Hall loomed before me, abandoned. The door was in splinters, and hung by a single, loose hinge. Reign had said she was below Merchants Hall. That's where her grandfather had been, and he wouldn't be there unless there was something worth protecting. If I wanted to find the knife and the lodestone quickly, I needed to descend. I approached quietly, unwilling to draw attention to myself after what I'd done to the city. Every shadow and dark place no mortal dared gaze acted as my shroud.

As soon as I passed the threshold, I felt the magic of what I knew to be the Palisade glyph. It tingled across my skin in that annoying way most mortal magic did—twice as annoying because I knew it would make teleportation *very* unpleasant, though not impossible, for me. I gritted through the nuisance of taking several flights of stairs down till I reached the last floor. I stepped over two mortal bodies at the landing and advanced down the long corridor of cells. This had to be where she had been. She had thought the lodestone and knife might be waiting for her here—a trap set by her grandfather.

The corridor was quiet. If there had been enemies here when Reign arrived, they had clearly gone. I glanced back at the two bodies I had just passed. Had she killed them? A memory flashed of *Grace* across from me at the dinner table, lightning lacing from her fingertips, poised to strike with the lethal edge of an adder. I loved the utter beauty of that dangerous, deadly creature. How I longed to see that feisty nature in Reign now. My heart twisted with pain and sorrow, realizing I *had* seen it in her—back then.

I peered into each of the empty cells as I tread deeper down the corridor. Then I passed one with an occupant—an elf, her wrists shackled and chained above her head. She was covered in bruises and cuts, like she'd been tortured. Her lavender eyes shot up to me just as I passed out of view.

"Wait, I know you!" she called after me.

I kept walking. I did not have the patience to deal with prisoners. Finding the lodestone and the knife were my highest priority.

"You're Leander, Prince of the Fire Circle! I know your soul mate!" Her voice echoed in the corridor as I created distance between us. "I know Grace!" she shouted.

I stopped. Did everyone except for me know her fucking name had been *Grace?* I turned on my heel and walked back to the cell. She flinched upon sighting me, as if she realized now it was a mistake to hold my attention. The corner of my lip turned up at the fear in her eyes as she beheld me.

"You have my attention now," I said darkly. "Do not waste it, or I will end your suffering prematurely."

She took in a quick breath, trying to quiet the trembling terror rattling her body. "I was with her here. I was trying to help her find the lodestone, but she vanished. Is she okay? Where is she?"

I loosened my jaw as I thought about what to say. *"Tell me where the lodestone and the knife are,"* I said with a magic-laced *Command.*

445

She frowned, flinching and gripping the chains that held her dangling against the stone wall. She clenched her mouth shut.

Hmm ... interesting.

"I see you've developed the skill to resist magical commands." I felt the fire inside me stoke hotter. "No wonder you are so beat up. Should I take a turn at torture as well?" I watched her pull the chains, pressing herself into the wall at her back.

"It wasn't as bad as what they do in Veldrasyl." She spat. "But I said nothing." She drew in an exasperated breath. "They told me they'd leave me here for three days, and if I wouldn't talk then, I would die."

I tapped the metal bars with my fingers impatiently. This elf had practice resisting *Commands*, but was she practiced enough to resist me reading her mind? I stared at her, sending my metaphysical fingers out. They met a mesh-like steel that I could not press through. But, devils are clever. We thrive on manipulating and bending a creature's mind for our gains. I followed the mesh until I found a weak point in the weave that was just loose enough. A few moments later, I slipped in.

"Tell me where the lodestone and knife are, and I'll release you from this prison," I said kindly.

My offer surfaced thoughts and I picked through them. A view from where this elf watched from the shadows as Lydia was cut down in front of Reign. Reign's grandfather's words announcing that he'd moved everything to the estate.

The elf's eyes flared as if she realized my dark presence in her mind. She struggled to fold the mesh of protection under me to push me out. I laughed. I had learned what I needed to know.

"Thank you for your cooperation," I said, tapping a finger on a metal bar before walking back in the direction I had come. "Good luck in three days."

Her voice rattled in the corridor behind me. "Wait! Leander, I need that knife and lodestone!" I could hear her voice cracking.

"Someone I love died! I need to change what happened. I can't live accepting that he's dead," she sobbed.

I stopped again at the raw sound of her pain. It was exactly what I felt—that I couldn't live without my Reign. That I refused to accept the fact she'd been torn from me in every way.

I raised my hand and, with a sharp snap of my fingers, released her restraints. Another snap, and I unlocked the cell door. I continued down the corridor saying nothing, and the elf must have been smart enough to wait till I was gone to emerge.

CHAPTER SIXTY-THREE

REIGN

We kept finding ourselves entangled together, just like when I was mortal. I was resistant at first but, when he cornered me and purred things in my ear like,

I need to taste you again, so I don't forget you when you leave.

I want to touch every part of you so I can paint your body in my memory.

as well as the less poetic,

Let me fuck you on the verandah.

I melted into him, and at times didn't even think about if what I was doing was the same as what *Grace—I*—had done before. Each moment made me realize how important she—I—was to him. No wonder he was so devoted to me once he'd given in and we had united our souls. We hadn't known it, but we'd found each other again, and everything had been as it should be.

I was curled in the library again when I began thinking about when I should try to walk back into the lake of glittering flames—when I should attempt to go home to all the problems that for now seemed frozen ... my grandfather, my dead mother, Freda—who was who knew where—and Alàn ... poor Alàn. Left in that room with my grandfather when I had been teleported away to Remodeus.

Shining through all of those problems was the reason for going back. *Him*—my Leander. The one that had all the memories of our time together, not just the ones with *Grace*. Now that I had also experienced those moments, when we united again it will be like the crashing of worlds. Two threads not tethered, but woven together through time. I would always be his, and he would always be mine. We'd thought this entire time we'd been forced into this, that we didn't get to choose. But I chose him—would always choose him. Here, as *Grace*, I'd done everything I could to ensure that we would be together.

My thoughts on the subject subsided in the pages of a book about drakes. I wondered how my friend was doing. I supposed I could *Command* the drake to return, but I didn't want to. He deserved to be free to fly the skies. I would let him enjoy that for as long as he could. I learned from the book that drakes, like the one I'd healed, were often mis-identified as juvenile dragons. I smiled at the possibility of that thought. According to the text, it was common to never know until they grew beyond the size of a drake. Dragons were rare and powerful creations of the Nine Circles, often hunted for their scales to enchant weapons and armor—or, in the case of the Primordial Father, enslavement. Because of this, they would not self-identify for fear of being captured or killed.

I passed a couple more chapters of my book before I heard footsteps and Leander entered the room. At first, I wondered if he came to whisper more sensual things to unravel me, but he looked to be in an ill mood.

"Remodeus is here, and would like to speak with you."

My stomach twisted, but I followed Leander to a sitting room where Remodeus was waiting. We sat on a plush sofa across from his spot in an armchair, and he placed a teacup on the nearby table.

"Hello again—*Grace,* is it?" Remodeus smiled, using what I imagined was *all* his concentration to seem pleasant. He looked almost exactly the same as I remembered him in my time. Not like Leander, who had clearly been affected by the results of their failed war a mere twenty years ago now. Remodeus hadn't seemed to suffer at all.

"Yes, that's right. And you are Remodeus, The First Prince stewarding the Prime Circle." I inhaled. "It must be nice to receive such a significant promotion at the expense of others."

His displeased expression yielded to a slight upturn of his lip at my taunting. "Right place, right time, really," Remodeus replied flatly.

"What can I do for you?" I said, disinterest in my voice.

"I wish to speak with you alone."

Leander growled low in his throat, but I sent him a *Mindtell.* *"I'll be fine. If he annoys me, I'll turn him into a frog."*

Leander's eyes met mine in acknowledgement. He stood up from the seating area and replied to my message, tone wary. *"He's the commander of this plane. You might be more at his mercy than you think."*

"The only one at mercy on this plane is you—to me." I sent the message with a light caress to his mind—and felt his internal, fluttering reaction. I had entered in his thoughts a bit further than I'd intended. Was this what it felt like when he'd send me messages as a mortal, caressing and stroking my mind?

He smiled at me before speaking aloud to the two of us. "I'll be outside." Then he exited the room, casting a quick glance back at me.

"Well," Remodeus began, "I wanted to speak to you in person out of respect, as you are clearly a powerful creature. Would you mind if I asked you a few questions?"

I nodded.

He snapped his finger and an imp ran to pour more tea into his cup. Then the imp scuttled over to me and handed me my own full cup.

I smiled down at the imp. "Thank you." It was a gesture I had yet to see anyone in power on this plane offer the constructs.

The imp blinked at me, wide-eyed in surprise. Then it cracked a pointy grin.

Remodeus shifted at the reaction. "First, I'm curious about your family. Who are they and where are they from?" Remodeus took a sip from his cup.

"I'm not from this plane, so you've probably never heard of them," I replied, taking my own sip.

Remodeus pressed his lips together and leveled a look at me. "Please do not lie to me. I am not a lesser devil you can fool with deception."

I tilted my head, thinking. What could I say to satiate his ability to determine a truth from a lie, yet still keep my secrets?

Remodeus looked me over as if trying to catch my thoughts.

"Alright ..." I took a sip from my cup, considering. "I am *originally* not from this plane. My family is a complicated and personal matter." All truths. Was it enough?

He furrowed his brow. "Your aura, whatever magic you have access to, is completely primordial. You originated from the Nine Circles." He leveled an unamused glare at me. "So why don't I know you? And how did you escape being imprisoned?"

I was hit with the painful reminder that in the Nine Circles, powerful females were often imprisoned for the Primordial Father to use solely for creating powerful progeny.

I kept my eyes on him, pressing my hands into the cup and saucer in my lap. "I've been able to stay out of trouble," I offered. "I know what the risk of making myself known is. Now is probably the safest time for me to roam, given the Primordial Father's banishment."

"Hm." He took another sip of tea. "Since we've established you are from the Nine Circles, I have a proposition for you."

I raised my eyebrows. Was he seriously—

"The Primordial Father imprisoned creatures like you and forced them into bonds. Personally, I found the entire process distasteful. I find existence much more enjoyable without the oppression of binding females to me." He sat the cup down in its saucer. "So, my proposition is for you to give me a progeny, but you'd be free from any sort of contract, as well as any sort of committed relationship. You can stay here and fuck the Fire Prince as much as you want, but you will only bear me a progeny—no one else."

This was nine levels of fucked up—but of course he didn't realize. I tried not to let my disgust show completely. Sure, he was my father by magical means, not biological, but I had absolutely zero interest in this regardless. Especially after I knew what he'd end up doing to Leander.

I sat my teacup down across the table from his. "No."

He blinked. I was sure the shock on his face was not only from being rejected, but from the way I'd rejected him, after he'd spun his little web.

I recognized it for the insult it was.

"Your reason?" I could hear the frustration laced in his words.

"I don't need to give you one," I replied flatly.

"Then what is your intention with Leander? Are you going to give him a progeny?" His voice rose slightly, and I realized now how much of a threat to his power it might be if I did as he suggested.

The truth for this answer was complicated, knowing Remodeus could detect my lies. All I'd ever wanted was my own family. Someday I would like to make that a reality—with *my* Leander. However, in this time, my purpose for being with him was not about that.

"No. Why? Would it bother you if I did?" I needed to gain a higher initiative in this conversation. Baiting him would distract from asking follow up questions that would be difficult for me to answer.

"Bother? I would forbid it," he replied with the confidence of someone who ruled an entire plane.

"I see. So you have a distaste for oppressing the females on your plane so long as their choices align with your own desires?"

He narrowed his eyes and his voice grew quiet with malice. "I can see what is between you. Either you accept the offer, or you can find another plane to live on."

The threat was full-bodied, though internally I laughed at the thought of him actually attempting to banish me. In the end, he'd get one of the things he wanted—I couldn't stay here.

"Actually," I said, "I am leaving this plane soon. It was never my plan to stay here." I leveled a stare at him. He knew Leander couldn't leave this plane, so I'd be going alone. There was something else in his eyes, though—disappointment.

"I see ..." He glanced over me while his primordial magic pushed against me, prodding, searching for any weaknesses.

I let him explore. He should see what I was capable of. I felt his magic slide close like the glass he'd abducted me in when I was mortal. The memory sparked my agitation. I found the edge of his glass and tapped it with a glittering, arcane finger, shattering it before it could press down around me.

He sat back, adjusting his posture to cover his surprise, but I could read the underlying fear. Fear that *I* was the more powerful one here. When he spoke again his voice held a tremor.

"What are you?"

I narrowed my eyes on him, fire blazing behind them. "That's none of your business. Now that you've received the answer to your proposition, I think you should return to the Prime Circle."

"You do not *Command* me," he seethed.

"Go home!" I felt the arcana heat the words. I meant it. I wanted him to go back to the Prime Circle, *now*.

Remodeus stared at me in shock. His body went rigid as he sat there, still as a statue. Could he feel it, too? Maybe not that I could actually *Command* him, but something was there that allowed for the possibility of it? His hand lifted and he snapped his fingers. There was a puff of arcane smoke and he was gone.

He'd retreated ... obeyed my *Command*.

Leander swung the door open wide, striding over to stand right in front of me. I looked up, and he crossed his arms with a devious smirk.

"You know," he said, his voice melancholic, "I've wondered the same thing. I had hoped you would just tell me and I wouldn't have to ask, but I'm thinking that I won't get an answer at all."

My heart fractured a little more. "Leander, the truth is, I don't know exactly what I am, or how I got here. I just know I have this primordial magic that seems stronger than most."

"Stronger than all, is more like it. I've never seen Remodeus crawl away like that. He's probably never going to forgive you."

Oh hell, was this the start of the feud that would lead Remodeus to torturing Leander in my own time?

He sat down next to me on the sofa and ran his fingers along my arm till his hand met mine, and he held it. "I think you know what you are. You just don't want to admit what it is." His infernal eyes blazed at me. I had a hunch he'd developed the same suspicion as Amias.

"Don't say it." I said. "I just want to be Grace right now ... till I leave." I couldn't keep my voice from cracking. I hadn't asked to be made into a goddess or whatever Erebell had done. I wanted more than anything to get back to my Leander. I knew that with him, we'd figure it out together.

"It doesn't change anything for me—what you are, or what you could be." He lifted his hand to stroke my hair back from my face.

I could see in his glowing orange eyes what he was referring to. He still wanted me—wanted to be bonded with me.

I pushed myself into his chest and hugged him tightly. "I love you dearly," I said, quietly squeezing him.

He squeezed me back. "No one has ever said that to me," Leander breathed against the top of my head.

"Really? Not even your mother?" I tilted my gaze up to him.

His face scrunched in confusion. "Perhaps she did, but I don't remember what it sounds like. I ... don't even remember her voice. I was so young when the Primordial Father killed her. I suppose she did love me," he said quietly. "I want to tell you the same." His voice was wavering, as if the words were difficult to get out.

I squeezed him tighter. "It's okay. You don't have to say them for me to feel them."

He kissed the top of my head. "I'm in agony, not knowing when you will leave. That I might turn a corner one day and realize you are gone ..." he trailed off, hurt in his voice.

"I won't do that. I won't leave without seeing you first."

He planted more kisses atop my head and held me.

I needed to leave soon, but for now, I wanted to live for this. His embrace, and the knowledge that soon we'd be together again.

CHAPTER SIXTY-FOUR

LEANDER

The coach ride to the estate took excruciating hours. If only Reign had shown me a painting, anything, so I could teleport there. Alas, after rummaging through the minds of a few mortals and making a deal with a carriage driver, the long, half-day journey began. Had Reign suffered a similar length of time just sitting in a buggy every time she had to travel between her academy and the estate? I tried to imagine her in such a situation and saw her simply curled up with one of many books she'd likely bring to occupy her time. She probably loved it.

I occupied my own time with thought. The past month of my existence had transpired so quickly. Before that, it was endless years of mundane devil activities. Just enough soul collection not to alarm anyone, the occasional manipulation of mortals for either entertainment or gain—typical infernal toil. They were the centuries where I'd given up, really. I thought I would never cross paths with the soul mate Grace had promised.

Then I'd finally met her, my Reign, and life had suddenly felt accelerated—like coasting the clouds as some great flying beast before it took a sharp plunge. She had since occupied my thoughts every second of every day, like some kind of eternal hymn. I'd never been so obsessed over something. It had been like that with *Grace*. Something about her drove me mad, and now I think I finally understood why.

I replayed all my memories with Grace, searching for Reign in them. I had not slowed down to think too deeply about the implication that they were the same person before, and now it was all that consumed my thoughts.

When Grace had told me about her soul mate, had she been talking about me? All those centuries ago, she'd poured her heart out to me about how she wanted to follow him, to find him. But he ... was *me*. It was why she'd had to leave—to be with *me* again. My heart twisted, hating that I had not known—*could not have* known—back then. How painful had it been for her to see me like that? And to have me *beg her relentlessly* to be mine? She'd told me all the things I had needed to hear. All the things that had healed how horribly broken I'd been.

She had saved me.

Then another thought crossed my mind. What was she now, *a goddess?* I couldn't begin to even understand how that could have happened. My worst fear was that in the end we could not be together. Deities had a duty to their plane, and they tended to spend eternity in the ethereal planes with the other gods watching from afar. It was why they were so disembodied from the creatures of the physical planes. They did walk the physical planes sometimes, but it was rare. I knew all about that, unfortunately ... it had taken one such deity to slaughter me. If Reign was one of them now ... I couldn't imagine facing all of my immortal existence without her. Praying to her would not be enough, but I would. I would worship her all the way to my last breath.

I watched the landscape change as the sun set on the last leg of my journey. Grace had left to follow our bond, to be with *me* again. I was not sure what it would take to bring her back to this time—*our time*—but I resolved myself to do anything to see that she arrived here. I could likely get lost in the ever-turning wheel of time myself, but if she was stuck there, I would gladly trade places with her to save her.

The coach slowed to a stop and the driver called back to me, "This is as close as I can get! The Vendelfrey's are private people."

I emerged from the coach door. The path ahead was illuminated with silver light from the moon. Further was a gate, with about a dozen guards floating in and out of the lookout tower.

"You are dismissed," I snapped my fingers and a velvet sack of coin landed in the driver's lap.

He said nothing and made to turn the carriage around.

It was a slow annoyance to walk through the three gates, slaughtering the mortal guards as I went. Seeing the same leathers I'd seen Cyrus wear and the matching black leather garb the wizards wore enraged me. I knew one thing was for certain: this hunt would end with me burning this estate to the ground. My Reign had said she'd wanted to burn it all herself, but not a day ago she'd asked for my help. I would be her weapon and execute her divine will.

I saw a driveway ahead with large columns of marble and a massive door. I snapped my fingers, and my form altered into the appearance of one of the guards I'd just slaughtered. I passed the threshold and began sorting through the magical auras, following the tingle towards what I hoped were the items I was looking for. The estate was quiet. I barely saw another soul, but eventually I turned a corner and saw it.

The lodestone was a massive, rectangular rock laying flat on its longest side. I walked the length of it, observing. Then a glint caught my eye, and I saw the knife resting in a case behind it.

How arrogant do you have to be to leave all this shit just sitting out unguarded?

I strode to the knife. When I picked it up, it hummed in my grasp.

Interesting.

No one had mentioned that the knife these mortals were creating such a fuss over was *infernal.* I twisted it in the light. The curved blade was a warm, silver metal, the hilt wrapped in a dark leather. Aside from its infernal aura, there was something ... else to it. A familiarity I couldn't place.

Footsteps sounded, and a leather-clad human rushed into the room. "What are you doing, guard?" he barked at me.

I turned to face him, twisting the knife in the light, watching how it glittered. "How many souls do you think it takes to activate this rock?" The knife hummed louder, as if it yearned for the soul ahead of me.

The human looked at me in confusion. "You are not supposed to be touching that. Put it down before the Master finds out," he said sternly.

I glanced over at him and extended my hand, pointing the knife in his direction. My hand tingled with warm primordial magic as I pulled his body towards me—and onto the knife. A soft, wet crunch, and he was seizing, the ability to breathe driven from him by the impact. I dropped my altered appearance and watched the guard's eyes widen. When his face slackened, I kicked him off the knife.

The silvery essence of his soul was stuck to the blade, as if the edge had ripped it from his body. The soul sank into the metal, its color shifting from a warm silver to a darker, infernal violet glow.

How many souls would be enough?

Everyone here had been complicit in hurting my Reign—I would clear the entire estate if necessary to get her back. I certainly didn't want any ... interruptions.

I suspected Reign's grandfather was not here—yet—but I hastened. Every time he arrived, he complicated things. I didn't have *time* for complications.

It took surprisingly little effort to dispose of every guard and wizard he'd left here to protect the artifacts. I used the knife to take the killing blow, but otherwise enjoyed igniting each corner of the estate with burning hellfire.

The estate crackled as air rushed to feed the flames. I smiled at the warm, enjoyable sensation of pure hellfire. I felt the knife vibrate as I approached the lodestone. I didn't know what kind of spell or ritual was required to travel through time. But this was an *infernal* blade, so, in the absence of any other information, I would do what devils did best.

Command.

CHAPTER SIXTY-FIVE

REIGN

It felt harder and harder to leave every moment I lingered here. Days went by, and all I wanted was to steal one more glance, one more touch, one more kiss from him. But my Leander was waiting—thinking I was dead. Probably wrecking havoc on the planes ... I needed to rip the bandage off and at least *try* to go home.

Leander and I were sitting at another little breakfast on the verandah, clothing included this time, when I told him.

"Today I will try to go home."

He sat there frozen and didn't reply for a long while.

I looked down into my tea as if it could protect me from the pain in his eyes. It was the same amber-colored one I liked, still filling the cup.

When he did speak his voice sounded brittle. "What can I do to help you prepare?"

"There is not much I need to do. Make sure that you convince Remodeus to write a contract for you to bind your soul. His specialty in contracts should be able to handle that." I finally raised my eyes back to him, and the look on his face was heartbreaking.

"How will I know when I've found her?" He seemed impossibly far away as his hellfire eyes dimmed to embers. "How will I know I'm not just waiting to find you?"

My eyes burned with tears that spilled over the edges. Was that really what he had felt all these years? He'd been waiting to find me ... then Remodeus had tied him to a mortal who looked like his Grace, and his fear was realized—waiting for me, only never to have me.

My sweet Leander ... you did wait for me, and you will have me again. I promise.

"Trust me," I said after I had wiped the tears from my face. "That's it. Just trust me." I smiled through the feeling even though more tears threatened to roll down my face.

His gaze softened on me and he nodded.

I decided to keep and wear one of the casual dresses I really liked, the one with a high collar and sleeves down to my wrists. I gave away the extras, then dismissed the imp I'd taken into my service on my first day here. As I took care of my tasks, the sky darkened.

I was breaking his heart.

After Leander let the night completely descend, I found him in the library sitting in a chair by himself. He looked wretched, like he was letting the despair suck the last life from him. I took his hand, kneeling before him in the chair.

"Don't let this circle return to night after I leave," I said softly.

He merely glowered at me, his head propped up by his fingers on the arch of his brow.

I continued. "If you keep it day here, it will be how I loved to see this circle. How I want to remember it forever."

He sat there unmoving, refusing to tear his gaze from me. Nothing I said seemed to cure the absolute ache plaguing his body.

"Are you not going to say anything to me before I leave?" I pleaded. I couldn't leave him like this. It would still be over 900 years before he found me again.

"Please don't leave," was all he said, staring down at me with the glow of his orange eyes all but a flicker now. It tore at my heart again and I could feel the tears building.

"You will be alright without me—better without me. I'm not saying this as a comfort to you—I know it." I stared into his eyes and felt the glittering primordial magic behind my own well up, attempting to give reassurance. Trying to tell him wordlessly that when I said I knew, *I meant it.*

Some of the glow came back to his eyes as if he understood.

I pulled a small note sealed with wax from my pocket and handed it to him.

He glanced at it, turning it over to read the writing on the back. "What is this?"

It hadn't taken much thought for me to create the note—the one that spoke about the mortal me. I hadn't realized at the time that I had been its author. But earlier, when I had put pen to paper, it felt right, and word after word had spilled out. When I read it at the end, the strokes of ink on the parchment had caught me off guard because I realized I had penned it with that magic—the arcane translation for any who viewed it. That had been why it looked foreign to me when I'd read the note in my own time. There was no handwriting—only a transcription of the words in the viewer's language. Then I'd closed it and focused on my primordial magic.

A deal.

A deal using this new magic. The Primordial Mother's magic. *This letter will not open until he meets me. Mortal me.*

... Simple.

"You can open it once you meet her," I replied to his question.

He ran his finger along the edge, feeling the magical resistance keeping the seal from breaking.

I stood up and Leander followed, shoving the letter in his pocket.

"Goodbye, Leander." I offered a sweet smile, attempting not to add to the sadness weighing down the air around us.

"Goodbye, Grace." He leaned his forehead down to mine.

I pushed myself up to my toes and gave him a kiss. He wrapped his hands around my lower back, pulling me deeper into the kiss. Before he could kiss me senseless, I leaned my face slightly away.

"I'm going to teleport down to the lake now," I said.

He squeezed me tighter and whispered, "I'm glad we met, Grace. I'm not sure exactly what sort of future you can see for me, but it's reassuring to know it's one you want for me."

"Trust me, you will have no complaints." I smiled at him. "I'm glad we met, too. Please take care of yourself. No more parties ... try to leave the palace every once in a while. Take care of Silas too," I added. I kissed him on the cheek, pushing myself away.

"I ... hope you find him," he said quietly.

I trailed one hand along his cheek. *If only I could tell you ...*

"Will I ever see you again?" His infernal eyes blazed over me, taking me in as if it truly was the last time.

"Not like this." I smiled. I took another step back and brought my hand up in a little wave.

He brought his own hand up and waved in return.

Just as I felt my magic warm to teleport, he called out.

"Grace—" His eyes trailed across me. "I *do love you.*"

I smiled. "I will always love you dearly, Leander."

Chapter Sixty-Six

In the darkness of the night, the lake really was a sight to behold. It provided the only light—a shimmering, multi-colored reflection that highlighted the shore and the walls of the nearby buildings. As I surveyed further down the shoreline, I noticed the absence of the garden where the path simply hugged the shore, with no bridge in sight. Would he build it in my absence?

I swung the toes of one foot into the shallows of the flames. There was no heat, not like when I had been mortal. Strange. I knew that the immortals of this plane had felt the heat by how they avoided entering it—how they had gaped at me when I'd emerged from it.

A small crowd was gathering again, standing in clusters and watching. None approached me, but I could hear them whispering quietly among themselves.

I took in a deep breath and closed my eyes. When I had first traveled through time, I'd wanted nothing more than to follow Leander's soul—which was something I'd done on instinct and thought little on the mechanics of.

I traveled through time.

Had I invoked Chronomancy? There had been no knife, no souls spent. I'd just done it. I wished I could ask the Primordial Mother—why couldn't I? With a prayer ... like a *Mindtell*.

"Erebell, if you can hear me, please give me a sign."

Her voice flared across my mind like a welcome heat—like home. *"My child, you do not need signs like a primordial cleric. We may simply speak."*

"You recognize me as your daughter?" I said, a little confused. *"That hasn't happened yet."*

"For you it has happened. For me it always was," she replied. *"This is the way of a true goddess."*

"Is ... that what I am now?"

"To the residents of the Physical Planes, perhaps. In truth, you are a Divine Incarnate. Your body is of the Physical Planes, so that is how you perceive time, but I gave you almost all of my primordial chaos."

Primordial chaos ... her primordial magic. The glittering flames inside me and before me.

"The gods were born of the chaos of the cosmos eons ago. The oldest gods swirled and massed themselves of that first bounty of chaos—it's why we are called primordial. I made your soul from my own primordial chaos." The glittering lake flared briefly around me.

So ... I was something on the level of a goddess, but not quite one at the same time. I let out a soft laugh. Of course it would be like this for me. Never completely human, never completely hellborn or devil—and now, not completely a goddess either. Perhaps when it came to the Transmutation of living things, there was always a bit of paradox sprinkled in. A chaos.

I opened my eyes and saw two large, arcane eyes staring back at me from in the flames.

Erebell's eyes.

"It doesn't mean you are not special," Erebell continued. *"You are my greatest creation, unmarred by the influence of Erethor. Free to walk among my other creations, to guide and protect them on their plane. You are the first of your kind. Even mortals who have ascended to godhood had to leave their planes behind to reside in the Ethereal Planes."*

"But you are not with the other gods. You are in a dungeon," I stated.

"Yes ... because Erethor binds me here," Erebell replied, a pained sound to her voice. *"But through you, I am free."*

"Is that why you made me into this?" I had never wanted this for myself, and I certainly didn't know how I was going to guide or protect anyone if—or when—I returned to my own time.

Her eyes squinted slightly at me, wreathed by the flames. *"The way the gods experience time and the cosmos across the planes is infinite, non-linear, and contains all possibilities. It's not the same as seeing fate. We observe all threads through time and choose to our liking. However, there are rare anomalies to that. Small loops, where the chaos of the cosmos has organized a form—a will—and no god can alter it. That is how it was for you. I had to make you to fulfill that design, because you were always going to be made."*

"So that's it? Everything for me is predetermined?" I replied a little sourly.

"Because you experience time linearly, the loop is a line. Once you return, you will have reached the end of that line. Your life begins anew—ripe with all the possibility and determination of any goddess."

I took in what she was saying for a moment. Then I realized ... *"Leander is part of that anomalous loop, too? Because we were soul bound?"* My heart started pounding in my chest as I tried to process all of this.

"The chaos wove your lives together. It had nothing to do with whether or not your souls are bonded. What you are is magnitudes beyond that. You'll always be cosmically intertwined."

Was that how I'd found him across time? Because, even though I didn't have his soul to tether me, our paths were still woven? It made sense. Even when our bond was broken, I still desperately—madly—wanted him. There was no influence of the thread now, no mechanical tug to drag me to him whether I willed it or not. We needed each other, like any symbiotic force of nature needs the other for life.

"Use him as a constant across the loop." She added as if she could hear all my thoughts. *"All you need to do is focus on him through time, and the chaos of the cosmos will make what you see comprehensible to your mind. When you reach him again, every choice you make from that moment on is purely at your freedom."* She blinked at me in the flames, and then faded away.

My freedom.

I had wanted to be free from the control of others, but I never truly could be until this. That was why Erebell had said she couldn't help me *escape* the dungeon, but that she would help set me *free.* I wondered what would happen to her when I returned. She was still in that dungeon, depleted of almost all her power.

Then my mind raced to what she had said about Leander—what we were to each other. That our bond was so much more than a soul bond. It all seemed to make sense now. Why, when we'd met, everything had moved so fast, like there was something driving each of us towards each other—screaming that we belonged to one another.

We were literally each other's purpose for existing.

I was frightened to think of what life outside this loop might be, to have true freedom not guarded by the chaos of the cosmos. But it also excited me. It burned like a wild flame from my soul.

I would make my own choices, knowing fully they were mine to make.

I breathed deep and took a single step into the flames. Then a second step, a third step. I felt compelled, then, to take one last look behind me, at the time I was leaving behind. So I turned.

The rather sizable crowd was still gathering, watching me. I looked beyond them to the clay buildings, then the sky—it was shifting. I had not noticed because I had been staring into the flames, but the sky was lightening to a pink dawn. I smiled, knowing it was him, that he was doing it for me.

Then my eyes drifted down again and caught on a shadowed alley between the buildings behind the crowd. There, I saw Leander's orange, glowing eyes cloaked in darkness staring out at me. I glanced down the lakeside where I remembered the bridge being and then back to him before reaching out to his mind.

"I think a garden would look great down there," I said with a soft caress.

"Anything for you, Grace."

My heart swelled. Soon we would be back in each other's arms, both with the full knowledge of this experience. I locked eyes with his for a moment, burning one last look at him into my mind, before turning back around and facing the flames. I picked up my pace till it was so deep I began to float as if I were swimming. The colors flashed around me chaotically. It was disorienting, the light between colors melting across my vision till all I could see was waves of sparkling patterns. I thought of him, *my Leander.* My guiding infernal star in the night of cosmic chaos.

Then suddenly, the flames began snuffing out, and I was falling—no, whirling into a dark expanse. Whipped wildly around here and there in the chaos of time. The ground was gone from under my feet and I was flung with no sense of what was up or down. The roaring of wind and rushing water and static assaulted my ears. Sparks and glittering dust pelted me as I looked for anything to orient myself with in the relentless, cosmic winds. I was alone, swirling in a vast expanse of black oblivion. I concentrated my thoughts around my chosen gravity as I shook violently.

Leander.

I belonged to him. I would find him no matter what.

The black expanse fell silent. The chaos winds stilled and the sparks and glittering dust drifted like suspended snowfall. It hovered for a moment, and then flowed forward. Slowly, in the oblivion ahead, a path lit in front of me. It shimmered like the glittering flames of the lake.

Erebell's flames, the primordial chaos.

My chaos.

It flowed like a sparkling river with a current of purpose, and I took a step forward on that glittering, cosmic road.

CHAPTER SIXTY-SEVEN

LEANDER

I pressed the knife blade flat on top of the lodestone. The entire stone vibrated as the violet glow from the blade was sucked into its surface. I placed my other palm flat on the stone and bent to rest my forehead against it. Warmth rushed across its surface, like the souls were pulsing through it. My eyes closed as I focused on her, *my Reign*. Not the Reign of this time, but the one that had walked into those glittering flames. The one that hadn't known how she'd get back to me. I would find that Reign and I would guide her here, to me.

There was no soul mate bond to hold on to. There was, however, an overwhelming feeling that I still belonged to her. Something otherworldly dragged at me, just as it had when I had first met her a thousand years ago. It wasn't a thread, but it would work. It would lead me to her.

The *Command* to bring us together was not constructed of words, but a disembodied, arcane desire that demanded it. The stone hummed, a whirring, rushing sound like being pushed beneath water. I felt the *Command* well up like a fire in my soul, and I willed it upon the lodestone.

I fell forward quicker than I expected, landing on my hands and knees against cold, dark dirt.

It was night, and I was outside. The knife, the lodestone—even the estate—were all gone. Ahead of me I saw orange lights from torches around what looked like a small settlement and a road. I glanced behind me and was met with the dark formations of trees. It was the same tree line I had seen upon approaching the estate. I was in the same place, but the estate was not here. Either not built yet, or long gone. I didn't stop to contemplate what the latter meant and walked towards the squat buildings.

A melody carried through the open windows of one inn, and I angled towards it. Emerging inside, I saw a crowd of humans, some listening intently to a bard singing, others drinking. Barmaids handed out refills, and some set plates before the patrons under the sounds of the ballad. Then my gaze fell on one human sitting in the corner wiping her face as if she'd been sobbing. I tilted my head. There was something different about her. I had seen her before ... in that elf's mind. Then I realized. This was Lydia Vendelfrey, but she was much younger ... and with child.

The time travel had clearly worked, but it seemed to have brought me to the mortal Reign still within her mother's womb. There was no knife, no lodestone, so was I now stuck in this time? This had not been that long ago. Where was I—the version of me that already existed here? Surely we could not co-exist. Just as I had the thought, I felt a twinge of heat in my body as if in answer—a warm, tingling heat, like when I had pressed myself against the lodestone. Then a ripping anxiety flooded my body, turning into a push—as if I was being rejected from this time.

Lydia noticed me, and she quickly pushed herself up from her seat and rushed to me. "Excuse me, sir? Are you a devil?" Her voice was hoarse, as if the sobbing I suspected had carried on a while. "I've been trying to find one for three days. I need to make a deal," she pleaded.

"What sort of deal?" I replied. What should I do? I knew Remodeus had written Reign's contract, and yet here was her mother talking to me instead. How much interference would prevent us from ever being bonded?

"The father of my child is a low born human. My father is going to kill him as a punishment for *ruining me*." She said the last sourly in opposition to the threat. "I need to make a deal to save him so he can meet his daughter."

"You haven't been able to get an audience with any devil?" What *could* I do here without changing the course of history?

"No, I've tried for days. My father is going to kill him tomorrow. There's no more time. Please, help me." Tears spilled down her face with the words.

This was all wrong. Remodeus had taken an audience with her. He had written the contract. Was this some kind of alternate time? *Unless ...*

I pursed my lips before speaking, feeling the painful irony well up my throat with my words. "Would you like a referral?"

"Please, if you know *any* devil willing to make a deal with me tonight ..." The tears soaking her cheeks glistened under the bar sconces.

I reached into my jacket pocket and pulled out one of my Calling Cards. I re-enchanted it to send to Remodeus instead of myself.

"This is a Calling Card. Write your story and request on it, then burn it. It will be sent to a devil willing to make a deal with you." I handed her the card.

Her eyes grew wide, and the tears ebbed as she blinked down at it. "T-thank you." She took it and looked back up at me in gratitude.

"There is something else—" The twinge in my body started to burn, as if it was trying to rip me apart from the inside. "He's not a pleasant devil, but he is sentimental. Tell him what you will name the child and he will take an audience with you."

"Thank—"

I fell again—at least, I had the sensation of falling—then there was bright light all around me. I blinked, looking forward down an opulent hallway. I was inside. These walls were taller than the inn, cleaner. Like ... the estate. Then I heard Lydia's voice behind me, tired and gravely.

"I wondered if you would return at all after what you did to her in our contract," she said flatly with disgust.

From behind, did she think I was Remodeus? I was never suppose to be here. I cast quick magic so that as I turned, my form from the front shifted smoothly to that of Remodeus. If she believed I was him, perhaps it all still worked out. I could talk my way out of this mishap.

I noted the dark circles shadowing her gaze now. How long had passed?

"It's her birthday. I imagine you want to see her?" she said with hate in her tone.

Realization slammed into me, and my nerves threatened to send me to my knees.

It was ... me.

Remodeus said that he'd not traveled to this plane since he had made Reign's contract. He hadn't forgotten about visiting Reign or taking her to ... *my circle* and giving her *my button* because he'd never done those things.

I had done those things.

"Lead the way," I replied.

She led me to a room with seating and offered the large chair at the end to me. Then she backed to the door and crossed her arms. "What is it you want?"

"Bring her to me." I said in my best imitation of Remodeus, sitting and leaning back into the cushion of the chair, forcing my body to relax.

She stared back at me through her frigid, blue eyes. I could see she was already broken—her expression consumed with loathing. She exited the room, and, a few moments later, I watched her drag a child through the doorway by the arm. A child with black hair, two small horns, pale red skin with dark flecks—and *her* eyes. They glowed like little, infernal roses.

It was Reign ... but she was so small. So young. My heart twisted with sadness for her. Then a sudden, overwhelming instinct of protectiveness for the child before me surged. Instead of glimpsing the past, I was glimpsing the future—a future of my own daughter standing before me. A perfect little version of Reign to protect and cherish together. Lydia left the room, and this tiny Reign stared up at me.

I stared back.

"Are you my father?"

A tremor raced through my body at the sound of her voice. It was hers, only higher pitched, delicate and innocent. Reign had told me about this moment—how she'd had no father, received no love from her mother—but seeing it broke my heart. She'd said that Remodeus visiting her had been the start of *everything*.

I would be her father today. I would do anything to help her on this path, a path where she sets herself free.

I nodded to the child. "Would you like to see where we are from?" I extended one hand to her and opened a portal with the other. I was not sure how much time I would get before the twinge and burn returned to rip me away, but it had to be enough to do what she needed.

She wobbled as we arrived on the other side of the portal. Clutching two of my fingers, she steadied herself as we looked out at the lake. There was no fear in her eyes. She had this expression

... as if she knew it was where she belonged. I'd never realized how deep it actually had been for her, to want to be in the Nine Circles of Hell. No wonder she'd cried when I had finally brought her back here.

She looked up at me and I smiled. I led her silently down the walkway around the lake. I wasn't sure what to say. Eventually, I realized I was simply retracing the steps we'd taken together the first time I had brought her here—well I suppose it had been the second time for her. At the end of the garden path, I still did not feel the twinge that signaled I would be plucked away.

Just a little longer ...

"Would you like a sweet treat, little Reign?" I said kindly.

Her eyes widened, and she smiled, showing two, tiny little buds where fangs would grow in. "Is *Reign* my devil name?"

Fuck. Why did I call her that? *Did I just change everything?*

"I mean—*Grace*, why don't we get ice cream? You like ice cream, don't you?" I tried to recover, ushering her along to the shop.

She sat quietly in the chair eating her ice cream while I had my own. I knew it was the only food here she could eat safely, and I was suddenly very grateful it was something as enjoyable as ice cream.

"Can I live here with you, father?" She looked up at me with those rosy, infernal eyes.

I couldn't lie to her. "I'm sorry, but you can't stay here with me. I was not supposed to meet with you like this."

Large tears started rolling down her face, and I was utterly broken. I felt my own tears spill down my cheeks as I kneeled down to her, hugging her tightly. I couldn't let go of her without telling her, and I knew I had because Reign had told me that this was the first time she'd ever heard the words said to her. Just as she was the first to give them to me all those centuries ago.

"I love you," I whispered. "Even if we can't see each other for a long time, please do not forget how much I love you," I pleaded to her, wiping my face.

She sniffed, rubbing her own cheeks with sticky fingers.

I snatched a cloth napkin from the table and wiped the streaks. I should send her home soon ... It was time. "I have something for you."

The spare button had been sewn into the inside of my jacket for millennia. It had been my father's. There were a few, the only things left of him, one sewn into each of my jackets as a tribute to him. I pulled on the button inside this one, breaking the threads, and held it out in front of her. Her eyes sparkled in awe and I placed it in her tiny hands.

"Whenever you feel alone, I want you to look at this button and think about me. We're special, and you are more powerful than you think. This button will help you if you keep it with you."

She clutched the button in her hands.

I felt the twinge start in my body. What if ... I could not find her after all this? What if this was the last time I ever saw her?

"I love you so much," I squeezed out, somehow managing not to sound absolutely shattered.

She sniffled, holding the button tightly. "I love you too, father."

Then the twinge turned into a burn. I opened another portal and took her back, releasing her into the care of her mother. The burning tingle intensified as I pushed myself down the hallway. I got halfway through it before I fell again.

The hall looked the same, but the light was warmer. How far had I gone? I heard voices—a group of men—from a room just ahead. I approached slowly as a familiar voice spilled out.

"Allow me the pleasure of introducing you to my poor grand-daughter, Grace. A hellborn raped my daughter, but we didn't throw the babe out when she was born. We knew we could give her a good life despite being a victim of such a violent act."

The muscles in my body tightened. I knew what this was. Reign's grandfather would parade her around as a tool to manipulate arrangements and trade agreements. She'd never told me about any time in particular though. What was it I was supposed to do here?

I passed a mirror hanging on the hall wall and saw that I was still magically altered to look like Remodeus. I checked my surroundings for witnesses before snapping my fingers, altering myself to look like an ordinary, human nobleman. Then I strolled into the room.

There was a table spread with all kinds of food and drink. Beyond it was the wretched man himself, standing on a slightly raised area. There were about twenty men in wealthy clothing circled around him, goblets in their hands. But I glimpsed her through the crowd.

Reign ...

She was a little older now, perhaps nine or ten. She just stood there, silently, without saying a word. She looked up at her grandfather with fear in her eyes—eyes her grandfather had altered to look hellborn with white sclera like a human's.

"Her skin is not very red," one of the nobles remarked. "If you have her horns and tail removed, and her fangs filed when they come in, she may be able to pass as human."

It took every ounce of control not to *shred him to pieces* and burn this *entire* estate to the ground in that very moment. I fisted my hands into my pockets, attempting to hide my utter rage at the comment. I slipped into the man's mind, learned who he was, and where he lived. If I ever returned to my time, I would pay him a visit and take my time removing each piece of *his* body one by one till the pain alone killed him.

"We accept her how she is, of course." Her grandfather smiled.

What a fucking lie. No wonder my dear Reign always hid herself.

"Now, Grace, why don't you excuse us so we can discuss property lines and boring adult things." He motioned to a nanny among the servants standing ready nearby, and the woman grabbed Reign by the arm, pulling her away from the crowd.

I watched her be dragged towards the exit right in front of me. She didn't even notice me because those two, walnut brown eyes were glued to a cake on the banquet table.

The same creamy cake she'd once instructed Emrys to retrieve for us.

I raised my voice over the lot of men beginning to mingle. "At least let the young miss part with a slice of cake." I sounded a bit more aggressive than I had meant to, but her grandfather nodded to the nanny and she took a slice on a plate before leading Reign out the door.

The twinge erupted in my chest, this time shooting to a violent, heated vibration. I rushed out of the room and down the hall. My concentration on my modified self broke with the pain, and my appearance fluttered back. Rushing down a flight of stairs, I entered an opulent foyer, and my feet slid slightly on the glossy, white marble. I heard footsteps and retreated to an attached hallway, ducking into a shadowed corner near a closed door.

A door I had shattered when collecting souls for the lodestone.

It was then I realized each jump was bringing me closer and closer to my original time. I was going in the wrong direction to reach my Reign. This had been her life before she'd met me. What might I see next? Could I course correct my path?

The burning twinge seized me again, and I fell.

I opened my eyes to candlelight flickering in darkness—and immediately sensed some kind of magical tampering—preventing it's use around me. I listened to footfalls echo just outside of where I was.

"Did you think I'd really let you travel there in a mundane way?" The voice of her grandfather echoed with his steps.

I crept to the edge of the corner I'd been hiding in and peered into the foyer.

There she was. Was this my Reign?

She stood there, shifting nervously as her grandfather turned away from her. I took in her clothing, the pack she carried—they were the same ones she'd had before she met me.

This was still the past.

I felt a shift in the air—a tingle in my fingers. That magical prevention, had been removed. What was happening? I peered back around and saw her grandfather fishing around for spell materials in his pocket. Reign looked ... terrified.

What am I supposed to do? I can't kill her grandfather right here. I can't abduct her ...

Pressing my back against the wall, I closed my eyes, trying to narrow down an acceptable option—any option. If I was here, I was meant to be, and I felt an overwhelming need to interfere somehow.

The twinge came behind my eyes this time, and I knew it wouldn't be long before I fell again, so I whipped my head back around the corner. When I caught sight of her, I flicked a finger. A shadowed door to a demiplane rose up through the floor behind her. She cast a *Arcane Twin* of herself that she sent running past her grandfather. It snagged his attention and she pivoted, rushing through the door.

Such a clever girl ... Now, I would *Scry* on Freda and deliver Reign to her—but the twinge thrummed through me and I fell with no warning.

Fuck. Fuck. Fuck.

I dropped into a dark hallway. Where was I? How far had I gone? How long has she been inside that demiplane? I whipped my hands up to *Scry* on Freda. The vision focused, and I saw her stuffing items into a pack on a bed in a house room. Behind her was a window, a green lawn next to a dirt road visible. I focused on that patch of green and summoned my shadowed door once again.

Please let her be alright. Please let her not be dead in dimensional space.

Then the door swung wide and Reign tumbled out onto the grass. I sighed when Freda took notice and rushed out the door.

The heated twinge returned with a thunderous crack. Pain erupted down my body as if it was being split in two.

I fell and fell.

This time, I reached out my hands for purchase and felt cold stone under them. I opened my eyes.

Both my hands were splayed across the lodestone—which was cleaved completely down the middle. The heat of the flames from the fire I'd set to the estate warmed my back. I breathed in and out. A glint of light drew my eyes to the knife resting to the side of the broken lodestone. It was still and cold, dull and depleted of all souls.

No ... this could not be it.

I couldn't be back where I started.

Alone.

Without her.

"Fuck!" I screamed, punching the lodestone, sending cracks and fissures through one side. The pain of broken fingers seized through my hand, but I didn't care. I slid down to the floor and cupped my head in my hands.

I had failed.

I failed her.

CHAPTER SIXTY-EIGHT

REIGN

The light of the road dimmed as I walked, cosmic flames extinguishing to the darkness of oblivion. But I could still feel him. He was so close. Colors and shapes bloomed around me like bright drops of ink in water. Light stretched across a floor like it were cast from a window. A plume of ink yielded a chair, then a small table, and a door. The space had a strange familiarity to it—ethereal and blurred, as if my presence were no more solid than those drops of ink dissipating.

I knew this room ...

The door flung open, and I saw my mother—my human mother.

She twisted a young child's arm behind her, then released her in the room.

It was ... me.

The color bubbled and bloomed around the younger me, and then spread to the chair to reveal my father—no, that wasn't my father ...

The ethereal haze shifted ... and my eyes went wide.

Leander?

I could see right through the illusion he'd cast on himself. I blinked, tears rolling down my cheeks.

This was that moment.

The moment that started everything—and it had been him? All this time? He clearly had no memory of this ... or ... it had not happened for him yet. I watched him like an uninvited specter as he looked upon the much younger version of me.

His eyes ... something about the shape of his brow over them ... he looked absolutely heartbroken. His hands twitched and his posture in the chair looked forced, like he hadn't meant to be here and was improvising. The voices of young me and my Leander were muffled through whatever thick, ethereal air separated me from this moment. He extended his hand and opened a portal, guiding the younger me through it.

This was ... not a memory. It was happening. I was watching it happen.

It was him.

He had been the first person to tell me that they loved me. He had been the reason I'd wanted to learn arcana and seek out the Nine Circles. He was the reason why those pink skies blazed in my memory.

The forms before me dissipated into the dark oblivion. New drops spilled like rain all around me, bleeding into objects—multiple moments—*memories.* All happening in real time before me.

He stood disguised among men, watching my grandfather use me for manipulation. I turned and saw him rushing down the estate staircase. The moments flashed, here and then gone. I turned again and saw him back against a door, watching my grandfather preparing to send me away to the Gisenwald's. Had it been him that sent that shadowy door? It must have been. My eyes darted back and forth as the moment played on and he turned away, hesitating.

Leander! I shouted across the ethereal fog between us. I reached my hands out to him, trying to touch his face, but they slipped through him as if he—or I—were a phantom. *Do it! Help me!*

He looked around the corner again and flicked his finger. The door appeared.

Enough of this.

I threw my hands to my sides, my magic—*my primordial chaos*—burned through my body.

Take me straight to him.

My Leander.

My soul mate.

Where I belong.

The drops of color gave way, narrowing, buzzing around me like little sparks taking form. Warmth bloomed all around me, then the blazing orange of hellfire flooded the space. The shifting colors bubbled till the forms they took became heavy and solid. This ... this was the estate.

My eyes widened.

I saw him slumped against a large stone, hands covering his face. That—was that the lodestone? It was split down the middle, the knife we'd been looking for resting beside it. He had used it, had tried to find me—that had to be why he'd become so intertwined in my life.

We'd both woven ourselves in each other's lives. Both influencing and acting with a single, driving purpose—to ensure we'd find each other. The Primordial Mother had said our bond transcended the fate of the gods and had been laid out by the chaos of the cosmos. Even before that, when our soul bond had been contracted, we'd thought we hadn't chosen each other. But how could that be? Even if it was always meant to be ...

We created this.

We chose each other.

The space continued to materialize around me until the ethereal fog broke and all but faded away. I felt myself drift down and my foot solidly tapped on the stone floor.

Leander looked up at the sound, eyes wide and face wet with tears. His gaze traveled slowly, unbelievingly, up the folds of my dress. I felt my own tears run down my face as I thought of everything we'd experienced throughout time.

Our wide eyes locked together. I watched the breath fill his chest as my own lungs grasped for air. We spoke our next words to each other in complete unison.

"It was always you."

I sunk into him as he wrapped his arms around me, squeezing me tighter than I'd ever felt. He kissed my head over and over again, crying. I pulled away just enough to look at him, to cup his face in my hands. Our eyes met, and it confirmed what I'd suspected.

He knew it all now.

That I was the Grace he'd met a millennium ago. That he'd been the one who'd first told me I was loved, spoken out for me, sent me a way out. I leaned in and wrapped my arms around him, melding my lips with his, falling into a deep kiss. His hands gripped my back as he held me closer. He kneaded against my flesh, as if to savor every softness of my corporal body.

"Thank you for guiding me back," I said, pulling away from him. Those moments had been like breadcrumbs, to lead me here.

His expression softened on me. "Thank you for saving me," he replied coyly.

Oh, we would have so much to talk about when it came to *Grace*, but that would have to wait.

"Leander—" I barely got his name out when his eyes flicked to something behind me. He threw me to the ground away from him as the room flashed.

A deafening crack of thunder shook the room. It echoed through my body, weighing down on me until it ebbed. I pushed myself up and saw the remnant static of the white lightning rippling over Leander's clothes. I'd never seen him look so enraged as he pushed himself to stand, his wrathful eyes locked on where the lightning had originated. I whirled to follow his stare and found my grandfather standing in the doorway.

CHAPTER SIXTY-NINE

"Are you okay!?" I sent the question to Leander's mind.

"I'm fine ..." he growled in return.

My grandfather lifted his hand and the knife flew across the room, handle landing in his grasp. "That stone was tedious to get here," he seethed, looking over the enormous crack running through the stone.

I rose slowly to my feet and heard Leander's voice enter my mind.

"That knife is infernal. I don't know what else it can do—if it can hurt you," he said in a worried tone. *"You should run now."*

Ha! Like hell I would leave him here. Besides, whatever being a Divine Incarnate included, it had to mean that *I* could protect *him* for once.

And set *myself* free.

My own lightning sparked between my fingers and I threw my hand out towards my grandfather. Leander stared at me in surprise as the crackling electricity erupted from my hand.

Thunder rattled the room. Crackling remnants of electricity snaked around a spherical arcane shield around my grandfather. He held the knife against his rolled-up sleeve, his gaze shifting to me before he made a cut along his forearm. Blood pooled in the carved flesh, then rolled up the knife in sanguine beads. My grandfather's voice vibrated with arcana as he spoke.

"Dark Echo, let your will be heard again."

My eyes widened as energy reverberated through the room. It pressed down on me, like an arcane ceiling lowering against us. What was happening?

"Go, Reign!" Leander said, rushing to my side as if he'd push me to leave. I could see the red coals in his eyes. He wasn't just on the edge of becoming that colossal hellhound of shadow and flame—he was terrified.

"I'm not leaving without you!" I argued.

"Please—"

"Leander ..." A dark, cruel voice grated on my ears.

My eyes whipped back to where my grandfather stood. He was staring at us still, eyes wide—only his left eye was a solid black void that seemed to suck in all the light around it. His head shifted to me.

"What are you?" The cruel voice poured from my grandfather's mouth. It wasn't his voice. It was heavy with power, aged from millennia. *"I did not make you."*

Leander growled as his shadows licked up his back like hackles.

My grandfather's head tilted back to Leander, and that punishing voice growled back, *"Sit, boy!"*

Leander arched in pain, muscles straining, fighting, as he dropped slowly to one knee to the floor. He was shaking, trying as hard as he could to resist. Panic flooded my mind as the pieces clicked together.

It had to be the Primordial Father.

Erethor.

And his possession of my grandfather enabled enough of his power flowing through to *Command* Leander. My stomach turned. This was not like how I *Commanded* Remodeus, or threatened Julian in the past. It was more ... crushing—oppressive.

"I won't allow my favorite weapon to be used as a key for the portal, but whatever you are ... you are ripe with primordial chaos."

I felt that arcane weight around us advance in, driving the the breath from my lungs.

"You will work nicely."

My eyes shot to Leander, wide with both fear and concern.

"He won't kill me, go *now!*" Leander pleaded through gritted teeth from the floor.

I backed away. I could still feel the Palisade glyph at work, so I rushed to the nearest wall where I cast *Passage*. My primordial magic heated within me, and an opening bloomed across the wall. I emerged in the hall cast in hellfire, and halfway down I heard the crackle of lightning and looked back.

He was pointing after me.

I cast again, diving through another passage opening to a room, and rolled to take cover as the lightning lanced down the hall after me. The boom of thunder that followed it caused glass and furniture to explode and the ground to shake.

I scrambled to my feet and pressed back against the wall. I just needed a second—a second to *think*.

"Where are you hiding, little primordial thing?" I heard the echo of my grandfather's shoes click in the hall.

My body rattled as I clung to the wall, panting for air. It was the first time I'd felt fear since my mortal soul had been destroyed and Erebell had filled me with her glittering fire. Even if our power as divine beings was matched, I didn't know anything about using my primordial chaos outside the spells I had learned at Midor's and from Leander.

That's why I needed to think like a *wizard* instead.

I opened another *Passage* and bolted through to my grandfather's office. I passed the spot where the woman had disintegrated, and rounded his desk, racing down the hall. Once I reached the door between the drawing room and the foyer, I froze, hugging the inside wall and listening. The fire consuming the building was still raging, and here, at the foyer, the heat of it glowed along the floor.

Fingers snapped, and the doors to the estate vanished, replaced by an expanse of more wall. Flames licked at it, spreading eagerly to the new fuel it provided.

"Even if you try to leave, you won't get far." The Primordial Father's voice echoed down the hall. *"I'll send my dog after you."*

My eyes drifted up the twin staircases. I could just barely see the corner of the wood table up there. Beyond it was the archive, the place where my contract had been stored—where my grandfather stored all his useful arcane objects. I reached out with my mind.

"Leander, I have a plan."

"Reign ..." His voice was desperate. He had to be afraid—and angry—being held by the Primordial Father's *Command*. *"If he Commands me to kill you I will resist, but do not trust me. Run as far as you can. Go to a different plane if you have to."*

The thought of Leander being forced to harm me sent a silent rage rippling through my body. It would *break* him. Worse, I knew, than how being slaughtered had broken him—how losing me *twice* had broken him. I crept quietly up the stairs towards my grandfather's archive.

"You are mine," I said with a gentle caress. *"I won't allow you to be commanded by him to do such things."*

I knew I could *Command* infernal creatures like the Primordial Father could. If it came to it, I would test the theory of its strength on Leander, the most powerful creature of the Primordial Father's creation. Something told me Leander would not mind one bit if my theory was correct.

I surveyed the foyer from the top of the stairs. Perhaps I could attract the Primordial Father this way. I couldn't give him too much time to think or communicate with my grandfather. I sent out my *Mystic Hand* across the foyer and pushed over the marble bust of my grandfather. It rolled across the short table and crashed to the floor, shattering, sending jagged cracks across the marble tiles. The diamonds from each eye were flung in opposite directions.

I smirked. *Foreshadowing.*

I leaped into the hallway that led to the archive and listened as the Primordial Father brought the clicking of my grandfather's heels to the foyer. The sound of building, crackling lightning followed.

I sent my *Mystic Hand* to press against the small wooden table at the crown of the twin stairs. The wood creaked slightly. In half a heartbeat, the lightning flashed up in that direction, sending splinters of wood from the banister and the table flying across the floor beside me.

I moved down the hall to my grandfather's archive and cast *Passage* again to enter. Some smoke poured into the archive before I could close the arcane opening behind me. This room was cold and dark, just the faint blue glow of the Palisade glyph from across the floor. The fires would likely touch here last thanks to the way my grandfather had designed the room with its double, insulating walls.

I searched for the tools I needed among his most prized possessions. I lifted my right hand, summoning them like I had pulled materials from the enchanted pouch. A red glass orb the size of a small melon flew into my palm. *Mordoch's Void Orb.* I held out my left hand, and a curved knife from the large collection above flew down to me. I bit the knife blade between my teeth and summoned a second knife to my waiting palm.

"I can smell the trail of chaos you leave behind, little primordial." He was near the stairs if I had to guess. Good.

I listened to the tapping of his heels as he approached the door. There was a desk close to the wall farthest from the door, and I crouched behind it, setting the knives on the floor.

The door handle jiggled.

I bobbed my head up above the desk. I needed to bait him before he found out how to unlock the door—or what the consequences of the Palisade glyph were.

"What, a little locked door stops you? Are you too weak possessing an old man to even teleport? Pathetic!" I ducked back down quickly. I put one of the knives back between my teeth and held Mordoch's Void Orb in both hands. I ran my fingers over its smooth surface and found the flush button.

I heard him growl, then the Palisade glyph surged with a bright blue light. Blue electricity erupted in the space he teleported to on the other side of the door, triggering the glyph's consequence. My grandfather's head reared back at the bands of blue electricity rippling up his body.

I used the distraction to activate the anti-magic field and set the Void Orb on the ground under the desk. I rose, a knife in each hand, and lunged for him.

The Primordial Father snarled at me with my grandfather's face. *"What did you do?"*

I didn't give him time to say anything else, sinking one blade into his chest. The infernal blade he held clattered to the floor. Without arcana, this was simply a fight between a woman and an old man. I adjusted my hold on the second knife as he stumbled back from the pain in the mortal body. I advanced and arced my knife up just as I had done to Victus in the cemetery. My grandfather's hands clamped down on my wrists. I pushed my entire body weight, my straining muscles, my anger, the years of neglect—everything—towards him, till the blade tip sank into his throat.

He stumbled backwards, coughing up blood, hands clenching and unclenching before finding purchase against a cabinet.

The cruel voice laughed as more blood gushed from my grandfather's mouth. *"A minor setback."* The black void of his eye narrowed on me. *"I won't forget your face, primordial thing."*

My grandfather crumpled to the floor. The black void of the Primordial Father's eye faded, revealing the original blue. The icy ring was crowded by burst blood vessels, the pupil slowly dilating.

I stared at his corpse, waiting to see it. Finally, the wisp of my grandfather's soul appeared. I lifted the Void Orb and deactivated the field, then took a step forward and extended my hand. It floated up into my grasp. It was a cold and malevolent thing, writhing at my touch. I closed my fingers over it and it vanished, tucked away wherever I assumed my mother's soul had gone.

"Reign?" Leander's concerned voice rushed through my mind. *"Where are you?"*

"I'm upstairs in the archive," I replied. *"He's dead."*

"Stay there, I'm coming."

I broke my gaze from my grandfather's corpse and turned.

It was done. He was gone.

I unlocked the door and opened it. Seconds later, Leander was there. He reached out and embraced me. My arms went around him automatically, welcoming the warmth of him. I felt him look around the room before his eyes focused on the body.

"You did well, my dear." He squeezed me tightly.

I kept my eyes closed and pressed against him. Even without the soul bond, feeling him warm against me helped quiet the shock of what I had just done.

"Did your grandfather always have a false eye?"

"What?"

Leander pulled me away from his chest and turned us to face the body, gesturing towards my grandfather's right eye—the eye that had not turned into a void.

I looked at it more closely. It was pristine and glassy. The pupil had not dilated like the other had. I sent my *Mystic Hand* to it, tapping on it to test it. It was solid. I grimaced as I slid an arcane finger into the eye socket and popped the eye right out. It bounced heavily on to the floor with a sound like a glass marble. I shifted away in disgust, but Leander picked it up.

"It *is* false. He probably used magic to make it behave real," Leander mused. "I didn't noticed any illusions on his eye before."

"I don't even recall him having lost his eye. If he did, he kept it a secret."

He looked at the body, the eye still between his fingers. "Reign, mortals can fragment their souls. They use dark magic to do it, and they must remove parts of their body so that the soul can reside there. Given the context here, I expect he attempted it."

A fragmented soul contained to a body part ... could it call back the portion of the soul I'd taken? "Are you saying that there's a chance my grandfather is not actually dead?"

"His eye—wherever it is—and the small bit of soul resides in it—yes. This body however, is dead." He looked back up at me with a devilish grin. "Did you take the rest of his soul?"

"I did," I replied sweetly.

His finger drifted under my chin, pointing it up towards him. "That will make it harder for the eye to be useful. But we need to make sure this body is destroyed. We should also take the infernal knife with us."

I glanced down at the body and the infernal blade nearby on the ground. I held my hand open and the blade flew to my palm. It hummed in my grasp, sending shockwaves through my hand. It was unsettling to hold. Leander held out his hand. I placed it there and watched it vanish in a puff of smoke.

"It will be waiting for us at home," he said.

I smiled. *Home.*

I looked back down at the body and waved my hand over it, calling to my primordial chaos. Flames rose up around it, the clothing and skin crackling from the heat. Leander flicked the glass eye into the flames. I watched it for a moment before Leander drew my attention back to him with the velvety caress of his voice.

"I told you that you would set yourself free."

"Almost," I said quietly. "There is one more thing I need to do."

"If you don't list *me* as the thing you need to *do,* I don't think I'll recover." His devilish grin turned saccharine.

I leveled my eyes at him. "Don't worry we'll get to that—but I need to go to the Prime Circle. I promised the Primordial Mother I'd visit her."

Leander gave me a confused look.

"She's the one that made me like this," I added.

"What does that have to do with your freedom?"

"Because ... my freedom, is her freedom."

Chapter Seventy

We traveled through a portal together leaving behind the burning estate and who knew what calvary my grandfather had waiting. I was sure I'd be able to cast a portal between planes, but I'd never done it before, so I held on to Leander as the flashing colors whirled by us and we arrived in a foyer at the Prime Palace. It was so familiar yet slightly different to the parts I had seen at the party centuries ago. I wondered how much of it was still here.

Leander glanced down at me, noting the expression on my face. "I wish I could still read your mind," he said, both a little playful and solemn.

I grinned. "You like to hear me say what I'm thinking anyway, so I guess you'll just have to ask."

"Alright," he purred. "What has this purely devious and divine expression all over your face?"

"I was wondering if that study was still here," I replied a little sheepishly.

"Oh it's most definitely still here. I can take you to it right now if you like." His arm slipped through mine, as if he planned to drag me there immediately and finish what he had started almost a thousand years ago.

Just as I was about to reply, Victus turned a corner in the hall. His eyes met mine wide in shock, then flashed to Leander where the shock shifted to a nervous fear. I broke the link made from my and Leander's arms.

"Victus!" I said excitedly, rushing to hug him. I was so glad whatever I had done in the past had not literally stopped him from being born.

He stood awkwardly for a moment before lightly patting my back. "You're alive? I thought you had died."

"I did die, technically. I think? But the Primordial Mother adopted me, so now I'm a Divine Incarnate. I'm still trying to figure it out." I broke from our embrace and looked up at him. "Freda is okay, right?"

"Yes, she is safe. I left her at Midor's. It took a little longer than expected because I've never been there before. That's why I didn't make it back before ... father intervened." He glanced at Leander before dropping his gaze, as if in apology.

"Thanks for making sure she was somewhere safe." I smiled up at him.

"Father is in the tea room. He'll probably want to talk to you," Victus added unenthusiastically.

"I want to talk to him too." I pushed Victus and he led us both through the palace until I arrived at that lounge I had found refuge in before—the one Amias and I had made our deal in.

Remodeus was seated at a small table set with confections and drinks for one along with a stack of ledgers. His eyes went wide when he saw me. He must have sensed it—my primordial aura and realized who I was—who I had been.

"Are you ready for a real conversation now?" I said.

He seemed frozen—as if from the shame of the meeting we'd had a nearly a thousand years ago.

I closed the distance to where he sat and took a seat across from him at the table. Victus joined us, pulling out a seat for himself, and Leander stood behind me protectively. We sat in silence for a moment. Perhaps Remodeus was waiting for me to speak first.

I looked over his cup and tea kettle, then the ledgers, before making it back to his eyes. Eyes like mine. "I know now you didn't intend on me actually being your daughter. I'm grateful, though, for your part in all this. You made me," I said easily. Even if it had been to torture Leander, or be part of this grand loop of chaos, I never would have existed like this without his part in it.

"I didn't make you into *this*." He gestured to me tensely.

"No ... Erebell did." I smiled.

I watched Remodeus's face go soft. She was not just the Primordial Mother—she was *his* mother.

"I'm going to set her free," I concluded.

He blinked, a spark of awe in his eyes along with something else. Perhaps he was questioning if it were truly possible. The way his eyes scanned me, it was as if he could sense her primordial chaos flowing off me.

"I can't imagine you have any objection." I continued.

"What will you do after that?" His tone was cautious.

"I just want this plane to be different. To not be *Commanded* by the Primordial Father's sadistic rules. To have her rules instead," I said with conviction. I could hear Leander shift behind me. It would mean everything to him to be free from the Primordial Father.

Remodeus straightened in his chair. "What makes you think her rules will be any different?"

"It will be different enough to allow you to all be free of him."

Remodeus looked down to his hand resting on the table. "What do you need from me?" he said flatly.

My face lit up. "Oh I don't need you. I remember the place you sent me to, so I can just teleport there. I just wanted you to know that I don't hate you, and that I'm going to set someone we both care about free." I stood up abruptly from the table and caught a glimpse of his jaw dropping before I vanished in a puff of smoke.

I appeared in the darkness of the dungeon cell I had been in once before. I'd like to think I recognized it, but I couldn't see a single thing. The smell however ... that dank, wet smell lingered with some kind of smoke—ah. Smoke and the smell of the parts of me that had burned.

"Erebell?" I called aloud in the darkness. My voice echoed slightly among the dripping.

"You came," her disembodied voice was a weak drag, "to visit me ..."

I smiled. "I'm going to do more than that," I said excitedly. "I'm going to set you free."

"This ... this is not part of the loop," she replied, more so in surprise than argument. "You would choose this thread? This possibility?"

"Yes." I cracked my fingers. "What good am I as a Divine Incarnate if I can't dispel the primordial magic that holds you—holds all the females of power—down here?" She was silent, so I added, "I want you to take over this plane instead of the Primordial Father. I'll do whatever I can to help you, but we can do better and be better than this."

"I've never used my chaos in such a way. I am weakened now because of what I did to create you. If I pour myself over these lands, it will be the last bit of me," she said solemnly. "I would be simply a layer over what was old. No more thoughts, no more long waiting in darkness. Just a warm embrace of all."

Could I really ask her to do that? To stop existing how she does now? I wouldn't be able to talk to her, or seek guidance from her. Before I could respond she spoke again.

"It sounds ... quite nice. I've spent a long time simply existing, yet not being able to do anything. I think I quite like the idea of being everywhere, being used by everyone. I would finally get to live."

I could feel tears welling in my eyes. "Are you ready?"

"Yes," she replied quietly.

I wiped my face. "I'll miss talking to you."

"Talking will simply be different. You'll hear me in the sound of wind and see me in the expanse of the skies. You'll still have my primordial chaos inside you to urge you on."

It was true. There had been a few times recently when I'd known something was possible, and it felt like that deep, ancient well of primordial chaos was stirring to do it. Like now.

I held my hands out, thinking of the spell that I used to dispel arcana, and focused on the Primordial Father's thrall all around me. It was claustrophobic, heavy, and cold. Warmth flowed out of my finger tips, and chased it away. Light bloomed in the cell. Then, before me, I saw her.

She looked like a devil, if one could be crafted out of pure, arcane light. She seemed almost as if she might be made out of liquid, red crystal, illuminating the entire cell in a warm peaceful red glow. Her two void eyes held center points of glittering flame—*her flame*. Her hair was like sheets of shadow that spilled down her head and covered her bare body. She was the most beautiful thing I'd ever seen. How could the Primordial Father keep her trapped down here all this time and rob everyone of her light?

"I met Erethor, for a moment," I told her. "You never deserved to be abused by him the way you were."

She extended her glowing hand to my own and held it. It was so warm and soft, and full of energy. I realized that energy was the same feeling I'd had deep inside me when I became aware of my new magic—that primordial chaos she had given me.

"He will always try to find a way back here," she cautioned. "But he will not know how to deal with you. You don't think like a god as he does. Still, you must be careful. He created this plane, and he is forever bound to it. What we are about to do will suffocate him, shove him away to be forgotten, but at the core he will still exist because this plane does." She looked out at the surrounding cell as if she could see for eons past it. "I wondered if I could do such a thing as him, create an entire plane—or truly adopt this one. Perhaps if I had not made you. But I think I prefer having you instead anyway."

I smiled. I drew my eyes over her, memorizing her form, trying to take in every second of her. The edges of her were floating off like when a bonfire flared on its last log. I would be the last person to ever see her—to ever feel her eternal love so directly.

She offered me one last, gentle smile as the flickering of her form shifted away. "See you again on the wind and in the skies." She squeezed my hand and at last extinguished. A small tingle radiated up my wrists in the absence of her.

The ground below me began to rumble. Glittering sparks floated up around me. She was leaving this place, bringing her whole self from far underground, and breaking free.

I teleported back to the tea room. As soon as my feet touched the ground, I felt the tremors here as well. Remodeus and Leander were arguing about something as dust and shards of ceiling fell around us.

I shouted over them. "We should probably go outside before she collapses the building!"

"This is not *your* doing?" Remodeus demanded.

"It's your mother." I smiled.

Leander smirked at me and hooked his arm through mine, teleporting us to the garden outside of the palace. As soon as we arrived, a thunderous crack sounded. The spire nearest to us shifted to the side before tumbling back onto the architecture of the palace.

Leander chuckled. "Remodeus is not going to be happy about that."

Speak of the devil—he appeared several feet away in a puff of gray smoke, Victus not far behind him.

Remodeus sighed. "I *am* happy she is free, but was destroying my palace necessary? Is it even my palace anymore?" His infernal eyes narrowed on me, an accusatory look on his face.

I blinked with realization. Oh no. I wrung my hands together. "Am ... I in charge now?"

The entire section of the palace we'd just been in collapsed in on itself, sending a wave of air and dust flowing out from it. I swore I could feel her in that gust as it reached us, my skin tingling from its presence.

Remodeus sighed and crossed his arms. "Not every Circle will accept her magic. They will try to continue their own ways. What is your plan for that?" he said sharply.

I pondered the notion. I had assumed that everyone hated the Primordial Father as much as Leander and Remodeus did. That they would welcome the Primordial Mother's magic to this plane, even if to just layer over the remnants of him. But what if ... some preferred the Primordial Father? A sinking feeling grew in the pit of my stomach. I hadn't really thought this through at all. I had just wanted her to be free and right a wrong an eternity in the making.

"I ... don't really know," I said a little anxiously.

Leander's hands closed around my sides in a reassuring caress. It calmed me a little, but I wondered.

"Wait, so am I really in charge now? Because I'm more powerful than you, and both the Primordial Mother and Father are unavailable?"

Remodeus rubbed the space between his eyes and swore. "Gods spare us ..."

I had no experience ruling anything. I needed him on my side. I turned to him with a fanged smile. "I'll make you a deal."

Remodeus's knitted eyebrows bent up in concern.

"You can remain the steward, and I'll act as an advisor, in exchange for helping me convince the other princes to accept the Primordial Mother's magic and influence over this plane."

Victus shifted, looking between his father and me. "Obviously you'll need termination clauses for when you'd like to take over after the princes have been won," he added.

My smile went wide in response. Remodeus shot him a sharp glare at pointing out the weakness of the deal. I shook the remaining nerves from my hands and began dictating all the clauses—leaving it mostly open-ended on my part. I wasn't sure if I even wanted to rule this plane, but I sure as hell didn't want to be contractually prevented from doing so. Remodeus begrudgingly agreed to all of it. It really wasn't such a bad deal for him.

I stood there for a moment, watching the last section of the palace collapse, when he spoke sternly. "I'm going along with this for now," his voice softened, "because you freed her." He quickly adjusted his tone back to his flat, stern—almost fatherly—voice. "But that gift alone will not have me giving you any other preferential treatments."

Victus groaned behind him. "You've already been nicer to her in the past five minutes than you have ever been to me in five hundred years," he complained.

"Did *you* free my mother from eternal banishment?" Remodeus asked sharply. "What is it you have done except make a mess?"

Victus began arguing back, and I watched them go at each other. It was endearing, in a way. Warm in the way of a family I'd always wanted. I turned around to Leander.

"Where should we go?" I said in his mind with a sweet caress.

He responded without skipping a beat, knowing exactly why I had asked.

"I can take you to my room," he purred. *"Or anywhere in the Palace of Flames that you desire. Anywhere that is fond in your memory."* He pressed his fingers under my chin, lifting my face to him.

"I kind of want to go somewhere we haven't already ... you know."

"Do you now?" His eyes shifted to a deep, glowing burn of orange. *"I never got to enjoy you in the first place we spent time alone. In that room at the Bon Mar."* His voice was now a sinister purr.

I simply smiled wide, showing him my fangs. He folded me into him and pulled me backwards into another shimmering portal. We fell till I landed on top of him, on that same bed he'd left me on after our first kiss.

The portal burned to nothingness, leaving behind Remodeus and Victus, still arguing.

CHAPTER SEVENTY-ONE

"Tell me what you desire," his velvety voice demanded as we were covered in the warm darkness of Novus. He snapped his fingers, lighting a few candles. I was already melting into him, straddling him, my lips hovering over his.

"I want you," I replied desperately. It was everything I had wanted to say a thousand years ago when we'd fought in the library and he'd begged me to bind our souls. "I want you to bind yourself to me."

His hands trailed up my sides slowly. I watched him remember the moment when I'd denied him. Then that devilish grin curled his lips. "Right now?"

His favorite way to tease me ...

"Right now."

The devilish grin twisted to a wicked delight, his infernal eyes blazing so brightly I thought they might erupt. I dove against him, kissing him and writhing at the pleasure of him simply squeezing my body. After a few moments of deeply and thoroughly enjoying the taste of him, his hands slid around my head and he pulled me away slightly.

"You are sure you can still do it?" Leander asked, a little concern painting his face.

I smirked at him, placing my finger under his chin in a playful stroke. "You know, that was only like a week ago for me," I crooned.

A look of smug satisfaction melted across his face as if he were remembering what he'd done to me back then. "Then, as I recall, you have a bit of a concentration problem that I have just the solution for."

He twisted and threw me onto the bed, rising to remove his shirt. He pulled me to the edge of the mattress and surveyed my position.

I squirmed wanting him on me, *in* me.

"May I tear it off of you?" he asked darkly, eyeing the dress.

"Tear it off me," I panted.

He dove towards my neck, puncturing the fabric with his fangs and ripping it. He then continued the work with his hands, freeing my body from the dress. The air rushed in and I arched for him, his body. My core began fluttering when I instead watched him drop to his knees.

His mouth pressed into me, his arms wrapping around my thighs and hips, gripping me, winding my tail around his arm. My legs arced over his shoulders and I exhaled sharply with pleasure. He brought me to a climax swiftly, my moans filling the space between us. He rose once more to remove his pants and threw himself on me. We pressed our palms into each other, both craving the other, driven by the need to be united again.

It was easier to find his soul this time as he pounded away at me. If I could follow him through a thousand years of time, I could easily take a piece of his soul this close to me—and so willing to be mine. Then I followed my primordial chaos to that warm flame deep inside me, and split my soul with half a thought. I took his half and gave him mine. I didn't need a contract like Remodeus did. My primordial chaos orchestrated it all, a divinely executed will. Once the exchange was complete, I felt it rush back in—the thread between our souls. This time it was more powerful and concrete, wheeling between us. We didn't part until it settled in again, so that we could make this bond permanent.

For eternity.

I wasn't sure how or if a Divine Incarnate—or whatever I was—could be killed to end this bond, but our bond as soul mates was now my divine prerogative. He would be mine, and I would be his, for every age of existence. I could face it all, if only with him.

We fell asleep from the exhaustion of making love over and over again. It was bliss, to feel the thread tugging against me again, humming in his embrace.

I woke later as he ran his fingers along my ribs and up to my breasts, savoring my soft, pale red flesh. We'd talked a little bit about our experience together a thousand years ago. Mostly Leander told me how much he had wanted to fuck me from the moment he'd heard my *Mindtell* in his head after I had emerged from the lake.

As he nestled against me in the bed, I could feel him already hard and pressing against me. I ground into him and he squeezed me.

"Should we continue where we left off before we collapsed?" he purred in my ear. The sound of his voice in my ear had me already melting.

"What sort of things do you wish you could have done with me back then?" I said instead.

His hand returned to my ribs, then slid down the curves of my body till it pushed my legs open wide. "So many things." He kissed my neck. "Though I suppose I was curious to see if you could give me a magical *Command.*" He dropped more kisses at my neck, trailing to my ear. "No one has been powerful enough to do it when I am at my full strength, except for the Primordial Father. So I've never really known what it feels like in the context of being pleasurable."

My memories swam back to when I had been a mortal and cast *Command* for him to teach me to *Scry*. He had been so enthralled with my attempts to *Command* him with arcana. I imagined now that I outranked him, my *Commands* would undo him completely. I flipped over and sat up on the bed with my legs folded back and to the side.

"Would you like me to?" I said sweetly with a fanged smile.

He propped himself up and his gaze fixed on mine. "Have me do whatever you like," he purred.

Hmm ...

I pondered whether I should pick something simple and easy to fulfill, or something I knew would require effort—and possibly give him more satisfaction. I lowered my gaze to his hard cock between us. My lips curled in a devious smile before my eyes flicked back up to those blazing, infernal eyes. He was so eager for me to speak my next words. Fortunately, I only needed one.

"*Come,*" I said in an arcane-laced *Command*.

His body tensed and he shuddered. "Fuck ..." he moaned.

I looked down between us again. Oh, he had definitely come. The evidence was all over the bed. My eyes went wide with surprise, then I smiled up at him. "Like that?"

His eyes turned feral on me as he panted. "I can't believe you did that."

"Are you displeased?" I teased him.

His expression went sinister. "Displeased?"

He pressed me down into the bed, his body spreading my legs wide as he pinned me beneath him. "I want you to do it again. Except this time," he leaned into my ear before rasping in a warm breath, "*you are going to wait till I'm inside you, like a good girl.*"

I went molten.

He was already hard again and pushing into me. He ravaged me, winding me closer and closer to another climax.

"When you are close to release, *Command* me to come again," he breathed in my ear. I clutched him as that pressure built. Closer and closer it came to spilling over the edge. Just as that release barreled into me, I moaned and gave the arcane *Command* again.

"*Come.*"

BONUS CHAPTER

FREDA

Somehow I'd been blessed with this over-six-foot, absolutely sculpted drow loitering around in my dorm room. It was not like I was complaining, but *hell* Emrys's drow form was something to admire. Like he'd been a star the Veldrasyl gods decided to pluck from the sky to be around us mere mortals.

After Victus had left me at Midor's, Emrys had found me. At first, I had been terrified of him, but then something in the sparkle of his drow eyes helped me recognize him as Reign's infernal cat. We both worried for Reign. We didn't know what was going on or where she was. She'd disappeared like this before, and Leander had found her. I had to trust he'd find her again.

"Don't worry, I'm sure our Mistress will be fine." Emrys smiled.

"*Our* Mistress?" I cracked a grin at him.

He rolled his eyes. "*My* Mistress," he corrected.

I watched him sprawl awkwardly across Reign's old bed, staring at the ceiling with his hands tucked behind his head. They'd never given me a new roommate.

Not yet anyway.

"What do you think happened to her?" I said. "Tell me the truth."

Emrys held his stare on the ceiling. "I ... think something bad might have happened." He paused, worrying at his bottom lip. "That's why I will not leave you. She would want me to make sure you are protected."

"Why do you think something bad happened?"

He took a deep breath before replying. "I can't feel our familiar bond anymore—the one that Leander granted to me when he gave me to her. Which means she's dead or really, really far away. I've tried asking Leander, but he's ignoring me."

I felt like if she were truly dead I would know, somehow. Leander would make it known anyway. "Why haven't you taken me to the Nine Circles? Wouldn't it be more comfortable for you to protect me there?"

Emrys's eyes shot over to me. "I don't think you'd like it very much. It's not very friendly to mortals."

"Does it ... ever *snow* in the Nine Circles?" I asked timidly. I had to know. I had to know if that dreadful vision Lumoniel gave me would happen if I went there. Reign was in it ... and snow ... and my hair loose in the wind ... It reappeared night after night as I slept like a nightmare, and its theme had slowly revealed itself.

Death.

It was why I hadn't protested when Reign seemed like she was doing her own thing. I was happy to return to Midor's and put distance between us, just in case. It never snowed here. After I had been snatched from Midor's and placed in that prison cell, I'd half expected my next view would be of a snowscape, red wisps of my hair crowning my vision, and Reign ... screaming. Perhaps her rescuing me had thwarted that likely consequence.

"Hmm ..." Emrys mused. "It does snow on the Ice Circle. I think it might also snow on the Ash Circle? Or was it the Bone Circle?"

At least it didn't snow on Leander's Circle. I supposed that was obvious, it being the Fire Circle. Maybe it would not be so bad to visit her then. I missed her so much, despite how greatly that vision had shaken me.

"Freda?"

I bolted upright at the voice that sparkled across my mind. It wasn't just any voice, it was *her* voice.

"Reign?" I spoke the reply aloud as I responded to her message. Emrys shot up and went rigid, only his chest moving with his breath, waiting to hear my recounting of the *Mindtell*.

"You're okay!" she continued. *"I was so worried about you. I'm safe. We're at the Palace of Flames. Is it alright if I come get you after I find Emrys? There is a lot I need to Faizan's Tiny Closet you."* Her voice glittered warmly in my mind.

Wait, if she was in the Nine Circles, how was she sending me *Mindtells?* First thing first, and I reached out with the free response.

"Actually, Emrys is here with me! I'm sure he can bring me there. I can stay for the weekend at least, so I don't miss any more classes."

"Yes! Good. I'll see you soon! I'm so glad you are okay."

I relayed the messages to Emrys and immediate relief washed over him.

"Ahh, she's okay ..." he sighed. "And she wants you to come visit? Should we leave now?" His eyes had relit with a new energy. I had never understood a familiar bond to be like this, but then again, I'd never had one.

"I need to pack first." I held a finger up to him. "Try to contain your excitement for at least thirty minutes?"

He grinned back at me.

I packed my things, checking and rechecking that I had everything, then I stared into the mirror on the back of the door as I braided my hair carefully. I used to only wear it up sometimes, but ever since the vision ... I just felt more at ease if my hair was tightly coiled in a braid. Finally, I turned to Emrys with my pack on my back.

I smiled at him. "One round trip to the Fire Circle, please!"

Acknowledgments

Thank you to my husband for reading the first eight chapters I ever drafted of this book, and encouraging me to keep writing. Thank you for putting up with and supporting me writing into the dark hours of night, like I might be the one under a spell of possession to get everything in my brain into a Word doc. I would have quit a long, long time ago, if it were not for you.

Thank you to my very first round of alpha readers, Liz, Paige, Virginia, Sam, Jacy, Lindsey, Bridget, and Amanda. Your feedback led me to fearlessly red pen my book and get it to its final polished state.

Thank you to my amazing editor, Kiri Rabina, who probably left me over 6,000 revisions in the rounds we put this book through. I learned so much from working with a professional editor like you, and working together really helped make me a better writer (along with, you know, making my book amazing).

Thank you to Patricia Gutierrez, the wonderful illustrator of the cover. Thank you to K.M. Alexander for creating the high quality map brushes used for this book's map.

Thank you to my publisher, Seven Sisters Fables, and my fearless business partner Liz Swartsel, whose special skill is helping others achieve their dreams. This wouldn't be possible without you.

Finally, thank YOU for reading this book. I wrote this for myself, never knowing if another soul would ever read it. But I am glad you did and I hope you enjoyed it.

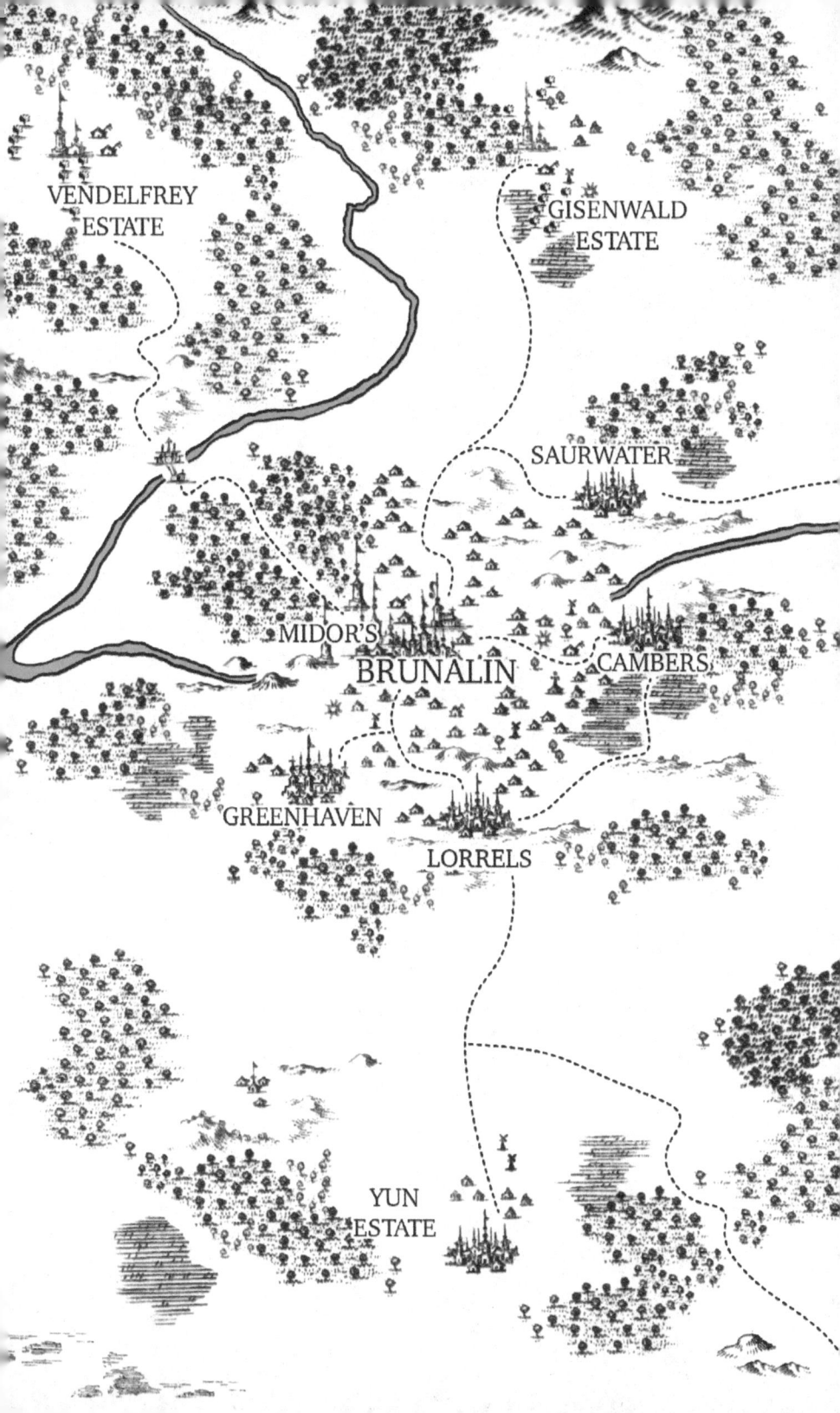